THE SOUNDS
OF SILENCE

JUDITH RICHARDS

THE SOUNDS
OF SILENCE

G. P. PUTNAM'S SONS   NEW YORK

SBN: 399-11950-7

Library of Congress Cataloging in Publication Data:

Richards, Judith.
    The sounds of silence.

    I. Title.
PZ4.R516So   [PS3568.I3155]   813'.5'4   76-56396

PRINTED IN THE UNITED STATES OF AMERICA

To Mom and Dad:
WILMA ANDERSON RICHARDS
and
R. JACK RICHARDS

When I see the wrinkled lines
Of an old face marked by time,
Good things and bad are therein etched;
The artist: Time hereon sketched
Of hate and pain, harsh words spoken,
Of gentler things and loves betoken.
Laughter, tears, in creases fast
Visible echoes from the past.

THE SOUNDS
OF SILENCE

Chapter One

Aramenta Lee stood a moment looking at the house. Paint curled from gray wood, the victim of humidity, wind, and sun. The windows were wavy panes of elongated glass, dark, stained with mildew. The shutters, some with slats missing, hung askew. A remnant of eave gutter hung in ragged and rusted stalactites of metal, the lower portions long ago fallen. There were forty-one rooms, divided in a tripartition of east wing, west wing, and main house, each of which loomed two stories high with a full attic above. It was one of the few houses in Mobile with a cellar and the only one with a subbasement. This was possible in a city where the water level was inches from the surface, because Lee Manor was atop the highest elevation in the area—Springhill.

Aramenta hated it. She despised her past association with the family home, and most particularly the fact that she had fallen heir to it all. After thirty years of living in Paris since victory in Europe, she had been summoned home with a five word telegram: AM DYING COME HOME MOTHER.

Goddamn Mother.

As though lingering only for Aramenta's arrival, which no doubt Mother would have a capacity to do, the matriarch succumbed to emphysema less than twenty-four hours after Aramenta's arrival. Three decades without so much as a Christmas card between them, when suddenly she was thrust back into this cesspool of the South, surrounded by all the bitter reminders of pain and torment she had known all her life. Blood demanded nothing, not love, not respect, *nothing!* But it was blood alone that bound her to Mother and blood that brought her back.

"Blood tells, Aramenta—"

Put that thought away.

"Blood! Remember your station, child. Blood tells."

Aramenta turned as a vehicle crunched in the drive, coughed, dieseled as the ignition was turned off. A man with a perspiring bald head stepped out, smiling.

"Miss Lee?"

"Yes."

"Buddy Ellis here. Ellis Realty." When her expression remained stoic, he added, "You called me."

"Yes, Mr. Ellis."

"I know the funeral was today and all, but the note said come right out. If this is not a convenient time—"

"Now is fine, Mr. Ellis." She pawed through her large purse looking for the ring of keys.

"Largest house in the city," Ellis said. "Rich history. When I was a boy, I used to walk right past this house everyday on my way to school. I went to school right down the street there."

She examined the lock and tried a Yale key.

"I always wanted to go inside," the realtor said. "Do they still have the great big chandelier?"

"I'm sure," Aramenta said; then questioned, "If you've never been inside, how do you know about the chandelier, Mr. Ellis?"

"Oh, that was the topic of conversation with my grandmother for a month, after your granddaddy imported it from France. Seems like it was the largest crystal chandelier in the South back then, as I recall."

"Won't you come in?" Aramenta pushed against the heavy door and without a sound it opened. A musty odor assailed them.

"I apologize for the state of things," Aramenta said, not truly apologetic. "I only arrived night before last."

"Oh, I know that! Mrs. Lee was—well, reclusive is a good word. Her mind had slipped a bit, I suppose. You know, I tried to talk to her about putting the place on the market a few years back. She wouldn't even speak to me. Just shut the door in my face."

Aramenta clutched her pocketbook in both hands, watching the realtor blot his forehead and pate with a folded white handkerchief. He carried a hat, but it was obvious he seldom put it on his head.

"There it is," he said, looking at the cobwebbed and dusty chandelier. "Beautiful, isn't it?"

"Mr. Ellis, until night before last I haven't been in this house for thirty years. Then only in the hallway, living room, and Mother's bedroom before I called the hospital. I have almost forgotten my way about."

A lie. She could remember every detail from the wide plank, peg-pinned flooring to the rococo molding curling at corners near the ceiling.

"Well!" Ellis smiled. "Where shall we begin?"

"You may go where you will, Mr. Ellis. I will follow."

"Fine, fine. Let's see, this is obviously the library. Shame those books are molding like that."

He announced each room, "Kitchen, bathroom, hallway,"

and walked unhurriedly. "Every piece an authentic antique," he commented, running his fingertips across a silt-covered tortoise-shell inlay sideboard. It was Louis XIV, another of Granddaddy's French "imports."

"Lord, what a pantry," Ellis wheezed. "I've seen modern bedrooms with less floor space. And here we are in the foyer to the next room." He seemed at a loss to identify it.

"In those days," Aramenta said, "servants lived in. The house kitchen, which was brutally hot, was part of the servants' quarters. This was that kitchen. With the advent of high-priced labor—slavery had been abolished—the Lees were forced to install the existing family kitchen. This became a nonroom thereafter. She never forgave the North actually."

"Your grandmother?"

"And Mother."

For the first time, Aramenta realized his eyes had a piglike squint, two tiny blue orbs encased in folds of facial fat. He was not smiling, trying to determine how serious she was. After all, might she not be as looney as her mother? Aramenta did nothing to ease his doubts.

"Yes, those were the good old days, according to the Lee women—plenty of demand for Granddaddy Lee's imported French wines and the Lee schooners which sailed the seas. A standard of living impossible to maintain, of course, without that—ah—amenable labor. That's what Mother called slaves, you know—'amenable labor.' She meant, if they didn't polish silver or press crinolines just so, one of the men could beat them until they were amenable."

"I suspect most slaves were treated fairly enough," Ellis said, a typical southern response suggesting the blacks were "still pretty much cared for" and "adequately."

"Your family had slaves, Mr. Ellis?"

"No, no. We were the common folks, Miss Lee."

"Umm." Common folk. Blood tells.

"Shall we go on?" Mr. Ellis inquired, a hint of a bow now, hat in hand extended to indicate the way. He expressed surprise when he discovered they had made a full circle and were once again in the hallway. He opened a door.

"This goes to the basement?"

"Cellar. Yes. And subbasement. Do you wish to go down?"

"That won't be necessary. It's already getting too dark to see. Are the lights functional?"

"I'm not sure."

"It doesn't matter," he sounded suddenly hurried. "I can see the rest of the house another time. I'll have to make several trips to familiarize myself with the layout and the best selling points. I would like to see upstairs before I leave."

The oak stairs dominated the rear of the hallway, rising half a flight, then splitting into two separate and opposite stairways connecting the wings with the central section of the house.

"It must've been wonderful growing up in a place like this," Ellis huffed, his prominent bulk taking its toll.

"Do you wish to see the east or west wing?"

"Whichever. Go right, I suppose."

"Oh, dear." Ellis halted and Aramenta followed his eyes. A hole had been knocked in the bottom panel of a door. "Vandals, probably," Ellis suggested. He pushed against the door and it wouldn't move. He bent low, peeking into a dark hole.

"Can't see anything," he said. "I should've brought a flashlight. Looks like a tunnel of some kind."

"Tunnel?"

"Like through straw or something." Ellis reached through the hole and felt. "Paper. Somebody blocked the door with bundles of paper."

Then, as though Aramenta were delaying them, Ellis said, "Let's hurry along, Miss Lee. It's getting too dark to do this tour justice."

The next door was similarly blocked. And the next. Out of nine suites, only one was accessible. Furniture stood like ghostly apparitions in dustcloth covers, as though awaiting a witching hour when they could all spring to life and dart about the room between gossamer webs of spider's silk.

"I be damned!" Ellis turned abruptly. "Excuse me, Miss Lee. Slip of the tongue."

"What is it, Mr. Ellis?"

He was standing at the connecting portal to the next suite. "There's a panel knocked out of this door, too." Reaching inside, feeling, bent over, one pudgy hand propped against his own knee. "More paper, Miss Lee."

"The place is probably crawling with rats," Aramenta observed acidly.

"Listen, Miss Lee, it's really too dark to continue this. Perhaps I could return tomorrow morning, early?"

"If you wish."

They were walking faster now, the realtor setting the pace. "If you'd like, I'll call an exterminator."

"Understand, Mr. Ellis, I have not *seen* rats. It was a theoretical observation."

"I couldn't stand rats. Where are you spending the night, Miss Lee?"

"Here, Mr. Ellis."

"Here?" They halted at the front door. Pig eyes wide, Ellis cleared his throat. "You be all right here alone?"

"I think so."

"I'd be happy to drive you to town."

"I have a means of transportation, Mr. Ellis. I rented an automobile."

"I don't want to be nosy, Miss Lee, but maybe you'd be more comfortable at the Admiral Semmes Hotel."

"Thank you for your concern, Mr. Ellis. I'll stay."

She closed the door, heard the latch click, and released the huge brass knob. She took a measured breath, exhaled slowly, and turned to stare unseeing down the dark hall. She recalled a childhood memory of a gaslight, converted when electricity became available, and the switch oddly placed too high and midwall. She felt along the wall, the texture of paper made gritty by a residue of dust. There! She touched the switch plate, found the toggle, threw it up. A meager yellow bulb, fifteen watts perhaps, pushed vainly against the dark. By this light she located another switch, but nothing responded.

In the living room she found a Tiffany-shade lamp, which she turned on. Cobwebs and "dust mice" took cover in shadows. The blemishes thus rouged by the healing shade of night and the varicolored lamp cover, the place regained some of its lost aura, a bit of the class of the aristocracy which constructed it.

She walked over an Oriental rug, feet in steps recalled from infancy, to Papa's high-back Queen Anne's chair with majestic carved arms and legs. She could almost smell the scent of apple shavings in fresh tobacco again, the lip-lifting aroma of masculinity. If she closed her eyes and mentally discarded fifty years of her life, she could once again recapture the suckle sound of short puffs as he lit his favorite pipe with a preferred blend. Oh, God, how time evaporated. Fifty years! Two lifetimes, two vibrant lifetimes, gone. For what? What in heaven's name for?

The wide-bottom cane-back splayed-arm rocking chair had been Mother's. Nobody was ever allowed to sit in that chair. Like all things "Mother's ' they were not to be shared, but were expressly, explicitly, *Mother's!* Deliberately she sat down.

Her feet lifted with each backward push, Aramenta fighting memories, the gut-wrenching pictures indelible in her brain. It had taken most of an adult lifetime to consign such thoughts to niches where they could be locked away and slowly forgotten.

"Blood tells—"

"You can't play with that child, Aramenta. No sass, now. I shan't tolerate it. Don't you dare dispute my word, girl! I said no and I mean no. The Lees are aristocracy. The well-to-do don't palaver with the poor. They want what you have, Aramenta. You can never trust them. All they think about is money. Sooner or later, every one of them will ask you to loan, or give, money. Like wild animals seeking food, the indigent man seeks money! It obsesses him, Aramenta. If one dares ask for money, or even dwells on it, you will know his caste, child. Bitter lesson, but better learned than burned. Now, now, stop your tears and be a young lady. There! Mother hates to tell you this. But it is life. Life is not easy, even for the Lees. It's a price one must pay for being of the blood, child. Blood has its rewards—see your funny little nose? Like your grandfather and his father before him. That's a Lee nose, a mark of the aristocracy. Blood. Remember that, Aramenta. Blood. Blood tells."

Aramenta ceased rocking, head up, frozen. Ever so slowly, she turned, more to direct hearing than sight. There! There it was again. A thumping sound. Somebody at the door? She was in no mood for the hypocrisy of enduring condolences. Aramenta stood abruptly, walking toward the front door. "Who is it, please?"

Putting her ear near the thick portal, she called again, louder, "Who is it?"

The knocking had stopped. She searched the wall for an outside light switch, finding none. She pulled back the tatted lace curtains and, with a dry odor of dust in her nostrils, leaned near, peering out. The porch, which surrounded three sides of the main house, was empty. The columns and balusters were dimly silhouetted against darker shrubbery.

Again. Thump-thump-thump. Aramenta quelled irritation, threw the lock, and opened the door.

"Yes!" she demanded of the dark. Nothing. She stepped out. "Yes?" she called.

Children maybe. Or perhaps the place truly *had* rats.

Thump-thump-thump.

Enough of this nonsense! Aramenta turned toward the apparent source of sound, the kitchen now, and resolutely marched in that direction.

The refrigerator door was open, illuminating a rectangle of linoleum floor. She groped for one of the elusive and oddly placed switches she knew existed. Then with a muttered oath at her own ineptitude, she crossed the kitchen in the dark, bumped a heavy cutting-board table, and slammed the refrigerator door. Feeling her way back to the hallway—something touched her!

Not truly. Not *touched* her. More like a current of air stirred by something as it went past, that was it. Struck still, heart slamming, she shuddered and goose bumps erupted, racing around her body.

"Who's there?" Her own voice sounded hoarse in her ears. "I know you're there, now who are you?"

The strum-strum-strum was the pound of her own heartbeat. "I demand you identify yourself." Strum-strum-strum.

She made the final few yards to the living room with long strides and then wheeled to face the dark. She was breathing too fast, a primordial reaction to unreasoning fear. She wiped her hands down her skirt and suddenly realized she still wore the mourner's black hat, a veil covering her face. She snatched out the long pin, cast the hat aside, and shook her head. Better. Cooler. It was warm in here. She would open a window. Forget it. Go to bed! She had tons of things to sift through before calling a dealer. She had to get the house cleared somehow, get the place sold, and go back to Paris where she belonged!

Thump-thump-thump.

Ears drumming, a patina of perspiration now returning to her palms.

Thump-thump-thump.

Initial apprehension dissolved in anger and she stormed into the hall. "In case you haven't looked at me—I have horns, fangs, and I sleep hanging upside down. Come too near and I'll rip your heart out!"

Thump-thump—silence.

Beast or man, that would give it something to think about. She held the hatpin like an épée, adrenaline surging, and stomped defiantly toward the kitchen.

The refrigerator door was again open. Maybe the clasp is broken; Aramenta, be reasonable, for heaven's sake! She pushed the door shut, positioned a chair to hold it, and with continued bravado marched out into the hall again, treading hard.

"I'm going to have you exterminated, you creeps," she yelled. "Better start packing, you hear me? I may burn this dump to the ground."

Mother's bedroom had a musky scent of illness, rice powder, long-dried perfume decanters. The bed was exactly as the ambulance attendants had left it when they rushed Mother to the hospital.

Mother's bed.

Aramenta undressed and got between the covers.

Thump-thump-thump.

Hatpin in hand, she closed her eyes and willed sleep to come. It did.

Chapter Two

Aramenta awoke, chilled. Her eyes slowly focused on the ornate solid-wood canopy overhead. Startled, she sat up, confused. She had thought herself at home in Paris, but the feel and smell of this room were alien to nostrils and mind. She reassimilated her consciousness, surrounded by the past, in the heavy Empire-style mahogany bed with ormolu mounts. A dust catcher. Aramenta had never thought the nineteenth-century bed was attractive, but it had been Granddaddy Lee's favorite in a room full of ponderous dark pieces.

Aramenta opened her suitcase and removed the few things she'd brought. She hadn't come to stay. The dress she wore to the funeral, an alternate change for the return trip home, a "day" dress—that was it. Surely in this house there would be something she could wear, more appropriate for the labor she faced. She spread her clothing atop a cassone at the foot of the bed, a "marriage coffer" Mother always called it

Aramenta stood looking at the cassone. Sixteenth century. It occurred to her she should call Parke-Bernet in New York. She needed an appraiser. As the realtor, Mr. Ellis, had said, everything was "an authenic antique."

She opened the drawers of a lemonwood armoire, pushing clothing around, seeking something of a utilitarian nature. Mothballs permeated everything. She closed the drawers and stood, naked, considering going out to buy slacks and blouses. From the corner of her eye she saw something move. She spun, breathless. Her own image in a smoked mirror looked back, hands clutching herself as though to fend off prying eyes.

"I've got to get out of this place," she said aloud. She dressed hurriedly, drove to a mall, and spent two hours purchasing clothing she had no intention of keeping after she'd completed the task of clearing Lee Manor. While out, she bought breakfast, an inedible sixty-nine-cent special at a restaurant open to the mall. It reminded her of a sidewalk café where she normally had morning coffee.

At a bank within the complex, she cashed traveler's checks into change and made a long-distance call to her lawyer in New York.

"This is Aramenta Lee in Mobile, Alabama."

"Yes, Miss Lee?"

"Is Bruce in, please?"

"He's in court this morning, Miss Lee."

"Please tell him I called, " Aramenta said, words clipped. "I'm in Mobile closing out the family estate. Ask him to telephone Parke-Bernet and get them to send down a representative. I have no idea of the value *in toto,* but it should approach half a million dollars."

"Yes, Miss Lee."

Aramenta gave the address, read off Mother's telephone

number, and hung up. Thirty minutes later she was back on Springhill. Mr. Ellis was waiting. With him was a thin, unclean man with bushy black hair and baggy trousers.

"Miss Lee, this is Jimmy Rountree. He deals in junk and stuff. I told him you might want him to make an offer on things inside."

Aramenta resisted a smile. "Very well, come in, Mr. Rountree."

"I'd like to walk the place over this morning, Miss Lee." Ellis smiled, eyes becoming slits. "I also have a conditional sales contract which we'll need signed."

"Fine, Mr. Ellis." Aramenta watched the "junk and stuff" dealer walk casually into the living room. His face denoted nothing, but there was an almost imperceptible change in his eyes.

"I don't think this place will stay on the market too long, Miss Lee," Ellis was saying. "According to the courthouse records there are twelve acres in all and some of it might be rezoned commercial. We may consider breaking it into parcels." He was watching her read the contract.

"You will do a little paint-up, fix-up, of course," Ellis said. "Superficial stuff, you know. First impression sticks with a potential buyer." He extended his pen.

"Ten percent is too much, Mr. Ellis."

"Ma'am?"

"Your commission rate is too high," Aramenta said, now looking at him, unsmiling.

"It's pretty standard, Miss Lee. Commercial property sales generally demand—"

"This isn't commercial property, Mr. Ellis. That is a possible change in status that has not yet occurred."

"All rightee." Ellis took back the contract and flicked his ball-point pen. He marked out "10%" and wrote "06%," then offered it anew, smiling. "No need quibbling over trivia," he said.

"Mr. Ellis, let me make a suggestion. You 'walk the place over' as you say. That done, submit a probable price you think you can ask and get. I'll arrange for an attorney to handle the contract for you."

"Yes, ma'am, but I will need your signature, Miss Lee."

"Possibly," Aramenta said, "but I'm going home to Paris as soon as I tie up a few loose ends. The attorney will still be here and he could better serve your needs. You understand."

He understood. His hopeful and erroneous assessment of her gullibility had vanished.

"No problem, Miss Lee. Now if you don't mind, I'll wander around awhile."

"Feel free, Mr. Ellis."

Casually, Mr. Rountree ambled back into the room. His trousers, clasped by a too-long belt, looked in imminent danger of bypassing his hip bones to fall away.

"It'd take a while just to haul junk out of here," he remarked to Ellis in passing. Then to Aramenta, "Miss Lee, I could probably squeeze out five thousand for the lot."

"The lot, Mr. Rountree?"

"Yes, ma'am."

Aramenta walked into the formal dining room. "Mr Rountree, what would you pay for the furniture in this room?"

He scanned the pieces, ten chairs, sideboards, and serving tables. "Oh," he said, "forty, maybe fifty bucks."

"I see."

He studied her. "Maybe five dollars more."

"For everything in here?"

"Yes, ma'am."

"Thank you for coming out, Mr. Rountree." Aramenta escorted him toward the door.

"I might could see a few dollars more, Miss Lee." Rountree smiled now for the first time. His teeth were stained, irregular. "I tell you, Miss Lee, the junk business has about peaked out. A few years back you could turn a table like that for a hundred dollars. But today, there aren't many houses that can take a table that size, don't you see?"

"Mr. Rountree, how long have you been in your business?"

"Forty years."

"Junk only? Or do you deal in antiques?"

"One man's junk is another man's antique, Miss Lee."

"Let me be frank, Mr. Rountree. I'm trying to determine whether you are unaware of what you see, or whether you think I am."

The dealer visibly stiffened. "Yes, ma'am."

"The dining-room suite you just offered sixty dollars for," Aramenta said, "is an original Charles Percier and Pierre Fontaine from Château Mamaison near Paris. It dates to about 1799 and my great-grandfather brought it over around 1835 when this house was constructed."

"It's had a lot of wear, Miss Lee."

"Yes. Well, thank you for coming, Mr. Rountree."

"Listen, Miss Lee, maybe I could offer more."

"How about thirty thousand more, for the one room, Mr. Rountree?"

Defeated, the dealer's smile turned ugly. "Forget it, lady. If you can get it, get it. You got a lot to learn."

"Good day, Mr. Rountree."

Cuffs scuffing, the dealer walked back to the realtor's automobile and got in, waiting.

"Ah"—Mr. Ellis descended the stairs—"here you are!" He mopped his brow with the folded handkerchief.

"Got a few problems, Miss Lee."

"Like what?"

"You know those tunnels upstairs?"

"In the suites."

"Yes. Miss Lee, they *are* tunnels. Apparently the rooms are packed solid with paper. I looked in and the tunnels go from one room to the next, evidently. Like kids had played in there. I can't begin to see the room itself, of course. Listen, why don't I make a cursory walkover outside and then come back after you've had somebody come in and haul all this junk away?"

"If you wish, Mr. Ellis."

"Listen, Miss Lee, this piece of property could bring you a nice price. As is, one price. Make a few repairs and a week or two of cleanup time and the price could be as much as doubled."

"Mr. Ellis, I intend to leave day after tomorrow."

Ellis shifted uncomfortably. "Let me be honest, Miss Lee. I don't care whether you need money or not. But to me, for my commission, it means the difference in twice as much. If you aren't willing to invest the time and energy, maybe we can work something out on a flat-rate deal acceptable to you and I'll assume the responsibility. But anything above the flat rate would be at a higher percentage. Would that be agreeable?"

"Possibly. Work up some figures, Mr. Ellis."

"Fine," Ellis said, curtly. "I assure you nobody is going to buy this place with every room jammed full of trash. It's that simple. You haul it off, have it hauled off, or pay dearly for the buyer to haul it off. And you have no idea what's in those rooms besides the paper! Hell, there may be several thousand dollars' worth of furniture, Miss Lee!"

"All right, Mr. Ellis." Aramenta felt better about him now. "I know you're correct. I'll stay long enough to get such things as the trash hauled away."

Ellis paused at the door. "And mow the lawn, Miss Lee."

He gestured at a lopsided shutter. "It wouldn't take a man but a few hours to do things like rehang the shutters. Oh! One more thing. Air the place out. The cellar smells like a tomb. Worse."

She watched the portly realtor get into his car, slam the door, and secure his seat belt. She read a vulgarity on the lips of the junk dealer. Blood tells.

Staggered with the immensity of the task ahead and unsure where to begin, Aramenta walked back to Mother's bedroom. She surveyed furniture, closets, all filled with family accumulations of more than a hundred and fifty years. She opened a dresser drawer and pushed around a tangle of necklaces, brooches, and earrings.

She picked up Grandmama Lee's favorite cameo, a diamond-circled brooch reputedly given to Josephine by Napoleon in 1807. The ornament bore Josephine's likeness. Given a license to steal, which Rountree sought with a flat offer "for the lot," he would have carted such things away en masse.

Forty-one rooms! Aramenta felt smothered. She went to a window. She tried to lift it but the wood was swollen and immovable. For an instant she was seized with an impulse to shatter the glass—then with forced restraint she strode into the hall.

To allow a man like Rountree, or anyone else, to come in here and carry things away without supervision was idiotic and irresponsible. It could mean a loss of things Aramenta had never known existed.

Well, she had to begin somewhere. But where? She felt impelled to do something constructive and physical, empty garbage, throw something out, clean a room, anything! She walked through the dining room into the kitchen. She stared at the refrigerator. The chair had been moved. She examined the latch. It wasn't broken. So how did the refrigerator door come open last night if the catch was not—

Her foot slipped and Aramenta looked down at pieces of bread, a spot of liquid that resembled milk. Don't be silly! Mother was nearly ninety, she would be prone to drop things. Her eyes going bad, she probably didn't even see this filth. But the chair? Aramenta remembered placing it against the appliance. Perhaps Mr. Ellis or Rountree had moved it.

She opened the cooler and the contents surprised her. Fruit, a gallon of milk, and sandwich meats. The top was off a mayonnaise jar. Aramenta looked around the cabinets. A vitamin jar, top off, with pills spilled along the counter. She replaced the cap, an automatic feminine response to waste.

In the pantry, every cupboard was filled with dishes, pots, pans, accouterments of the culinary arts. The drawers were locked, but Aramenta knew what was in there, sterling-silver service for sixty people, she'd seen them polished a thousand times. Behind glass doors, Mother's china, Sèvres porcelain, a family heirloom dating from 1810, purchased by Great-grandfather Lee for his new bride. Produced as a special order, the plates each had a gold-embossed replica of one of the Lee line of sailing vessels, which ultimately became world famous for quality, service, and record-breaking trans-oceanic crossings with maximum payloads.

"What am I going to do?" Aramenta asked aloud.

"Hello?"

She froze. "Who's there?"

"Hello?" Same voice.

"Yes?" She walked into the hallway. "Who is it?"

"Miss Lee? Miss Aramenta?"

"Yes, who is it?"

"Miss Aramenta, I'm Randy Beausarge."

"Yes?" She looked at him through the screened door.

"Beausarge-Mathis-Beausarge and Smith, Attorneys, Miss Aramenta. We've represented your family for more than a hundred years."

He said it as though asking, not telling her.

Dimly from the depths of her childhood memory, a name recalled—now and then there was a Judge Beausarge who came to dinner on special occasions. "Judge Beausarge?" Aramenta questioned.

Randy Beausarge laughed. "My grandfather. He was an attorney too. May I come in?"

"What did you need, Mr. Beausarge?"

"I have several legal matters to cover, Miss Aramenta. There's your mother's will, which must be probated, and personal property to be transferred."

He grinned, blue eyes under youthful shocks of auburn hair askew over a well-formed forehead. "I really need to sit down with you, Miss Aramenta."

Aramenta pushed open the screen door. "Come in."

Inside, he extended a hand. "Well, how are you?"

"As compared to what, Mr. Beausarge? I'm hot, this place smells bad, and I am faced with the distasteful and herculean chore of disposing of it all."

"Then you are going to sell?"

"Everything."

"I see. In which case, we do need to implement the will."

"Which entails what?"

"Oh"—the young attorney met her eyes levelly—"stocks, bonds, debentures, cash deposits, property, it's quite involved, I'm afraid."

"The will?"

"No, the will is a masterpiece of simplicity. I know it by heart. Would you like me to recite it?"

"Why not?" Aramenta said.

" 'To my only living daughter, currently residing somewhere in Europe, I bequeath all my worldly belongings . . .' signed Mrs. Arlington Edward Lee, the Third."

"I had hoped to fly back to Paris in a few days. Apparently that isn't going to be possible."

"No," Beausarge confirmed soberly, "I don't think so."

"Come sit down, Mr. Beausarge. Do you prefer a musty dining-room table with bad lighting, or a moldy living room? I can give it to you formal or informal, and in all cases archaic."

The attorney nodded, unsmiling. "Your mother had become quite a recluse, you know. I never once saw her face-to-face in the ten years I've been handling her accounts. But I have an image of her from the bills."

"Bills?"

"Yes, all bills from any source came to us. We paid everything. Good Lord, who would believe that a house this size would only have a thirty-dollar-a-month electric bill? My house costs seventy!"

"Mother obviously didn't believe in waste, Mr. Beausarge."

They sat in the living room and Randy Beausarge studied Aramenta openly.

"Is something wrong?" Aramenta asked.

"No. I'm pleasantly surprised. I expected a little old lady and I get you."

"I beg your pardon?"

"I came out here expecting a wizened old biddy and here you sit, vibrant, youthful, and attractive. I had constructed a mental image of an elderly woman."

"I'm sixty."

"Yes, I know."

Aramenta nodded. "Let's get down to business, shall we?"

Beausarge withdrew a sheaf of papers. "Miss Aramenta, have you found any cashier's checks around the house?"

"I haven't begun looking for anything, yet."

"Mrs. Lee confirmed receiving the checks, but she never cashed them. Checks from stock dividends mostly, maturing negotiable bonds, which are the same as cash."

"Senile most probably," Aramenta said.

"No, not senile," Randy Beausarge said, adamantly. "If that'd been the case we would have taken steps to protect her health and well-being. According to my father, she was very astute."

"She was?"

"Do you hear something?" Randy asked.

Thump-thump-thump.

"Yes," Aramenta said. "Let's get on with the business at hand, please. I have more work to do than I can handle."

"All right."

That noise again.

"IRS is going to demand a complete accounting, which, I think, will take months. For one thing, I have no idea of the value of some of these assets, all of which are subject to inheritance tax. The last time we had an accounting, the estate was valued at something like sixteen million and—"

"Sixteen million!"

"Cash or liquid assets. By the time you add the increased value of land and—"

Thump-thump-thump.

"Miss Aramenta, do you think there's someone at the door?"

"No," Aramenta said, vaguely. "Please go on."

"It's like the uncashed bonds and checks that are around the house. I'm reasonably sure they're here somewhere, since her checking account has been inactive for fifteen years. There's no way of knowing the value of such—"

Thump-thump-thump.

Go home to Paris! She hadn't come for this. Life had been

comfortable, simple, her annuity and trust-fund checks had been more than adequate.

"... and the various items such as family jewelry, which are most likely in the safe deposit boxes ..."

How long would this take to resolve?

Thump-thump-thump.

"... actually the tax picture isn't as gray as it sounds. The firm has carefully structured shelters and depreciating schedules which will ..."

Thump-thump-thump.

Mother had certainly managed to leave her affairs in a shambles ...

"... and then— Miss Aramenta? Miss Aramenta, are you all right?"

"Yes." Her eyes refocused. "Please go on."

Thump-thump-thump.

Young Randy Beausarge turned and gazed toward the hallway portal. "Is that a dog, Miss Aramenta?"

"Probably. A dog. Please go on."

Thump-thump-thump.

"Big dog," Randy said, sorting papers

Chapter Three

The house had always made noises. "Talking," Father called it: expanding wood, contracting terra-cotta tile, the sighs and whispers of varying air currents, shifting foundations, water trickling down a gutter spout. As a child, Aramenta recalled an eerie screech of an oak limb gently scraping against a window of her room. Like spectral footsteps coming down the hall, the floor creaked in a rippling progression as temperature and humidity changed. At a certain place near the old servants' quarters, doors had a way of unlatching and swinging open. Later, the same doors would close, click, and be secure.

Below the servants' area, a large well had been dug when the house was first built, long before anyone ever heard of city water. A hundred years later, the well no longer needed, they had filled it with stones to keep children and animals from crawling in and falling through. The cistern and well served as a moderating force, slow to cool and even slower to warm than the area around it. It was the effect of the well, cooling air currents on a warm night, which caused walls and floors to shift, doors to open, and later when the cool air was overcome by natural expansion, doors closed again.

When they'd discovered the cause, at last, the opening doors became a family joke: "Come in, Captain!" somebody would say. When a door later closed, "Good night, Captain, come again."

The same well was responsible for a phenomenon in winter which raised hair and prickled flesh of strangers who observed it. In the formal dining room, atop a four-inch-thick marble mantel, moisture collected by condensation. With a fire in the hearth, the wall would shift and a vase on the mantel would move as though shoved by an unseen hand—to the very edge, where it stopped. Later the vase would return to precisely the spot from which it came.

"That's the captain," the family solemnly declared. "He's our ghost. Drowned on a Lee schooner at sea and came back looking for Great-granddaddy Lee, who designed the craft."

It was guaranteed to hasten lingering weekend guests who had overstayed their welcome.

Thump-thump-thump.

So Aramenta didn't pay much attention to sounds which came with evening. No doubt the explanation was as simple as an opening door, invisible footsteps, and the moving vase.

Randy Beausarge had called the employment services and Aramenta spent a day interviewing applicants. She dismissed all but one, within a few minutes. "Mary, miss," said the thickset black woman introducing herself. Mary professed to have a high-school education, three grown children, and "a bad need for money."

Mary toiled with a systematic thoroughness which quickly impressed Aramenta. The maid was not talkative, took directions well, and had an eye to detail which Aramenta appreciated.

"Begin at the front door and work toward the rear, Mary," Aramenta had said. "Clean from ceiling to floor. Can you handle this kind of labor?"

"Yessum."

"Fine. I pay by the hour, minimum wage; is that acceptable?"

"Yessum. Never got that much afore."

"Well, you'll get it here. Anything you require, ask for it."

Mary required everything. Brooms, mops, vacuum cleaner, extension cords for same, buckets, a tall stepladder and a short one. After the first day, she also required her husband, Joe.

"Joe he don't mind upsteps," Mary explained. "He don't think so strong, but he bends real good. I need some muscles, Miss Aramenta."

"Very well," Aramenta agreed. "I shall pay him by the hour also, Mary. Minimum wage, the same as you. Is that all right?"

"Yessum." Mary seemed none too sure. "But he didn't finish high school."

"I don't think that will matter," Aramenta said. "I'll continue to look to you for results, Mary. You manage your husband. Agreed?"

Wide grin and a nod.

When Mary finished a room, Aramenta followed, sorting through everything. Like Mary, she started at the front door working toward the back. Aramenta found the cashier's checks and negotiable bonds. At least, she found many. Between the pages of books, in unopened envelopes in a desk drawer, behind a hatbox in a closet, in cartons filled with newspaper clippings which had been gathered over the years but never pasted into scrapbooks. "Thousands of dollars' worth," she telephoned Randy.

"They should be listed and deposited right away, Miss Aramenta."

"Will you take care of that for me?" Aramenta asked.

"I'll pick them up this evening."

Aramenta read every shred of paper before discarding it. Parke-Bernet called to advise that she throw away very little. The accented voice came in a businesslike, but soothing tone over the long-distance wire.

"Everything has a value, Miss Lee. Furniture, paintings, silverware, dishes, rugs, even books and magazines. We will send a team of people who will carefully catalog items. If you will concentrate on separating anything you wish to keep, from that which you wish to offer, we will take over from there."

Thank God for somebody who could take over.

"Our people are bonded, of course," a slight British lilt to the inflections.

"Then I shall begin throwing out trash," Aramenta suggested.

"Trash of what nature, Miss Lee?"

"Evidently the upstairs bedrooms are filled with old newspapers."

"I shouldn't worry about it," he said. "Let our people examine everything first."

"It's mostly junk upstairs, I believe."

"One man's junk is another man's antique, Miss Lee."

Hadn't she heard that somewhere before? Aramenta hung up, feeling for the first time as though she were getting a grip on things.

Young Randy Beausarge was ideal. Professional, courteous, efficient, he eased the legalities and helped smooth Aramenta's way.

"Miss Aramenta, we have a human problem," Randy noted during one of his visits.

"What is that, Randy?"

"Your grandfather bought stock in a small private bank. Over the years, it grew, split, and was eventually absorbed by a larger banking organization here in town. During the crash of '28, it was one of the few banks which survived and prospered. At any rate, by the time your father died, your mother owned a majority of the bank's stock. Yet she didn't attend board meetings, or sign away her proxy to vote the stock. Since her death, everyone at the bank is aware of your presence. It has produced a certain tension in the organization, if you understand what I mean."

Aramenta sighed wearily. "What do you suggest?"

He listed the options, all designed to put the board at ease.

"Randy, I want to get through all this, sell the property, and go home. What do you recommend?"

The attorney thought a long moment, then shrugged. "You've obviously walked into more than you anticipated. You're swamped with the house. In my opinion you aren't prepared to exercise judgment in an impartial manner."

"And you recommend?"

He smiled. "Let 'em sweat until you're ready."

"So be it," she responded.

Like an abstract in blacks and grays, fragmented images began to merge in Aramenta's mind with tiny clues as to the kind of existence Mother had lived. Mother had saved everything. As issues of magazines arrived, she stacked them unread in a corner until such time as they could be baled and stored upstairs. Morning and evening newspapers were similarly packaged.

On a pad by the old-fashioned French-style telephone, Aramenta found an extensive grocery list in a jerky scrawl, with a telephone number which she called out of curiosity. It was a small market on "the hill"—they delivered, charged, and later billed Beausarge attorneys. In drawers beneath the phone table, thirty years of duplicate billing attested to the span of time this had covered. Mother's outside activities had been curtailed sharply at the end of 1945. It was then that Lee Manor began to fall into disarray, settling into the death throes of a mansion no longer pulsing with life.

In trunks stored in a huge walk-in closet serving Mother's bedroom, Aramenta found letters dating back to a time when the only "stamps" were embossed envelopes, the datelines ranging back over one and a half centuries. On a shelf were the tattered and brittle logs of ships, ancient transcripts in cryptic codes only a seaman might decipher. Beneath dust covers, in round-top steamers, were carefully preserved records of family finances, life's joys and tragedies. Here Aramenta discovered a series of scrapbooks wrapped in protective covers which had succumbed to beetles, roaches, and silverfish. The pages were chronicles of ascending wealth and influence, personal achievements, marriages, births, obituaries—details of one Lee after another.

With a jolt, Aramenta uncovered a scrapbook spanning her own youth. Lips tightly compressed, stilling a quiver that sprang to them, Aramenta saw photographs of her sister, Annette, four years older than Aramenta; and brother, Arlington, eight years older. Aramenta sat on a dusty box, turning pages, watching time move from birth to—

Annette had always defied Mother. With Mother's lavender eyes and raven hair, Annette could be vicious in her counterattacks and yet, mysteriously, she'd been Mother's favorite.

Arlington, dear, sweet, gentle Arlington. From infancy hewed and honed to Mother's concept of what a Lee male should be. Aramenta stared at faded photos of Arlington in military garb, never smiling, from the first day at a local academy up to and through Annapolis, which he'd detested.

"I don't want to go there, Mother."

"What you want truly is not important, Arlington."

"I'm not going."

"You," Mother had replied coldly, "will go, Arlington. Your father manipulated every political string available to the Lees and you now have this wonderful opportunity. You will go, young man. And don't sass me, boy. I shan't allow it. I shan't tolerate it! Now get yourself dressed. Senator Mathis will be here this evening for dinner. Arlington!"

Aramenta remembered how Brother had turned, frail shoulders back, pale head high, eyes filled with loathing.

"Get that expression off your face, Arlington Edward," Mother admonished mildly. "Tonight I shall expect you to thank the good Senator for this marvelous and unique opportunity."

He'd left the room without answering.

As a child he had never enjoyed physical activities. Horses frightened him, tennis was exhausting, sports a bore. He'd been dominated and twisted by Mother, pursuing family tradition in military school. He was told about the lives of princes who became kings and how fate decreed one's station. "Blood tells," Mother hammered. "Blood has its responsibilities!"

The day he graduated from Annapolis, Arlington Edward Lee IV was found hanging in a senior-class locker room.

There was no obituary in the scrapbook.

Annette had vowed from childhood, she would someday run away. At seventeen, she had. When the letter came from her "husband," it was a misspelled epistle to a childless wife who died in her prime giving birth to their first — stillborn.

"Yes," Mother had rasped. "Yes, I told her, Aramenta. *Blood tells!* Listen to your mother, child. Why should you tread the mire all men must when Mother can guide you around it? Never forget your sister, Annette, God rest her soul. Dead! Dead, Aramenta, and for what?" Mother had wept and mourned for months.

Then as though Annette's demise had galvanized her, Mother turned to Aramenta, her least favorite. Time and maternal losses did not temper Mother, no indeed! She turned on Aramenta with a vengeance, as though salvaging one of the three would somehow rectify her errors with the first two.

After Pearl Harbor, Brookley Field became a training center for the nation's air force. It was in the summer of 1943 that Aramenta met, loved, and married Lt. j.g. James Darcy, fifteen days before he shipped out for the European theater of operations.

Fifteen days that should have been the epitome of romance and happiness. *Damn* her! Aramenta put the scrapbook aside, hands perspiring, trying to brush dust from her slacks. Each touch became a smudge.

"I cannot believe you have done this!"

"I love him."

"What is it?" Mother had cried. "Insanity? First Arlington, then Annette, and now you?"

"Mother, we're married and that is that."

"A—a commoner!"

"We are not royalty, Mother."

"Son of a mechanic—for God's sake, Aramenta!"

"Mother," emphatically, "I love him."

Stunned, James had stood by, listening

"Ungrateful, deceiving, lying—"

"I'm leaving, Mother."

"You stand right there!" Mother turned on James. "It is you who will be leaving, young man, this instant."

"No, ma'am, I'm afraid not."

"How dare you come into my home and defy me?"

"I married your daughter, Mrs. Lee. If I go, she goes It becomes a matter of your choosing whether you wish to continue a relationship with her."

Head shaking, hands knotted, Mother glared at Aramenta.

"I want you both to remember something," Mother had said, voice shockingly steady now. "I want you to remember that, in the final analysis, blood tells."

"Oh, Mother!"

"You shall see," Mother intoned.

"Let's go, James."

"Blood tells and don't you forget it!"

"Come on, darling."

"You'll be calling soon enough, Aramenta. Blighted and broken, but you'll call. You shall learn, just as Annette learned and just as—"

James later said, "Like a curse, almost."

And of course, it was.

Aramenta carefully resealed the scrapbooks, each move stirring silt that rode shafts of sunlight coming through small-paned windows which Mary and her husband had opened to air the large closet. She walked out through the bedroom, then down the hall, opening doors and closing them after a brief glance into rooms where time stood still Personal belongings placed as though yesterday, untouched for years.

"Miss Lee!" Mary's eyes were saucers of white punctuated by pinpoints of brown. "Something's prowling round this house, Miss Lee!"

"Rodents, you mean?"

"No, ma'am. Like ghost*es.*"

Aramenta told about the opening doors, the moving vase Her intentions were to mollify fears, but the explanations seemed to have the opposite effect. The next day, Mary called to quit. Depressed, frustrated, and angry, Aramenta threw on fresh clothing and went out. She had not come here for this! She didn't want it! She wanted to get on a plane and fly home to sanity, serenity, and the few friends she had acquired in the quiet suburb where she lived. She missed morning coffee on Montmartre, the flurry of pigeons taking wing and the music—not Muzak, God forbid, but live musicians wending through the streets, into cafés, playing with emotion and pleasure.

Returning from her solitary day, Aramenta parked her car, paused outside the front door, and with a faint urge to be ill as her impetus, returned to the steps and sat in the evening air. Listening to crickets in harmony, cicadas whirring, she took deep drafts of air, trying to still a twisting in her abdomen.

Thump-thump-thump. Distantly. Muffled.

What *could* that be? The cistern learning new tricks of contraction and expansion? Too insistent for that, she decided. It came in a pattern, too. Threes—thump-thump thump. Halt. Thump-thump-thump. Halt. Thump-thump thump. Like a one-legged man climbing stairs, pausing to catch his breath, resting on his wooden stump. Thump stump-stump. Stump-stump-stump.

Aramenta pulled at the front of her blouse with two fingertips, separating damp clothing from moist flesh. Mobile was not only warm, it was humid. As a child, her sinuses had given her much trouble, including violent headaches

Thump-thump-thump. Maybe a dangling piece of wood blown against a side of the house. Or a rear door. Aramenta arose, pushing through a privet hedge between the overgrown yard and walkway. She put aside any visions of snakes—her first thought—and made her way around the main house and east wing. She paused, listening, then walked on, circling a far end of the building.

In a full moon, like a Currier and Ives print, the livery stable and carriage house stood engraved against the sky Oaks murmured. Aramenta went to a stable door. It had been a stable, later a carriage house; then, too narrow for modern automobiles, it had become a storage building. She tried to open the door, but it was blocked by gravel washed against it over the years. She turned back toward the house, listening. Nothing. Whatever it was, it wasn't out here.

Chastising herself, Aramenta returned to the porch, found her keys, and entered. She had left the feeble yellow hall light burning. Eyes wide to admit more available light to her sensory system, she walked to Mother's bedroom. In the dark, she undressed completely. Mary's husband had opened windows with a crowbar, but it had not dispelled the mustiness. Aramenta closed the bathroom door partially behind her, squinting as she turned on the bright light. Mary had not cleaned the shower curtain adequately. Never mind. Take a shower. Go to bed.

The pelt of water was instantly relaxing. She stood, head hung, letting it beat against her neck and shoulders. It was amazing how therapeutic running, warm water could be. Very relaxing, very—

She jolted. Through the opaque shower curtain a shadow took form. She pressed back against the tile, watching. Water in her eyes. She blinked. Gone! Ridiculous! Stupid! She threw open the shower curtain, aluminum hoops squealing against an overhead rod.

Holding a towel before her, she looked around the corner. The door was open. Open? Water dripping, towel to her breasts, she stared wide-eyed toward the dark bedroom.

"Hello!"

Cursing her jittery nerves, Aramenta stepped completely from the tub. Had she made that wet track? Wind blew the door? She stared at the dark; water rushed in the shower; heart pounding. Don't stand here! Move!

"Hello?"

Chapter Four

Randy Beausarge sat at the spacious and unlittered desk that the firm had given him. Like Russian letters, his gilded name on the frosted glass door read, "Яandall Béausaяge" with smaller block letters announcing, "AттояиЕ-Y." That was him, all right. From the outside he was prosperous, with future guaranteed. But from within, like his name reading backward, he felt convoluted and misplaced.

As the youngest member of the organization, the petty and inconsequential things had fallen to him. Legal research for the firm, mostly, and trivial matters that the others refused to deal with. His own ability remained untapped, untested.

He looked like a man on top of the world—good firm, fine salary, and plenty of time to play golf. But golf was not what Randy wanted to play. He yearned to get out there and compete, rise, win, and conquer. There was more to a career than money! A man had to feel an inner reward that came only from seeing the fruits of his labor, from pursuing his ambition with positive forward strides. Randy had visions of a political career of his own, and fantasies of his day in court—but all had vaporized with the decade just past.

No point in fooling himself. At thirty-six he was still "the boy." He wasn't going to make city councilman, much less governor of the state. He wasn't going anywhere! He would continue poring through the legal library and paying the Lee household bills.

Then last night, out of the trivia that trapped him came opportunity. Miss Aramenta, voice trembling over the telephone, said she had been taking a bath and thought somebody was in the house. Randy had gotten up grumbling, but secretly pleased to have *something* which required his attention. He'd driven over, walked the grounds, house, checked back doors and windows, putting the lady at ease She'd thanked him profusely and he had stayed to have a cup of coffee, sitting in the kitchen at a meat butcher's-block able.

It was then that he learned that Aramenta Lee didn't merely dislike her mother, she damned well hated the old woman. Whatever the cause of their estrangement thirty years ago, it had been caustic and final. Aramenta had gone to Paris "widowed," as she put it, and had completely severed all ties to the Lees of Mobile, which then consisted only of the elder Mrs. Lee. When Aramenta finally came home, she came against her will. She arrived completely ignorant of what she had fallen heir to and furthermore she didn't give a damn. She truly did not want to be bothered with it.

Since her arrival, Aramenta Lee had become frustrated and even more alienated from anything Lee. As she said last evening, with tears in her eyes, "I want to go home, goddamn it. I want out of here!"

Randy's thoughts were interrupted as Rosa brought in a sheaf of papers. "Your brother asked that you study these contracts," Rosa related. Randy glanced at them. Oil leases. Since Getty Oil uncovered the find up at Creola, mineral rights had been changing hands in a flurry. He nodded, incensed; it wasn't his account. Rosa left the room and closed the door.

Okay, Beausarge, think this thing through. You've been doing research and legwork for ten years. A dull, thankless job and your largest responsibility around here. Now, unbeknown to anyone else (and thank God for that), you find yourself sitting on an estate that probably has a net worth approaching thirty million. Tidy sum, that. At 5 percent of earnings for the management of same, you could become very wealthy.

Money wasn't the major factor here, although it would be nice. The juicy prize here is Miss Aramenta Lee. She only wants to be relieved of an onerous and unpleasant task so she can go home. She is an unhappy lady who needs a gallant knight on a white charger to rush in and slay dragons on her behalf. And he could be that knight.

He would have to be willing to replace a housekeeper who quit because she hears spooky noises. He must be ready to contract painters and handle the disposition of the family home and assets. He must be willing to make decisions for her—always with her best interests at heart, of course.

What may the knight expect for a field of dead dragons? Money. Yes. But much more. He could expect to become responsible for things like the proxy vote which would con trol Marine Guaranty Bank with a mailed fist. He could anticipate a full-time position on such titillating boards of directors as Hanson and Hanson Realty, one state utility company, two independent telephone companies, one large insurance corporation, and a small oil company.

Therein might the brave knight find the flaming sword of political clout. More than money, a wise and courageous savior would probably assume all the unpleasantries which now so plagued Miss Aramenta Lee—and allow her to go home to the simple life.

Of course, he soberly reminded himself, he could also lose it all if anybody around here even sniffed the fantastic opportunities involved. He would have to win Miss Aramenta's undying gratitude and confidence.

Randy sat forward and flicked his seldom-used interoffice communications system. "Rosa."

"Yes, Mr. Beausarge?" Rosa sounded slightly startled.

"Call Mr. Morgan at Alabama Employment and see if he can have lunch with me. Suggest to him that it is more social than business, but it is business."

"Yes, Mr. Beausarge."

Randy leaned back again, smiling. He did something he'd never done before: he put his feet on the desk. Yessir, a wise and gallant knight could ride to the Governor's Mansion on what he would gain out of this account. He could develop political power virtually overnight.

Randy sat on the edge of a divan. Across the room, expression rapt, a young man from the Alabama Employment Service followed Randy's conversation with Aramenta.

"Miss Aramenta, Virgil Wilson is twenty-five, single, from a farm family in Lucedale, Mississippi. He graduated from school in Jackson, having completed the twelfth grade. He's had shop training, knows some carpentry, and according to a check I ran on him, he is honest, hardworking, and willing. I took the liberty of investigating him fully, with his permission. He's been in Mobile about a year, unable to secure employment. He has a good mind, strong back, and he needs a job. He is also free to move in here. I thought perhaps the carriage house could be converted into living quarters for him. He'll take that responsibility. After interviewing him three times and having interviewed a dozen other people, I feel he will be able to best satisfy your needs."

Aramenta gazed unsmiling at Virgil. "What rate of pay do you require, Mr. Wilson?"

"We agreed on a hundred dollars a week, Miss Aramenta," Randy added. "Plus his living quarters."

"I see." Aramenta smiled. It occurred to Randy it was the first time he'd seen her smile.

"Virgil," Randy instructed, "go around back and look over the carriage house. See what it needs to make it livable. Whatever it requires, make a list and I'll see to it."

Virgil nodded and arose.

"Miss Aramenta, you won't have to worry about him getting spooked by noises."

"Oh? Why is that?"

"Virgil is deaf."

"Deaf! Then how do I—"

"He reads lips, he is intelligent. He desperately needs employment. If all I've heard is true, the deaf make valuable and extremely loyal employees. Mr. Morgan at the employment service has been trying to help this fellow find a job for months. The fact that Virgil is deaf limits his capacity only where language is concerned."

Aramenta's expression altered slightly.

"If for any reason he isn't satisfactory, however," Randy said, standing, "pick up the telephone and call my office. I'll find somebody, somewhere, who can do what you need."

"Thank you, Randy. But surely you don't have time to be bothered with things like this."

Randy's eyebrows lifted. "Miss Aramenta, if you had a client who was worth thirty million, wouldn't you have time for things like this?"

Taken aback, Aramenta stammered, "I don't know."

"You would," Randy said. "However, if you would like to see a happy attorney, how about allowing me to take you out to dinner this evening? I'm afraid you have a jaundiced view of our remarkable city. It would give me pleasure to alter your opinion, if I can."

"Randy, I'm not going to remain here. I'm going home," Aramenta warned. "Nothing can change my mind."

"That isn't my purpose," Randy said, smoothly. "Frankly, it is in my best interest if you go. Somebody has to vote your proxy at the bank, and somebody has to handle your investments."

There it was. He could see the dawning light in her eyes now. He was after something and he made no bones about it. Aramenta Lee nodded, slowly, head going up and down as though each nod was a reaffirmation of what she was realizing.

"What time should I be ready?" she asked.

"Oh," Randy said, "sevenish."

"Seven," Aramenta stated. "Sharp. And Randy—"

He pivoted at the door.

"Please drop the 'miss,' will you? My financial adviser and confidant must not make me feel antebellum, much less southern aristocracy."

"So be it, Aramenta. See you at seven."

Thump-thump-thump.

Randy hesitated. "Must be the plumbing."

"What?"

"You didn't hear something?" Randy questioned.

"No, what was it?"

Randy laughed, shortly. "Now I'm getting spooked!"

"Get out of here," Aramenta snorted. "My nerves are frayed enough without you adding to it!"

Randy walked around the outside of the house, looking for the deaf man. Score one for him. He'd guessed right.

Aramenta not only appreciated absolute honesty, she demanded it. Now the cards were on the table.

Through the back door, Aramenta observed Randy speaking to the deaf man. Together, they went into the carriage house. There had once been a complete bath back there, and indeed a small apartment of sorts which a gardener had used during Aramenta's youth.

When Randy emerged again, he was smiling, Virgil nodding. Apparently, everything was satisfactory. They drove away together, returned later with cardboard boxes and a battered suitcase bound with an old belt. The deaf man took in various small cartons and an antiquated typewriter. Sipping coffee, watching from a bay window in the eating area of the kitchen, Aramenta observed Randy removing his jacket and tie, rolling up his sleeves. He and the deaf man spent the afternoon screening windows, making repairs, working side by side.

Thinking the men might want cold drinks and sandwiches, Aramenta went to the refrigerator to see what she could offer. The milk was gone, the empty carton still in place. No sandwich meat. In fact, no bread. She telephoned the grocery Mother had been using, ordering what she required. The drawling southern voice politely agreed to send it over "rat now."

By the time the supplies arrived, however, Randy had gone. Aramenta nonetheless went out, the sandwiches her excuse, to see how things were progressing. She found the deaf man putting away books, generally setting his house in order

"I thought perhaps you might be hungry," Aramenta said. His eyebrows lifted, a ready smile softening features which seemed accustomed to smiling. He nodded, gestured at a chair, and held it for her as she was seated.

"Your name is—Virgil?"

He nodded.

"Please understand, I do not know how to talk to the deaf."

His mouth formed a silent "Oh," and he brought out a pad of paper and pencil from his pocket. He wrote in block letters, "Speak naturally. Do not shout. I can read lips. We will learn together."

She read this. Read it again. Nodded. "Good."

Virgil offered her the plate of sandwiches and poured iced tea in her glass. Mannerly, courteous, agreeable. In silence, they ate, acutely aware of each other, their eyes meeting now and again followed by nervous smiles.

"You type?" Aramenta inquired.

He nodded and simultaneously shook one fist, palm down, which she guessed meant "yes."

"That's nice," she said. He shrugged his shoulders.

Swallowing a mouthful of food, Virgil's lips formed soundless words, "I want to be a writer."

"Say again."

"I want to be a writer," he repeated, now making the motions of using a pencil against his other hand.

"That's interesting," Aramenta observed. "I once wrote poetry, as a child. Not very good, I'm afraid."

His interest aroused, Virgil dug into a box of papers. He withdrew a manuscript and gave it to her.

"You wrote this?" she asked.

A nod.

"I'll read it," she offered. "May I take it with me?"

Animated nodding now.

"Very well." Aramenta stood. "If you are ready, we will begin work tomorrow."

"Good," his lips said it, one hand flipped from mouth outward in a flat palm.

"That means 'good'?" Aramenta questioned.

He nodded, pleased. Then pointing to the sandwiches, he made the same sign

Aramenta returned to the kitchen and the bay window. She saw Virgil moving things, cleaning. She was slightly disturbed and the fact of that disturbed her all the more. Why? Because he was afflicted? Didn't speak? She'd felt ill at ease, even awkward. Afraid she'd blunder, probably. Reminding herself he was "only human," she determined to be friendly and open. Their mutual needs could be satisfied with the rudimentary kind of exchange they'd just experienced. After all, how much language did one need to instruct a handyman?

The following morning at the break of dawn, Virgil was tapping lightly on the front door. Still not dressed, Aramenta dismissed him with instructions to "clean the yard."

Later in the day, Randy appeared with a Yazoo mower and Aramenta went out to find a mountain of limbs and debris already gathered. Virgil made a striking motion against one palm and she got matches for him.

"My word," she commented to Randy, "he works fast and hard, doesn't he?"

"As we had hoped."

"Randy, I enjoyed dinner last evening. The Chinese food was superb."

"We'll do it again soon," Randy said. "Aramenta, I have contracted a professional cleaning service. The employees are bonded, the manager assures me he will also take personal responsibility. I thought perhaps they could begin by cleaning the downstairs area as you sort out what is upstairs."

"Excellent."

"I also made a deal with a Negro man who does my yard

work. He has a pickup truck and he'll help Virgil load anything you want to be taken away."

"Good, Randy."

"Whoa!" Randy yelled at Virgil. "Hey, Virgil. Wait a minute. Oh, for God's sake, I forgot he's deaf."

Randy ran over to Virgil and shook his head, stomping out a fire Virgil had started. "It's against the law to burn," Randy said. The alarm slowly eased in Virgil's eyes and he nodded, glancing at Aramenta to catch her reaction, whether forgiveness or rebuke.

"In case of trouble," Aramenta commented when Randy returned, "I'd better plan to call someone else."

But that evening, Virgil ran a wire from the kitchen to his quarters. He demonstrated to Aramenta, by pulling the wire it shook a flag in his apartment.

"You want me," he said, hands gesturing with each mouthed word, "call me like this." He shook the wire.

"Very good, Virgil."

He left, the perpetual smile warming his face.

She was almost asleep, windows open, the thud of insects against the screen lulling her. Exhausted, she had dropped into that half-sleep where full unconsciousness won't come because of muscles aching with fatigue.

Out of the usual night sounds came one that brought her up, eyes open. She realized her hands were extended at arm's length before her, waving the air as though feeling for something. Bad dream? What?

She tipped a lamp trying to turn it on and groped up the base to the switch. She pulled a chain and soft light illuminated the room. In the instant she first gained sight, she could have sworn she saw something flash past the bedroom door. She threw on a robe and went into the hall, turning on a light there. She peered into the living room, dining room, and started back to bed. Glancing down the hall, she saw the basement door ajar. Remembering a flashlight Randy donated the other night, she got it from the bedroom. Thus equipped, she went to the basement door.

Thump-thump-thump. Aramenta turned the flashlight down the steps, a shaft of light probing darkness. Ah! A switch. She was ready to flick it, then hesitated. A faint illumination came from a far corner of the cavernous basement. She stooped low, trying to see. She took a cautious step lower, then another. Might break her fool neck! She turned the flashlight down on the dusty treads—but they weren't dusty! At least, not evenly dusty. Aramenta knelt, examining the stairs. Apparently, someone had been walking up and down—

The flashlight beam zagged as she threw it toward the full basement. Thump-thump-thump, coming from the back. Why should light be burning down there? She returned to the top of the stairs and activated the lights electrically. Now the basement fell silent.

"Is somebody down here?" she called, flashlight poking into shadows not vanquished by the light bulbs overhead. No thumping. Maybe it had something to do with the electricity. She walked toward the rear of the cellar. The lights were coming from the subbasement.

It was a wine cellar, actually. Built by Great-granddaddy Lee and embellished by Grandfather and then Aramenta's father too. Designed to house and protect valuable wines, the cellar was down yet another flight of steps. There were two doors one must enter, both heavy, barred, and designed to keep out servants or thieves. Looking down the steps, she saw that both doors were open. Oddly, a tray lay in a center of light at the foot of the stairs, between the doors. It was one of those partitioned trays such as a school cafeteria might use.

"Hello down there!" She glanced around. Directly ahead, between crates, discarded paraphernalia, and abandoned furniture, she saw thin circles of light rising from the floor. She remembered now, it was possible to change the light bulbs servicing the wine cellar only by lifting out the fixtures from up here. As a child, the wine cellar was forbidden for play. On rare occasions Aramenta had gone down there, always with Father. She recalled row upon row of wine racks, which Father had slowly diminished as he came more and more to depend on alcohol to keep away the demons which he saw when sober and living with Mother.

A faint clicking sound caught Aramenta's ear and she flashed light in that direction. She stared across the room at a clock mechanism. Moving closer, she saw tiny pegs of steel teeth jutting from the dial face. It was a timer device, the type used to turn things on or off automatically. Apparently set to start something around nine in the evening, it also cut off at six the next morning.

She laughed aloud. The very times when the thumping was most predominant. Whatever caused the knocking was associated with this timer. Aramenta returned to the stairs, doused the lights, and instantly the noise began again, more insistently than before—thump-thump-thump-thump-thump.

She flicked on the lights. The sound halted. Off again. Thump-thump-thump!

So simple. Probably a pump of some kind, or any of a dozen other pieces of electrically operated equipment. Like the moving vase and the opening doors—a logical explanation.

Mildly curious now, Aramenta listened as a new tone joined the rapping. A moan. A cog in need of lubricant, perhaps

She left the basement lights off and closed the door. As an afterthought, she turned the key, locking it Now at ease, she went to bed and quickly to sleep.

Chapter Five

Virgil Wilson sat at his typewriter, fingers poised. He stared at a single sheet of paper, white, void, as blank as his mind. Surely *The Earth Is the Lord's* and *The Source* weren't written by staring at clean paper! What did a writer do when his brain idled without thought? He pulled the paper from the platen, smoothed a crease it had gained from being bent so long. He centered the carriage, reset the margins, indented as though for a paragraph—and stared.

"Deaf folks can't write." That's what Papa had said, his coarse thick eyebrows pulled low. "It don't pay to be a dreamer, Virgil. Dreams don't come true. Be smart, son It don't take ears to till land and plant. You think plowing a straight furrow ain't something? How long you think it takes a body to learn about fertilizers and seasons and God knows what all? Being deaf is deaf, son. It ain't never going to change."

Mama had sat to one side, rocking slowly as she sewed, head down to hide tears. Papa put a calloused hand on Virgil's arm, his black eyes troubled.

"Me and your ma want to help you, Virgil. I wish we knew more and were wiser. I wish to God we did. We've prayed for guidance. Since you come home from deaf school we've watched you suffer, son. We want to help, but there's no way to help a man who can't be helped, don't you see that?"

Virgil signed, lips synchronized to produce words without sound as his gestures "spoke."

"I want to be a writer."

"Boy, listen to me." Papa's grip tightened on Virgil's arm. "Now get this through your head—people who talk, who know the language, they might spend a lifetime getting to be a writer. There ain't—you understand me?—there ain't no such thing as a deaf writer!"

"Why do you discourage me with everything I want to do?" Virgil accused.

"I don't do that."

"You are against anything I want to do!"

"No. That ain't true, Virgil. But if I lied, saying 'Yes, Virgil, that's a good idea,' how much would you trust me later when you found it is not a good idea?"

"I will be a writer!"

Papa nodded, face worried. "You could write some things, I suppose."

"No, not some—books."

"Books," Papa's lips formed the word. "Perhaps. Maybe some kinds of books."

Having beaten Papa into yielding, the cautious affirmations were even more painful than his former denials.

"Papa." Virgil had grabbed the older man's shoulders, "I must try."

Papa nodded, eyes downcast.

For six years after high school, after Gallaudet rejected his bid for college entrance, Virgil had tried.

"I didn't finish fourth grade, Virgil," Papa would say "God don't require no college degree to sow and reap."

Virgil's presence was needed on the farm. An extra hand where there are never enough for the work. But he was a daily reminder of "God's will." Somehow, they were never sure why, they had afflicted their only child with ears which could not hear. When Virgil sat alone, isolated, brooding and unhappy, it was a very personal reminder of their failure. Like hail shredding tobacco, or weevils in the corn Virgil was an act of nature that was quietly suffered with stoic forbearance.

In a world of speaking people, Virgil was an alien, segregated from daily communication, more an object than a human mind. His inner turmoil and frustrated ambitions soon made him a stranger in his own home. What he felt, his aspirations and dreams, were as remote to Mama and Papa as a distant star. Had he been endowed with an ability to speak clearly, he wasn't sure he could have explained.

To a man like Papa, born of the soil and son of a similar man, what sense could be made of Virgil's love of words? How could Virgil express the aching in his soul, the anger and futility? Not because he couldn't hear, he'd never known anything else. His thoughts were imprisoned. His mind was locked in a cell with no outlet! It was more than a need for expression, more than a desire to speak with other beings; he yearned for a sensitive response to his ideas, a sympathetic ear for his prose, and most precious, he needed to let someone know he was here, in this mute body, alone and lonely.

The torment to his spirit never truly subsided. He seemed destined to the same dreary and fruitless existence most deafs face. Trapped. Doomed. Desperate.

"I'm going to Mobile, Papa."

"For what?"

"To get work."

How many times had Virgil seen that expression now deepening in Papa's eyes?

"We need you here, Virgil." Mama's hands, stubby fingers clumsily signing.

"I must go."

"You mean you want to," Papa amended, almost angrily, "not that you *must!*"

Virgil nodded. "Want to," he corrected.

It had taken nearly a year. Coming to Mobile by bus, or hitchhiking to save the fare. Wearing a tie that was narrower than any he saw others wearing, his brogans scuffed and outsized, hair cut too closely at the sides and not short enough on top. He remembered studying his reflection in the employment-office window: a country hick, a—a deaf country hick.

Week after week he came, determined to take anything as a beginning. One job after another was denied him or soon withdrawn because he couldn't be "managed." After each failure he returned to the only recourse he had—the farm.

And now, this job. Mr. Morgan at the employment office had been cautious.

"I don't know how long it will last, Virgil," Mr. Morgan had warned. "But it pays good, a hundred a week. The lady's attorney will want to interview you and check up on you. Is that all right?"

Virgil had nodded, smiling, heart pounding.

"Go to this address then," Mr. Morgan had instructed. "Ask for Mr. Randall Beausarge. And Virgil—"

Virgil waited, trying to comprehend the expression he saw on Mr. Morgan's face.

"Virgil, tell Mr. Beausarge how hard you will work. Don't be ashamed to tell him how much the job will mean to you. It is physical labor. Tell him you are willing to do this. Do you understand?"

Virgil understood well enough. It had taken three meetings with Mr. Beausarge. He got the job finally, by begging with tears in his eyes when he thought it might get away.

Virgil pushed back from the typewriter, bitter memories bringing an acid taste to his mouth, a shiver to his muscles. All that talk in high school about a trade and the value of an education—total nonsense! Nobody had told him about the uneasy glances, the rudely cupped hands to hide lips, the torturous tests of loud noises behind his back to see if he was *really* deaf! No teacher had ever mentioned the open hostility of the hearing world, the way orals suddenly withdrew when they sensed they were getting too close to a deaf person. They should have told the students, "Forget all this emphasis on history and mathematics and typing, boys and girls. Your biggest problem is not going to be job qualifications. Your largest hurdle is going to be overt, crude, cruel discrimination. You see, orals all think you are *dumb!* You can't discuss politics, religion, or philosophy—you can't even ask a clerk where to find a loaf of bread! Language, that's your loss. Language so natural and learned so effortlessly by orals—it will be to the deaf a never-ending and constantly frustrating experience."

Nobody had told him that even a written note could give him away—awkward grammar written as he would sign it, because that was Virgil's lexicon: *signs.* He was enslaved by a language unique to him and his kind, and the mysterious melody of the spoken word was still incomprehensible to him.

He would never forget the heartfelt joy he had experienced at age nine when he enrolled in the first grade at the school for the deaf. All around him hands darted, fingers flying, communicating! Lips became secondary, sounds unimportant now. Virgil had seized a signing book issued to him and devoured it with such intensity he had learned the basic hand signs within a month. At last, he could tell of thoughts snared in his brain and he listened with his eyes as others revealed their minds to him! He dreamed of signing. He caught his hands talking to himself. He observed sleeping students in the dormitories talking in their sleep, hands like fluttering moths, incomplete in form and arcane to a viewer. "You talked in your sleep," they would tell one another. The standard response, "I hope I didn't keep you awake." Always good for a laugh, each student jiggling his shoulders to show the depth of his mirth.

Then came the printed word. Here was a link that could connect Virgil's mute world to a hearing mind. There was a word for every object, as there was a sign. And when there was no specific sign, the hand-formed letters of the alphabet with different finger positions, to spell out meanings. At age twelve or thirteen, Virgil began to master language, but it was never easy He discovered that "thing" words had "connecting" words which gave orals the lilt and flow of conversation. To Virgil's utter dismay, he had discovered that some things would be forever denied to him—the nuance of expression, the elusive tone of a voice which could turn an apparently innocuous statement into a joke. But worse, these jokes often incorporated such abstruse factors as "puns," always a deaf man's nemesis. They didn't make sense even after a lengthy explanation.

Virgil sat forward looking at the typing paper. He wrote:

Dear Marie:

I am Mobile now with job finally. I am a yard cleaner. That is funny for a writer to be a yard worker. I know. But the pay is 100$ each week. Good pay. I am very tired. I am happy. I work for Miss Lee. She tries to be nice, but she is oral and cannot sign.

Know I love you. Miss you. I very lonely Marie. It is hard most part of deaf to be so lonely. I wish we could use telephone. Then I would call to ask how are you and have you made any friends new? I am trying to write stories but cannot think of any. Do you know some ideas for stories? I gave Miss Lee something I wrote. She has not said anything about it. Maybe not good. I don't know. Each day I wait to see what she says and she does not talk about it. It must be bad writing. Oh. I miss you. Please write.

Love,
Virgil

He saw the grammatical errors, the stilted sentences, but was too tired to edit and retype the note. He put it in an envelope, addressed it, and used one of the stamps he'd bought in a roll of a hundred. He walked toward Springhill College, until he found a mailbox, where he posted the letter.

Aramenta sat on the floor replacing books in the library shelves. She was watching Virgil as he tenderly wiped mildew from each volume. Now and then, contrary to his usual manner of fast, uninterrupted labor, he paused to gently fan the pages of a particular book, hesitating here or there to examine a photograph or read a passage.

Brother handled books that way. The touch and feel of books did something to him. Almost as though he drew a tactile pleasure merely in the manipulation of them. She recalled how angry he once became because somebody dog-eared a page to mark the point reached in reading it. Left to his own, Brother always went to the library and there became engrossed in one book or another.

"Confine your mind to constructive things, Arlington," Mother would admonish. "One cannot consume it all, therefore be selective."

It always piqued Mother to find one of the children wast-
ing themselves on popular novels. "As one thinks, so one is,"
Mother lectured. "Words are to the mind as food to the
body, to nourish and mature. Trash is best consigned to the
garbage heap."

Aramenta tapped the floor, a signal Virgil had taught her
to gain his attention. He looked up, startled, then shamed
that he was not working fast enough.

"Let us finish the work, Virgil," Aramenta said. "You
may borrow any book to read in the evening."

The room was too dark to follow her lips. Virgil came to
her and cocked his head as though to better hear her.

"I said, Let's get the work done," Aramenta repeated.
"This evening you may borrow any book which interests
you."

Virgil nodded and returned to his chore with more delib-
eration. In the shadows, his back bent, he almost looked like
Brother. Get busy, Aramenta! Set the pace and you may
better expect a follower to emulate it.

"Miss Lee?" It was one of the Parke-Bernet men.

"Yes?"

"What a magnificent piece that is!" He referred to the
book cabinet. Aramenta was trying to recall his name.

"Veneered on oak with coromandel wood," he said, softly,
"showing marquetry of tortoiseshell on brass. Eighteenth-
century French, I believe."

"Your name escapes me, I'm sorry," Aramenta said.

"Smythe." He straightened a bit. "With a 'y' and ending
in 'e'—Smythe."

"Yes, Mr. Smythe. What may I do for you?"

"We have concluded that a systematic approach here is in
order. With your permission, we shall begin with the attic
and end with the cellar."

'Fine."

Mr. Smythe excused himself with an old-world gesture, heels together, a curt, quick bodily nod.

Virgil had paused again, leafing through another book. Temptation's way! Aramenta tapped the floor with her foot. He hastily returned to work. At this rate they'd be in the library for six months Aramenta tapped anew and gestured, "Come with me."

On the front porch, Aramenta asked, "Do you think you could rehang the shutters?" She pointed at one. Virgil smiled, nodded. Aramenta had noticed, no matter how incongruous the occasion, Virgil's first response was that smile! It gave him a certain expression of stupidity.

"Will the ladders reach the upper floors?" Aramenta inquired. Virgil shrugged his shoulders.

Christ! She was spending more money on tools or equipment than on the labor required to do the jobs. "If not," she said, "Mr. Beausarge will get one that will."

Thank heaven for Randy. He came at least once, usually several times every day. He had taken charge of Parke-Bernet the minute they arrived, arranging motel accommodations, transportation, relieving Aramenta of all concern. In the midst of professional cleaning crews, roaring vacuum machines, the static British-accented voices doing inventory, and Virgil requesting something *else* he needed to complete a task, Randy smoothly and firmly brought order to chaos.

His thoughtfulness went well beyond the call of duty. He had taken her to dinner, introduced Aramenta to his lovely young wife, Bobbie, and with witty and charming conversation he had miraculously crowded out Aramenta's worries, at least for a few hours. The attorney had done the impossible, he was actually doing what he said he wished to accomplish, changing her jaded opinion of Mobile. Each evening became a delightfully entertaining and, yes, educational experience. They had attended a remarkably professional piece of legitimate theater at the Joe Jefferson Players, a community theatrical playhouse. She had eaten delicious seafood at the Catalina in Bayou La Batre, and superb Oriental cuisine at the Chinese Palace.

"It is an exciting, growing city," Randy said, "destined to be one of the greatest metropolises in the nation. Our projected growth predicts a million population shortly after the year 2000."

"The city will lose something," Aramenta had commented.

"Umm," Randy said, casually, "but ideal for your investment capital."

Randy Beausarge was courting her and Aramenta knew it. But precisely *because* she knew it, she neither resented it nor did it diminish her enjoyment of their evenings together.

In New York, her own attorney nervously sensed a change in his client. Bruce Matthew had not only arranged for Parke-Bernet to come down, he flew in also.

"Aramenta, darling!" He held her hand with both of his. "Now, now, darling, I know what you've surely suffered down here. Don't you worry a whit, you hear me? I shall take over and you will be back in Paris in no time."

"I have someone to manage it, Bruce, thank you. Now let's go somewhere and visit."

"Someone to manage it?" Bruce's mock hurt was deeper than he would like Aramenta to believe, of that she had been certain.

"Yes, a young attorney here. He's quite capable."

"Darling, don't be silly! A Mobile attorney? There is no such animal. They hand out legal degrees the way we sell hot dogs in Manhattan. But don't you worry your head about that. I'll meet with him and—"

"No, Bruce. I'm really quite satisfied with his work."

"Ara-men-ta," Bruce spaced her name through pursed lips as though chiding a precocious child. "Darling, I know how distraught you must be. Let's not discuss business now, let's visit and enjoy! Do you realize it's been nearly ten years since you called me? Ten years! Can you believe—"

Despite his plea not to discuss business, that was all they did discuss. Bruce pressured, ridiculed Alabama and particularly any "legal beagle" as he put it, "who sniffs out a fortune to be fleeced."

Aramenta's reaction stunned her even more than the New York barrister. "Bruce, who's paying for your flight down here—you or me?"

"I—well, Aramenta, of course I came with your interests in mind, but anytime I can get together with you is—"

"Then you're paying for it," Aramenta snapped, more a command than a question.

"Yes, Aramenta, of course." Bruce looked into his drink "If you wish."

"Now Bruce," Aramenta softened, "go back to New York Stop worrying about me. I'm all right. I'll do fine. Thank you for talking to Parke-Bernet."

"No problem," Bruce said, draining his martini. He glanced at his watch. "Goodness, how time gets away, Aramenta. Shall we call it an evening?"

The following day, Randy didn't appear until late. When he came in, he was obviously disturbed. "Your New York attorney spent the morning with me," Randy related, evenly.

Aramenta masked erupting anger. "Oh?" she said, tone carefully noncommittal.

"I endured various insults concerning my lineage, heritage, and politics. I listened politely as he tried to drink my expense account dry. I answered his questions to the extent that I felt such questions did not violate your privacy. But when the sonofabitch insulted the University of Alabama football team I told him to take his Ivy degree and—"

"And?"

"Go back to New York."

Without awaiting a response to this, Randy turned and walked away. Later, Aramenta found him going over Parke-Bernet's initial inventory, making suggestions for the local help they required.

Thump-thump-thump.

It was louder than before. Aramenta stood in the hallway listening. She checked her watch—earlier, too. She called up the stairs for Randy, but he was beyond earshot. Where was Virgil? She went to the front door and, sheltering her eyes from the afternoon sun, looked up. Virgil was at the top of an extension ladder, struggling to straighten a warped shutter.

Thump-thump-thump.

She got her flashlight from the bedroom and walked to the basement door. A tingle of alarm stopped her short of the portal.

Thump-thump-thump.

Another noise, a drawn sighing—

Thump-thump-thump.

She put her hand out, touching the panel, and snatched away as though it had shocked her! The door was jarring, bumping. Trembling, she held her breath to better hear through the thick partition.

Thump-thump-thump—and that weird, almost strangulated sighing!

She ran down the hall. "Randy! Randy!" He was in the attic. Aramenta ran outside, the door slamming behind her. She started to call Virgil and paused—it had stopped! She stepped inside, listening. Muffled sounds afar, from the farthest wings and attic upstairs, nothing else.

She went out to Virgil's ladder and tapped the base. When he looked down, she motioned that she needed him. Virgil nodded and continued his chore.

Whatever it is, Aramenta thought, we're going to get to the bottom of it! She waited as Virgil secured a loose shutter. He was physically fit, strong, muscles rippling as he maneuvered the heavy sash.

Whatever it is—Aramenta restated to herself—we will get to the bottom of it! Virgil can handle it. Better even than Randy. Virgil would find it.

Virgil was coming down now.

If only— Aramenta saw her alarm mirrored in Virgil's expression. "Something wrong?" he questioned.

"I don't know."

He put a hand on her arm as though to steady her. Aramenta realized then that she was shivering.

"I heard something, Virgil."

His head cocked, that visible question mark that implied he needed more information or a repeat of same.

"Will you look in the cellar for me?" Aramenta asked.

Quick nod; determined, masculine strides now.

Chapter Six

Virgil turned the knob, shook the door, then realized it was locked. He rotated the key. Aramenta indicated the light switch and Virgil flipped it. Together they descended into the basement.

Aramenta flashed light into corners, both of them walking slowly. She asked Virgil to investigate the windows and see if there was any other entry. He took the hand light and left her standing in the center of the room, waiting.

"Come." He motioned. He pointed to heavy planking and thick bolts barricading each window. He swept aside dust-laden webs, pushing past boxes and crates to each of the boarded openings.

"You hear something now?" Virgil pantomimed the question with a hand cupped to an ear.

"No."

He followed the walls going under the east wing, then west. "Nothing." He shrugged.

"Do you mind looking down there?" Aramenta pointed to the narrow, steep wine-cellar steps.

"Lights?" Virgil asked, one finger making an upward flick gesture.

"I don't know," Aramenta confessed. She went to the timer mechanism and lifted her eyebrows, questioning. Virgil examined it, traced the electric lines, which terminated somewhere in the subbasement. He turned the clock dial one click at a time. At "9 PM" the lights came on below.

Virgil preceded Aramenta into the prisonlike wine cellar Aramenta stopped inside the second door. The room was lighted, except for a couple of overhead bulbs which seemed burned out. Along walls, from concrete floor to ceiling, racks for the storage of wine stood empty. As a child, she could remember thousands of bottles here, canted so the liquid kept corks moist and firm.

On the floor, in a fanlike pattern, reddish hair lay sprinkled as though someone had sat for a barber. She saw Virgil turn a corner and disappear. Aramenta followed. Casks, three high, of different sizes, were mounted with bungs intact. French symbols indicated *Vin doux . . . bordeaux rouge . mousseux . . .* and the year. Virgil looked beneath the casks, then climbed up and systematically searched the tops. He jumped down again and wandered among the racks arranged like library shelves. A fortune in liquids had once been stored here. The almost floral aroma was still evident after all these years. Following Virgil, wending the aisles between racks, she saw a bottle here and there, probably dry by now, or ruined for lack of turning, so essential to the keeping of such things.

There were no windows. No other door. From floor to wire-covered lights overhead spanned maybe eighteen feet. The wine cellar was surprisingly large, although Aramenta's childhood frame of reference had made it seem larger still. She bumped Virgil. He had stopped midaisle. Aramenta followed the point of his finger—what was that? A bathroom? For heaven's sake! Dirty, but complete and apparently operable, the enclosure included a legged, high-back cast-iron tub, a sink, and a commode with flush tank. Aramenta examined the fixtures and then looked around. Her expression made Virgil scan the room also.

"New plumbing," Aramenta said aloud. Virgil caught her lips moving and asked for a repeat. Aramenta shook her head. "Nothing."

The fixtures were old, typical of the first manufactured in America—but the plumbing itself, the pipes, were flexible copper!

Virgil opened a medicine cabinet. He held up a worn, natural-bristle hairbrush, a *plastic* toothbrush. Several corroded razor blades were there, an empty shaving bowl with a stiff applicator. Aramenta recognized it as her father's shaving brush—and here! She lifted a straight razor, no more rusty than if it had been used yesterday. On one wall, a strop covered with mold; beside it hung a dirty hand towel.

Virgil pulled her arm and Aramenta followed. Against one wall was a bed. Not a cot, a twin-sized bed. Sheets, soiled but in place, and a pillow. Beneath the bed were several pairs of shoes. All the signs of habitation and nothing to suggest it was a thing of the past. Dear God! Had Mother a boarder? And had Aramenta locked him in here the other night?

"You see anybody?" Aramenta asked.

Virgil shook his head. Together, they looked through a narrow clothes cabinet, a piece of furniture Aramenta dimly recalled as having been upstairs years ago.

"Is there anybody here?" Aramenta called. The room absorbed her words. She lifted her voice. "Is anybody down here?"

Virgil's breathing the only audible reply.

"What in God's name has been going on here?" Aramenta

questioned. Virgil watched her, his brown eyes following her lips.

"Somebody has been living down here," Aramenta said, fingering clothing in the cabinet. "Hello!" She pivoted. "Please come out now!"

She took the flashlight from Virgil and walked toward the back. "Hello—please come out. We know you're here."

But there was nobody. Virgil circled one way, Aramenta the other, like children playing hide-and-seek, deliberately positioning themselves so nothing would evade them. Not easily, anyway. There were so many casks, barrels, racks, and turns, a person might conceivably elude them, but he'd have to be quick, and quiet.

"What do you think, Virgil?"

He shrugged his shoulders.

"Do you think anyone is down here?"

He shook his head.

"I'm acting like a doddering old fool. Let's get out of here."

Virgil held her elbow as they made their way to the exit and up the steps.

"Turn out the lights, Virgil." He twisted the dial of the timer, putting it approximately where it had been.

Upstairs, the hallway now dark, the sun was settling outside.

"There you are!" Mr. Smythe called. "We were searching the premises for you."

"I'm sorry," Aramenta said. "What do you need?"

"Nothing. We're going for the day. We wanted to tell you. Mr. Beausarge left earlier. Miss Lee, I must say, this house is a veritable French museum circa eighteenth and nineteenth century. I've worked with the liquidations of castles, hotels, and many family estates in my years, but truly you have exquisite pieces here! A discerning taste is most evident. I should like to have known the person who brought it all together."

"My great-grandfather," Aramenta said, "and grandfather."

"Remarkable. Positively remarkable. Well! Good evening until the morrow."

"Good night, Mr. Smythe." She watched the assessor and two assistants go out to a car Randy had rented for them. Aramenta became aware of Virgil standing at her side.

"It's too late to continue working, Virgil," she said, absently. "Why don't you go ahead and borrow any books you want from the library?"

He made a thank-you sign. Aramenta went into Mother's bedroom. She telephoned Randy's office—no answer; then his home.

"Hello there," a child said by way of greeting.

"Hello yourself," Aramenta replied. "Is your daddy home?"

"No. He's had a hard day."

"Oh? Has he?"

"He said he needed a stiff drink and—"

The sound of bumping against the receiver and a mature female voice, "Hello?"

"Bobbie, this is Aramenta Lee. Is Randy there?"

"No, Miss Lee, and this child can thank his lucky stars for it! I'm sorry—"

Aramenta laughed. "I'm afraid I'm the cause of Randy's hard day."

A feminine link between them, Bobbie's voice relaxed. "I don't think so. Evidently things at the office are piling up. Frankly, I believe he's enjoying his work in your behalf. You're his main topic of conversation."

"Favorably, I trust."

"Definitely so. Miss Lee, is there some problem?"

"No. Not really. Could you have Randy call me? No matter how late, it'll be all right."

"Then there is a problem?"

"No. Not really. I was just wondering if my mother had a live-in here. A nurse, a handyman, perhaps."

"I'm sorry, Miss Lee, I haven't the slightest idea. I'll have Randy call for sure tonight."

"Thanks. Good-bye, dear." Aramenta hung up.

She walked to the library door. Virgil sat on a footstool, engrossed in a book. Aramenta started to renew her offer to loan any of these volumes, then held her silence. If he wished to stay here and read, why not?

She felt much better having him in the house.

Randy listened to his brother with a practiced expression denoting nothing. It was a studied reaction, a response to thirty-six years of domination. William was fifteen years older, more a father than a brother, and the firstborn—Dad's favorite. William the Achiever: cynosure of the Beausarge clan, a born leader with inherited political connections.

Tonight was a typical William the Conqueror stratagem. This afternoon he had issued a public rebuke before two secretaries, a senior partner, even a goddamned cleaning crew in the office.

"Randall, I specifically asked you to study these oil leases, didn't I? Did you relay that message, Rosa?"

"Yessir, Mr. Beausarge."

"Then, by God, Randall, why didn't you do it?"

"I was tied up—"

"Tied up? Jesus! Tied up!" William epitomized long-suffering management surrounded by ineptitude. "All right, Randall, tell me what is more important than the largest oil company operating in this state?"

"Perhaps nothing, William, but—"

"Perhaps? If there's something more important, enlighten me!"

"Nothing." *You bastard.* Randy repeated, "Nothing."

"Okay!" William dismissed the others with a backward flick of his hand. "Now let's see what we can do to straighten this out."

"Sure, William." It would never occur to Randy to call his brother Bill or Willie. Always, William.

William began by talking of the increased pressures which had befallen him since Dad's recent stroke. He alluded to multimillion-dollar accounts riding on small-print contracts, the importance of the most minute detail of an obscure subparagraph of the last "whereas."

"You're going to have to pull your load, Randall."

"I want to do that."

"More than ever, now you must. You've had it pretty good these past ten years, you know. We've tried to ease you into the firm."

"I'd like to get into it deeper, William."

"Yeah, but, first, you're going to have to learn the abso lute importance of detail! It's the essence of a professional attorney. Think like a thief who will someday be trying to crack your contract, then plan to choke him off before such an occasion arises. Understand?" William made himself a drink.

"I think so."

"How's Bobbie?" Abrupt change of subject, a typical attorney's ploy, preparing the witness for a coup de grace.

"Listen, Randall"—here it came—"I've been thinking What with Dad incapacitated and all, maybe the time *has* come for you to step into this thing a bit stronger. You're how old now?"

"Thirty-six."

"Jesus, at thirty-six I was a sitting judge in city court!'"

William swiggled his drink, tie loosened, hunched over a corner of his desk. "Dad's not likely to return full-time, you know that."

"Well, I wasn't sure."

"He'll never be back. Not full-time. He was losing his touch before the stroke; it showed up in a hundred ways. Unforgivable errors in procedure. Really apparent things. The brain begins to deteriorate at a certain point."

Randy stared, unresponsive.

"All right!" Tone indicated a decision made. "Now you're going to have to step in there, Randall. Take over."

Randy's heart skipped a beat, lifting.

"If I could assume more responsibility, that would be great. I despise all this legal legwork and research. I need something I can get my teeth into."

"Of course you do."

Randy waited.

"All right!" William slipped forward, now conspiratorial. "I have about five clients that eat up time, know what I mean? Lilly Lumber Company for example. It's a nice account. But everything is relative, don't you see? Now what I'd like to do is work you in—"

Bastard! Sure, step in here, Randall. Take over the most worrisome accounts. If they drop, forget 'em! But maybe you have enough on the ball to keep them in tow, we'll see.

Seething, Randy nodded mechanically, looking at the floor for fear his thoughts would be mirrored in his eyes.

"Imbeciles, that's what they are, but the retainer is—"

You wait, William. You huckster. Just by God you wait! He looked up, anger and disappointment hidden, nodding, all the while thinking, Wait, William. Bastard. Just wait.

Chapter Seven

When the thumping began, around nine that evening, Aramenta had called Virgil, using his wire-strung alarm system. Together they had once more searched the house, including the basement and wine cellar. They found nothing, although the lights were now on in the subbasement. She had nervously dismissed Virgil, apologizing anew

When it came again, that insistent knocking, she had determined not to embarrass herself with another command search. Whatever was there, she would locate it by herself Filled with trepidation, she thought about a weapon—kitchen knife, fireplace poker—and remembered Brother's antique gun.

The pistol was in Brother's bureau, top drawer, where he'd always kept it. It was one of the earliest manufactured revolvers, with a very long barrel. Aramenta saw the brass casings, knew it was loaded. Father always insisted that any gun on the premises be "always loaded." He believed that, knowing this, nobody would be shot by an empty weapon

Thus armed, she had come downstairs again, heart hammering almost as loudly as the thump-thump-thump drumming in her ears. Holding the pistol with both hands, stepping softly, she approached the basement stairwell and threw open the door. Feeling for the light switch, she was abruptly jostled, knocked aside! She screamed, the gun in her sweating palms skittering away, lost in the dark.

"Who is it?" she demanded.

Shaking uncontrollably, she pawed the basement wall for a switch and at last, light! She found the pistol, picked it up, and pressed against the wall, trying to regain control of herself. The police. She had to call the police! She ran to the bedroom phone and as panic ascended, dialed improperly. The pulse of the busy signal was the type telling a caller the circuit was overloaded, or that a call couldn't go through as dialed. She slammed down the receiver, waited, waited, then lifted it and listened. Buzz-buzz-buzz—*take your time!* Give the equipment a moment to disconnect!

She was dialing when the light of the room altered slightly. Like a creature responding to a hawk's overflight, Aramenta froze. Behind her, close enough to hear the rale of breathing, someone stood. She wheeled, a figure was framed in the doorway for an instant before darting aside into shadows of the hall.

"Who are you?" Voice quivering. "What do you want?"

She gripped the wiggling gun, the barrel shaking despite both hands and stiff arms to steady it. "I have a gun," she warned. "You better get out of here!"

Call the police!

"I'm going to call the police!"

The telephone rang as she reached for it and Aramenta screamed with the unexpected shrill. A movement at the door made her spin, gun at ready. "Please—get out of here!"

She tried to hold her breath, to listen, but a moan escaped

her throat. "Listen you," she said, "I'm so scared I might kill you Get out of here!"

Answer the telephone! She groped behind herself, hands trembling, found the receiver, and snatched it to her ear.

"Aramenta?"

"Randy, is that you?" Returning her call.

"Yes. Is something wrong?"

"Randy, I think someone is in the house. I thought—I thought I saw—" He stepped forward, the shadows melting away as full illumination struck him, staring at her.

"Randy! Randy!"

"Aramenta, what is it?"

He wore no shirt, no shoes, his trousers short and tattered. He was bearded, his hair tangled, beginning to bald—

"Aramenta? What is it?"

He looked at her quizzically, studying her as though it were she, not himself, who was the intruder here. He looked old, but was not old. Aramenta watched as he came into the room. His eyes were pale eyes like—and that nose, that sharply hewn nose—

"Oh, God." Her own voice, as though afar.

"Aramenta, what is it?" Randy's voice metallic, alarmed.

He was circling her now, the quaking pistol of no more concern than the telephone into which Aramenta was weeping. "Oh, dear God!"

She heard Randy's shout, "Aramenta! What is it?"

The interloper had halted now, head turning slowly from Aramenta, from her face to the bed. He stood looking at the pillow, then with lips aquiver, he reached out one hand, eyes aqueous. He went to his knees, hands out, long tapering fingers splayed, touching the pillow, touching where Aramenta's head had lain. A gurgling, choked sound came from him.

"Aw-aw." He barely touched the pillow, fingers lambent

his other arm going across the mattress, prostrating himself, knees on the floor, body atop the bed. "Aw-aw." A tortured, tormented, almost weeping—he was! Crying! "Aw-aw." Softly, imploringly, those delicate fingers searching, feeling, like a blind man seeking shape in a human face. "Aw-aw." The tears of a child for a loved one. "Ma-ma—"

"Damn Mother." Had she said that, or thought it?

"Aramenta?"

"Oh," Aramenta screaming now, "damn her!"

He stood, movements slow, his expression twisted by anguish. Dimly, distantly, Aramenta heard Randy speaking, " . police . . . hear me . . . I'll call the police. . . ."

"No," she whispered.

"What?"

"No. Don't call."

She watched him move through the door, turn toward the kitchen.

"Aramenta, what's going on over there?"

"Don't—" Get control. Control!

"Aramenta, unless you give me a straight answer, I'm calling the police."

"No." Strongly, with authority. "Do not call the police, Randy."

"I'm coming over."

"No! Randy! No—" The phone went dead in her hand. She put it in the cradle, ran into the hall. A sound from the kitchen. She went in, a rectangle of light from the refrigerator the only illumination just as before. She found the light switch, flicked it, stared at an empty room. Her senses keen, adrenaline surging, she heard a faint noise from the hall and ran back there. The cellar door was closing.

She moved with great care to be silent, following. Stealthily she went down the steps, seeing nothing but the mute and immovable objects stored here over the years. Aramenta eased farther down, a step at a time, across the basement, then into the wine cellar through aisles of racks. She saw him, holding the tray she'd seen at the foot of the steps. He was leaning against a supporting timber, tearing bread and lettuce, choking them down. From here, like an etched shadow in half-light, his profile was clearly cut against the lighter wall. A strong, high forehead, tendency to balding, a nose sharply cut from the flesh of—it couldn't be! He jerked upright, head turned, mouth stilled in midchew. His upper lip curved like an archer's bow, lavender eyes— God! Dear God! The baby—screaming, shrieking, no, no, no! Damn her! No! The baby!

She saw him put a hand to the post against which he'd been leaning, visually checking the room before scooping the rest of his food from the tray. As though Aramenta were not there, her hysterical screams unheard, he walked into the dark recesses of the cellar.

A pounding, so far away it could barely be perceived. An incessant hammering—then she realized it was somebody upstairs at the door. Transmitted from door to jamb to floor and sills, the reverberation carried to these remote posts.

Thump-thump-thump. By the intensity of it, she knew it came from the back door. Randy! No! Go away! If she did not come, he would break down the door, search the house, find her here gun in hand. No! Go away! Aramenta ran up the stairs, fighting for control over the mindless shaking, sobbing cries. She still clutched the pistol! She threw it onto her bed, clamping one hand with the other, willing her body to cease shivering. She grabbed a robe, threw it around herself. Wham! Wham! They were breaking the door! She ran into the kitchen and turned the lock.

"Aramenta!"

Virgil stood behind Randy, eyes wild.

"Are you all right?"

"Yes." Please go. Please God, make him go. "I had a—a bad dream."

"May we come in?"

Dare she refuse? They must not stay. Must not know. "I'm sorry I disturbed you, Randy. This is unforgivable of me. Virgil, it isn't necessary to stay, please go home."

Virgil looked to Randy and the attorney hesitated. "Would you like us to look around, Aramenta?"

"No." No, no! "It isn't necessary. I had a nightmare, Randy, I—"

He studied her face, then took her shoulders. Suddenly, Aramenta was crying, clutching him, Randy patting her back. He held her close, comforting, saying nothing.

"Mother—damn her—Mother."

Delayed grief? Guilt? Randy had seen it before. Brave survivors at a funeral who months later suddenly realize the finality of death. But Aramenta did not love her mother. Or so he thought.

"Damn her." Aramenta wept. "Damn her soul."

When Virgil's eyes met Randy's, the attorney made a sidewise tilt of head to tell him, "Go home." Virgil quietly departed by the rear door.

"Aramenta," Randy suggested, "let me get you a room in a hotel. This place is getting to you."

She stepped back, blotting her eyes with the lapel of her robe. "No, I'm all right now."

"This house is like a mausoleum," Randy urged. "Being here by day is bad enough, but at night even Dracula would be nervous. So why endure it?" Randy smiled. "Grab a few things and I'll take you to a fine hotel. Not a bat in the belfry, I promise."

"You're sweet, Randy. But I'll be all right now. May I offer you a cup of coffee?"

"Sure." His stomach was already upset from caffeine and

tension, but she obviously needed a companion for a while longer.

He sat at the butcher's-block table as she walked around the kitchen, slippers flopping. He could see she was here in body only, her eyes troubled, mind in some distant place. She went through the performance of setting out two cups, sugar, and looked in the refrigerator for cream. She stared into the cooler so long that he asked, "Do you see something?"

"There isn't much food in here," she said.

"Are you hungry?"

She shook her head and closed the refrigerator door. "I'm out of milk, Randy."

"I take it black anyway."

They sat waiting for the coffee. Aramenta, hands clasped, shoulders rounded, stared at the top of the table.

"Aramenta, I've been thinking about it and I believe it would be possible for you to go back to Paris day after tomorrow if you wish."

She lifted her gaze and returned to the present. "What?"

"I was asking, would you like to go home day after tomorrow? I have a few papers for you to sign, relating to the probate of the will, a few technicalities where some other legal matters are concerned, but you could be home in a few days, if you wish."

"Thank you, Randy."

He waited for more comment, and when none came, Randy said, "Shall I make airline reservations for you tomorrow?"

The coffee pot gave a gurgle. Aramenta arose, dreamlike, and in a trance stood staring at the percolator.

"Aramenta, this place is getting you down, you know."

"I know."

"Then go home. I'll take care of everything and if there's

any question I'll call or write. Nothing is worth this mental turmoil. You can go home and pull yourself together."

"My proxy at the bank?" Aramenta said, woodenly.

"It can wait. Everything can wait."

"Is that in my best interest?"

He felt a wariness akin to a moment when William was meticulously examining a legal brief Randy had prepared, seeking errors.

"Aramenta, have I done something to displease you?"

Long silence.

"Aramenta?"

"I'm not displeased."

"Is there any way I can help you further?"

Shake of the head, her back to him.

Clearly, this was not a time to bring about a decision. She poured coffee, pushed the sugar bowl at him, then sat staring into the ebony liquid untouched before her.

Randy sipped his coffee without conversation, then excused himself and walked to the front door alone. His backward glance at Aramenta saw her sitting, head down, shoulders slumped, hands grasping each other, coffee going cold.

Maybe insanity ran in this damned family.

If there was a netherworld, Mother must surely be there laughing in the flames of perdition.

When Aramenta looked back on her life, there had been precious few moments of happiness—and none without the specter of Mother looming, threatening, ever present to poison even the most carefree action or thought.

In James, Aramenta thought she had found her freedom at last. He soothed her fears, built her confidence, allayed her anxieties, and stood resolutely between Aramenta and the past. When she froze at his touch, cringed during their intimacies, he gently dispelled shadows of shame, tenderly subdued ugly thoughts rising from some nebulous warning issued by Mother. With an understanding and patience no frigid wife would expect, Aramenta melted in the warmth of James Darcy. He whispered of happy times to come, of home and love and family. He conjured images of tomorrow, and yesterday became a dream. Ever so slowly, so sweetly, he brought her into today and drove away the clinging tentacles of yesterday. There were times, during that wonderful period, when Aramenta passed through an entire day without the chilling ghost of Mother.

His letters from Europe spoke always of the future. Of a time when they would return to Paris, when war was done, when peace reigned. He wrote of his desire to someday become a writer, to tell the world of good things. Always, each sentence was a statement of hope, of tomorrow, of them and their love. James enjoyed life. He reveled in the act of being alive. Whole pages of masculine script spoke of beauty—never the savagery—even of war.

With victory so near, so sure, the wire had come. A terse series of letters on a yellow blank. Dead. In action. Enemy fire. On mission. Lies! It was not missile or mortar that had killed James Darcy. Aramenta knew why he died. Punishment.

She had vowed never to see or call Mother again. Never! She would not allow what James stirred in her to be destroyed. She would go to Paris, find a small place like James often described. She would use her mounting assurance and sanity as a living testimonial to the man who had helped defeat Mother!

Aramenta tried to halt the flickering images across her mind. The minipictured flashes of time so vivid they might have been today—not thirty years ago.

"I can't be pregnant."

The naval doctor grunted, "But you are."

She could still remember the way her abdomen drew taut, painful. "It's impossible."

The doctor laughed. "Then this is going to make headlines, Mrs. Darcy. By the way, I'll need some information on your husband, for the records."

"I can't be pregnant."

Humor vanished from the doctor's face. "Is there some problem, Mrs. Darcy?" He scanned the medical records, eyes lingering on "widow," then murmured, "Oh, I see."

He circled his desk, took her hand. "Is there someone we can call, Mrs. Darcy? A relative? A friend?"

"No." Then she implored, "Are you sure?"

"Yes. You are pregnant."

With the world rejoicing over victory, the autumn leaves going from green to gold, Aramenta mourned for James. Oh, yes, she knew why he had died. Just as she knew in her soul that this baby she carried was not right, even before the doctors began to worry.

"Measles don't always affect the baby, Mrs. Darcy. Let's not worry until we have to." But the doctor's concern was obvious.

"The baby doesn't move."

"He moves, Mrs. Darcy. I feel him move. You feel him move, don't you?"

There were moments when she thought it moved. Gas perhaps. Muscle contractions. Spasms.

How brave she was. So frightened, yet determined to endure this alone. James would be so proud if he could see how brave she was.

There was no air-conditioning then. The ward was breathless, gowns adhered to stretched flesh, an odor of antiseptic kept Aramenta nauseous.

Women tell women about the pain. Aramenta was steeled

for that. They seem to enjoy describing the rending of flesh, the crunch of pelvic bones pushing apart. Aramenta expected that. They spoke of breech births and stillborn fetuses; and in the delivery room Annette appeared through the ether whispering warnings about the baby—and Mother.

Aramenta had not dishonored James by calling Mother. How he had learned to detest that woman. "Get away, Mother," James would intone, seducing her, "get away now, scat! Leave my beautiful wife alone."

Coming out of the recovery room, nobody mentioned the baby. Aramenta did not ask. It was not enough that Mother had blighted them all, controlled and destroyed their lives, now this—

"Blood tells, Aramenta."

A thousand times told? Ten thousand? "Blood tells."

Like poor Annette, married out of her caste and punished for it in the throes of birth trying to bring a child from her aristocratic womb. Mother warned her. Mother said it—to Annette before, and Aramenta afterward—"Blood tells!"

They had not returned to her ward. She was in a private room. Devoid of flowers, gray from midwall down, cream from that point up, and deathly quiet, the room enveloped her in solitude. She was in her third day and still no mention of the baby, when Mother appeared in the door with a staff doctor.

"What are you doing here?" Aramenta demanded.

"Hush, child. We have bad news."

"Get out! Doctor, you get her out of here!"

"Aramenta, don't you speak that way to me. I shan't tolerate it."

"Get out, goddamn you. Get out!"

"Nurse . . . a shot . . . call . . . hurry. . . ."

Aramenta pushed up, looking past Mother. "What's wrong, Doctor?"

"Now just you lie back, Aramenta." Mother's hand pushing on her shoulder now.

"Tell me, damn you! I'm thirty-one years old! Tell me! What's wrong?"

"It was the measles, Mrs. Darcy."

"Oh, God—"

"The damage was beyond—"

"Hush, sir!" Mother wheeled on the doctor, voice sharp. Then to Aramenta, softer, "It is dead, Aramenta. You need not concern yourself further. Mother will take care of everything. You sleep. Rest. We'll go home soon and forget this entire thing. It's dead. Done and over. Rest now."

"James!" She threw back the covers, striking at Mother. "Help me, James! Get out of here, you cursed—"

"Hold her, nurse. Watch it. Give me about sixty cc's—"

"No! I don't want that! I don't want that! No! Get out! God—Mother—damn you—goddamn you!"

Mother must be laughing. Aramenta cried softly over the table, tears rolling down her fine aquiline nose, dropping into the coffee cup. Blood tells, damn her, blood tells.

Chapter Eight

She had not slept. Awake all night, hands quavering ungovernably, Aramenta ebbed from a numbed stupor to fits of wrath, cursing the ghost of Mother. Again and again she returned to the wine cellar; no matter how softly she crept, how surreptitious her approach, she could not again catch sight of—had he a name? Had they ever asked Aramenta for a name? The son of James, the misshapen, deformed, *dead* son of James—would Mother have named him? Not dead. Alive. The distinctive nose could have been carved from the flesh of the Lee ancestry, that delicate curved lip, the Lee forehead—if the genes and chromosomes of James therein lay, Aramenta had not yet seen them, but it was her baby, hers and his.

That poor being, lying across Mother's bed weeping for her. God knows he must have depended on Mother, for food if nothing else. Mother's aristocratic pride would not have allowed her to admit having a less-than-perfect member of the family Lee. Aramenta could imagine Mother secluding him, teaching the infant and later the child, "When someone comes—run hide!"

Aramenta remembered news stories of such things. A New Jersey woman died and authorities discovered a demented forty-year-old son nobody had suspected existed, hidden all his life because of the mother's shame that he was illegitimate. Parents who locked away the retarded and deformed, sometimes for decades, with no neighbor remotely aware that such tortured souls existed. Horror stories of insane and distorted minds—and now, Aramenta was a part of such an atrocity.

"It is dead," Mother had said. Why should Aramenta have doubted that? If not physically dead, then mentally so. She had *known* something was wrong. She had expected the worst.

Mother would be so capable of committing this terrible crime. It would be so like her to doom the damned to a lifetime of quarantine and darkness. Here at last, a person Mother could utterly control and manipulate. God bless him—Aramenta was crying again—God bless him.

Hunger alone had driven him up from his cellar bastion. Mother dead, the food ceased, he must have huddled at the head of the basement stairs for hours waiting for sustenance that would never come. Then a stranger came, Aramenta, and he reacted as Mother had taught him—hiding. Only when the pangs of hunger became an ache, when animal instinct for survival overrode the matrix of his infancy, then he had crept through the dark, confused and starved.

What to do? He must be brought up from the wine cellar. Bathed, shaved, dressed, and fed. Who to call? The police? The newspapers would disgrace them all, forever tainting the balance of her life, their lives! No, Aramenta must not call the police. Such a story would hum through press wires and leap continents. Surely, even in Paris, everyone would know—it was Mother and Aramenta—and Aramenta's abandoned child.

Wait, think. Consider all facets, reach conclusions only after deep and careful consideration. Randy Beausarge wanted to manage the estate, be her financial adviser and investment counselor. He had a service to offer and she needed him. He would help, she had only to ask. But what could she expect in the future? If a day came when she wished to withdraw her proxy, realign investments, would she ever be able to pull away from Randy Beausarge? Not easily. Not if he were armed with this.

She contemplated her New York attorney, Bruce Matthew. He'd been a college friend of James, had helped Aramenta escape to Paris in the postwar years. Bruce had buffered her from Mother. He had arranged to relay Aramenta's annuity and trust money. He had stood as a bulwark between Aramenta and Mother, a necessary link and needed buttress. Had it not been for Bruce, Mother might have come for Aramenta, haunting her even in Paris. Bruce would be discreet; he could arrange for institutionalization and—

Institution? Was she to compound Mother's dementia by committing this helpless soul to another caged existence, possibly for life? The progeny of James, the flesh of her flesh, the product of her love—God help him! Did he deserve this final renouncement from Aramenta?

And Bruce, what would he expect with the whiff of a fortune in his nostrils, avarice cloaking him unmistakably? When Aramenta telephoned to say "half a million" in furniture, Bruce must have run a quick check and discovered this was only the tip of Aramenta's financial iceberg. No, Bruce would be worse than Randy—his help would be suspended over Aramenta's head like the sword of Damocles.

In the cellar, Aramenta reasoned with the dark. "I want

to talk to you. I want to help you. Mother—your grand-mother—I am her daughter. You are my—"

She regained composure. "I will call a doctor, get you examined. You can come upstairs now, get out of here. You don't have to be afraid of me. Of anything."

From the rear of the east wing she thought she heard a susurrant sigh. "Please come out," Aramenta implored. "I won't hurt you. I will help you. Come out now, please."

Weeping, attempting to explain the inexplicable, pleading for understanding, offering help and friendship, she might have been alone. The electric timer cut off the lights and wrapped her in a darkness more complete than any she'd ever known.

Dear God, this cannot be happening—she tried to re-create a mental picture of the labyrinth, feeling her way down an aisle of racks, bumping a cask, a smothering blanket of total blindness choking her sobs, making her gasp as if for air. Something touched her and she screamed, jumped, bashed her shoulder, and overreacted by yanking back only to strike another unseen projection. She stood stock-still, her own breathing loud, a swallow adhered her tongue to the roof of her dry mouth, waiting for her eyes to adjust, seeking any glimmer of light. There! From a distant source, a faint glow. Enforced movements now, with deliber-ate steps around corners, through black aisles and finally . . . she stood in the portal, gulping fresh air as though surfacing from water. She realized there was a breeze through these doors, a draft drawn from the basement, down into the sub-basement.

Mother had planned it so carefully. A fan to circulate air, a clock to regulate hours. At Aramenta's feet was a tray, placed where she'd first seen it. A pattern. Mother prepared food, delivered it here, returning to get the tray for refill later. Like a keeper serving an inmate, like an attendant shoveling fodder to sheep.

She took the tray upstairs to the kitchen. Her eyes fell on the vitamins. Those would be crucial to him, living down there without sunshine. A balanced diet was imperative. She must call, order food, have it delivered fresh daily. Vegetables, rich red meats, and the vitamins! Milk.

She sat in the bay window of the dinette as dawn broke. The sky was a canopy growing pale beyond the tatted leaves of towering oaks. She watched Virgil leave the carriage house, walk down the drive. She was still there when he returned an hour and a half later. Out for breakfast, possibly. He busied himself hanging out clothing he had laundered.

She must coordinate her thoughts, plan the day. She couldn't remember what day this was. Mr. Smythe had said something about working downstairs, cataloging furniture. He had commented about the east-wing suites, paper stacked from floor to ceiling with tunneled access only. Aramenta had sent the professional cleaning crew up to carry away load after load after load.

"Little hollows in there," they had said. "Tunnels interconnecting ... like a child's playhouse ... burrows in a haystack. ..."

It struck her then, he had not been totally confined to the cellar! He'd had access to the house, upstairs, and over the years as Mother accumulated more bales of magazines and papers, he must have fashioned his own personal warren of sorts, a place to hide and play all at once.

Aramenta opened the rear door for Virgil, channeling her thoughts. The two of them sat, Virgil smiling, accepting coffee, which they drank without communication.

She needed time to think. She juggled the clues at hand,

trying to determine a probable system Mother followed with her charge. Mother's neglect was not absolute, that was obvious. The sheets on the bed were dirty, but in place. The toilet was unclean, but functional. Clothing must surely have been washed, his hair cut—the reddish hair spread barber-fashion on the floor was proof of that. He was unshaven, yet there were shaving utensils. Lack of lather, blades? Aramenta could only guess.

After Parke-Bernet and Randy came and set about their work, Aramenta returned to the cellar with a flashlight She'd left Virgil enraptured in the library, surrounded by books.

She found Baby sleeping. Even before she got there, she heard the masculine rale of snores. Using her skirt to diffuse the flashlight to a softer glow, she went to his bed and stood looking down at him. He lay on his back, one arm outflung, mouth agape. His teeth were surprisingly white, even, the shape of them reminding Aramenta of James and his beautiful smile.

She reached out as if to touch him, but some inner warning stayed her hand. He drew a deep breath, exhaled, teeth gnashing in his sleep. He turned on his side, slumber deepening again. Aramenta saw a roach motionless above the bed. She made a mental note to buy pesticide. How long she stood there, heart aching, she couldn't be sure.

Why did he not come forth now that he knew she'd seen him? Ask for what he needed, make his desires known—why persist in this childish game of run and hide? Was he a child?

When she went up again, the house was a bustle of activity as Randy and Mr. Smythe supervised movers, who were going up to the attic to begin crating.

"I'll need Miss Lee's signature," Mr. Smythe said.

"I'll sign for her," Randy replied.

Without greeting to either of them, Aramenta went to the kitchen and inventoried the food supplies. She then telephoned Mother's grocery store, list in hand.

"This is Miss Lee," she said. "I wish to order for delivery, please."

"Yes, Miss Lee."

Her glasses on her nose, reading from the list with the slightly clipped tones of one accustomed to service, Aramenta chanced to glance at the smoked-glass mirror. Mother was on the telephone ordering groceries, aloof and authoritarian. The image was younger, but unmistakably Mother. Anyone who had known her twenty-five years ago would not deny that.

As a child, people often remarked, "Aramenta, you are the very picture of your mother!" To which Mother would sharply and quickly amend, "No, Aramenta is a Lee. She looks quite like her father and grandfather. She has the Lee nose, and her eyes—" So many times Aramenta had heard Mother's recitation of genetic similarities, she believed it. Not until James, had she become aware of her resemblance to Mother. "How can something so lovely be a copy of something so ugly?" James had once mused. Meaning, of course, Mother.

Into the telephone, Aramenta altered her inflection to more of a request than an order. "I shall be calling frequently," Aramenta explained. "How often do you deliver?"

"Tuesday, Thursday, Saturday, Miss Lee," the southern drawl replied. "But if you need something badly, we can make a special trip."

"Thank you. You may continue billing as before."

"Thank you, Miss Lee."

Aramenta disconnected and sat staring at her reflection

Yes. It did look like Mother. Damn her.

Virgil bounded into the kitchen grinning. He slapped a book and gestured vigorously.

"Whoa!" Aramenta commanded. "I can't follow that "

Virgil placed the soft-bound book in Aramenta's hands. Stunned, she studied the title: *Talk with Your Hands*.

"Deaf?" she whispered. "Deaf talk?"

Virgil was like a child who has discovered a favorite toy, an old friend. Chortling, grinning, nodding, he watched Aramenta turn the pages. The leaves were soiled, worn, several had come lose from the binding of the old book.

"Deaf," she said.

Virgil pointed to the book, pointed at Aramenta, then himself. His lips shaped words, "We learn talk now."

"Yes," Aramenta said, dumbly, "yes, we could."

Virgil left the room and returned with several more books from the family library. *Say It with Hands* and *Talk with the Deaf,* each with photographs and/or drawings showing the movements needed to produce signs. "American Sign Lan guage," a foreword explained.

Virgil patted his foot, asking attention, and Aramenta looked up. "You learn this?" Virgil said. Aramenta wasn't certain whether it was past or future tense.

"I'm not sure I can, Virgil."

He nodded, animated, excited. Yes sign.

"Well"—she gave back the books—"put them on my bed-side table, Virgil. I'll glance through them."

There was no mistaking his joy. In his lonely world, a person who could learn his language would be a welcome relief. Aramenta began putting away groceries just delivered.

"What is happening to me?" she said aloud. "What am I going to do? I'm not ready for all this!"

Virgil worked until late to compensate for a day of sloth. He understood now why Miss Lee had not discussed his article with him. She was waiting until she knew *his* language! His spirits were soaring as they had once soared when he enrolled in the Mississippi School for the Deaf in Jackson. Somebody who cared enough to learn signing! Wait until he wrote Marie. No, on second thought, he wouldn't do that. Marie was the only deaf in the small town where she lived. For Virgil to be too happy and satisfied—it might be unkind to brag about this to Marie. She was miserable enough now without adding jealousy.

He had returned to the house several times after leaving, hoping that perhaps Miss Lee would ask advice on the forming of this sign or that. Once he found her coming up from the basement. She didn't seem to be hearing noises, and although she appeared distressed, it was not fear Virgil saw in her eyes.

Abstractions and lengthy conversations were beyond them, so he asked no questions. But not for long! If she mastered the basic five hundred signs, only those five hundred, he would soon be telling her his thoughts and she would be telling him hers. This was so smart of her! How much better she could direct his labors now. No mistaking an order if Miss Lee knew signs.

He began to build a fantasy around it. He imagined her coming to the carriage house, her long fingers flicking off letters and symbols. "I have studied your story," she might say. "It is warm and sympathetic. I like this story very much. Do you have something more I may read?"

"Truly!" He would give her the short story about a deaf girl entrapped by a professional beggar, a deaf man who made slaves of his employees. The girl was a girl Virgil knew. Mentally deficient, she was taught to go into public places handing out cards showing the American Sign Language alphabet. The other side of the card was a request for donations. The girl's food, travel, and lodging were paid by her boss. She brought him as much as six hundred dollars in a week, and she was but one of eight people working for this boss. For this she received forty dollars, part of which the boss took back for clothing, cigarettes, and other extras. Virgil wanted to tell the world never to give to such people. It did nobody good, not deafs, not the person begging, only the boss man waiting around the corner. Such men were intelligent, ruthless, extracting sexual favors and forever using the dim-witted people soliciting for him.

"This is so?" Miss Lee would sign.

"Yes. Worse," Virgil would explain. They would discuss this terrible thing, a source of embarrassment for all working, self-respecting deafs. Miss Lee would see that Virgil was perceptive, with thoughts, aspirations, ambitions.

He would tell her his ideas for so many things. He would tell her his idea for liberating deaf people over the entire nation by teaching signing in public schools from kindergarten through high school. Thereby, orals would learn a language, a linguistic feat comparable to Spanish, German, or French, surely! But more important, by learning signing, orals could allow deaf students into their classes, instead of relegating the deafs to state-operated specialty schools. Deaf students could stay home, go to local schools, make oral friends.

A rich woman like Miss Lee could probably get such a thing started here in Mobile.

He invented conversations that would take place: his comments and Miss Lee's responses. Learning signs so she could make him a more valuable employee. Virgil felt a rising wave of admiration, more than respect alone, almost adoration. Maybe God had kept him from getting a job all these past months, waiting for this specific time. Waiting for Miss Lee to come to Mobile. Maybe together, Virgil the writer and Miss Lee the patron, perhaps together they would do many great things.

She was trying to be friendly, from the beginning she had tried—the sandwiches and iced tea she'd brought out to him the day he arrived. He had been uncomfortable with her, not really attempting to span the chasm of language. Too often such efforts drew rebuke and hostility from strangers But this was different! This was Miss Lee, with a library filled with books and the titles told Virgil the depth of her sincerity. Books on the psychology of the deaf, demographic studies, reports relating to job training, social problems, teaching a deaf child, everything a person would want to know about deafness.

More than language alone, Miss Lee wanted to understand the man, Virgil. She wanted to meet him on his ground. Virgil could scarcely wait to exchange thoughts in a meaningful way. He was too excited to sleep. He had to force his brain to idle, before he could doze.

Chapter Nine

Randy listened as Buddy Ellis spelled out a plan for the subdivision and subsequent sale of Lee Manor. The realtor turned pages of his proposal, tone and delivery reminding Randy of a schoolboy reading homework aloud. But Randy wasn't really interested. He had made his decision on the matter even before Ellis arrived to make a presentation.

"Mr. Ellis," Randy spoke at a propitious pause, "may I be frank?"

Ellis saw it coming, it showed in his slitted eyes. Randy sat forward, cleared his throat. "Miss Lee acted hastily in contacting you, Mr. Ellis. She came here sole heir to her family estate. She was not aware of the extent of her holdings. For example, she is a major stockholder in several businesses—including a realty company founded by her father."

"I'm out, that's what you're telling me."

"I'm afraid so."

"I've spent a lot of time on this. Money out of pocket, researching zoning and the like."

"Yes. Well, the hazards of business—"

"Nonsense, Beausarge! The woman called me on the phone, asked me to come out, and I did. She verbally indicated she wanted me to handle the sale. I went to the courthouse for specifics, had an assessor make a market evaluation, got a copy of the plat—she ought to at least put the property on a competitive basis, let me make a bid."

"You may make a bid if you wish," Randy offered.

"Then I will. Right now. I'll handle the property for less than anybody in this city, by God."

"Less than three percent?"

"Go to hell," Ellis fumed. "Any realtor making that kind of a deal will lose money." He began putting papers into his briefcase.

"That's the point, Mr. Ellis," Randy said. "Miss Lee owns stock in Hanson and Hanson Realty. If they handle the sale for her, she is in effect paying a commission to herself. It is too good a picture, businesswise and taxwise, for her not to do it. I'm forced to advise her accordingly."

"I should've known." Ellis stood angrily. "Anytime a rich bastard is involved they cheat the common man."

"I'm sorry, Mr. Ellis."

"Good-bye, Beausarge."

Randy was still standing when the door slammed. For days he had been fending off angry people who had dreamed they might latch on to Aramenta's money. Ellis, several other realtors who had gotten wind of the estate, and contractors who saw the activity at the Lee home.

"Mr. Beausarge?" Rosa's voice on the intercom.

"Yes?"

"Mr. Riley from Marine Guaranty on the telephone."

Randy lifted the receiver. "Good morning, Mr. Riley."

The man's tone was casually cordial, as though he

and Randy had been chatting back and forth for years

"Randy, how are you?"

"I'm fine, Mr. Riley. What can I do for you?"

"I'm calling about Miss Aramenta Lee, Randy. When I telephoned her house, she was short with me." He chuckled, a sound designed to ameliorate the situation. "She referred me to you, my boy."

"Yessir. What can I do for you, Mr. Riley?"

"Yes. Umm. Actually, I was wondering if we might have lunch together."

"It can't be today, I'm afraid." Randy thumbed his empty calendar as though seeking an opening.

"At your convenience," Riley said, mildly.

"Day after tomorrow then?" Randy suggested. "Say about one?"

"Excellent! Does the Trade Center suit you?"

"Very good, Mr. Riley. I'll meet you there."

They had said good-byes when Randy interjected, "Oh, Mr. Riley, I have dark auburn hair, stand about—"

The banker's laughter stopped Randy. "I know what you look like, my boy. But to avoid fumbling, I shall be at my usual table. Ask the maître d'."

"Look forward to seeing you then," Randy said.

He cradled the phone as the intercom buzzed anew.

"Line one, Mr. Beausarge. A gentleman from the newspaper."

"Mr. Beausarge?" A slightly effeminate voice. "This is Tom Diehl over at the paper."

"Yes, Mr. Diehl."

"We're doing a piece on Miss Aramenta Lee. I called her house and she suggested I telephone you. I'm afraid we have annoyed her."

"How is that, Mr. Diehl?"

"One of our cubs went out there for a bio and he took her photo unawares. She chased him off."

"I daresay."

"Yeah, well, the kid's green and he's got about as much tact as a Brahma bull with a herd of heifers."

"And what do you need from me, Mr. Diehl?"

"Corroboration of a few things, mostly. Can you give me Miss Lee's age?"

"Not if I want to stay in her good graces."

"We have sixty-eight."

Randy coughed, then amended, "Sixty. Better accurate than insulting, I suppose."

Diehl's lilting titter came over the phone. "I have a list of the various Lee enterprises, the stocks they control, things of that nature. I'd like to run through and confirm them."

"I can't do that, Mr. Diehl. I'll have to ask Miss Lee's permission to release information of that nature."

"It's a matter of public record, Mr. Beausarge."

"Then perhaps you should quote those records as your source. What kind of article is this?"

"It started out as a simple human-interest thing," Diehl stated. "But mention of the lady's name stirred up a hornet's nest. The chief now wants a full background, scope of influence, political impact—the works. Miss Lee's old lady was a mystery sort and it must run in the family. Aramenta Lee ain't talking to nobody about nothing, so far as we can tell. Riley at the bank sits as chairman of the board, and, hell, he can't get her on the telephone, he says."

"I see."

"A few more questions here—"

"Diehl, let me make a suggestion."

"Shoot."

"Let me talk to Miss Lee. Maybe I could arrange an interview. She recently went through the tragedy of her mother's death. She is faced with reams of legalities. She is probably too busy to want to talk to anyone just yet. But I'll be happy to try in your behalf."

"Okay." A cautious note. "How long will it take to get a go or no go?"

"A few days. Call me back Monday."

"Okay. The chief may not wait. Or it might make a good follow-up, I'll ask."

"No," Randy said evenly, "I suggest you wait and run nothing until after an interview, if I can arrange one. If you print something that incenses her, there'll be no interview."

"Makes sense. Okay, Beausarge. I'll call back Monday."

Randy hung up, hands perspiring. Damn it! The intercom was winking again.

"What is it, Rosa?"

"Mr. William Beausarge wants to see you, sir."

"I don't have time right now, Rosa. I— All right. Where is he?"

"In his office, Mr. Beausarge."

"Ring it."

William's voice, efficient, timbre smooth: "What the hell's going on in there, little brother?"

"Same old stuff, William. What do you need?"

"I don't need anything. But I've spent more time telling people to see you than I've spent on my own accounts this morning. What's the big deal with the Lee estate?"

"No big deal. She's trying to liquidate her house, things like that."

"Did you talk to Diehl at the *Press-Register?*"

"Yeah. Human-interest article on the Lee family."

"Oh." Randy heard a rustle of papers, an aside to William's stenographer. "All rightee, Randall. Nothing you can't handle then?"

"Got it by the horns, William. Mostly legwork and nit-picky legalities."

"That's what it's all about."

Randy disconnected. He wasn't going to be able to keep this thing under wraps much longer. If William even guessed what—he snatched up the phone.

"What is it now, Rosa?" he demanded too sharply.

"Mr. Bruce Matthew from New York calling."

"Jesus! Listen, Rosa, hold my calls after this one, will you?" Randy pushed the blinking button. "Good morning, Mr. Matthew."

"Bruce," the New York attorney corrected, "call me Bruce, Randy. How's the weather down there?"

Randy glanced out at blinding sunshine. "Snowing, Bruce."

"Snowing? In August? In Alabama! For God's sake, I thought—" the attorney paused. "Oh, you're putting me on are you?"

"Yeah. What can I do for you, Bruce?"

'I've been trying to call Aramenta, Randy. She isn't answering. Is everything all right down there?"

"Yes."

"No problem?"

"No."

"I don't understand then—"

"Understand what?"

"You know, Randy, Aramenta and I go back a long way Her husband was a classmate of mine. I was four-eff, draft exempt, but James Darcy went in the day after Pearl. James was killed in a Berlin run. Navy pilot, but they transferred him to air force—you're too young to remember when there vas no air force, I suppose.

"When Aramenta came to me for help, I helped, know vhat I mean? Not for a fee, for friendship. Over the years I monitored her annuities, forwarded her mail, arranged to have her trust-fund monies sent to Paris. Never for more than my cost, know what I mean? Now, since she got down there, she's pulling back as though I had a curved beak and talons."

"Aramenta is quite well, Bruce."

"Good, good." The use of Aramenta's first name had not been lost on the northern attorney.

"She's up to her chin in settling the estate," Randy said.

"Parke-Bernet says it's a gold mine in eighteenth- and nineteenth-century French," Bruce noted.

So Bruce had been keeping tabs, had he? Randy kept his answer noncommittal. "I think Aramenta is planning to return to Paris shortly."

"That so? Hmm! Would it be a breach of professional mores to ask what the ultimate disposition of her holdings will be?"

"No," Randy said, "but perhaps you should get that from her. She hasn't told me all her plans yet."

"No, no," Bruce's tone altered, "this isn't the time to bother her. Maybe I can see her as she comes through on the way home."

"Perhaps so. I'll tell her that you called."

"Do that, my friend!"

"Will do, Bruce. Thanks for your interest."

Randy sat, hand on the receiver, staring at nothing. He could feel the vultures soaring overhead, prepared to pounce on the kill. Sure Bruce Matthew would wait to see Aramenta! Like hell he would. He was on top of every development, you could bank on it.

Randy walked to the liquor cabinet in a corner of his office. Dad had given the bar to him on the first anniversary of Randy's association with the firm. Inside were various expensive brands of rye, Scotch, bourbon, and gin, waiting to entertain important clients. But there had been no important clients. Randy took out a glass, rinsed it in the half-bath off his office, and poured himself a jigger of bourbon.

He sat again, looking out the window. All he needed was what Aramenta could give. Yet somehow, now, he felt more estranged from her than he had at the onset of their relationship. Randy sipped the drink, winced, then took it as he would medicine, all at once.

If he was going to effect this coup, he'd better get busy, before William, Bruce, the newspapers, the bank, all and sundry jumped in and began tearing the estate into shreds.

All with Aramenta's best interests in mind, of course.

Aramenta put the telephone receiver under a pillow on her bed. She could still hear the faint hum of a signal. She placed another pillow on the first. There.

The calls had started before dawn, while she was still in the cellar, taking down a breakfast tray. She'd placed the food on a step, running back to catch the phone—purely a reflex action—and whoever was calling had hung up. When she returned the tray was gone. She went into the wine cellar, but couldn't find Baby. She'd been anticipating this meal in hopes that she could lure him out, gain his confidence, establish a beginning contact.

All morning the telephone had rung. Painters, roofers, some idiot from the board of the bank wanting her to come to dinner! Then that moron from the newspaper shooting flashbulbs in her eyes as she answered the door.

She'd spent most of the night in pensive thought. She had taken clean sheets, towels, a bar of soap, toothpaste, and shaving supplies into the cellar. But as with the trays of food, she found an empty room. As she made the bed, cleaned the bathroom, taking clothes to be laundered, she talked soothingly, constantly, hoping to impress him with her sincerity and friendliness.

Actions speak louder than words. She had sprayed for insects, set our rat poison, in case there were any, swept the area, which was surprisingly free of dust. In a basement and house honeycombed with webs, silt, dust, and dirt, the cellar was cool, clean, fresh. Had Mother done that? Aramenta remembered her mother as a fastidious person, demanding cleanliness. In her declining years, though, she apparently had changed.

He was thirty-one. Was he aware that October 23 was his birthday? Were there any holidays he observed? Aramenta asked these questions of the dark as she tidied his living area.

"You have a birthday soon, you know."

She could feel his eyes on her movements.

"What would you like for your birthday?"

Questions posed as though to a child. Was he a child, in a man's body? Normal intelligence? Below? Brilliant?

"I wish you'd come talk to me," she said.

She had taken the clothes, bed sheets, everything, to be washed. She had discovered a modern washer and drier off the back porch, in the old servant's wing. Mother may have been a recluse, but she'd managed to conduct her business well enough to install the niceties of modern life. The electric timer for the cellar lights, exhaust fan, washer, drier, and in an anteroom off the laundry room, an empty chest freezer.

How could she have ordered his clothing, if all bills went to Randy? Wouldn't he notice that men's wear was what she had bought? Thinking about this, Aramenta saw that the fly of the trousers buttoned, the cuffs were turned and bulky. There was not a new garment among them. He had been wearing hand-me-downs forty years old.

The books on the deaf which Virgil had found in the library lay untouched on Aramenta's bedside table. She was too busy trying to penetrate the barrier between her son and herself. She checked all the electric lights walking over the reinforced ceiling of the wine cellar, pulling up fixtures one at a time to change burned-out bulbs.

If she sat by waiting, with his food tray clearly visible, the food would spoil and he would not come forth. But leave him alone for half an hour and the tray would be at the foot of the stairs between the two security doors of the cellar, every bite eaten, the vitamin pill gone, glass rinsed out.

Using Mother's past grocery bills, Aramenta soon had a diet fixed in her mind, carefully balancing the meals. She tried to vary his food and discovered he would not eat certain things. Any deviation from old to new was left unsampled on the tray. Aramenta found a cookie batter repeatedly ordered by Mother, and she included this in her food purchase. She spent an hour preparing the cookies, delivered them piping hot, but found them untouched when she returned. Perplexed, she rechecked Mother's lists and determined the ready-mix batter to be the same. Then why had he not eaten her cookies? Mother had never cared for sweets. In fact, she forbade them to Aramenta as a child, stating that "sweets do pimply faces make."

She remembered those rare occasions when Mother did allow them cookies—Christmas, birthdays. Mother never rolled them out, cutting them, nor did she ladle them onto a pan to spread wafer thin. Mother had always mixed a coarse batter, very dry, and formed little rolls of dough between her hands similar to link sausages. Brother hated them, Aramenta recollected. "Mother's rocks," Brother called them.

She again mixed batter, careful to add less milk than the recipe called for, and made a batch of mother's rocks. These she took below and left. When she returned, every cookie was gone and the plate was at the bottom of the steps.

He won't vary his routine one centimeter. Not one iota, Aramenta realized. So entrenched were the patterns of behavior, so firmly ingrained his training, the elusive figure in the cellar was not likely to yield to her overtures. Mother had subdued the child, taught him to "run and hide," and now he would not be confronted by Aramenta or anyone else.

This revelation plunged Aramenta into a deepening depression, born of frustration and seething anger toward Mother.

Wearily, amid moving men, Parke-Bernet assessors, cleaners, Virgil, Randy, and the now ringing telephone, Aramenta came to the conclusion she wasn't going home this week, or the next, or anytime in the foreseeable future.

She was trapped, caught in Mother's clutches and the shameful, horrible crime committed against her own child. She must somehow lure this man from the cellar and transport him to professional help in a city where she was not known. She reconsidered calling on somebody for outside help.

But whom?

Chapter Ten

Randy sat at the bay window in the breakfast area, watching Aramenta. Her eyes were the haggard orbs of an insomniac, dark circles giving them a sunken appearance. He saw her hands tremble as she spooned coffee into a percolator. She went about this in silence, her movements mechanical. He recalled her, as she was at their first meeting, vibrant, self-assured, and poised. Now here she was, still in robe and nightwear although it was late afternoon.

"I have no cream," Aramenta stated. "Will milk do?"

"I take it black, Aramenta."

She poured their coffee, sat across from him. She gazed out the window, watching Virgil mowing the lawn.

"Aramenta, there are several important things we need to discuss."

She sighed, still peering out the window.

"Have you found any keys, Aramenta, that might go to a bank lock box?"

"No."

"We need to locate those," Randy said, softly. "There should be eleven of them somewhere."

Aramenta's head shook slightly, a mannerism common to the elderly when age weakens the neck muscles.

"We need to inventory the contents of the safe-deposit boxes," he noted. "It's about the only thing remaining before we offer the will for probate."

"I'll look for the keys." She clamped a little finger to the handle of her cup to stop a tremor.

"Aramenta, this morning a newspaper reporter called me," Randy said. "They're doing an article about you."

"The bastards. They came out here and took my photo as soon as I answered the door! I want that story stopped, Randy. I also want them to know if they run that horrible picture of me, I'm going to sue them for trespass. I'm tired of invasions of my privacy."

"I don't blame you."

"I want them stopped."

"Aramenta, they want an interview with you. A human-interest story, they said."

"Absolutely not."

"They plan to run an article with or without the interview," Randy warned. "There's nothing we can do to stop that."

"Sue them."

"It would invite countersuit, Aramenta. They have a right to publish an article. You are now a newsworthy item."

Aramenta glared at him a moment, then gazed out the window again, watching Virgil.

"You see, Aramenta, you have become a powerful woman. Whether you like it or not, your existence touches many, many people. Your whims and fancies can affect thousands of lives."

"Thousands of lives? That's absurd!"

"Not at all. Stop and think about it. You are the rightful chairman of the board at Marine Guaranty. Mr. Riley, who has held that position because he was elected by the minority stockholders, is quaking in his boots. He's in jeopardy of losing prestige and power with a snap of your fingers. But even more than that, he worries about the bank, an institution he's spent a lifetime building. Hundreds of employees, thousands of accounts, and millions of dollars ride on you— and you are an unknown to him."

"He's safe."

"He doesn't know that."

"Tell him."

Randy squirmed uncomfortably. "Frankly, I'm not sure he is safe, Aramenta."

"What do you mean?"

"I mean, if I were the holder of those proxy votes, there are some serious questions of policy I'd like answered. Marine Guaranty has become stultified, stagnating, while other banks in the area are growing steadily. Total deposits have fallen, loans decreased—"

"Randy! Please. I don't even want to discuss it."

"All right, Aramenta. But hear me, you are like the princess who became queen. You my not want to give up fox hunting and skeet shooting, especially for something as dull as affairs of state. But somebody must handle such affairs You control, or influence, thousands of people—realty, banking, insurance, oil-company decisions. If you are a prudent and wise executive, these organizations will breathe a sigh of relief. But if you were to be erratic, wild—"

"If I scandalized them, you mean."

"Yes. Stocks would plunge, contracts would falter, jobs would fail, and it would affect many families."

"Oh, dear God." Aramenta put down her cup and covered her face with both hands.

"A person in your position is, therefore, a newsworthy individual. There is going to be an article with or without your consent and assistance. It seems to me that it would be wise to control your publicity, rather than allowing speculation to run rife—and the publicity thereby to control you."

"I can't do it," voice muffled.

"Aramenta, you and I are going to have to talk. I will do whatever you wish. I will help anyway I can. But I'm slightly confused. Whatever is bothering you, let's put it on the table and work toward a solution."

Aramenta's hands dropped, one to either side of her coffee cup. She stared at the attorney a long time, then looked out the window again.

"What do you recommend?" she asked, hoarsely.

"I recommend we get the will probated as quickly as possible, that you sign over your proxies to the various corporate stocks to me, in trust for a period of not less than three years with an automatic renewal unless canceled in writing. I also suggest you sell this house, go home to Paris, and enjoy your wealth and your life. You are too young, too beautiful, too—"

"Bullshit!"

Stunned, Randy asked, "What?"

"Don't try to flatter me. I resent it."

"Flatter?" Randy felt his face warming. "Listen, lady, I call the shots as I see them. I don't flatter anybody! Don't get the impression I'm licking boots, nothing is that important to me. If you want a sycophant, call Bruce Matthew. What I tell you is the truth as I see it. That includes my assessment of your business and financial picture and most definitely my opinion of you as a person, particularly your physical attraction. But I'll tell you one thing, you stick around here much longer and you will be a trembling old woman—a basket case!"

It was a calculated risk. He'd won. Aramenta had turned, jolted, listening, then quietly nodded.

"I shall follow your recommendations," she acceded. "Implement them as soon as possible. Except for one thing."

His heart caught in his throat.

"No interview. And that photo had better not run in the newspaper."

"All right. I think," Randy said, "disposition of these business matters will silence almost all conjecture, including a newspaper's desire for a juicy intrigue."

"Intrigue?" Aramenta looked up with alarm.

"Yes, certainly. Right now you are a mystery woman. That's precisely what they'll say in the article. It is the doubt over the corporate decisions that is exciting them all."

He left her sitting at the table, brow wrinkled, watching Virgil cut grass.

Virgil saw Mr. Beausarge wave, going to his car Virgil returned the gesture, the mower humming in his hand. The scent of freshly mown grass rose pleasantly into his nostrils He was aware of Miss Lee sitting in the bay window observing him. He took special care around the plants and remnants of flower beds. He didn't want her to think him careless and irresponsible. True, the flowers were gone, but with pruning, fertilization, and weeding, the rose bushes would bloom next season.

Virgil knew the magic that proper care worked on a shrub. He had already noted several remarkable camellias and azaleas which grew in profusion along the street front of the property. As for the lawn, once a thick mat of Bermuda grass, it would regain luster with weekly mowings. Actually it was good for a lawn to go to seed as this one had done.

He felt her eyes on him as he adjusted the carburetor, one hand atop the motor to judge the purr. He knew how amazed orals were when a deaf man could detect a faulty piece of equipment by touch. But, in fact, tactile judgment was probably more accurate than any hearing person's audible assessment of the same machine. Another slight turn of the screw. Again, hand on the motor, he nodded to himself

"He certainly pulls his share of the load," he'd once read Miss Lee's lips as she spoke to Mr. Beausarge.

"That's what we want," the attorney had responded.

There were so many things he wanted to say. Not about his job; he wanted to tell her about a new idea he had for a short story. He wanted to ask her opinion of the plot and characters.

He would like to talk to her about Marie.

Marie had written him that she wished to come to Mobile for a visit. She was very lonely. Her parents did not sign They were ashamed when Marie used her hands to talk When Marie was a child, they punished her for using gestures. They did this because an educator had told them "Unless she is forced to learn to speak, she never will. Using her hands becomes so easy, she will not try to use her voice."

It was a cruel hoax which deafs bitterly resented. Marie, like Virgil, had come to the school in Jackson, where she'd discovered signs, communication, and the joy of expressing herself. In her small town, in north Mississippi, Marie was the only deaf person. Nobody could talk with her.

He wondered if Miss Lee would allow Marie to come and stay in the carriage house. Virgil was afraid to ask. He had decided to wait until Miss Lee could sign, so there'd be no chance of making a mistake, causing a misunderstanding With signs, he could easily tell her what a nice girl Marie was, and how they planned to be married someday. Perhaps Miss Lee would like to hire Marie to work in the house!

He had no idea what Marie might earn. But it wouldn't take much for the two of them to live. He tried to imagine what kind of questions Miss Lee would ask about Marie

Can she cook? Does she iron? Does she know how to purchase food and household supplies? Things which Virgil did not know how to answer. He decided he must write Marie and ask these things before he could talk to Miss Lee about hiring another person.

He saw the kitchen lights come on and Miss Lee moving around, getting food from the refrigerator. She carried a tray to the butcher's-block table. It seemed strange for her to eat off such a thing as a tray. With beautiful dishes all over the place, why would she select a battered old tray?

However, Miss Lee did many things which struck Virgil as strange. Her fear of noises in the basement, then her attraction to it. Several times he'd gone in seeking her and found her emerging from the cellar. Sometimes she ate down there, on that tray she was now preparing. And she didn't seem to sleep at night. He would often complete his evening of writing, stories or letters, and see the lights burning in the house. When he got up to go to the bathroom before dawn, he found her light burning and even saw her walking around—with that tray.

Lately, she had been different, moody. She'd sit for hours staring into a void, her mind absent from her body He would tap the floor and she would not respond. She seemed lonely. Virgil empathized with loneliness. Deafs knew the meaning of that word, as no other word in the world The painful, aching desire to have someone who cares, someone with whom to talk. Yes, he knew how she must feel, and his sense of attachment to her strengthened.

Miss Lee had many things to worry about, Virgil saw that. The men making roof repairs; the painters spilling blobs on the floor and speckling window glass; the daily visit of Mr. Beausarge, who always seemed stern when he spoke to Miss Lee. And he discovered that she left the telephone off the hook to avoid incessant telephone calls.

He stopped mowing when darkness prohibited doing a

good job. He put the mower into the carriage house. This was Friday. He had his pay. Mr. Beausarge had been kind enough to cash the check. He took a bath, brushed his teeth, put on the new Hush Puppies he'd bought last week, and a still-stiff pair of Levi's.

It was a seven-mile hike to downtown, and half that distance to Bel Air Mall, where several movie theaters were located close to one another. Although he set out for town, by the time he reached the mall it was already close to nine o'clock, so he stopped there instead.

He should have bought a newspaper to see which theaters were showing what, but decided it was a dime better spent on something else. It was a bad choice.

He went to this movie because he saw people coming out smiling, laughing. If it was funny, it must be puns. Much of the film was shot in the dark shadows of late evening where the lips of the actors were hidden. Also, there were long shots of an automobile winding up a mountain highway with crucial dialogue dubbed in, and lost to Virgil. The story made no sense, lacked action, and was *not* funny. He had watched other patrons with his peripheral vision. They didn't laugh either. He came out feeling cheated. He'd spent two and a half dollars to watch shadowy images in a nonsensical montage. He should've bought the paper.

He wandered down Airport Boulevard to Sambo's, a restaurant which stayed open all night. Here, for one price, he could drink as much coffee as he wanted. Sitting in an orange upholstered booth, he watched people reflected in the window glass, so it appeared he was observing passing traffic outside.

He spent a lot of time watching people. He would see a mannerism, a quirk, and in his stories he would blend these true-life motions into his characters. One thing he did not do. He never judged a person by his appearance. Too many times he had been judged accordingly.

It was a noisy place, the floor vibrant with scuffling feet, chairs scraping, table responding to background music, people bumping around. The unsettling vibrations kept Virgil tense. It was this sensitivity to his surroundings which made many orals think a deaf person wasn't truly deaf. Any deviation in the harmony underfoot was a clue to turn, look.

A waitress stopped beside him and Virgil chanced to see her lips moving. Thick lips, barely mobile, stiffly pulled in a mechanical smile. He lifted his eyebrows, a physical question mark. She carried a coffeepot. Whatever her words, Virgil nodded. She poured more coffee. Still talking? He nodded, smiling. She put sugar and cream on the table

Fog was coming in, shrouding streetlights in halos of suspended moisture. It was a long walk home. He paid his tab, shoved his hands in his pockets, yawned, and walked toward Springhill.

Aramenta stood by Baby's bed, talking.

"Mother was sick, perhaps. Her mind was sick. She did things which were sometimes cruel. Everybody had to meet her expectations. Sometimes, usually, her expectations were impossibly high. She—"

Aramenta turned. A sound? She stared into the maze of casks and racks. She had to make him understand!

"When you were born," Aramenta said, "the doctors called Mother because they knew your father had been killed in the war. Your father was a fine man. A good man. He would have been so proud to have a son. James was his name, did you know that? James Darcy. He was a handsome man. A good man."

Please listen. Please hear me.

"When you were born, they saw something was wrong Mother told me the baby had died. I believed that. Maybe I wanted to believe that. I—I ran away. Try to understand me, and if you have any questions, I will answer them."

Silence.

"Mother brought you here. She did a terrible thing. She kept you hidden. That's what happened, isn't it? She taught you to hide if anyone came to the house. Isn't that what she did? The reason—" Oh, God, was he listening? Angry, filled with loathing? "The reason Mother would do such a thing is because of her pride. She would hide you so nobody could think a Lee was less than perfect."

She waited, listening; a sigh, a breath, anything to indicate his presence. Nothing.

"Do you understand what I'm trying to tell you?"

Silence.

"You are—" Tears ran down her cheeks. She swallowed, cleared her throat. "You are my child. I am your mother The woman who raised you was my mother. Mother did not ever tell me about you. She kept you hidden from me. If I had known, I would have come home. I would have taken you with me. I didn't leave you here deliberately. When I ran away, I truly thought you were dead. She told me you were dead."

A strange sound that made her hold her breath. It was the rebounding of her own sob from a far wall.

"Now we must get to know each other. We must become friends. You don't want to stay down here. Come upstairs with me. We will talk. I will tell you about my home across the ocean."

She stopped speaking, chest heaving, shoulders pulled by contracting muscles. Could he ever forgive her?

"Baby?"

Why didn't he answer?

"Baby, I beg you to forgive me. I would not have put you through this. I knew what Mother could do to people. She twisted me. She hurt me. She hurt my father. Brother, your uncle, was driven to his death by Mother. My sister, too, ran away. Mother was too demanding. She was angry because I married your father, James. Your father and I had promised each other never to see her, or write her, or call her, again. When she came to the hospital, I did not call her. The doctors called her."

Voice choking, almost a whisper, Aramenta pleaded, "Baby, please come out and talk to me. Let me see you. I will do whatever you wish, I promise. If you come upstairs, it is more pleasant. We will go into the kitchen and I'll make some cookies for you. A sandwich? Would you like a sandwich? Let's go upstairs."

Aramenta waited again, still as stone, saying nothing for a very long time. Scarcely breathing, holding involuntary sobbing, listening—the room was so quiet it was the blood of her own heartbeat she heard. He gave no sign of hearing her. Finally, she went upstairs.

She crawled into bed, in the dark, staring unseeing toward the ceiling. Sharp images of Mother formed in her mind, tyrannical, insane, the depths of her madness never quite accurately discerned.

She thought about the "thousands of people" her "existence" affected, as Randy Beausarge had said. She thought about the stocks that would fall, the contracts that would falter, and the jobs that would fail. Nobody could know, not about this terrible entrapment Mother had perpetuated, and the misshapen man she had created of poor Baby.

"Dear God," Aramenta whispered, "what should I do? If anyone finds out, it will disgrace us all. Mother has disgraced us all!"

She turned on the bedside lamp and sat up, head throbbing. There was no aspirin, she'd looked earlier in the day She scribbled a note to herself to order some. She sat on the side of the bed, head aching, throat raw from weeping.

Her eyes focused on a small stack of books. *Speak with the*

Deaf, one was titled. *Talk with Your Hands.* These were the books Virgil had chosen from the library. And they were well worn, as though by long use.

Deaf. Her heart leaped. Were these mother's books? Was it possible that Baby did not answer because he could not hear her? Could he really be deaf? Aramenta seized the top book. Every page worn, soft from handling, crinkled and straightened from heavy usage.

Deaf! He was huddling in the dark encased in a silence not of his own making, doing as mother had taught him, and Aramenta had been speaking to a vacuum! Fingers trembling, she turned a page.

She looked up "I." "Little finger extended from a closed fist, the thumb of the fist against the chest." She checked the index and found "love." "One or both hands over the heart." "You," she now sought. "You: point at the person."

Aramenta ran down the hall, into the basement, and to the cellar. The timer connected to the lights indicated another fifteen minutes before cutting off. She went down the subbasement steps, through the double doors and back to Baby's bed.

Without a word she gestured, "I" and "love" and "you." She faced the shadows of the opposite wing and repeated the signs, "I love you." Again to the casks and racks, "I love you."

This done, she left him still hiding, her heart racing with new hope.

Chapter Eleven

Aramenta was wearing slacks, a cool blouse, her hair drawn into a neat bun behind her head. She greeted Randy with a smile and coffee.

"Sleep well last night?" Randy inquired.

"Not a wink," she said, cheerily.

"Would you like to see a doctor about getting something to help you relax?"

"No." She motioned to Virgil to come in, even before his knock sounded.

One fist circling over the other, Aramenta made a grinding motion. Virgil's mouth fell open and he stepped back. He nodded. Virgil came to the table, grinning, and sat opposite Randy.

"I see his language is rubbing off on you," Randy commented.

"Somewhat." Aramenta served Virgil and with her free hand made a pantomime of grasping and pulling which even Randy interpreted as "milk."

Barely able to contain himself, Virgil nodded, laughing, a softly rippling sound. When Aramenta returned with the milk, Virgil suddenly jumped to his feet and hugged her

"What the hell's going on here?" Randy asked.

Aramenta submitted to a bearish embrace and smiled at the deaf man. When Virgil sat again, she explained, "He's happy that I'm learning to sign."

"Yeah," Randy grunted, "obviously."

The scene disturbed Randy throughout the day. The fact that it *did* disturb him was all the more distressing because it seemed to have no basis in rationality. That evening as he prepared for bed, Randy hardly heard Bobbie's rambling discourse on her day as wife and mother. He took a long shower and returned to Bobbie, sitting up in bed reading

"Something bothering you, honey?" Bobbie asked.

"Business."

"Aramenta Lee?"

That's how restricted his damned business was; Bobbie knew it, William knew it, Rosa at the office knew it. Randy had developed an image of a child given a new responsibility which he avidly clutched as a pseudo-mark of ascending maturity.

"Yes. Aramenta."

"Want to talk about it?"

He went so long without reply, Bobbie returned to her book. Randy was in bed, chewing his lower lip. He finally formulated the question he wanted answered.

"Bobbie, Aramenta is learning to communicate with her deaf yard man. She's learning to make movements with her hands which stand for words."

"Oh?"

"I don't know why, but it is bothering me "

"Oh."

Randy twisted to face her "What does that mean?"

"You're surprised to see her take that much interest in something or someone, perhaps."

"Okay."

Bobbie was nibbling his earlobe. Her lack of attention to his thoughts was Randy's rationalization—her overture was also irritating him. "Bobbie! Please talk to me."

She drew back, the tone of his voice a warning. After due reflection she said, "You are possibly a little jealous of the gardener."

"Aw, for God's—"

"Up to now Miss Lee has been turning to you alone and you were her stalwart and resourceful mentor. Now, although it is a bit silly, you are offended that she should be interested in this man enough to put herself out and learn his hand-talk."

"Bobbie, I'm serious!"

"So am I," Bobbie said, soberly. "You are a closet chauvinist anyway."

"Now what the hell does that mean?"

"It means," she said, now resolved to a loveless night, "you are a male chauvinist who wants a woman, albeit a sixty-year-old woman, to be a slave to your manly better judgment."

He turned out his lamp, thumped the pillow, and threw his head into it, his back to Bobbie. He lay waiting for more comment, and when none came, he turned to look at her over his shoulder. She winked.

"Male chauvinist," he snorted.

"Pig. I forgot the pig part of it."

He slammed the pillow into a hump and snuggled his head into it again. "Iroveou," he intentionally mumbled

"What, darling?"

He repeated the slurred remark.

She came closer, bending across him, "What?"

Cutting his eyes up at her, he enunciated now, "I love you."

"Of course you do," Bobbie rejoined. "I'm a lovable slave. Deprived and neglected, but ever loyal, like a Saint Bernard."

He pulled her over, biting her neck.

"Easy, piggie," Bobbie whispered, "remember I bruise and that makes the children ask questions in the presence of company."

"I'll give you a hickey," Randy threatened.

"You do," Bobbie said, "and you'll draw back a crimped appendage. Stop all this talk and get serious."

Walker Riley was a small man, lean, courtly, one of the old-line southern gentlemen of a type Randy had learned to distrust. Over the years he had seen men like Wally Riley use their positions, money, and political pull to keep the South from growing, except of course when it behooved their financial interests. Pillars of the church, honorary colonels, members of the governor's staff, the Wally Rileys were anathema to expansion, higher wages, and progressive government.

On the top floor of the International Trade Center, in the exclusive club section, Randy was led to a table which overlooked the docks, shipbuilding facilities, davits of unloading vessels, and the panorama of Mobile Bay. He had correctly guessed that Mr. Riley would keep him waiting a suitably demeaning time before making an appearance. Randy in turn had allotted five minutes to suffer this. Any longer and he would be gone, leaving the banker to stew in his own juices.

"Randy, my boy!" Five minutes to the second after Randy's arrival. Riley smiled, bushy white eyebrows pulled low, a liver-spotted hand extended to shake.

"How are you, Mr. Riley?"

"Don't get up, sit down," Riley intoned. The waiter now placed two menus before them.

"The flounder here is *par excellence,*" Riley suggested, to which Randy nodded.

Their order placed, and with typical at-ease preliminary conversation so common to southern tactics, Riley held forth on a need for improved docks, a pending deepwater port facility, and the effect all this would have on the economy. Over lunch, the banker did most of the talking, his conversation sprinkled with aw-shucks humor and anecdotes. Despite a nervous stomach, Randy ate, accepted a refill of coffee, and with ten minutes of his hour remaining, waited for Riley to get to the matter at hand.

"I knew Aramenta's mother," Riley mused. "Remarkable woman. Every inch a lady. The Lee home was at one time the social hub of the city. Gentility was the watchword, hospitality the theme. Aramenta's father died an alcoholic, but he was nonetheless a force in this community, believe you me. I did a lot of hunting with Arlington Senior—her father.

"Yes, sir, old Arlington and I go way back. He was a fine man. Tragic man. I always tried to look after Aramenta's mother after Arlington died."

Riley sipped hot tea through pursed lips, then gazed pensively at Randy. "I can't even remember Miss Aramenta. How old is she now?"

"Sixty, I believe."

"Sixty—" Riley sipped again. "Times flies all right. Here I am nearly eighty. Seventy-eight to be exact."

"Yes, sir."

"I've watched banking go from a simple vault and guard to what it is today," Riley said. "Amazing how things have changed. These days, computers are the crux of the trade.

Information and money changes hands so fast it staggers the mind. Nothing is simple debit and credit any longer. We're boxed in by rigid controls, federal regulations, and a tight money market."

Randy watched Riley sip tea, thick eyebrows lifting.

"I don't really know what happened to Miss Arlington, Aramenta's mother. She wasn't the same after Arlington died, then the death of her son—a tragedy that, too Suicide."

"Yes."

"Her oldest daughter died in childbirth, I seem to recall Then Aramenta married and left home. Miss Arlington quit having parties, stopped seeing old friends, withdrew into that big house like a hermit crab. She wouldn't answer her telephone, wouldn't come to the door. She ceased communication with us at the bank altogether."

"Yes, sir."

"We've been a minority-controlled bank ever since, you know that."

"Yes, I do."

"I sit as titular chairman of the board, and have for twenty-four years."

"Yes, sir."

"My son, Wally, Jr., is right behind me. I always told Wally he'd step into my shoes someday. He has a lovely wife and four fine children. Do you know my son, Wally?"

"No, Mr. Riley, I don't."

"He's been in banking all his life! Grew up in it. Why, hell, that boy could balance a ledger and pull a D and C before he was twelve years old! Fine mind, astute, with a genuine talent for banking. Way ahead of an old codger like me."

A long pause as Riley measured part of the package of

artificial sweetener into a fresh cup of tea. Stirring, he asked, "Your brother William will most likely be taking an interest in the bank now?"

"I wouldn't know, Mr. Riley. He's very busy with other accounts."

"One of the senior partners in your father's firm?"

"I doubt it, Mr. Riley."

The banker nodded, still stirring. "I'd have to insist on a mature, seasoned man. Too much of my life has gone into building Marine Guaranty."

Randy waved away another cup of coffee.

"What kind of—woman—is this Aramenta?"

Randy lifted one shoulder, dropped it, "She's intelligent, harried, eager to return to Paris. I don't think she has much interest in her business holdings."

"That always vexes me." Riley's eyes glowered. "People like that inherit the hearts and wallets of other folks, then totally ignore their legacy."

"Yes, sir."

"All right, my boy!" Riley smiled again. "I'll be meeting your brother William about all this. But since you are seeing this woman now and then, I wanted your opinion of the situation."

"My brother isn't involved in the matter, Mr. Riley."

"Oh? I see. I assumed your father was too ill, my boy Well, fine, I'll call your father then."

"No, sir," Randy said, properly tempered. "Dad isn't handling it either. I am."

The change in the banker's eyes was ever so slight, a flicker of dawning awareness and cold calculation followed by a disarming sparkle. "Good, good, son! In which case, I'll be seeing more and more of you, then?"

"It seems that way."

"Well, tell me," Riley asked, as the check was being presented, "does Miss Lee intend to exercise her right to vote her stock? Or is she going to ignore it, like her mother?"

"I don't know, Mr. Riley. We're swamped with technicalities and tax problems over the probate of will. When that's out of the way, we'll probably set up some sort of trust with a board of directors."

Visibly relieved, Riley shook Randy's hand, "Good thinking! Fine thinking. Well, keep me informed, my boy. I take a keen interest in my bank. I wouldn't want any problems which might cast a bad reflection on a lifetime of work. You understand that, don't you?"

"I most assuredly do."

Randy parted company from the banker, walking the several blocks back to his office. He felt the onslaught of a headache. When he entered his office, Rosa greeted him with the bleak look of an employee about to face an angry employer—an expression she exhibited more and more of late.

"Mr. William Beausarge wishes to see you, Mr. Beausarge."

"All right, Rosa. Is he in his office?"

"Yessir. Mr Beausarge?"

"Yes?"

"He's mad as smoked-out hornets."

"Okay, Rosa."

William exploded the instant Randy shut the office door. "Goddamn it, I asked you a week or so back if you could handle the Lee thing!"

"I said I could."

"Said you could and doing it are two different things!"

"What seems to be the problem, William?"

"I talked to a very unhappy banker—need I say who?"

"No."

"He is threatening a minority revolt, charging this firm and Miss Aramenta Lee with negligence, challenging her choice for a sitting board member."

"All right."

"All right? What does that mean, little brother? Who the hell has she selected?"

"Nobody, yet."

"Nobody? Randall, I think we'd better go over this woman's holdings. I want a full report on my desk, the dossier on her and everything relating to her. Get it for me by six. I'll study it at home."

Randy leaned against the office door, mind whirling. "I should think you'd have more to do than mess with a tangled estate, William. But if you want that account, thank God! I've had to hire domestic help, a yard man, secure a realtor, contract building repairs, meet with IRS, and bring all the files current. I've taken her out to dinner, checked her house for prowlers, and helped her handyman mend his plumbing."

"What? Jesus, Randall! You don't have to put up with that kind of thing!"

"William, you said to pay attention to details. One detail here I have not overlooked."

"Which is?"

"Every time I go trotting over to her house, she is paying us one hundred dollars an hour. I keep close records and she'll get my bill."

William smiled. "Good boy. Okay, little brother. Stay on top of it. Any problems, let me know. As for Riley, that bastard is sucking eggs and he knows it. But if he gives you any flak refer him to me."

"Thank you, William."

"Get out of here, kid. I'm up to my Adam's apple in work."

Randy returned to his office. "Any calls, Rosa?"

"Yes, Mr. Bruce Matthew from New York again. The Mobile *Press-Register,* two calls from Hanson and Hanson Realty, one from—"

"Hold those," Randy said. He went into his office and dialed Aramenta's number. The line was busy. Off the hook again most likely. He called the telephone company and ordered a new unlisted number for Aramenta. Then he went down to the garage and got his car.

Until he probated the will, Aramenta could do nothing. Therefore, nothing was more important than the final tax valuations and settlement. If he had to, he'd spend the weekend helping Aramenta search for those safe-deposit-box keys.

Randy turned out Springhill Avenue. Hot air gusted through the window. The air-conditioning in this car had never operated properly. He felt perspiration being blotted by his collar and Randy loosened his tie. The headache was approaching now on pounding hobnail boots.

Aramenta appreciated honesty. Perhaps he should sit down with her and go over all this. No, that wasn't possible. She valued candor, but she was not the least bit interested in hearing about his problems where her business was concerned. If he couldn't manage it, he knew she'd find somebody who could.

Randy parked in the rear near the carriage house. Men laden with hods of terra-cotta tile were climbing ladders to the roof. Virgil paused, pruning shrubbery, and waved Randy returned the greeting and walked inside

"Aramenta?"

He let himself in, hearing hammers from upstairs. The upper floor had taken on the hollow sound of unoccupied rooms as the movers crated and carried things out.

"Aramenta!"

He searched all of the downstairs first, then up where the Parke-Bernet people were overseeing the packaging of oil paintings. He nodded in passing, asking if anyone had seen Aramenta, then went on to the attic, which was now bare. A person could get lost in this house. Randy returned to the first floor, then saw the open basement door.

The lights were on. Drawn as much by curiosity as a desire to find Aramenta, he descended the steps. The place was huge! It reminded him of one of those castle dungeons he'd seen as a kid in horror films. A pleasant aroma of clay and mustiness mingled here as Randy strolled toward the rear.

What's this? Another, lower basement? He went below, through heavy steel doors and down an aisle of racks. The place was fascinating! He heard a voice.

"Aramenta?"

Now silence. Randy moved through the winding rows of racks. What a building this was. "Aramenta!" he called again.

Unhurried, he followed the line of least resistance, came to a dead end, and doubled back. "Aramenta, are you down here?" He was momentarily confused. Which way was in and which was out? He turned and gasped.

"My God, Aramenta, you scared me half to death!"

"What do you need, Randy?" Aramenta was almost whispering.

"Well"—he laughed—"I was looking for you." She was ushering him out. "Are you down here alone?"

"Yes."

Alone? Then who was talking? Randy studied her face, now shadowed and disturbed. "I thought I heard voices."

"You did. I was talking to myself."

141

Trying to inject levity, Randy said, "You know what that's a sign of, Aramenta."

She nodded, unsmiling. Soberly, she paused to lock the basement door. She put the key in a pocket.

"Now," she said, smiling at last, "what did you need?"

Chapter Twelve

Exhausted, Aramenta asked Randy to let her find the keys. They had ransacked the obvious places, desks and visible containers. With a den, study, Father's old office, much of the library, and Mother's bedroom, the task would be one of tedious and systematic hunting.

When Randy left, Aramenta went into the yard and found Virgil clipping the privet hedge. She scanned the grounds, pleased, and childhood memories of lawn parties briefly engrossed her thought.

"I want to talk to you," Aramenta signed clumsily.

Yes-sign.

She fumbled for the proper gestures, then abandoned the effort, speaking, "Why don't you go take a bath, come inside, and spend the rest of today with me. I want to ask some questions if you don't mind."

He hurriedly put away the tools. Aramenta went into the kitchen, made coffee, and baked Mother's rocks. When Virgil arrived, clean, shaven, wearing fresh clothing, they sat by the bay window. Aramenta had placed paper and pencils on the table, along with cups, sugar, cream, and cookies

"Virgil, how much do you understand when I speak?"

He shrugged his shoulders, grew thoughtful, then with a series of gestures and mouthed words, replied, "Sometimes little, sometimes much."

"Can all deaf people read lips?"

He held up thumb and forefinger, very close together.

"Could they learn to read lips?"

He stumbled, faltered, then wrote a lengthy note in careful longhand:

"It is complex. Some things cannot be read on lips Examples: gun, sun, none, done. Lips do not move. Nothing can be seen. You say some words and lips move well. Examples: we, who, what—but the same lip movement for all three, it looks alike. Some lips easier to read. Sometimes people look away. Some lips stiff. Some talk and laugh at the same time. Chewing gum. Eating. Cannot understand then."

She studied the note, struck with the truth. Virgil was still writing. "English, 40% cannot be read on lips."

"Then you misunderstand much that I say?"

He lifted his eyebrows, sighed, nodded.

"How do deaf people talk to one another?" she asked

He held out his hands, smiling.

"How many signs are there?"

He wrote, "Thousands. But 500 enough to talk most things. If you know alph—" He scratched out the last word and penned, "A B C's."

Aramenta had seen the one-hand signs for the alphabet in one of her signing books. She poured coffee, offered a cookie She wondered if Virgil would laugh at the same things she found funny. She decided not. His humor was probably more visual than verbal.

"Do you think I could learn to talk with my hands?"

Virgil nodded enthusiastically.

"Could you teach me?"

Yes! Yes!

"Will you teach me?"

"Yes! Happy to teach you." To be sure she comprehended this, he wrote the message, each letter carefully transcribed.

"Then," Aramenta replied in writing, "beginning now, I want you to plan a lesson for each day. I want you to spend no less than three hours each day teaching me. Will you be agreeable to this?"

Animated, overjoyed, "Truly!"

"What should I first learn?" Aramenta questioned.

Virgil used one hand, lips in unison with the gestures, "A-B-C-D-E—"

"Would it not be faster to learn the meaning of word signs?" she asked.

"This too," he resorted to writing. "But many words have no sign—then you must spell."

"And you think I can learn?"

Exaggerated nod, up, down, up, down.

"How quickly can I learn this?"

He put down his coffee, writing, "This depends on you. How much you practice. When I was 9 and had never met another deaf, I learned from a book in 1 month. I was in first grade then."

"First grade? At age nine?"

Laboriously, each word carefully considered, each sentence tediously formed, Virgil wrote, "Yes. Deaf boy and girl must learn talk before can learn anything. You learn talk by age 2, 3. Nobody knew signs to teach me. For long time Mama and Papa thought me slow, but not deaf. Then thought me dumb. By time know better, I am 9. Deaf worse than blind. Blind learn like boy and girl with eyes. Deaf do not learn so fast. Because must learn talk first."

Aramenta read this, from a corner of her eye seeing Virgil massage his writing hand, soothing a cramp.

"You will be my teacher," she said.

He grinned. Then with his hand he signed her words.

"What does that mean?"

He wrote, "You will be my teacher," and signed it slowly Aramenta mimed, and he nodded approval.

He asked her to bring in the signing books he'd left by her bed. He selected one, *Say It with Hands* by Louie J. Fant, Jr. Herein, the signs had been broken into lessons. There were forty-five lessons in all. Virgil had suggested a lesson a day, but Aramenta insisted on three!

They set aside each morning, having breakfast together. The first hour was a review of past lessons, the second hour devoted to new signs, the third hour practice, with Virgil asking questions with signs only, Aramenta attempting to reply. It was wearisome work, hands aching as she used muscles unaccustomed to the flex and twists.

As with all orals, Aramenta signed slowly, spelled even more slowly, and deciphering her meaning was depleting to mind and body. Nonetheless, Virgil taught her with a regimen of carefully planned sessions. He saw her willingness and determination to learn each sign properly. Knowing this, he demanded the perfection she sought.

The alphabet came slowest, as it had with Virgil as a student. Each letter a pause, hand jerking, floating instead of remaining still so it would be easier to read. With Randy Beausarge and the moving people constantly interrupting, Virgil watched Miss Lee's patience wear thin and finally break with an angry exchange. Thereafter, everybody left them alone.

The attorney did not like this. It was evident in his eyes, open resentment, his lips compressed. He was no longer as friendly. This was upsetting and beyond Virgil's comprehension. But any deaf was accustomed to orals suddenly withdrawing, blocking off further contact for reasons known only to themselves.

Miss Lee's will to learn made her practice, even when the lesson for the day was done. Virgil observed her doing homework, hands moving, talking to herself. It would not be long before they could talk about anything. But, for now, their concern was the critical working signs which allowed a person to express his basic needs. Abstractions, inner thoughts with more than surface depth, these must await a time when signing was as fast as speaking, when the fingers did not grow stiff from drawn tendons.

Virgil entered the kitchen to find Miss Lee soaking her hands in a dishpan of steaming water.

"Hands hurt?" he signed.

She nodded, her eyes telling him even before she withdrew a hand to slowly fingerspell, "Arthritis." Virgil winced. Rheumatism, arthritis, even a minor sprain of the wrist was comparable to orals suffering a loss of voice.

"You want to wait until tomorrow for a lesson?" Virgil queried.

"No." She dried her hands gingerly. From a cupboard she took a bottle of Bufferin and of these she swallowed four. As usual, she had the coffee ready.

"Perhaps we should wait until tomorrow," he urged.

Her face twisted, a flash of irritation. "No! Let's begin."

But as the days passed, the weather cooler these mornings, the house drafty and almost empty of furniture, her hands responded slowly, knuckles swollen. She had stopped the moving people after they cleaned out the living room. Still furnished, but sparsely, were the library, Miss Lee's bedroom, and of course, the kitchen.

Virgil felt a chill in more than the morning air. He saw

Miss Lee snap at a repairman, again at a plumber who had gone into the basement to mend Miss Lee's bathtub. While Virgil went through a morning class, Miss Lee kept Mr Beausarge sitting in the hall, waiting. Finally, the attorney had come in, face flushed, and angry words passed between them. Virgil's belly contorted. Anger was terrifying, especially when he did not understand the cause of it.

He remembered being surprised as a toddler when Mama suddenly descended on him from behind, snatching him up, mouth working, shaking his shoulders in her anger. But as quickly as such anger erupted, it might also evaporate, melting into breathtaking hugs and weeping. He was never quite sure what had caused the outburst, or when it might recur. Thus he was molded into the cautious, wary child many deafs become, maintaining a strict schedule, fearing any change in routine, dreading new people and situations. It was the infant-toddler relationship, erratic and unfathomable, which engendered the simpering smile. Virgil was smiling now at the attorney and Miss Lee making shout-faces, anger-faces. He wiped the smile from his lips.

"Aramenta, for nearly three weeks I've been asking about the keys for those lock boxes!"

"I have not found them," she seethed.

"Aramenta," Randy moderated his tone, "may I look for them?"

"I said I'd do it. I will."

Randy glanced at the deaf man, that idiotic grin now gone, eyes down, sober. The bastard actually seemed to be enjoying all this.

"Aramenta, we cannot probate the will until—"

"I know that," Aramenta said, too loudly.

"You do see that it's holding us up, don't you?" Randy reasoned.

"I see it."

"Does it matter?"

"Of course it matters."

"As much as learning that hand gibberish? Everyday I come over here and—"

She wheeled, face flushed. "Don't ever say that again, Randy. Hand gibberish. Virgil can read your lips. He is a human being. He is a thinking, sensitive human being."

"Yes, Aramenta—you're right. It was thoughtless and completely uncalled for. I apologize. But I did have my back to him."

"Nevertheless," Aramenta said, coldly, "I do not appreciate such remarks."

"All right, Aramenta. I'm sorry." Randy sighed. "I am truly sorry."

The air was thick with emotion. Randy mustered a smile and nod for Virgil, then excused himself and departed.

"What in God's name is happening here?" he asked aloud, walking to his automobile. Was the kid like a pet? Some single, many elderly, and most lonely people were prone to take in animals or plants upon which to pour their affection. Randy knew it was a basic need, to be needed. He'd seen doting septuagenarians with spoiled Chihuahuas, goldfish, and even African violets. But, Jesus!

What was Aramenta doing here? Couldn't she see that Virgil worshiped her? Surely, with her intelligence she must realize what a fall she was setting him up for! Virgil had probably never had so much attention in his life. He came here a waif, unemployed, drifting, crying and begging for a job. He'd been a damned good employee, too. He worked his tail off, required little supervision, and was competent But look at them now! For God's sake, Aramenta was feeding him breakfast, sitting for hours making those hand signs, and then for the rest of the goddamned day she wasn't worth shooting as she walked around in a stupor practicing in front of people who had no idea *what* she was doing.

And the newspaper! Those guys had been stalled off about as long as they were going to stall. Already Diehl had interviewed somebody who'd seen Aramenta wandering around waving her hands in the air.

"Is she off her rocker, Beausarge?"

"No, she definitely is not."

"Then who's she conjuring up?" Diehl grunted.

"Nobody, Diehl," Randy had fumed, "she has taken an interest in learning signing."

"Doing what?"

"It's the way deaf people talk."

"Is she deaf?"

"No."

"Going deaf?"

"No."

"Just wants something to do with her hands?"

"I suppose."

Diehl's giggle rose and fell. "Okay, Beausarge, I'll wait another few days. This babe is getting more interesting all the time."

Damn it! Randy slammed the car door, backed around, and drove from the yard. He was spending his day—all day of every day—with things relating to Aramenta. He didn't mind that. He wanted that. She saw him pretty good and he thought he understood her, too. But lately, the past few weeks particularly, he'd found himself tensed and nervous when he had to see her. Crazy things she was doing, like this thing with Virgil. What the hell had possessed her?

He jammed on the brakes, narrowly avoiding a collision at the driveway exit into the street. Wake up, stupid! He accepted the verbal barrage, unheard but clearly understood as the other driver pulled around him. Randy took a deep breath, exhaled. Horns blowing. His temples were throbbing. He'd had a headache more often than not for a month. He'd gone to a doctor. Tension. No cancer, no tumor, no high blood pressure—tension! He'd never had headaches until Aramenta Lee came into his life. Randy was breathing hard as he halted at a stoplight. A car pulled up beside him and the lady driver jabbed a finger at him. What the hell had he done now? Her lips were moving behind air-conditioned windows. Everybody's goddamned air-conditioner worked but his. Finger jabbing. His wheel? Tire? No? What then, lady?

He opened the door and looked down. He swore softly, then managed a smile to the now smiling lady. He had shut the door on his suit jacket which had fallen down behind the seat. The jacket was muddied and torn. He yelled his annoyance. People turned to look and he didn't give a damn, teeth clenched. He ought to turn around, go back there, and tell Aramenta Lee to take her estate and—

Hey! This wasn't doing the headache any good. Cool down. Hands sweating. Easy does it, Randy. He carefully planned each physical action: foot on gas; accelerate; look left, right; all clear, more gas; easy, boy; watch traffic.   .   He shouldn't have to bear all this alone. He ought to have some help. That's what business associates were for. William and the other attorneys talked over their problems, debated alternatives. But not Randy. Hell, no. If he went in and tried to discuss these problems he'd walk out with no estate, no proxies, no account, and be back doing legal research

Aramenta watched the clock, impatient for nine, when the cellar lights would come on automatically. She prepared Baby's tray, poured a large glass of milk, put the vitamin tablet where he'd easily see it next to the bread.

Aramenta proved to herself that he was deaf while he was asleep. Creeping downstairs, within a few feet of him, she had shouted and he had not stirred a muscle. But if she bumped a wine rack, stomped on the floor, he might be gone when she arrived, flashlight in hand.

Her preliminary joy and optimism had waned as she continued going down, gesturing, talking, pleading for his company. Not once had he revealed himself to her voluntarily. She spent hours each night cleaning for him, washing and folding his clothes, making herself available, obviously in his behalf. No response. She wrote notes, pinned to his tray. Another dismal failure. If he read them, he ignored them. If she was making progress, she couldn't tell it.

In frustration, she became angry, quick slashing gestures of hand and unmasked facial expressions. "Why don't you come out?" she demanded. "What is wrong with you? Are you not thankful for what I am doing? I do the best I can!"

Silence. Dark shadows unstirred by movement or sound She had stomped away and for several days had taken less care with his feeding. Then it dawned on her that food was her only means of provoking a response from him. So she would withhold it from him until he gave some sign of answering her. All the next day she went no farther than the closed portal, looking through the bars which allowed free circulation of air, watching for movement. By the end of the next day, the frantic thumping had resumed. She refused to yield, determined to see this thing through.

Thump-thump-thump.

Aramenta sat in the kitchen watching the sweep second hand of the clock. Thump-thump-thump. Now we'll see. If he wants food, he must come and get it. If he does not come, he does not eat. Like an animal—she put that thought out of her mind. All right, *like* an animal! Either he gave as she gave, and it became a seesaw of give and take, or he suffers as she was suffering.

Aramenta carried down the tray, hands trembling with

anticipation. Thump-thump-thump. The knocking ceased when she turned on the basement lights.

"I know you're there," she said aloud. "I know you're there and you know I'm here. Food. You want food, Baby? Come and ask for it!" The timer clicked, the wine cellar lights shone from below. Aramenta descended to the foot of the steps, standing in a brightly lighted area under an overhead light outside the door. She turned the heavy key, the tray balanced on one forearm. She pulled open the door Inside, she waited for her eyes to adjust to the sparse illumination. He had run away. She walked through the racks to his sleeping area.

"Want a banana?" she asked the shadows. "Want milk?" She put the tray on his bed, freeing her hands. Gestures joined lip movements as she asked, "Are you hungry, Baby?"

She held out the banana, turning to east wing, then west, offering the fruit. She'd known the extent of his pleasure over bananas when she'd found he had chewed the peel of one.

"Come get the banana, Baby. Come on."

She quelled mounting irritation. "Listen to me, Baby. If you don't come get this, I'm taking it back upstairs."

She put down the fruit and signed with both hands, "Want banana? Come. You not come. I take banana with me."

She repeated the message to the opposite wall of shadows. She then held out the banana again, silent, waiting.

Nothing.

She threw the banana on the tray and snatched it up, spilling some of the milk. Resolutely, she marched back toward the door.

An animal cry, a moan, ascended behind her. The hair on Aramenta's arms and neck tingled. She stopped, waiting, then turned and looked back. She still did not see him. She returned to the lighted sleeping area, put the tray on the bed, and repeated the offer, holding out the banana.

The sound was discordant, a frightening and choking wail, the vocal manifestation of an animal pinned in a trap. It subsided as she came back, now a low whimper in the darkness. The reverberations of sound made detection of source difficult—it was there—no, there.

"Come. You want. Come."

She grabbed up the tray again, moving toward the door. She left the cellar, heart pounding, the moan becoming a shrieking, mindless, terrifying, disembodied scream from the dark.

Aramenta closed the cellar door, locked it, and went up to the basement, then to the kitchen. There, she burst into tears and threw the tray against a wall.

Chapter Thirteen

"Well, hello there, Randall Beausarge," Ted Jones greeted Randy, entering the office. Golf, tennis, and poker partners as time and familial responsibilities allowed, the lanky attorney and Randy had been classmates at the University of Alabama.

"I have a thorn for Miss Aramenta Lee," Ted amiably related. "One Buddy Ellis wishes to sue her eminence for the worldly sum of one hundred and fifty bucks."

"Oh, Christ, Ted."

"I know it. Anyway, before taking it to small claims, I thought maybe you'd want to settle it."

"I do. Come in. Let me call Miss Lee."

Aramenta listened, then exploded, "I won't pay that man a cent!"

"Ellis seemingly feels cheated, Aramenta," Randy placated. "He claims he spent money for a survey, plat, and other out-of-pocket expenses which—"

"He said he was common," Aramenta's voice crackled on

the line, "and he is. That's a low-down lack of breeding if ever I saw it."

"I know, Aramenta."

"Let him sue. We'll fight it."

"Aramenta," Randy kept his tone sympathetic, "it'll cost five hundred to fight a one-fifty total. It isn't worth it."

"Nevertheless, fight it."

"If you insist."

"I damn well insist. I told that man to take a proposal to you. I refused to sign a contract because he wanted too much commission—which he altered with a pen on the spot. I saw trouble in the making and turned him away. Now he's trying to steal. Because he knows I have it. The bastard."

"Okay, Aramenta." Randy hung up and looked at Ted The opposing attorney wore a bemused expression.

"You won't believe this, Ted."

"Yes, I will. She wants to contest it."

"That's right."

"That's what keeps us in business, old friend. If there's one thing a rich client can't abide, it's a poor client trying to get something unearned."

"I'm tempted to pay the thing myself and be done with it," Randy said.

"Take my advice," Ted countered, seriously. "Fight this suit for all it's worth. Go to the Supreme Court with it if you can find an angle on which to do it. Wealthy folks loathe and despise losing."

"You're probably right."

"Mighty right I'm right," Ted said, standing and extending his hand. "By the way, I finally got my new Brunswick regulation pool table. How about shooting a few?"

"Love to, but I'm snowed this week, Ted."

Ted touched his forehead with a jaunty salute. "The price of success."

Randy returned to his desk, tossed the Ellis suit aside

Perhaps he could reason with Aramenta at a later date Until then, let it ride. Aramenta seemed to be losing a grip on herself. Doing idiot things. Mistakes that were going to result in enemies of long standing. Ellis, for one. He was a small-timer, but such independents could least afford to put out cash on an if-come deal. Because Ellis thought he had the property, he had gone ahead on good faith. To Aramenta, the money was nothing. To a guy like Ellis, one-fifty was a month of groceries.

And that deaf kid! It didn't take a prognosticator to foresee what the ultimate outcome of Aramenta's actions would be. Virgil Wilson was soaking up her attention, savoring the warmth of her compassion, assuming more than Aramenta intended. What would Virgil do when Aramenta tired of this and flew home to Paris? His source of beneficence inexplicably gone, respect would sour, resentment would fester, and Virgil would become a bitter, angry young man. He would hate Aramenta Lee.

Randy had read somewhere—Aldous Huxley, he thought—that making enemies by accident was unforgivable. It was the insulted elevator operator who grew up to own the building, the trampled aspiring actress who someday ruled the studio. If enemies you must make, for the sake of wisdom and the future, make them with careful consideration and then by deliberate choice. It was something Randy personally lived by. Well, Aramenta was creating her enemies with reckless abandon.

Randy opened a desk drawer and withdrew aspirin. He took three, poured a shot of bourbon, and drank it. Throat scorching, stomach upset, he leaned back and closed his eyes. One more thing to think about, Beausarge. If the lady is this unstable—how much can you depend on her?

He poured another shot of amber liquid and threw it down, face contorted, chest burning.

If he'd been smart, he would've paid off Ellis without

calling Aramenta. Stupid move. So, okay, he was getting smart. She was too shook to handle her own affairs, he'd handle them for her. Aramenta wanted to sit out there in an empty house and talk to the deaf, so be it. In the interim, he was being a yellow-maned tuck-tail dog, simpering around here waiting for her to do what she could not, *would* not, do!

Randy lifted his phone and dialed Rosa, so his conversation would be for her ears only.

"Rosa, bring in all files on the Lee estate. I'm going to need you for the balance of the afternoon."

"Yessir, Mr. Beausarge."

All right, Aramenta. You can be as tutti-frutti as your dear departed mother. But your obligations are going to be met. Forcefully, decisively, and now.

"Now Rosa," he said, as the secretary entered, "what happens in this office is confidential. That means totally confidential."

Rosa's lips pulled, a suggestion of a smile. "You may depend on it, Mr. Beausarge."

"Good. Let's get to work."

With the furniture gone, the house felt colder, looming larger than Aramenta ever remembered it. All of the upstairs was now being repainted, water-stained wallpaper removed, faulty plumbing corrected. By day, a din of workmen's coarse voices and laughter covered the thumping from the cellar. Tonight would be the third day. How long dared she deny Baby food? What if he became ill?

These past two days she too had forgone sustenance. The hunger he might be feeling was best judged by what Aramenta felt herself. But for her, belly knotted with tension, there were no appreciable pangs of hunger. The thumping became harder, more intense, and for these two days sleep had come to Aramenta only in the exhaustion of the first dawning hours. Her nerves were raw, temper short.

The thump-thump-thump drumming in her ears, Aramenta tried to imagine herself in a world of absolute silence. No music, no songbirds, no moan of a locomotive on the rails. Baby would never hear the baritone of a tugboat's early-morning foghorn. He would never keep time to Khachaturian, Sousa, or Strauss. Seeing herself through Baby's eyes, Aramenta was shocked at the image he must perceive. His routine altered, the only human contact he had known suddenly gone, deprived of food for a reason he could not understand, locked in the cellar for a wrong he could not recall—to Baby, Aramenta was a silent jailer, ruthless, cold, uncaring. She was a stranger. He could not hear the words of a mother's love, the tone of her soothing reassurances. Her gestures must seem uncertain and awkward, her motives mysterious and sinister.

Aramenta turned the key and pulled open the wine-cellar door. Jaw set, determined, she walked the aisles of racks to Baby's sleeping area. She placed the tray on his bed. Picking up a single banana, she turned full circle slowly.

"You want," she signed, without speaking. "Come get."

She thought she heard something. She faced that way. "You want?" she gestured anew. "Come get."

He was there, his breathing coming like the rale of liquid in a drinking straw, air through saliva—how close? Aramenta waited, banana held out.

The panting rush of his breathing seemed to give life to the entire cellar. The walls rebounded with the sound as though they were sighing. She could visualize him hiding, driven by hunger and stayed by fright, not comprehending why this was happening to him.

"Come," she signed.

She stilled the tremble of her outstretched hand. Please come. She didn't want to do this. Please. Come, Baby. Come out now.

"Come. You want? Come." Hand signs.

Was he nearer? She thought she heard a gurgle, a choked swallow. She squinted her eyes, the shadows made darker by the light in which she stood. Was he there? A scraping sound, like a plank rubbing along another board.

"I want to give this to you," she signed slowly. "Come You want? Come to Mama."

A noise behind made Aramenta wheel. Had her hearing misled her? She held out the banana, arm beginning to ache from the enforced position.

"You want? Come. Come!"

The faintest scuffle reached Aramenta and again she turned a quarter circle. Sounds down here played tricks. Not echoes, not exactly. Bent by angles and racks, floor and ceiling, the indistinct breathing and movement of feet came as if from everywhere. She was now confused. One instant she thought him in the west wing, the next in the east. Now she stood facing the exit.

"Please, come out," she said aloud, the volume of her own voice inordinately loud. "Baby, please don't make me do this. Come out and take the food. I only want to see you, touch you. We can't continue like this—you must come out to Mama."

Silence. Aramenta's throat constricted.

What was he doing? Sneaking closer? Retreating? The door!

She grabbed the tray and hurried down the aisles, round the corners, moving as quickly as possible with the tray gripped in both hands.

He had circled her! She ran up the steps, sides aching.

She reached the kitchen and the refrigerator door was still swinging as it found the lowest point of gravity's pull.

"Where are you?" she shouted. She put the tray on the butcher's-block table and ran back through the pantry. Spilled milk. A piece of bread on the floor. Aramenta threw on the lights in the old servants' kitchen. She caught a flash of movement and raced after him. He'd gone into the hallway—where? The basement door was still ajar. Back to the kitchen? Bedroom?

Corner him. Trap him. Force him to meet her! She locked the basement door. Get him in the hall and he must confront her. She searched the bedroom, closed that door, and latched it. One furtive glance around the other empty rooms, and she knew he was not there. She walked through the dining room and into the kitchen.

The tray was gone. She ran the circle from pantry and servants' kitchen, into the hall. Block him off. She shut the connecting door from pantry to old kitchen.

Then a scream tore through the upper floors, caroming, echoing, and as it faded, another! Goose bumps raced down Aramenta's arms. Another scream. What was happening to him? She mounted the stairs seeking direction. Would any neighbor hear this? Blood-chilling, heart-stopping screams!

She went from suite to suite turning on lights, her footsteps hollow, floorboards creaking. Her ears rang with the incessant shrieks.

It stopped. Abruptly.

Aramenta stood unmoving, listening for a clue to where he was. She tiptoed down the hall, back toward the stairway. From below a crash. Aramenta began to run, lungs burning, sides aching from exertion. She reached the main floor.

He was at the rear of the hall, nude, the food now scattered, the tray upside down. He gripped the door handle with both hands, snatching, gasping.

"Baby, this is Mama. Let me talk to you. Baby, let me talk to you. Wait. Wait, I'll open it for you."

He was frantic! Muscles corded, beard flecked with saliva, shaking the door with a frenzy. He threw himself against a far wall. Aramenta approached very slowly, talking softly, as though her tone would soothe his deafened ears. Her hands out, reaching, imploring.

He ran at the door, fingernails clawing, and for the first time Aramenta saw how long his nails were. He kicked the door, a thunderous barrage that rumbled through the building and returned from upstairs like spent lightning.

"I won't hurt you, Baby. I only want to help. Let Mama help you—"

He whirled, a swinging backhand blow sent Aramenta sprawling headlong among the foodstuffs. He stepped on her as he ran. First to the bedroom door—locked. Then to the front door, and for a second she thought he might escape into the night. But after an instant of hesitation, he turned slowly, teeth bared, a growling rasp coming between curled lips.

He wasn't trying to flee now. He wasn't trying to evade her. He was no longer thinking of food. One foot lifted and moved forward with the delicate precision of a stalking cat.

"Baby?"

His shoulders rounded, his body almost hairless and sleek with sweat, his posture and advance grew ominous.

Aramenta tried to rise, and her leg, where he'd stepped, gave way as she put her foot on something slippery. Baby panted, growling like a mongrel with hackles raised. She fumbled for the basement key, crawling toward the door. Her movement caused an instinctive tensing, his arms out as though to head her off.

She missed the keyhole, jabbed again, and sought a point where the key would turn. It jammed. Oh, please! She glanced back. Baby took another wary step toward her.

The lock gave. Aramenta grabbed the handle, turned, snatched, and fell back into a corner, wedging herself against oak wainscoting. He stood over her now, sucking air between clamped teeth, his face shrouded by shadows.

"Baby, please—please, Baby—"

Abruptly, he pivoted and began to gather the smashed bananas, crumbs of bread, scooping beans with his fingers, putting these in a partitioned receptacle of the tray. He found the tomato halves and dropped them on the carrier.

"Oh, God!" Aramenta cried. "Oh, God! Help me! Help me!"

He walked down the basement steps, sucking his fingers.

Aramenta sobbed, leg hurting, her clothing smeared with food, cursing herself—cursing Mother.

Chapter Fourteen

Randy sat on the small, brick-walled patio awaiting Sunday breakfast. Bobbie had correctly guessed the limits of his endurance and managed to feed the children early and send them out on a day of activity designed to keep them gone and happy. He watched her serve coffee, orange juice, and poached eggs.

"Have I told you lately that I love you?" he asked.

"Last Tuesday."

"Well, I do."

She placed a thick Sunday edition of the Mobile *Press-Register* beside his plate. "Bacon, sausage, or ham?" she inquired.

"Bacon." Then, mildly surprised, "You cooked all three?"

"No."

"What if I'd said ham or sausage?"

"You never do. Ask the blessing."

The trees had begun turning, donning fall raiment of rusts and reds, the air came cool and fresh. No insects. A perfect morning for eating out here.

"Is today something special?" Randy cautiously queried.

"Nope." Bobbie had dressed more for spring than autumn, her hair looked as if it had been recently cut and set

"All this special service leading up to something?" Randy asked.

"Yep."

"What?"

"I have planned the day, by the hour, and with great care," Bobbie reported. "When you finish breakfast, have read the paper, and taken a bath, I am going to rape you "

"Umm, I see."

"Maybe twice."

"I like the way you handle my itinerary," Randy said.

The meal was unhurried, excellent, coffee aromatic and delicious. They divided the newspaper and enjoyed the silence of each other's company. It was the first time in weeks that Randy hadn't had a knot in his stomach. He was suffering a vague uneasiness, as though he'd forgotten something or had some place to go. Then he realized it was because he had nothing to do and nowhere to go. It made the morning all the sweeter.

"Oh, dear," Bobbie said.

"What is it?"

She peeked over the newspaper. "Oh, nothing."

Her expression said otherwise and Randy insisted, "What is it, Bobbie?"

"I refuse to allow anything to get in the way of this day," she said, vehemently. "Do you have a match?"

"A match?"

"I want to burn the paper."

"Give me that." Randy took her section and turned it. He scanned the headline and said, "Damn."

"MOBILE MYSTERY WOMAN—WHO IS SHE?"

166

"Want some good advice?" Bobbie suggested, seeing his face coloring. "Stop reading it."

"The Lees of Mobile," the article said, under Diehl's by-line, "have been plagued by tragedy, mystery, and money." Photographs pulled from the newspaper morgue pictured several Lee men in high stiff collars and handlebar mustaches, launching a schooner. Other photos enforced the text with family shots, social parties in progress, and a presidential visit by William McKinley. Aramenta's mother and the three children stood in a pose familiar with photographers of the time.

"Money doesn't buy everything," the article stated. "Alcoholism, suicide, and death by childbirth have haunted the Lees."

"Oh, for God's sake!" Randy snorted. "This is insulting and unnecessary."

Bobbie was now standing behind him, reading over Randy's shoulder. There was a complete family history, dwelling at length on the era of their growth, rapid accumulation of wealth, and the expansion of political power. "Then," the story related, "something happened to the successful and gregarious Lees."

Randy read of Aramenta's sister, Annette, who ran away to marry and died in childbirth. Her brother's suicide, her father's death from excessive drinking, and Aramenta the war bride and widow, "escaping the curse of the Lees." She had gone to Paris and oblivion. The article gave her Parisian address, the name of a housekeeper, and artist friends quoted as though interviewed. Randy read the dateline anew and groaned: Associated Press. What Diehl had begun, the wire service had expanded.

"Mrs. Arlington Edward Lee III," the article stated, "closed her shutters, withdrew her welcome mat, refused to see or speak with anyone, and became a classic recluse. Not even her attorneys could penetrate the wall of silence she erected around herself. All the while, as money will, the Lee fortune grew of itself."

Randy cursed aloud, reading detailed lists of stocks, bonds, corporations, realty holdings, and other financial interests. Board members had been contacted. Riley had elected to be quoted as saying he "hadn't seen the decedent in thirty years, and had never met Miss Aramenta."

Meticulously, the article spelled out the ramifications of the Lee holdings, the untouched but potential power now vested in Aramenta's hands, the scope of her wealth, and the "inherited tendency to mystery and seclusion."

Two full pages of words and pictures, a comprehensive biography, interviews with past associates, and allusions to her present attorney, "who delayed, stalled, and finally requested that this article be withheld."

The photograph of Aramenta in her robe and hairnet was not included, but a series of other photographs were. Aramenta as a debutante; riding a Mardi Gras float as a high-school senior; in a ballet class with other students; a stock photo from Agnes Scott College yearbook, showing an attractive, unsmiling woman who graduated *summa cum laude.*

"A personal estate variously estimated from 16 to 40 million dollars," the article reported. "Control of the Marine Guaranty Bank of Mobile, Axiom Insurance Company of Nashville (a company which loaned the government of Mexico a mere 100 million dollars), and the largest female stockholder of—"

"Well, damn," Randy whispered.

"She's not going to like this, is she?" Bobbie noted.

"No, she won't. But for me personally, this means trouble."

"Trouble?" Bobbie's face became a lovely mask of concern.

Randy pushed aside his half-eaten eggs, poured more coffee, and gazed thoughtfully at Bobbie. He seldom discussed business at home—the advice of his father years ago. If Bobbie suspected the resentment Randy felt for William, it was despite Randy, not because of him.

"Are you going to leave me hanging or are you going to explain?" Bobbie asked.

"I was debating that."

"It'd better be good," Bobbie warned. "Breakfast is shot, my sex life is faltering, and I'm developing a short fuse."

Without emotion, Randy began with his unhappiness at the office, William's domination, how accounts were being shuttled his way only when such accounts were nuisances. He confessed his hope of securing the Lee proxies, the potential power and political dominance he would attain.

"Management of the investments alone would bring a fortune, so far as the money goes," Randy concluded. "I would receive five percent of the net."

"Which is what?"

"Conservatively," Randy calculated, "thirty million earning only five percent produces a before-tax gross of one and a half million. My part of that would run about seventy-five thousand a year. That's minimum."

"Lord, Randy."

He nodded, stirring sugar into his coffee. "But it isn't the money I want as much as the prestige her account would bring, Bobbie. I'm sick of being a flunky. William is already jockeying to take Dad's best accounts."

"And now?"

"Now," Randy said, softly, "when he sees this article he's going to realize the potential and he'll try to take this from me, too."

"You can't allow that."

"I'm not certain I can prevent it. He's the senior partner and the other senior partners will make the decision. Oh, it'll sound high-and-mighty enough. 'Randy is too young, too inexperienced, and this needs the wisdom of the entire firm behind it.' The result is, I'll lose it."

"You can't allow that," Bobbie repeated.

"If I buck them, you know what could happen, don't you?"

"I know I don't care what happens, Randy. You get in there and fight. You worried with this when it was a nothing chore, now that it's about to bloom, you should not—you *cannot* allow it to be taken from you."

Randy put his hand over hers. "Have I told you lately that I love you?"

Her brow smoothed. "Want to make love?"

He didn't. But he did.

William summoned Randy. By way of William's secretary, who called Rosa, who in turn called Randy, William announced he would meet Randy at the office *this* afternoon at five-thirty. Randy hung up, trembling with rage. Bobbie's hand ran up his back as he sat on the edge of the bed.

"William is a jerk," Randy seethed.

"I never dared say that out loud," Bobbie agreed.

"Well"—Randy began dressing—"this is where the war starts, I guess."

"Randy, don't yield."

"I'll try not to."

She reached out and pulled him back to the bed, looking up at him with troubled, dark eyes. "Darling, don't give in Don't rationalize that it is for the children, or me, or your father, or for the sake of brotherly harmony. Go down there and stand your ground. Do *not* give this up. No matter what happens. I am with you all the way."

"Even if I lose?" Randy questioned. "It could mean leaving the firm. Hard times."

She touched his cheek. "Even if," she said.

When he reached the office, the garage was empty except for William's tan Mark IV in its stall. Randy tapped the thick glass doors and a watchman opened up.

The office always felt different on holidays. All desks were neat, the artificial plants looked fresh, almost real. The carpet had been cleaned, the air-conditioner set low, and all the lights were dimmed. Down the hall, past Randy's office, he saw William's door open.

"Hello, William."

William gestured at a chair, unsmiling, placing several folders on his desk. Resentment mounting, Randy saw these were the files on the Lee estate.

"Randall, suspicion is a cancer, did you know that?"

"Yes."

"When a man begins to doubt something, he simmers like a caldron of nitroglycerin, getting more explosive by the minute. Suspicion is, I long ago learned, a very reliable indicator, it usually presages ominous tidings. I once suspected my first wife of having an affair with my best friend. It was a valid suspicion which I ignored for several very expensive years. I figure that oversight cost me another thousand a month in alimony and child support later."

Randy laced his fingers together, elbows on the arms of his chair, slumping slightly.

"Call it ESP, if you will," William continued. "Call it instinct, call it the assimilation of minutiae in the mind that eventually clicks and produces a printout—suspicion is the one thing that a good attorney possesses in abundance."

Randy's eyes never left William, as his brother paced around the office, peered out a window, then returned to his desk. He fixed his gaze on Randy.

"You know, of course, to what I am referring," William said.

"Since I'm not stupid, yes," Randy said, evenly. "You have gone into my office, into my files, and there lie the Lee folders. By now, I assume you have read what I have been doing and why. You've probably seen the proxy signatories prepared for Aramenta Lee. Therefore, judging by your statement to the jury just now, you suspect I am doing something without your permission."

"More, little brother. Much more."

"That I am somehow depriving you of something which is rightfully yours?"

"Correct me if I'm wrong," William said, voice deepening, "you are plotting a masterful coup, using Aramenta Lee's money, power, and political leverage to catapult yourself into instant prominence."

"But of course."

"Like hell!"

"Oh?"

William slammed a hand down on the Lee folders. "You think you can get away with this? I could break this god-damned contrivance in the lowest court in about thirty minutes!"

"Maybe you see something I don't see," Randy said, calmly. "What is there to break and why would anyone want to break it?"

"You are so young." William laughed. "So naïve. Do you really think that having a majority of a stock gives control? Wrong, little brother. Wrong. Respect is earned as much as demanded. Minority stockholders have legal rights too, you know."

"I know."

"They will not allow this."

"They can't stop it, William."

"They can. They will. I spoke to Wally Riley this noon He wants me to represent them in this matter. They're going to demand that Aramenta Lee's stock be broken, sold, or realigned to maintain the stability of the institution."

"I see," Randy said, perspiration seeping between his fingers.

"The woman is apparently irresponsible, possibly incapable of exercising good judgment. Mr. Riley will claim, and I think prove, that she should be divested of her stock and such stock be liquidated as part of the mother's holdings."

"You know she can win that," Randy stated.

"At the expense of destroying the bank, perhaps. This article in today's paper is a good step in that direction. However, Miss Lee is going to be inundated with legal problems. I also spoke with Harley Young at Axiom Insurance. He is under the impression that he has Mrs. Arlington Edward Lee's power of attorney, dated 1944."

"A lifetime power of attorney?" Randy countered. "When was it last exercised?"

"A good point, but Mr. Young feels the need to bring litigation—pretty much as Mr. Riley wishes to do, asking that Miss Lee place her stock on the market for sale."

"William, these are nuisance suits and you know it."

"Ah, but what a nuisance, little brother. Millions of dollars at stake, entire corporate markets juggled and unsettled, perhaps for years."

"Not to mention the countersuits for millions, which Miss Lee will win."

"Possibly. But it will take years and a fortune to do it, Randall. Do you see what I mean? Now I can go on and on with the problems Miss Lee faces. Or is it Mrs. Darcy?"

Randy took a deep breath, exhaled slowly. "William, a local two-bit realtor wants to sue Aramenta for a lousy hundred-fifty. She said fight it, although it will cost three times that amount. Does that give you any idea of the lady? She won't take to all this very kindly You are obviously stirring up trouble and you're doing it to force me to release the account to you. Now you correct *me* if *I'm* wrong."

"Do you honestly think you have the expertise and experience to handle something of this magnitude, Randall?"

"I will handle it, William."

"No, Randall, you won't. I'm sorry. I've met with the other partners and we've all agreed this is quite beyond you, my boy."

Randy stood, voice quaking, "William, I think it only fair to tell you that if you persist in doing this, I will not forgive you."

William affected a sad expression, shaking his head "Then I am sorry, Randall. Truly sorry."

"Not as sorry as you will be, however," Randy warned, "if you try to mess me up with this account."

"Is that a threat?"

"Absolutely."

"The line is drawn then. I'll see you in court. When can you vacate your office?"

"I'm not going anywhere, William." Randy reached across his brother's desk, gathering Aramenta's folders. William seized Randy's wrist, fingers crushing.

"Leave these here, Randall."

"One more thing, William," Randy's voice was rising, face flaming. "Push me about another inch and I'm going to fight you within an inch of your life. Let go my wrist."

William straightened. "What a pity. You would have made such a good attorney someday."

"We shall see soon enough," Randy said, at the door, "how good or bad I am. Oh, William, if I catch you going through my files again, for any reason whatsoever, I am going to react with indignation and a certain degree of physical violence. I've taken your crap, done your legwork, waited patiently for you to toss some accounts my way. Now that you have clearly revealed your selfishness, I will have to honor your advice and follow my suspicions. I suspect you are a whore, William. But it won't be me that needs your services. Do we understand each other?"

William was smiling, confident. "I think so, little brother."

Perspiring heavily and more angry than ever before in his life, Randy carried the Lee files back to his office and put them away. Tomorrow he'd order a new file, with locks. He heard William whistling down the hall. It was a psychological ploy and Randy knew it. Still, it infuriated him further— William's amused and benevolent response to the little-brother stand. Okay, damn it all, Randy wasn't as cool. He shook like a leaf, voice cracking, as though he were about to weep. He nearly did, too. He'd like to go back to William's office and smash the bastard right between the eyes!

"Are you going to answer the telephone, little brother?" William calling from afar.

That was so typical. William won either way. If Randy shouted back, "No," William would chuckle and answer the phone. If Randy answered the phone without debate, it was a continuation of William's big-brother–senior-partner domination. Randy stood staring at the blinking light.

He heard William's voice, cheerful, distant, "Hello?"

Randy wiped his hands down his trousers, waiting to see if the call was for him. Apparently not. He closed his office door, locked it, and started for the exit.

"Hold it," he heard William say into the phone. Then lifting his chin, William called, "Randall! Let me see you a minute before you go."

Apology? Acquiescence? Or more nonsense and pressure? Randy walked to William's office. Don't talk. The trembling voice was the worst of all—so don't talk.

"Right, right," William said, his best telephone tone. "I

see. Now when was this? I see. Yes. Yes. It was thoughtful of you to call." William waggled a pencil at the chair where Randy had been sitting, pulling his eyebrows low, lips pursed, now listening to the caller.

"I'll take it from here then," William said. "Thank you."

William hung up, tapping his desk top with the pencil eraser as he gazed at Randy. He lifted his eyebrows, took a chest-expanding inhalation, then nodded. All for effect. The bastard. Always stage center. Always before a jury. Jesus!

"That was the hospital," William said, his words ringing in Randy's ears. "They said Dad had another stroke. He's unable to move, cannot speak, and they aren't sure how long he has to live."

"Providence Hospital?"

Of course, that's where he'd been all along, William's expression stated.

"You might drop by and see him," William said. As though Randy wouldn't.

Randy left the office without another word.

Chapter Fifteen

The telephone had been ringing all morning. Aramenta could not leave it off the hook, as before, because the workmen so often required use of the phone. She'd no sooner hung up than it was ringing again!

A strange voice greeted her, "Aramenta Lee, where have you been keeping yourself? This is Donna Belhaven Baxter, you remember! Wright's School for Girls? You and I were the two princesses in the play that year and—"

Aramenta didn't recall the play or the woman. She was polite, then more blunt, "Please forgive me," Aramenta said, "I seem to have an emergency with one of the workmen repairing the house. Thank you for calling." She hung up.

Others had phoned, asking her to head up the United Fund Drive, yet another inviting Aramenta to a "welcome-back party with all our old friends." Some man who claimed he knew Mother "intimately" had spoken in a whispery voice about what a "good sport" Mother was. Whatever Mother was, a good sport she wasn't.

Salesmen arrived at the door! Not paint, home-furnishing, and decorating salesmen who had shown up in the first few days of renovations. These came with portfolios, representing investment firms. Aramenta was successively more curt, dismissing them.

What had happened? She was being deluged with "old family friends" she barely remembered from childhood! They were courting her like a schoolgirl. Aramenta also detected a change in the manner of the men working on the premises. Heretofore jovial, boisterous, almost flirty, the men had arrived with somber faces and gone to work quietly.

"Good morning, Aramenta." Randy let himself through the kitchen door.

"Randy, has the world gone crazy?"

"I don't think I can refute that," Randy grunted "Do you have any coffee left?"

"Yes. I made a gallon so the workmen would have plenty, and for some reason they haven't been down to ask. Is something wrong? You didn't see a quarantine sign out front did you?"

Randy tossed yesterday's Sunday paper on the table. Ara menta unfolded it as he poured his coffee.

"All right," she finally said, quietly. "That explains it."

"I'm sorry, Aramenta."

She didn't rant. She didn't explode as he had expected. She just sat there with a sheen of tears in her eyes, looking out the bay window and seeming to withdraw within herself.

"I always hated it here," Aramenta said, very softly. "I grew up with no friends, not even good acquaintances. I always felt so alone here. I wish I'd never come back. I wish Mother had given everything to charity."

"Aramenta, let's work together to get you out of this city I brought the papers for you to sign regarding the will. You don't have to be present in court, I'll do that in your stead."

He explained about the court order required to enter the family safe-deposit boxes, and asked her to sign these. Mechanically, she put her signature in each designated place.

"Aramenta, these are the stock proxies, giving the right to vote to me, in your behalf. I'll need your signature here, and here, and here." He pushed these under her pen. She sat staring at them.

Randy's chest felt as though it were clamped in a vise. He wasn't sure whether she was seeing or not seeing the proxies. Did she recognize what she was yielding? Did she care?

"Randy, I don't feel like reading all this today."

"All right," his voice sounded like it came from someone else.

"Please forgive me, Randy. I appreciate all you're doing But I can't think about this right now."

"I understand. It can wait a while longer." Goddamn it He rose and refilled his coffee cup to calm himself "May I pour coffee for you, Aramenta?" You stupid—

"Yes, please."

He had to steady himself to keep from spilling it. His hands shook so violently he didn't trust himself to deliver the filled cup to the table. He used a worn tray from the counter and placed this between them.

"Aramenta, I think we can have the will probated within the month. Wouldn't you like to move to a hotel until then? Or, for that matter, would you like to leave for Paris right away? It would give me a grand excuse to fly over and have you sign the proxies and so forth."

"No. I want to oversee the work around here."

"I'll be happy to take that responsibility. My wife, Bobbie, has superb taste in such matters. We don't mind at all."

Aramenta shook her head. "No. Thank you."

Randy gathered the papers. "I have to go down to the courthouse, Aramenta. Is there anything you need?"

"No."

"I enjoyed the coffee," he said, his tone carefully controlled. In departing, he saw Virgil wave from the far end of the lawn.

Aramenta took the food tray only as far as the two security doors now. She was afraid to enter the wine cellar. Afraid. She placed the food in the pool of light on the floor, and walked back up. Standing there, she could see his two arms appear from the dark, take the tray, and withdraw. Later, rinsed, the tray would be returned to the same spot for the next meal.

She couldn't handle this. Her foolish dreams of luring him out, communicating with him, were now gone. The other night in the hall, she had seen an animal. Prone to flight, always evasive, once cornered he was a frightening and dangerous creature.

Her leg still hurt where he'd stepped on her, in trying to escape. There was a large, deep purple bruise where his foot had come down. He hadn't meant to do that, Aramenta was sure. He had not tried to hurt her, once he saw the basement door was open again. But if she had not opened it? If she had not scurried aside giving him passage to the cellar—what would he have done?

After the incident, she had gone into her bedroom, her thoughts whirling. Call the police? A psychiatrist? What did Baby need? What would it take? Force, certainly. Strong men to wrestle him down, put him in a restrictive garment such as a straitjacket. They would have to haul Baby away in a wagon, his anguished screams bringing the curious to see what was happening. There'd be no way to keep this quiet, to hide Mother's terrible crime against an afflicted boy.

"How long have you known about this man in the cellar, Miss Lee?" the police would ask.

How long? Seven weeks now? Had it been seven weeks?

"Miss Lee," they would persist, "why did you not call us at once?"

Why indeed? She would have to admit her doubts, fears, shame. She would have to tell them, Baby was hers. Her son, long thought dead and buried. For thirty years a prisoner in his grandmother's clutches.

Aramenta reread the story in the newspaper. Eyes stinging, she knew this was "good copy," as a reporter would say. All true, but unkind; all very legal, but a painful reminder of family failings. This article, she knew, was nothing compared to the one they'd write about Baby, and Aramenta, and Mother. Oh, damn you, Mother. You have damned us all.

Had Aramenta broken any laws? Locking Baby in and her efforts to drive him out with starvation? That's what the newspapers would call it, "starvation."

She could not even cut his fingernails or give him a hot bath and trim his hair. There was no way to shave him. Aramenta could well imagine a news photo of the bearded "madman" from the Lee wine cellar. With a macabre fascination she toyed with titles as they might appear in *The Star* or the *National Enquirer:* "JAILED THIRTY YEARS BY OWN MOTHER." Or "A LIVING DEATH FOR DEAF BOY IN TOMB."

Aramenta rocked slowly to and fro, eyes blinded with tears. She didn't deserve this. Father and Grandfather and all the other Lees did not merit the defamation which Mother had brought upon them.

She couldn't sell the house. The business of repairing, painting, all were efforts to stall, buying time to resolve the problem with Baby. She had hoped to take him to a hospital, to get him the best therapy possible, to somehow make up to him for all the wasted years.

Through the bay window, Aramenta saw Virgil coming out of the carriage house. He had a wooden chair he'd found in the loft. He was sanding the dowels, reinforcing and gluing them. Baby could do that.

Virgil wanted to be a writer. Every night he sat before his typewriter, thinking, typing, searching for words in a thesaurus, seeking definitions in a dictionary. Baby could do that.

Virgil could tune the motor of the mower, the vibrations telling him whether the engine was faltering. Baby might learn that. He might. Virgil worked hard, earned his living; menial though his job might be, he aspired to greater things; Virgil had dreams and hopes and a good mind. Baby? Was his mind good? Who would ever know? His brain more caged than the body in the cell below, Baby had been contorted, exiled, his personality malformed. What thoughts lay behind those luminous eyes? He might be a genius, but in these circumstances nobody would ever know. Could he be tested? Helped? Taught?

Aramenta watched Virgil reassembling the chair. He had also upholstered another chair, which he now used. He never asked for a single piece of furniture from the main house. What Virgil had, he had gleaned from the carriage house attic, repairing and rebuilding. Aramenta had examined the upholstered chair. She did not miss the pride in Virgil's eyes.

"Very good." She had smiled.

He nodded. He knew it was good. He enjoyed giving good work. He took pride in his ability. Aramenta had observed Virgil tending the flower beds. With obvious knowledge he had ordered fertilizers and plant nutrients which he applied. He worked living things as though he loved them. Those living things responded by prospering. Aramenta almost wished she'd be here next spring to see the fruition of Virgil's labors.

A chilling thought struck her. She might be here to see

the azaleas bloom! She might be here until she died, or Baby did! And if he died, what then? Dear God! She would have to call in the authorities and Mother's crime would have become Aramenta's by inheritance and perpetuation.

She found herself incapable of untangling her worry-clogged mind. Aramenta got a piece of paper and pencil from a kitchen drawer. She wrote names: Bruce Matthew, Randy Beausarge. Did she not know anybody else she could call upon for help? An old friend, a doctor, anybody?

She felt the floor jar and looked up. Virgil was standing in the back door, smiling.

"You want lesson signing?" he gestured.

"No. Not today. Too tired."

He looked disappointed. "Want me do anything?"

"No."

He shifted from one foot to the other, reluctant to leave. 'I repaired chair. You want to see?"

No. She didn't want to see. She had watched him mend it, but this was too complex to explain. Aramenta followed Virgil out to the carriage house.

"Very good," she noted.

"You want this for you?" Virgil asked.

"No." Aramenta tried to smile. "You keep this. Enjoy."

He rubbed one hand across the polished wood. "Feel," he signed. "Smooth."

Aramenta touched it, fingers sliding over wax. "Yes, you did a good job."

He invited her into the carriage house with an extended hand. Aramenta wished only to go back to her worries, but like a robot she entered the snug, small apartment Virgil had fashioned for himself. It was surprisingly pleasant. He had bought material for curtains and hand-sewn these; Baby could have done that.

"Beautiful," Aramenta signed.

"Yes." He knew that. He was watching for facial clues to her inner thoughts. Whatever he saw must have disturbed him. Virgil's smile vanished.

"Something wrong?" he asked.

"No. No. I have things on my mind. This is all."

"May I make tea for you? Coffee?"

"No. Thanks. I must go back."

He was blocking her exit. Virgil searched her face, mirroring the troubled expression he saw.

"You read my—" His hands were suddenly a flurry, too fast for Aramenta to follow.

"What?" she questioned.

"You read my essay?"

Essay? What essay? Aramenta glanced around to see what he meant. Then she remembered. The manuscript he'd given her weeks ago! It was on a bureau in Mother's bedroom. Or was it? Good heavens, what if the moving people had taken it, or one of the cleaning crews threw it away?

"Not today," Aramenta signed, carefully. "I will do this soon. I have been very busy."

He looked hurt and Aramenta signed anew, vigorously, "Busy, busy!"

He mustered a smile, nodded.

Aramenta had an instant recollection of an incident from childhood. Brother had written a poem. He took it to Father. Father was sitting in the den; he'd been drinking for days. Blearily, he took the sheet of paper from Brother and stared at it uncomprehendingly. The drink in Father's hand shook, the tinkle of ice cubes tiny bells ringing, as Brother awaited a verdict.

"Leave this with me, Arlington," Father had said. "I'll read it later."

When Arlington asked about his poem the next day, Fa

ther didn't recall getting it. He'd fumbled, apologized, said he'd read it "this afternoon for certain."

Brother asked again and Father retorted brusquely, "I haven't had time, Arlington! Be patient, please."

Several days later, it was obvious the poem had been lost and never read. Arlington went to his room crushed, disappointed, angry. "If he wasn't going to read it," he cried to Annette and Aramenta, "why did he take it and promise in the first place?"

Aramenta returned to the house and immediately went to the bedroom. She sighed with relief—the paper-clipped manuscript was still there on the bureau.

She began the article that evening, after delivering Baby's tray. But she fell asleep. The next morning the manuscript was strewn across the floor where it had fallen. Ten pages total, neatly typed; Baby might learn to do that.

Over breakfast she started again. This time three telephone calls consecutively interrupted her. She left the phone disconnected and returned to the breakfast area. Once more she undertook the reading.

"Miss Lee, have you seen the stepladder we had upstairs?"

"No."

A voice from the upper floor, "Here it is!"

"Sorry, Miss Lee."

Randy arrived and Aramenta laid the manuscript aside, defeated. It did not cross her mind again for several days. When she remembered it, Aramenta arose from bed, got the article, and returned to prop herself up and finish the thing! Virgil had written:

Imagine, if you can, a world with no sound. An existence without the laughter of children, the babble of a brook, rain on a tin roof; a world akin to outer space, devoid of a thousand audible signals the ears perceive in a single day. A pollen-laden bee buzzing backward from a blossom, the whirr of tires on a wet pavement, a lonely man's sigh, the whispered sweet nothings of a lover—all fall on unhearing ears. Gone and never known would be a mother's comforting tone, the pride in a father's voice.

But it is not these sounds a deaf man misses—he has never heard them. The deaf man can only wonder whether a tinkle is softer than a clang, a murmur is warmer than a whisper. He can only guess at the meaning of melody, rhythm, and harmony. Although in school, he was taught to keep time to the thump of a stick on the floor as he struggled to learn the mystery of a dance.

It is not sound he misses most. One cannot truly miss what one has never known. Sound therefore becomes an intrigue. To the man born deaf, some sounds come with such force he wonders how those who hear do not pain from them. The squeal of a diesel, the piercing shriek of a low-flying jet, the scream of a whistle, the throb of a bell—sounds which pulse in bones of the skull, strum unpleasantly in the sinuses beneath the eyes and across the nose. The thumps of unknown origin in a busy, noisy café, the assault of music in a cabaret—disquieting, unnerving jolts which set the marrow of the bones to sympathetic responses. If it feels like this without ears, what must it sound like to those who hear?

No, sound is not something a deaf man yearns for, except when somebody tells him what he is missing. As eyes do not always see, most sounds are noise best ignored. True, the deaf man is a silent habitant of a riotous planet. Without his ears to guide him, to judge the resonance of his own voice, the efforts to speak come high-pitched and distorted. Seeing the shocked reactions his speech evokes, the deaf man soon abstains, preferring to be mute and unnoticed.

Surrounded by motion, the deaf begin to *see* sounds. The clatter of a plate shatters in silence, the sudden turn of a hearing man's head, and the expression it brings is the sound the deaf man hears. Lips without voice smile, purse, twist, tremble, curl in anger becoming ugly red gashes accompanied by faces filled with rage—visible "sounds." A waterfall silent and a brook without babble are no less beautiful. Children at play, teeth flashing with joy, are no less joyful. Love without words becomes tactile, touch and caress, lips upon lips, a hand holding hand, and a pat on the back, a firm handshake and a hearty wave hello! All no less meaningful than audible words of love.

Sound is not what he needs. He does well in his silent world What the deaf man needs is something that transcends sound alone. He needs language. This is his greatest loss. In a universe dominated by motion, naturally he assumes gestures as a practical method of communication. A flick of a finger, a chop of the hand, a twist of the wrist, and with appropriate expressions of face and body, he talks! Like dancers, such deaf speakers vary. Some mumble, stumble, hesitate, and falter. Others speak with a motion so fluid, a rhythm so exciting, the hands become a symphony—a joy to watch.

Signs are the deaf's mother tongue. He thinks of things not as letters and sounds he's never heard articulated. To him, even something as personal as "mama" is an image, a feeling, an entity. When he thinks, his brain sees symbols and the gesture that means the object. In rapid pictorial sequences, the deaf man's mind sees words, draws on his intellect and powers of reason, and is no less deprived than a foreigner who speaks English but thinks through his problems in his more comfortable and familiar native tongue So the deaf have a language as viable as any spoken, as unrestricted as his ability to sign it, as beautiful and expansive as his education and imagination may allow, except when he must cross the line and communicate with orals, who speak and hear. Now the deaf must write. There is no way to portray the gesture which says precisely what he means. He is faced with the legerdemain of syntax and grammar and most damning of all—spelling, all of which betray his printed efforts as "dumb" and "uneducated."

A foreigner with a doctorate, learning English, may be forgiven for misspellings and poor grammatical structure. Everybody knows he is a doctor! They don't judge him by his misuse of words because in his native language he may be more fluent than his present English-speaking listener. Yet, a deaf man is branded first as "different" (he does not hear, he does not even speak, usually) and then as "dumb" because he cannot spell and the rules of oral and written communication evade him.

"Why doesn't he study and learn these things?" the oral asks.

Because, without hearing, the task is impossible. Imagine yourself learning Russian: oddly shaped letters and mysterious spellings. "How do you say this word?" is your first question. The deaf cannot ask. Without phonics, the word "Christmas" is a jumble of letters very similar to the word "chicken." What the ear cannot hear, the mind has difficulty remembering. Deprived of the ability to use the mind's ear and phonics, to help master spelling, "phone" and "phony" require careful visual study wherein nonsensical letters must be placed one behind another for no other reason than that is the correct way to spell it. But the deaf tries! Laboriously, with great effort he struggles to commit to memory the accurate spelling of tens of thousands of words—and fails. He enters a grocery store and discovers QUIK CHEX counters, OK brands, and E-Z payment plans. He learns to distrust all advertisements and billboards which jumble his hard-earned properly spelled terms: 4-U, U-Haul, Sudz, Duz, Sno-white, Kool, Kwik-clean—the list is endless and excruciatingly confusing.

Nouns, verbs, even adjectives, eventually make sense. But there are words which are never comprehended by the deaf. Because in the oral-hearing world, a word may mean many different things Pick one from a dictionary, learn one or two of the definitions, and you soon discover that is only the beginning with such words as "done" or "row" or "act."

A deaf educator once commented that the difference between knowing the definition of "justice" and the "meaning" of justice were worlds apart. The deaf man stands on a world of literal definition, the oral on an ever-changing world of meaning.

When a tone of voice implies what words alone do not express, a deaf man is lost. Puns become nonsense, nuances escape him, and he is forever mired in the morass of language—unless it is his own: signing.

So don't think you can imagine a world without sound, simply by omitting *sound*. If you mentally hear a single word and know the proper pronunciation of it, if you mentally hear a thought related to sound, you cannot possibly imagine a deaf man's world

Aramenta placed the manuscript aside.

Virgil Wilson. Virgil could help Baby.

Chapter Sixteen

Aramenta searched the family library for books relating to the deaf. There were seven. All of them were on the breakfast table when Virgil arrived.

"You know these books?" Aramenta questioned.

He examined each, nodded, indicating three he had never seen.

"Are these good books?" she asked.

He set aside two. "These. But old."

"Old?"

He opened the covers and put a finger on the copyrights, the latest was 1951. "Old," he signed again. "Many things different now, much more learned since then."

"I am going to the library this morning for newer, better books," Aramenta gestured. "Will you come with me?"

"Truly."

Aramenta drove through heavy traffic down Government Street beneath large oaks overhanging both sides of the thoroughfare. They arrived at the library before noon. She examined sixteen books concerning deafness. With Virgil's help, she narrowed her choice to four, one of which Virgil said was "excellent!"

They ate lunch at McDonald's. It was Aramenta's first appearance in public with Virgil. His behavior surprised and dismayed her. In private, he gestured with full, sweeping movements. Every sign was carefully formed with a pause between each, so Aramenta could realize the figure before Virgil went to the next.

Now, Virgil positioned himself so that the crowded room was more or less behind him. He kept his hand low, his gestures abbreviated and hidden. When Aramenta signed, each movement amateurishly exaggerated and large, Virgil cast sidelong glances at people around them. Aramenta involuntarily dropped her hands, keeping her movements close to her chest. Back in the car, they returned to normal.

Thinking about it, she decided he must feel oddly out of place, a strange object of interest to everyone. Aramenta asked, "Back there, did I embarrass you?"

"No."

"But you did not like my signing in public."

"No," he protested, genuinely surprised.

So, she thought, he was not even aware of it, himself.

They spent the entire day together. Virgil had apparently read everything Aramenta was currently undertaking. He fanned the pages, paused at passages he considered paramount, and sometimes signed as his eyes read.

Except for taking down Baby's food, Aramenta studied as she had not studied since her college days. And she worried. Baby's sheets and clothing were becoming dirty. She left clean linen and garments for him along with the tray, but these were ignored. She tried to gather her courage to go in, as before, and make the necessary changes. Each time a nameless fear overcame her and she turned midway and fled, locking the outer security door after herself.

She discovered the automatic locking system by accident. Replacing a bulb which refused to burn, following the wiring visually, she spied a switch at the top of the wine-cellar stairs. She flicked it and was startled to see the outer security door swing shut. Simultaneously the errant light began to burn. Indicating what? Aramenta flicked the switch down. The inner door opened. The switch had yet another position, one more click down—the inner door closed, locked, the outer door opened. Like the synchronized bars of a jail cell, from here Aramenta could control passage. And the light? Bitterly, she recognized it as a signal to a deaf mind that the doors were about to be opened, or closed. She cursed Mother.

There were things here which Aramenta did not understand. The books. The signing books Mother would read to facilitate her communication with the prisoner below. But why the others? Books dealing with the psychology of the deaf, another with psychotic behavior as relates to the deaf. Had Mother *cared* about the problem she had herself engendered? Certainly Baby's grief in Mother's bedroom had been telling. He had come past Aramenta to prostrate himself on the bed, moaning, weeping. Was this not an expression of love? And did Mother return this "love" by studying all she could find on the problems of the deaf?

Now Aramenta studied these books for answers, for a clarification of cause and effect, seeking a way to handle Baby. But instead of answers, Aramenta found more questions. Hundreds of things could be the cause of deafness, she learned. Heredity, genetics, adventitious deafness, the books called it—deafness occurring after birth. Had Baby ever heard a sound?

The following morning Aramenta asked Virgil, "Have you ever been an oral?"

"No. Born deaf," he penned. "No deaf in family ever before. Why? They do not know truly. Because of disease maybe. Because of unusual thing between mother and father maybe. Birth defect maybe. Fever may cause this, when baby in crib. Not sure why. No sounds I can remember Deaf always."

It was apparent that the early childhood of a deaf person was a critical period. It determined adult personality, poten tial for success, and ultimate lifelong happiness.

"Too often a parent refuses to accept deafness," one book stated. "Grabbing any dim hope extended by misinformed or misguided doctors, friends and family, the mother often refuses to admit that her child *is* deaf. When finally she does, then rehabilitation may begin at last. The best advice this doctor can give such parents is: realize the child is deaf. Deaf is forever different. Deaf is forever."

There were tests to determine the extent of hearing loss. Many times, Aramenta read, a deaf person can gain some hearing through amplification. Had anybody ever done this for Baby? Aramenta asked Virgil if he'd ever tried a hearing aid.

"Yes. In school." His face contorted, eyes betraying unhappy memories. "No good. For some, okay. For me, no good. Sometimes deaf hear sounds, but sounds are"—he fingerspelled—"distorted."

"Could you hear any sound?"

"No. But made head hurt. Eyes painful with such sound in my ears. Bad. Very bad. I did not like this."

Aramenta continued to study, jotting questions to herself

which she would later put to Virgil. She was amazed at his scope of knowledge.

"You surprise me," she signed. "You have read many things about deaf."

He gazed at her, face solemn. "If you were deaf, would you not read everything?"

She looked away. Nodded.

Aramenta now watched Virgil more closely, analyzing his actions. She spent as much time as possible in his company. She tried to draw him out, pull him into conversation that would reveal the fiber of the man, his ambitions and motivations. If she was to use Virgil, what would he expect in return? Money, certainly. But money was not enough Aramenta needed him, his physical strength and knowledge, but more, she needed his loyalty and dedication. She now sought the method to develop such allegiance and devotion.

She had to know him. What impelled him? What did Virgil Wilson want that Aramenta could help him achieve?

He yearned for success in his writing, a field in which the individual writer is destined and doomed by his own ability and inventiveness. Nobody, not even a wealthy woman with a debt to pay, can create a successful author. But Aramenta found Virgil excited when the subject of his writing arose. Her comments about his first article brought a glow to his face, a smile that was more than the usual mask of geniality. He was genuinely pleased that she had liked it.

She read everything he had written and much that he had tried and abandoned. She found the style stilted, forced, awkward, sometimes incomprehensible—except when he wrote about the deaf. Then his words flowed and the ideas took form and rose on powerful prose to make his points. He was intelligent and sensitive, could have been a teacher, psychologist, a welfare worker for the deaf, with the proper education

"Would you like to go to college?" she asked, one morning.

"No."

"Why not?"

"Too old. Learn to write by writing." He glanced at her, grinned, and added, "I read that."

He often tempered his observations with, "I read that." How much had he actually read, she wondered. Was he merely a mirror of other scholars? Or were his opinions his own, distilled from his reading, evaluated and refined to become really original, creative?

His typed words, revealing his thoughts and motivations, became Aramenta's best clues to Virgil. She encouraged him to produce more, channeling his mind to the subject he knew and handled most proficiently. With editing as her guise, she delved all the more intimately for what lay behind the words he wrote.

"Do you dislike your parents?"

"No!"

"This piece makes it seem as though you do."

"No!" He took the pages from her hands and reexamined them, frowning.

"You state that the mother is most responsible for the deaf child's inhibitions," Aramenta pressed.

"She is. But cannot help this. Mother does not know what damage she is doing."

"You blame her," Aramenta persisted. "See here you wrote this: 'A mother builds resentment, then guilt for her resentment, then remorse and anger which may all be directed at the child. She punishes the child and then may overcompensate by indulgences, with confusing and damaging results to the child.' "

"This is true," Virgil argued. "But she cannot help what she does. My mother did not know what was happening to her. To her, my deaf is God punishing her. She feels somehow she invited this. With sin, maybe."

Bit by bit, piece by piece, Aramenta constructed a three-dimensional picture of the man: intelligent, perceptive, a thinking man with introspection, a man tormented by his own feelings of guilt for what he did to his mother. By what Virgil did not say, she learned almost as much as she did from what he did say.

Slowly, doggedly, Aramenta penetrated the smiling, almost simpering exterior which Virgil displayed to the world. Using his writing as her vehicle, she became more blunt in her inquiries. If he were to help Baby, she had to trust him. She needed proof of his loyalty and dedication. And much of what she learned saddened her.

"Why did you go home after high school?" she asked.

"Only place to go, home."

"No adult lives at home six years," Aramenta accused.

"No job! No money!" His face flamed.

"You did not look."

"I look. Come Mobile almost one year. I look!"

"That is one year. You lived at home five years before."

A shifting of eyes, face red. She had hit a nerve. "I was child," he confessed. "Weak."

It was her clearest and most poignant glimpse of the real Virgil. Like so many ambitious people, he was not disciplined enough to drive himself. He was—like Aramenta had been at the same age—trapped by parental influences, ensnared in childhood dependencies well beyond his legal age of adulthood.

He seemed determined to be a writer. But she sensed that he might be equally as happy as a teacher, or a welfare worker, or even a shop foreman. It was not his chosen vocation which drove him, but rather his determination to make his way on his own. He was afraid he would be driven back home to the farm. Virgil most feared that he would fail, not at *something*, but at anything and everything.

The only way to reach Virgil Wilson was to ensure that he would never, so long as he lived, be forced to go home Exactly, Aramenta remembered vividly, as she had once been herself.

She had come full circle. She was back to money. Money would make this possible for Virgil. And Aramenta had plenty of money.

"Do you have friends?" Aramenta questioned him.

"Yes."

"Who?"

Virgil blushed. "Marie Bell," he fingerspelled.

"Oh? Sweethearts?"

He nodded, grinning sheepishly.

"Tell me about her."

Succinctly, each statement slightly more revealing than the last, he spoke of high school, dates, the dormitories where boys slept in one, girls in another. Over lunch hour and class picnics, they had come together. Marie was, Aramenta learned, the only girl Virgil had ever called "girlfriend."

"You love her?"

Hesitation. A nod.

"You do not seem sure."

"No."

"Why? You do not know love?"

An embarrassed shrug of the shoulder. "She say she love me. I love."

Aramenta considered this, another tile in the mosaic, like all the other pieces of Virgil: indistinct, undriven, almost resigned—Marie loved him, so he loved her. Obligatory! Was there no fire in this man? Did he have no passion about a single thing in life?

It wasn't the writing, Aramenta grew more and more convinced of this. Virgil was a man on an island, a mind seeking expression. Starved for conversation and companionship on his intellectual level, he had turned to writing and thereby poured out his mind to the eye of an imaginary reader. She knew this by the volume he produced, at first a torrent, then a waning trickle. Each morning she asked, 'What did you write last night?"

Sometimes a little. More and more, nothing.

"You cannot think of anything to write about?"

"No."

"Write about Marie."

"There is nothing to write."

"Write what you feel for her," Aramenta suggested. "Write what your problems are, her problems."

He looked away, sighed. "I am tired of writing today. I will work the yard for you."

Aramenta remembered Brother sitting up all night some nights, poring over a lyric, sharpening prose. Brother once remarked, "Writing is a condition, a disease. There doesn't seem to be a cure." James called it "an unscratchable itch."

Virgil had all the appearances of such a writer. He studied his dictionary, leafed through a thesaurus, sat for hours at a typewriter. Now with Aramenta reading it all, his need for expression satisfied at least temporarily, he had written himself out.

Aramenta prepared Baby's tray. She took it down to the wine cellar, where she placed the food between the security doors. Standing at the switch, she watched the outer portal close, lock, and the inner open, which activated the warning light as a signal to Baby. She waited until he came, two pale arms reaching from the shadows to take the tray and disappear.

She could not delay much longer. If Virgil did not work out, if he refused to help, even if he tried and failed, this could not continue Then, Aramenta knew, she would have no recourse but to call in the authorities. She would have to confess the whole sordid story. And if she must—

She went to the commode at the head of Mother's bed She pulled open a drawer and sat staring. Brother's pistol lay waiting.

Chapter Seventeen

Aramenta sat in the kitchen bay window sipping coffee, the lingering miasma of night lifting, the sky growing pale. At home, about this time, she often strolled narrow cobblestone streets past quaint shops with shuttered windows. It was her favorite hour of the day, a peaceful time, the transition between nocturnal solitude and diurnal bedlam. Vendors prepared their wares, old men shuffled to park benches where they'd meet friends, Aramenta walking aimlessly but always ending up at a sidewalk café where the waiters knew her by name.

After three decades in France, she had few friends. Dozens of people spoke to her, hundreds were accustomed to her face, but close relationships had eluded her. She had never cultured them, that's why, and without the concerted effort to develop friendships, acquaintances remained just that.

She remembered something Annette once hurled at Mother: "You will be a lonely old woman, Mother. You will have nobody who cares! You'll pay for your 'blood,' but I shall not suffer for mine. I'm leaving. I'm getting married I'll have children and grandchildren. You will have nothing but your pride."

Aramenta sipped coffee, eyes distant. Not quite. Mother had Baby.

She saw Virgil emerge from the carriage house. When he spied her sitting here, he waved and came over.

"Good morning!" she greeted him as he came into the kitchen.

"No rain today," Virgil noted. He always offered to help with breakfast, Aramenta always declined. Virgil sat, waiting, coffee before him.

"Virgil," Aramenta's lips spoke as she busied her hands with scrambling eggs. "I have been thinking about you."

"Oh?"

"If you could do anything in the world you wanted to do, what would it be?"

He lifted his eyebrows and shook his shoulders, his laughter more physical than audible. Finally, when she glanced up, he was looking at her with an intensity that lifted Aramenta's heartbeat. He was not going to give a flip arbitrary reply, she could see that.

His hands flew and Aramenta motioned, "Slowly!" He began again.

"For long time I think this," Virgil expounded. "I have plan to teach signing in schools. To do this would make possible for any deaf to sign with many orals. It would open jobs, give hope to deafs."

He continued, often too fast for her to follow. If he wished to teach, why had he rejected college? It was one of those idealistic notions young people are prone to get. Aramenta placed his breakfast before him and sat, vaguely following his motions.

"This would be good thing," Virgil gestured. "To do this

could change all of nation. Maybe world. Deaf could go to public schools, stay near home."

Aramenta indicated his plate with a nod. "Be cold," she signed.

"First- and second-grade students learn fast," Virgil continued, eyes sparkling. "No trouble to teach such orals."

Whatever she had hoped, Virgil was not harboring some covert desire for personal gain. Here he sat, rambling on about a grandiose plan that "didn't cost much" and how it would help "the three million deafs in America." Then, jolted, Aramenta saw him ask, "Will you talk to school-board people? You do this. I teach teachers how to teach signs."

"I doubt that I am qualified to present such a thing, Virgil," Aramenta said.

"What?" he'd missed her lips.

"That is interesting," Aramenta hedged. "You should talk to my lawyer sometime about this."

"Beausarge?" Virgil fingerspelled.

Aramenta poured more coffee, nodding.

The meal was completed without further exchange. As Virgil helped rinse the dishes, he asked, "Something you want me to do?"

"Not truly," Aramenta signed.

"You okay my town?" It was one of those strange sentences Virgil lapsed into now and then, his signs dropping the grammatically correct formation.

"Do you mind if I go into town," he was saying. Aramenta could think of no reason why not. He seldom asked for time off.

"Okay," she signed. He nodded, grinning. Ten minutes later he was walking out the drive, dressed in his best clothing, his hair neatly combed.

The house felt damp. Mildew was again accumulating on

the library books, shoes in the closets, and along the cracks of the bathroom tiles. Aramenta briefly considered a day of cleaning. Then, filled with a sudden ennui, she walked through the house, looking at the recently completed work. Upstairs had the feel and smell of paint and mastic. The floor gleamed with the refinishing and buffing done last week. She had spent a fortune on it all. Doing things which, as Randy had cautioned, "A buyer may wish to have done differently."

She did it anyway. Nor did she regret it now. Even if it was all lost, for a short period of time there was a suggestion of the splendor regained. This would have made Grandfather Lee very happy. He had always worried about a day when a childless couple would "sell it away to another childless couple."

The irony of life was, by the time a family could afford such a home, there were no longer children and the need for the space was gone.

She stood in the west wing now, gazing into Annette's old room, which adjoined the room Aramenta had used as a child. Across the hall, Brother's room. A deep sadness settled over her, standing here. A sense of futility, of waste and lost years.

"Close the doors in case of fire," Mother had always harped. "Should flames begin it would go like tinder. Close the doors always!"

Aramenta walked from room to room shutting doors. The thumps, clicks, and scrapes reverberated through the building as if it were a hangar or a warehouse, not a home. Of course, it had never really been "home," had it? She started down the stairs, depressed.

Pray God somebody found more happiness here than she'd known.

*   *   *

The meeting was an orchestrated farce. The senior partners listened to William conjuring visions of Aramenta's latent power and the scope of her holdings. Randy felt perspiration on his forehead and upper lip. With the practiced hand of a master, William presented his case, set the wheels in motion, then indicted Randy more by innuendo than accusation.

"Little brother was given this account by our father," William said. "For ten years he has been paying this bill or that, petty details usually assigned to a first-year law student. While we were all busy with the bread-and-butter business, Mrs. Arlington Lee died. Dad's stroke was occupying my mind. Now we find ourselves with a serious situation. Randall does not wish to yield any part of this account. He wants it to be his alone part and parcel."

"Who did the taxes?" Alec Smith asked.

William turned to Randy. Randy said, "I did."

"You feel qualified to handle something of this magnitude?" Alec snapped. "I've spent thirty years specializing in taxes and by God I don't know all there is to know. What do you know that I don't?"

"Nevertheless," Randy said, "I did them."

"At an expense to the client of millions, possibly," Alec accused.

"You are welcome to go over them," Randy said, hotly.

"You goddamned right I will! If this woman discovered she'd lost as much as I suspect she lost, she'd be out looking for new legal representation this morning."

"Randall, you surprise me," William said. "Nobody is more qualified to cope with the complexities of an estate like this than Alec."

"The taxes were actually quite simple," Randy argued.

"That I doubt," Alec fumed.

"The IRS has worked with me and—"

"Oh, Jesus!" Alec stood angrily.

They had him. Randy knew they had him. He tasted an acid bile, mouth caustic.

"Randall," Chad Mathis inquired calmly, "I assume you also took it upon yourself to place a market value on the various stocks, bonds, and so forth?"

"Yes."

"For God's sake, Randall!" William shouted. "Did you consult with anyone about anything? Or did you simply sell your trusting client down the river?"

"I think I have protected her interests adequately."

"Do you believe this?" William asked the others. "This young—stupid—"

"Randall," Chad maintained a level voice, "perhaps we should go over the stocks. There are several things you may not have considered. Many times an apparently healthy issue is weak. Valuation which is high in the minds of IRS could be deflated by a quick sell to unload the stock, driving the price well down. You understand?"

"Yes."

"Let me tell you how I see it," William offered. "My little brother has had visions of power. Not money. He draws eighteen thou a year for sitting in an uncluttered office with a private secretary—all that is for ego. He does around here what any minimum-wage law clerk would do. He's a full partner because he was born to it, not because he earned it."

"Yes, and what the hell do I get handed to me?" Randy's voice lifted. "Menial jobs nobody else will touch; I'm stymied! I can't go out seeking new business, I'm trapped in a firm where anything I get is filtered down by way of everybody else."

"Then when you get something important, this is how you handle it?" William stormed.

"What would you have done, William? In my place, what

would you have done? As soon as your older brother found out what was happening, he'd come grabbing for the juicy stocks and proxies and return you to more of the same old tasks! Now tell me you wouldn't have done exactly what I did."

"You see, Randall," William's voice lowered, "there's part of our problem right there. You have this Freudian hang-up whereby you assume I am out to strangulate your interests. Nothing could be further from the truth. I have waited, watched, hoped, and prayed you'd show some initiative."

"Now you see my initiative, William."

"Hold it, boys." Chad lifted a hand, the arbiter in dormancy, waiting to mediate. "Let's not reduce this to a family brawl. Sibling rivalry should be dismissed altogether, regardless of what either of you think. The value of a firm like this is, the members are each specialists. I with stocks and market analysis, Alec with taxation, William is the best corporate attorney in this state."

The inference was not lost. And Randy—Randy is a flunky. He should interview the lady's yard man, secure domestic help, pay the monthly bills . . .

"At the same time, we've all been where Randall is at this moment," Chad said. "Ambitious beginners aiming for that big account and dreaming of an important case in court someday. Actually, for some time I have felt that Randall should be given a more responsible role in this organization. I have several accounts myself I have considered turning over to him. Weaning them over, so to speak."

Randy saw it coming. The names of this concern, or that corporation, raised for consideration—some of them very promising. He also saw the trap. If he refused, he would surely be paving the way for his eventual separation from the firm. If he accepted, he must give up part, if not all, of the prize.

Randy had spent days thinking this out. Hours of considering his advantages, recognizing his weaknesses. He wasn't a fool. He held a very untenable position. With a quick vote and a separation check, these men could send him looking for new offices. The Lee estate was a firm account, not a personal one. It went back to the origins of the firm itself He had no legal claim. But he did have Aramenta Lee and that's what stopped them. How much did he have her? Would she bolt and take her account with her, if Randy were withdrawn? Not only did they not know, they couldn't go to Aramenta and ask. To do this might precipitate a split, and these men did not gamble unless they were desperate or very sure of winning.

"What do you have to say for yourself, Randall?" William pressured.

On the other hand, Randy reminded himself, if he elected to break away and get out, and Aramenta did not come through, he might be chasing ambulances and arguing divorce cases for years. Forever, if William and his partners decided to give Randy a hard time.

"Gentlemen." William had waited long enough for a response. So long that the wait itself *was* a response. "Gentlemen," William repeated, "Randall is my brother. I want what is best for him. But at the same time, I cannot allow a client to be given less than our corporate name implies. Randall has made mistakes here, but together I think we can rectify most of them. The Lee will has been filed for probate. We have about two weeks. Alec, do you have time to look over the estate and meet with IRS for any adjustments?"

"I'll take time."

"Chad," William intoned, "how about you? Can you take a few days to go over all this with Randall?"

"I think so."

"Good," William said. "Settled!"

They smiled at Randy with everything but their eyes. He sat like stone, defeated. A client like Aramenta had a right and the privilege to the best money could buy. There was no refuting the strength of the firm as a unit. The bastards had him. Randy knew it.

His head splitting, Randy returned to his office. He had an overwhelming urge to vomit, which he downed with a drink. He was shaking, sick to his stomach, soaked with sweat, and he saw himself all too clearly—a neophyte, a fumbling, bumbling, inept beginner!

He had resented William for years. Dislike would be a better word, and no less accurate. Now a seething hatred was building in Randy and he had a momentary, idiotic vision of killing him. Schoolboy fantasies—murder the bastard—

"Mr. Beausarge?" Rosa's voice on the intercom.

"Yes, Rosa?"

"Mr. Vigil Wilson to see you."

Vigil? The name had a familiar—oh! *"Virgil* Wilson."

"Yessir. He doesn't have an appointment."

"It's all right, Rosa. Tell him to come in."

Randy massaged his temples, and when Virgil entered, he gestured at a chair, without a word. Finally, he sat back, easing his head against the rear of the chair and looked at Virgil, unsmiling. Immediately, Virgil grinned, head nodding.

"What's the problem, Virgil?"

Virgil's eyebrows lifted, questioning.

"I said, what-is-the-problem? Why do you want to see me?" He enunciated each word carefully.

"Miss Lee told me to see you," Virgil's lips formed soundless words, hands gesturing. Then, withdrawing a tablet from his pocket, Virgil carefully spelled out words. As he completed each page, he tore this out and pushed it across Randy's desk.

"I have a plan. Teach signs to boy & girl in all school. This way deaf people can talk to many orals." He scratched out the last word and substituted, "hearing peoples."

What the hell was this? Randy subdued impatience, waiting for the next page, tediously and carefully being composed.

"Miss Lee tell me see you about this. I am here. Can you see me now?"

Randy sat looking at the boy. Man. He wasn't a boy. Nearly twenty-six, if Randy's memory of the work application was correct. Educated in a deaf school, incapable of communication except through these penciled notes—and Aramenta was building this kid for the fall of his life. He watched Virgil's self-conscious smile falter, eyes now cast at the floor with only furtive sidelong glances at Randy. Still Randy stared at him, unaware of the lapse of time. He took a very deep breath, puffed his cheeks exhaling, and massaged his temples anew.

Virgil pointed at Randy, then his own head, and drove together two pointed fingers.

"I don't follow all that, Virgil, I'm sorry."

Another note. Jesus.

"Head hurt?"

"Yes."

Virgil's expression flowed into an appropriate, "I'm sorry," and he shook his head slowly.

"Virgil, must I write notes, or do you think you could read my lips?"

Virgil nodded. What the hell did that mean? Note? Lips? Randy spoke slowly, "Virgil, I don't know what is happening out there. I don't know what Miss Lee has in her head. But I do know you are about to be hurt, if you aren't careful."

Did the kid understand? He stared at Randy's lips, eyes intent, nodding.

"Miss Lee is going to go home, Virgil. She's going to go back to Paris, where she lives. Do you understand?"

Randy halted, seeking confirmation. After a moment, Virgil's eyebrows lifted and he smiled.

Resigned, Randy continued, "You remember when I hired you? You remember?"

Virgil nodded.

"I told you the job was temporary." Randy turned one of Virgil's used notebook pages and wrote, "Your job not permanent. Temporary." He pushed this at Virgil. He watched as Virgil's eyebrows lowered, face souring.

"Miss Lee will be going home," Randy said. Again he wrote, "Miss Lee will go home soon. To Paris. Another country." He gave this to Virgil. He didn't remember having this much trouble talking to the guy when he'd hired him. Maybe Virgil never understood a word—always smiling, nodding, and doesn't catch a third of— Virgil's face was coloring. He looked at Randy, glowering.

"Miss Lee doesn't have time for things like your idea, Virgil. I don't have time for it, either. I wish I did. But I don't. Do you understand?"

A quick, short nod.

"Miss Lee has been very busy, very worried. She only wants to go home. Back to Paris. You should," Randy wrote now, "find another job soon."

Virgil's lips pulled, quivering. The poor bastard was really hurt. Damn Aramenta! If she could see what was happening to this poor deaf sonofa—

"Miss Lee my friend," Virgil wrote, pencil slashing. He tore off the paper and thrust it at Randy.

"Miss Lee," Randy wrote to avoid any misunderstanding, 'your employer. Pays you salary. You do yard work. She likes you. Yes. But soon she will go away. You find job. Go today. I will call Mr. Morgan at the Alabama Employment Service."

He held out the note to Virgil, watched the words sink in, the agony and disappointment welling up behind moist pained eyes. Randy tried to smile sympathetically and his lips pulled. He clamped his jaws.

"I'm sorry, Virgil."

Virgil's eyes slowly settled on his pad and the now trembling pencil. "This is true?" he wrote.

Randy nodded. "True."

Virgil swallowed, his prominent Adam's apple bobbing again and again. He looked away, toward a far wall, eyes brimming with tears, swallowing over and over. Randy's headache was ascending by pounding, pounding leaps.

Finally, the deaf man stood, nodded at Randy, and let himself out the office door, very tenderly closing it behind himself.

"Oh, for God's sake," Randy groaned aloud.

Chapter Eighteen

Long before evening Aramenta began watching for Virgil's return. Several times she had gone to the carriage house, found it empty, and returned to the kitchen. He had been away since midmorning. An accident perhaps?

Weeks of worry, lack of sleep, and improper diet were depleting her. The most visible evidence of what was happening inside her mind was her personal appearance. She had gone for days without the energy or inclination to bathe, brush her hair, or go out. She would stand before a closet unable to decide what to wear when it didn't matter in the least one way or another! Aramenta recognized the danger signals of a breakdown, the mental stupor to which she succumbed.

There were times when her hands shook so uncontrollably she couldn't hold a cup to drink from it. Oh, yes, she was in trouble mentally. With a shock she caught herself feeling a distrust of "common" people that bordered on paranoia

Stupid suspicions which extended to Bruce, Randy, even Virgil!

It had reached a point where she doubted her own sanity Something had to be done. It had become a matter of her own health and well-being, as much as Baby's. She must make a positive move. She must take action. A decision was imperative.

Virgil would help her, Aramenta reassured herself. He might be horrified, repulsed, not understanding the *how* of it all—but Virgil would help. If not for Aramenta's sake, then for the sake of the tormented creature hiding in the cellar. He would at least try. Should he fail, Aramenta would have no choice but to call in psychiatric help, men with nets and canvas restraining jackets.

Aramenta had been contemplating the approach she should take with Virgil. Of the various alternatives, she had determined the oblique was better than the direct. She would ask Virgil to accompany her into the wine cellar. She would take down fresh bedding, clean clothing, then scrub the toilet and sweep Baby's sleeping area. By this, Virgil would know somebody was there. Everyday she would go down with Virgil, for as long as it took to make him ask, "Who? What? Why?"

She would confess then. She would beg his pledge of secrecy. She would plead for his help. She knew Virgil would do this. Please God. He would do this.

At nine o'clock, Aramenta took the food tray below. As soon as Baby had grabbed it and disappeared, she returned to the kitchen bay window. The carriage house was still dark. Where could he be? He had never remained away this long. An accident? How could he call her? Did he even know her telephone number? Dear God! Randy had ordered an unlisted number! Virgil couldn't call unless he'd made a mental note of that. He had never used her name to her face, did he know her last name?

Aramenta's fingers interlocked, squeezing until her hands hurt. Ridiculous! Silly thoughts. Another indication of how her mind was suffering.

She had one quantum move to be implemented, and Virgil was her only hope. She had to remove Baby from the horror of this house and place him in the care of professionals. Once he was in a hospital under the best therapy money could buy, Aramenta might atone for what Mother had done. Until then, she, Aramenta, was a part and party of it all, as damnable as Mother for having abandoned Baby in the first place, releasing him to the care of a madwoman Once Baby was with audiologists, psychologists, and teachers, Aramenta would have done all that was humanly possible. It was the step from the cellar, from the physical evidence of past abuse that was the crucial one. Virgil was her only hope of doing this without spreading the story across every newspaper in the country. After Virgil saw Baby, if he couldn't handle this, then Aramenta would abandon all hope of keeping it quiet. She would then call in the padded wagon and the men who would chase down Baby and haul him away.

Shortly after two A.M. Aramenta began calling the hospitals. She telephoned the highway patrol, sheriff's office, and city police. No reports of accidents involving a man of Virgil's description. No arrests. She now imagined that he had been picked up as a hitchhiker, robbed, and beaten; he wouldn't have left town, surely, without telling her!

Four A.M. Aramenta penned a note, "Please see me when you come home." She walked across the graveled drive to the carriage house. Opening the door, she groped for a light switch, flicked it. The room flooded with light. Aramenta jumped, frightened. Virgil sat staring at her, eyes wide with sudden illumination.

"I was bringing a note," she said. His expression was strangely hostile. Aramenta smelled the fetid odor of beer. Was he drunk?

"Are you all right?" Aramenta signed. He did not respond. "Virgil, are you okay?" signed again. "Is something wrong?"

"No."

"Have you had supper?"

"No."

She smiled. "Would you like a sandwich?"

He looked away, sullen.

"Are you sure nothing is wrong?" Aramenta persisted. He shook his head.

"Come to the house with me," Aramenta urged. "I want to talk to you."

He followed her into the kitchen. She opened a can of soup and began heating it. Virgil sat at the bay window peering out into darkness. She had the feeling he was watching her reflection. Aramenta got down two bowls and opened a package of saltines.

"Would you like something to drink? Coffee?" He shrugged his shoulders. After they'd eaten something warm, perhaps his mood would alter, that odd expression in his eyes would vanish.

"Please eat," she said.

He stared at the steaming soup. Vegetable. She knew he liked vegetable soup.

"I have friend Marie," he signed, without looking at her. "I have told you this."

"Marie? Yes, you told me."

"A girl."

"Yes," Aramenta replied. "I remember."

"She come here to live with me?" He made the formal zigzag sign to indicate it was a question.

Here? Aramenta put down her soup spoon. "For a short visit?" she inquired.

"No. To live with me."

His deaf girlfriend.

"Virgil, I would really rather not have someone else coming here right now." Aramenta spoke this. He stared at her without expression. Misunderstood? Aramenta signed, "For now, it best no person comes here."

His head slowly turned and he looked out the bay window again. Aramenta watched for perceivable indicators of thought. She finally tapped the table to get his attention.

"Truly this girl can come later," she signed. "Not this week. Wait. Understand?"

She saw a subtle change in his face, a hardening of the eyes, lips thin.

"I have many things to worry me," Aramenta fumbled. "I wish to talk with you about this. I want to ask you to—"

"You friend?" Virgil interrupted, signs quick, slashing.

"To you?"

"Yes! Me!"

"Yes, yes. I your friend," Aramenta signed.

"I want this," Virgil mouthed the words as his hands spoke. "I wish Marie come here. Marie deaf. Not oral. Oral people not friends." He shoved the soup bowl away so hard the hot liquid scooped out onto the table. His face was flushed.

"Friends ask and friends give," he signed rapidly. Aramenta missed the next symbols figuring out these few.

". . . many times orals do this thing . . . cheat . . . lie . make deaf think . . . friends . . ." Virgil stood abruptly.

"I ask one thing and you not give!"

"That Marie come here to—" Aramenta halted, his hands a blur too fast to follow.

"Slowly!" Aramenta commanded.

But he wasn't going more slowly. Emotion poured through hands flitting like fighting birds!

". . . not love . . . not interest . . . deaf alone . . . only friend deaf . . lies!"

"Virgil, please, I can't understand—"

"You!" He jabbed a finger at her.

"What?" Aramenta asked, drawing a finger across the other open palm.

"You!" He stabbed at her with a pointed forefinger. "You!"

"Yes, yes," she snapped, "what?"

"You not interest."

"About what?"

"Deaf."

"Not true. I interested."

"Lie."

Taken aback, Aramenta grabbed his shoulders, placing herself firmly before him. His attention fully on her, she released one hand and signed with deliberate emphasis, "My interest for you."

He snorted, an exhalation of beer breath, glowering. Aramenta questioned, "What is reason for this? Come sit. Tell me."

At the table again, she watched him sop spilled soup with a napkin. She pushed her napkin across to him. He met her eyes.

"You not want help deaf," Virgil signed. "I tell plan. You not want."

"Your idea for teaching schools?"

"Yes!"

Aramenta considered her words. "You go see attorney?"

"I hate him."

Aramenta queried again, "You go see him?"

"I hate this man!"

"He made you angry? Hurt your feelings?"

"Bad man!"

"What did he—"

"You go home?"

"Home? Paris? Yes, I will when—"

"He said this."

"Virgil, let me tell you something you don't know."

"He say my job soon finished."

"Virgil, there are other jobs. I will help you—"

"He say go seek new job."

"No! I want you here."

"You sell this house?"

"If I can, but—"

"Marie cannot come here to live?"

"Virgil, I have a problem. I have a worry. I need your help."

"You need. You want. You! What me? What I need?"

"You mean the girl. Virgil, I will help find a place for her She can come to Mobile later. If you will help me with my—"

He erupted with a jumble of gestures, the faintest sound of a voice coming in emphatic squeaks from his throat. She lifted a hand to stop him, but he continued. She reached out to stay his hands, and he pulled away, face livid. This was accomplishing nothing! Virgil stalked the room, shoulders forward, gestures lost by speed, his sentences reduced to essential thoughts without concession to grammar. He signed with his back to her, and when he halted, hands quivering, lips discolored, he glared at her with an expression approaching hatred!

"Please," Aramenta reasoned, "I wish not to make you unhappy. I want to help you."

"Why you lie?" Virgil took a step forward. "Why oral always lie?"

"Lie? Virgil, I'm not lying."

"Lie!" A finger snatched across the lips. "Lie!"

"Now wait a minute, Virgil." Aramenta frowned, speaking. "We have a misunderstanding here."

"I not understand! Sign! You sign! I cannot hear. Sign to deaf!"

"I'm sorry," she said. Then signing. "What is wrong I do not know. I do not want to make you unhappy with me. What is wrong can be fixed."

He spun, halting conversation, back to her. Jesus! Was the girl this important to him? If he would only wait—get Baby out of here. When he again faced her, it was obvious the anger had been replaced with something else.

"I sorry," he said. "I go bed."

"Virgil, we will talk about this in the morning. I have a very big problem. You will understand. I will show you. If you help me, I—"

Virgil slammed the back door, going out.

What in the name of God caused this? Randy? Whatever had transpired, she was seeing a side of Virgil she had not seen heretofore. The muscles in his neck drawn like taut cables, face ugly, so consumed with anger he was beyond reason!

She saw the light in the carriage house go out. The coming of dawn would clear the way for calm discussion. Morning worked wonders, Aramenta believed that. A new day would bring fresh light on Virgil's thoughts, whatever his problems. He would revert to his usual sensible self.

Aramenta undressed for bed, then propped against several pillows thinking. The girl, Marie. She could not come here until the business with Baby was settled. Aramenta had enough problems without one more.

She extinguished the lamp and lay in the darkness; a

sliver of moonlight filtered through the oaks and window, making dappled patterns on the bed and floor.

It wouldn't be long now. A few days, a week or two, possibly. Baby would be gone. Virgil—well, Aramenta would look after Virgil, financially. She'd make it so he'd never have to go home, if Virgil helped her with this. Dear God, please, Lord, please—help me to help myself. Help Baby.

Aramenta dressed, went to the kitchen, and looked out back. Virgil was up. She could see him stacking several boxes atop one another outside the carriage-house door. She put on a pot of coffee, fried bacon, and scrambled eggs. Having buttered bread and heated the oven to make toast, she went to the rear door to call Virgil for breakfast. Stunned, she saw more boxes, a suitcase.

She walked out, peered inside the carriage house. He was carefully sorting his books, packing them.

"What this?" she signed.

"I go home."

Her chest constricted. "Why?"

He ignored her.

"Why?" she demanded. "I make you angry? You can talk with me about this. Come eat breakfast. Talk."

"No."

The muscles now pulled so sharply, Aramenta had pains in her rib cage. She grabbed his arm, shook him.

"I need you. I need help!"

He stared at her a moment, continued packing.

"You angry with attorney," she reasoned, more slowly. "I will fix this. I will talk to attorney."

He closed a box, tying it

She touched his arm. "I need help. Help. You help me. I help you. Come talk with me."

221

He glanced up with obvious sarcasm, continued binding the box. Aramenta fought a surge of panic. This could not happen. Must not happen!

"I talk to school people. You want this. I do it."

He recognized the lie.

"You want money?" Aramenta questioned. "I give you money to help me."

"I go home," he signed emphatically.

Damn Randy! What had he said? Aramenta blocked Virgil and they stood eye-to-eye, him holding the box of books.

"I wish to be honest," Aramenta stated. "I want to please you. You talk to me. Tell me what is wrong. I will make right." She used the sign "legal" for "right."

He stepped around her, took the box outside, and put it with the others, She followed, standing in the door. "I ask this of you. Come to house. Talk with me. I need you. I need your help.

"You get help," he replied coldly. "Pay good. Help come easy for you."

"No! No, I need you! I need you help me!"

Gently, he moved her aside with one arm and went back to packing. Breathless, chest hurting, Aramenta ran to the house. She found Randy's telephone number and dialed, fingers trembling.

"Is Randy Beausarge in, please? This is Aramenta Lee calling."

"One moment please." Aramenta heard the click putting her on hold.

"Miss Lee?" A deep, masculine voice. "This is William Beausarge. I'm Randall's brother. He's out this morning. Is there anything I could do for you?"

"No. I need to speak with Randy. When will he be in?"

"I don't expect him, actually. You know, I owe you an

apology, Miss Lee. My father had a stroke and that has burdened all of us—"

"Mr. Beausarge," Aramenta said quickly, "is there anyway I can reach Randy by phone?"

"I don't think so, Miss Lee. Do you have an emergency?"

"I need to speak with him immediately." Aramenta thought she heard a car door.

"I've been meaning to get out there and meet you, Miss Lee. I apologize for that. Actually, we were going over the estate and we've come across a few minor problems we'd like to discuss with you. If I could—"

"Mr. Beausarge, I can't talk about that right now. Is there someplace I can reach Randy?"

"I'll have to ask his secretary, Miss Lee. If I could drop by and—"

Aramenta hung up, running toward the back porch. She halted in the kitchen. Virgil was there, waiting for her

"You call taxi for me?" he asked.

"Virgil, please." Aramenta struggled to suppress the breathtaking constrictions across her chest. "Sit down Please. I beg this. Let me talk with you. I need help. I have problem. Please sit. Talk."

He was so cold! His expression distant, he signed again, "You call taxi for me?"

"Yes!" a sign. "Yes!" she shouted. She pointed at the bay window table. "Sit down!" she ordered.

"I go home now," he signed evenly. "You call taxi, good Not call taxi, I walk to find person who will do this."

"I will, but first, sit down!"

"Am deaf. Must sign to deaf."

"What's the matter with you?" Aramenta snapped "What is all this I am deaf and cannot understand? You read my lips and I know it."

223

"Must sign to deaf," Virgil signed, eyes hard.

She signed, hands shaking, "I ask you and you do not tell me what is wrong. Sit, talk with me. I tell you I have much trouble. Much worry. Problem. I am beg—please—ask—help me! Sit down, talk."

He turned, leaving. Aramenta grabbed his arm, tears in her eyes. "I ask you help me. Will you help me?"

"Do what?"

Anything! Something! Delay him! Make him talk to her. "Box."

He studied her.

She fingerspelled, "B-o-x."

He hesitated, nodded, "Where?"

Her throat closing, chest now so painful she could scarcely speak, she was gasping for air. She sobbed, sucking air into burning lungs.

"Box," she fingerspelled stupidly.

Impatient he asked, "Where? Where box?"

Oh, God. Oh, dear God! Aramenta sagged against the door jamb. She blinked her eyes, one hand on her chest, her knees threatening to buckle. Oh, God!

"Where?" Virgil demanded, lips compressed. "I not wait. Where box?"

She nodded, weeping. "Please," she said. "Help me."

He moved as if to go and she seized his arm, her teeth clenched. "In the basement. I wanted to tell you. I have—"

"Where?" he slashed his hands, now angry.

"Basement!" Damn it! "In the basement!"

Chapter Nineteen

Aramenta pointed at the wine-cellar steps. Virgil adjusted the electric timer and the subbasement lights came on. He walked down the narrow passage past the security doors and turned.

"Where?" he signed. Above him, Aramenta motioned, "Back, left." Virgil waited a moment for his eyes to adjust to the dimly lighted interior. He saw no box. He turned to ask for more explicit instructions, but the door was swinging closed. He groped for a handle to open it, grasping the bars with his other hand. He felt no handle. Aramenta was descending the stairs now. Good! He waited impatiently.

She stood in the brightly lighted area between the two doors. He saw her lips moving, her face a relief of starkly defined flesh and shadows created by an exposed overhead light. What was she waiting for? Standing three feet from him, not signing, talking. Her eyes were orbs of black, her nose looked particularly long, the lighting throwing a dark shadow across her lips and under her chin. Lips saying—something— Virgil lost his temper.

"I cannot see lips! Sign! Open door." Dumb woman!

But instead of coming nearer, Aramenta stepped back, the shaded mask of her face altering. He saw her lips now, working beneath obscured eyes. Her hands made signs here, there, senseless.

"Teach ... what you know ... do this ... pay you ... anything ... help me ..."

"Open door!" Virgil commanded. He seized the bars and attempted to shake the barrier. It did not give so much as a fraction of an inch. He stuck his arms through the bars, signing, "Open!"

When his hands came between the bars, Aramenta retreated another step. Now he could see her entire face. She was crying.

"Sign!" Virgil ordered. He was impeded by the bars, only able to get his arms out as far as the elbows. Had she gone crazy? Weeping hysterically, it seemed. Virgil gestured again, "Sign! Sign! Sign!"

He saw she was trying to compose herself. Why didn't she open the door? Irritation rising, he waited, watching, his arms still thrust through the bars. Deliberately, slowly, he signed again, "Open door."

She shook her head.

What? Virgil felt a surge of emotion akin to claustrophobia. Tell her again. He signed, palms together, parting, "Open."

Another shake of head. What was this? A game? An effort to force him to listen as she spoke? Very well, he would listen. He withdrew his arms from the bars to hide the anger now taking possession of his senses.

She stood six feet away, weeping subsiding.

"You can be rich," she signed. Her hands were more controlled now. "You do this for me. I pay you much."

"This? What this?"

"Teach Baby." Baby? He turned for an instant, then froze as he stared into the dark. He thought he'd seen something move. He faced Aramenta again.

"Teach all you know," she was signing. "Make like you. Do this. Help me. I pay you much. Need you."

Was he dreaming? Had she gone insane? Virgil put his arms through the bars. "What? What?" he asked. "I not understand what. Why you not open door?"

She had undergone a metamorphosis. Gone were the tears. Gone the shaking and hysteria. In its stead, Virgil saw a set expression, a frightening determination. He read her hands, "Stay. When teach Baby all you know, come out."

"Come out?" Virgil glanced around the dark, up the aisle between wine racks, back to Aramenta, who was still gesturing. Come out? He wasn't staying in here. He was not staying one more minute. He grabbed the bars and yanked. The effort hurt his wrists.

"Need you . . . help me . . . Baby . . . teach . . . pay . . ."

She turned and started up the steps. The tremor of his own voice rose in Virgil's throat. He screamed, rage overwhelming him, hands extended as far as he could reach, fingers clawing space. She looked back, and he saw her hands move, "Teach Baby. All you know. I pay for this. Much money."

Virgil's voice was a chortled shriek following her. She walked toward the timer and panic made him lunge at the immovable barred door, scraping his arms. He jerked back. A board, a pole, something to rip this door apart!

He ran down the aisle, turned, another aisle, down this one, another, down this—the bed! He tore off smelly sheets, mattress, and springs. He disassembled the frame and took a sidebar. He needed a fulcrum. He bashed the end of a cask, using the steel rod as a battering ram. The boards scarred, but did not splinter. He ran back to the bed and got the opposite sidebar from under the fallen springs. The rods banging, bumping racks, he put them together and carried them upright.

Extending both rods through the bars, he braced himself with a foot against the wall and twisted, seeking leverage. The angle iron bent. Damn! He used the shorter, unbent section now, placing the opposite angle iron more carefully. He pulled—it bent. The bars were bigger than his thumb, embedded in steel, reinforced by the thick wood and plated on either side. It was like a medieval prison. He cursed with voice loud as he could. He banged the door with the warped rods, using the unbent one as a sledge and swung it to crash a wine rack.

Crazy! Crazy woman! Fool! He had allowed her to bring him down here and trap—a change in the light made him wheel again, facing the door. He held the bed support like a lance, waiting. When she came near enough, if he had the chance, he'd split her skull with this—

Stunned, he saw her delivering his boxes, which he'd packed and left outside the carriage house. She put them down just inside the first door. Too far to reach with this rod. She went back up with his cries rending the cellar. Several minutes passed. Virgil awaited his chance, the bed-stead support ready. Aramenta came again, another box, this one filled with his books. She actually meant to keep him! To hold him in this prison! She walked back up.

If he hit her. Killed her. What? She would lay eight feet away if she fell where the parcels were. Virgil extended the rod. He could barely reach the packages. If he dropped her with a well-aimed blow—who would unlock the door? He might be here days, weeks!

He felt the enveloping shadows closing in on him. Anger gave way to a senseless fear. Again he thought he caught a movement, a flicker of—what? He dropped the bed support and stood holding the bars, waiting.

She had his typewriter. "Please—please—" Virgil used his voice now. She put down the typewriter and turned as though he were not speaking. "Please!" he shouted.

She was bringing it all down. Books, boxes, suitcase, her mouth open, breathing hard from exertion, systematically delivering everything that was his. When she reappeared, he begged, demanded, signing with forced calm, but as she departed, he succumbed to enraged ranting, a vocal protestation that was as unnoticed as the rest of his gestures.

He tried physically and mentally to control himself, frantically seeking reason out of this madness. She had to open the door. How else could he reach his belongings if she did not open the door? He surmised what must happen. This door would open, the outer door would close. He could throw the bed rod, hit the crack before the outer door secured, keeping it from locking. Yes. Yes, that would work! He took deep breaths, estimating the most opportune moment. If he had even a split second for a good throw, using the rod as a lance, he could do this.

Aramenta placed the balance of his possessions inside the first door. She gazed at him, the extent of her calm more frightening than her former hysteria.

Where was she going? What about this door? Virgil saw her stop at the top step, turn, and reach for a switch. Turning out the lights? How could he do this in the dark? The door moved and Virgil jerked away, gripping the rod. The outer door was closing as the inner door opened. The free swinging end of one door faced the hinges of the other! Defeated, rod in hand, he stared at his belongings.

Watching above him, Aramenta kept her finger on the switch.

Trapped. Overcome with the realization, he was dumbstruck, everything he possessed lying here waiting for him to take it. Take it? Where? He looked up. Aramenta was gone.

Aramenta sat on her bed staring at the telephone. Ringing. A shrill unremitting note, punctuated by silence only to ring again. Who? Questions. Outsiders. Could they hear the faint sounds behind her? Thump-thump.

"Hello?"

"Aramenta, this is Randy."

She said nothing.

"Aramenta? Are you there?"

"Yes."

"I only now arrived at the office. You called me?"

The receiver was slick with the sweat of her hand.

"Aramenta?"

"Yes."

"Is everything all right?"

"Yes." Long pause. "Fine."

"You telephoned me?"

"Yes." Had she? Yes, she— "Yes, I did."

He waited. Then to fill the void, he explained, "I was at the hospital visiting my father."

"How—how is he?"

"Not good. The doctors say he has a fifty-fifty chance of living. But"— his voice charged with emotion—"there will be brain damage they say. We don't yet know how extensive. They said it could leave him paralyzed, unable to speak possibly, even blind."

Aramenta held a quivering breath.

"He was always such an active man—"

She had had nightmares after James was killed. Horrible dreams where she couldn't move, paralyzed, or injured in such a way that she couldn't care for herself. In the dreams, she always ended up with Mother. Mother feeding her, bathing and dressing her, the rest of her life to be spent trapped in an immobile body, the victim of—

"We aren't sure whether he even recognizes anybody." Randy's voice sounded far, far away. "He lies there staring at the ceiling, unresponsive."

"I'm sorry." Did that sound sincere? Aramenta said, "I'm very sorry, Randy."

"Thank you."

Long pause.

"Aramenta, did you call me?"

"Yes." She couldn't make her mind function. Nothing would come. Thump-thump-thump-thump—

"What did you need, Aramenta?"

"Nothing."

"Are you sure you're all right?"

"Yes."

"Where's Virgil?"

Yes. There would be questions about Virgil.

"He left."

"Quit." Randy didn't seem surprised. "That's probably best for him, Aramenta. After all, it was a temporary job. He's an adult. He needed to find more gainful employment."

"Left this morning."

"Aramenta," Randy's voice softened, "wouldn't you like to go home to Paris? There's nothing to hold you any longer. I could get your tickets to—"

"No."

"Aramenta," an edge to his tone now, "you shouldn't remain out there alone. At least move to a hotel."

"No."

"Is it Virgil? Are you upset because he quit?"

"I—he—no. I'm not upset."

"I could hire another caretaker for you. But, Aramenta, I don't really think you need that. I think you should go home. Wouldn't that be best? To go home?"

"No. There's more to do."

Randy sighed. "All right. Anything else?"

"No."

"Would you like me to drop out there?"

"No."

Another painful silence. Randy's tone lifted, "Say, how about having dinner with Bobbie and me tonight? We'll go down to Bayou La Batre and eat at the Catalina again. That was the seafood restaurant you liked so much."

"Not tonight, Randy. Thank you."

"Very well," Randy said. She heard him speak to someone on his end of the line. Back to her now, "Aramenta, my brother, William, is insisting that he meet you."

"Randy, you are my attorney," Aramenta said, abruptly. "I have no desire to socialize. I have no need of another attorney. Can you handle my business or not?"

She expected a hurt response, but Randy laughed.

"Well?" Aramenta demanded.

"You bet your boots I can, Aramenta. Here, you might want to speak to my brother."

"I do not!" Thump-thump-thump.

"Miss Lee?" a deep, smooth baritone.

"Mr. Beausarge, I consider your brother my attorney. Anything to be transacted must be done with him. I don't wish to be rude, but I shan't tolerate any further waste of my time. I assume I am paying your brother handsomely. Therefore let him do his job!"

"Of course, Miss Lee. But in our firm, every man is a specialist. Our tax man and marketing analysts are—"

"May I speak to your brother?"

"Of course."

Randy spoke, almost jovially, "Hello, Aramenta."

"Tell your brother I said go to hell."

His laughter told her volumes. Aramenta spoke more gently, "Randy, please protect me from such things. I have too much on my mind for frivolities. Please."

"I will, Aramenta. Was there anything else?"

"No. Thanks for calling back."

Randy grunted, still cheerful, "I'll begin looking for another caretaker right away."

"No! You're right, I don't need that."

"All right," Randy said, cautiously.

"I won't be here much longer," Aramenta protested. "I'll do fine. You just probate the will and take care of your end of this matter."

"I will. Good-bye, Aramenta."

Aramenta sank to the bed, watching her image in the smoked mirror. What was she doing? She couldn't keep Virgil down there!

But what else could she do? What other recourse was there? She had seen the raging anger in Virgil's eyes, his screams in her ears.

Thump-thump-thump, a thunderous crashing of wood, wine racks shattering. Eerie, high-pitched screams now and then, followed by more drumming and destruction.

She had gone too far now. She couldn't let him go. He must stay. They must do this thing together, she and Virgil. It had to succeed. It would've been better another way, enlisting his assistance willingly, but this would work. When Virgil had more money than he'd ever dreamed of, then he would forgive her. What was a week, two, a month even, to such a young man? He would agree.

But even if he agreed at this point, she could not let him out—until Baby was ready to come too. She could not trust Virgil. He would change, though. She nodded to her mirrored image. He would change. He would be thankful she had done this, soon enough, Oh, yes. This would change his entire life.

"They'll do anything for money, child," Mother had said that often enough. "Money is everything! Not to abuse, not to waste, not to flaunt, never. But it is the power the poor man seeks—money will cure his problems, all his cares, he thinks. The fools! When they get it, if they ever do, they learn soon enough, money does not change anything. It is blood that tells. Breeding and character flowing through the veins unseen. Break an aristocrat and he bounces back. Why? Because of the blood within him, the friends and associates of blood. Never forget that, Aramenta. Blood tells. Blood tells."

Aramenta stared, no longer seeing, the room going dark as the sun set. The throbs and splinters from below were only sporadic now, the cries fading.

There was no other way. Virgil would understand. He would forgive her.

Thump-thump-thump.

Coming! A thought, or a sound? Coming, Baby!

Her arms felt leaden, weighted, her footsteps an effort. She somehow reached the kitchen. Standing, doing nothing, standing in a stupor. Get yourself together, Aramenta. Do what you must now. Two trays. Two hungry mouths to feed. Damn it. Do what Mother would have done.

Thump-thump-thump.

She took the trays below, placing them both at the head of the wine-cellar steps. She saw Virgil's belongings were still stacked as before. She flicked the switch and the inner door shut as the outer opened. The overhead light signaled this. She delivered the trays to the area beyond Virgil's things, his piercing unintelligible voice babbling. "Please," the only word she caught. "Please!"

Aramenta climbed the steps, threw the switch, watched the doors change positions. Virgil stepped over both trays to the closed portal, gripping the bars, yelling at her.

She left him screaming, cursing, and went upstairs. As she walked away, Virgil kicked a box, kicked another.

There had to be a way out. A way to freedom, to the outside, to reach her! He kicked the box again, lifting a parcel to throw it at the inner door. He stopped, midair.

The trays. The food neatly compartmentalized, a single red vitamin tablet beside the bread—he'd seen her prepare such trays before. She brought it down here, down to the—bed! The toilet. Shaving paraphernalia, clothes hanging—fear welled up like a rush of flood waters, threatening to drown his last ounce of reason.

In the dark, something stirred. Virgil pressed back waiting, waiting.

The visage took form as taloned hands outstretched. Alabaster skin, shaggy hair, and bearded face, his eyes transparently pale reflecting nothing, the ghostly apparition took a tray and withdrew.

Virgil sagged, his back to the bars.

Chapter Twenty

Virgil awoke with a start. He was huddled behind his belongings, mind blurred, confused. His shoulder ached from pressing against the bars of the door. He sat up, realized where he was. The wine cellar was dark now, the only illumination coming from the light overhead. On the floor, two food trays, empty and clean. He turned to look up the stairs. Aramenta was watching him, a cup of coffee between her hands.

"Coffee?" she offered.

He nodded. She held it out and waited to see the reach of his arm before coming closer. He took the cup by the handle.

"We talk now," she signed, then made it a question with another gesture. Numbly, Virgil nodded.

"This can be long time," she motioned, "or short time. This depends on you."

"What?" he asked.

"My baby in there." Aramenta signed, lips and hands

working together. "Thirty years ago born. My mother told me he dead. Not dead, I find this when I come here. All years, down here where Mother kept him. He is deaf, I think. I try to see him, to sign to him, and cannot get him to come out. I need you for this. You teach Baby what you know. Make Baby do as you do. You make Baby come out, upstairs, be with me. Do this and I pay you much money. You never work again if you do not wish to work again. For now, you ask for something to do this, I will give it to you. I did not want to put you here like this. But I could not let you leave. Understand?"

He controlled his facial expressions, sipping coffee. When he did not respond, Aramenta continued.

"I know nothing about Baby," she signed. "Smart, not smart, this I do not know. Dumb, I do not know. This you must learn. You are strong. You know deaf language. You know how deaf man thinks. Teach this to Baby. Make Baby like you."

"How I do that?" Virgil questioned, angrily.

"I do not know."

"How long this take?" Virgil demanded.

"Not know."

"You will keep me here until I do this?" Virgil signed rapidly. "It takes one month, one year, you keep me here all time?"

"Yes."

"Police get you."

"No."

"Attorney come. Find me. Police get you."

"No."

"I do not want to do this!"

"You must." She stood. "More coffee?"

He held out his cup and she motioned, "stretch," making him extend his arm as far as he could. She put in sugar and milk before pouring coffee from a carafe on the steps. Virgil quelled an urge to throw the hot liquid on her. She was insane!

"This Baby hurt me?" Virgil questioned.

"Not think so."

"Think so!"

Aramenta wasn't sure whether Virgil was impugning her opinion or stating his own.

"You stronger than Baby. You can handle Baby."

"Where I sleep?"

"Bed there."

"Where he sleep?"

"When he come to you, I bring another bed."

"Let me out."

"No."

"I not doctor of mind!"

"You can do this."

"Let me out!"

"No."

He gripped the coffee cup with both hands, trembling More calmly, "Leave all lights on."

"Today yes. One day only. Next day," Aramenta explained, "lights only night, off day. You must sleep. Baby must sleep. I will set clock up here."

"Eighteen hours' light," Virgil bartered. She considered this, shook her head. "Sixteen!" Virgil demanded. Aramenta agreed. She mounted the steps, turned right, and a moment later the cellar lights came on. Virgil vowed to find a way out. She stood at the head of the cellar steps, face set. Her expression did not change as she came down to get the coffeepot, and left Virgil making sounds she did not understand, angry noises followed by the crash of the plastic cup as he threw it after her.

*   *   *

Virgil armed himself with a stout piece of board broken from a wine rack. He followed the walls seeking a window, crack, any place for a beginning. Crawling over casks, behind them, he traced the contours of the room. Into the shadows of the east wing, then west, from floor to ceiling, fingers groping into dark recesses, he searched while watching for this "baby." He discovered a ventilating fan, but the aperture was too small to allow passage. Looking up the shaft, he saw no light to suggest an opening. He put his hand against the grille and felt the faint tremor of a motor, a steady breeze drafting upward.

He found tunnels beneath and behind storage racks, the backs of casks broken out to provide hollow hiding places, a blanket forming a nest, all telling him he was not alone. Somewhere in this maze, moving out of sight and reach, the unknown cohabitant of this prison effectively avoided detection.

Virgil came back to center point, to the bed beside the doorless bathroom. He turned full circle, peering into shadows cloaking Baby. He wondered about the man's strength, sanity, size. Virgil gripped the crude club prepared to defend himself.

Hour after hour he retraced his steps, testing the walls and ceiling. Solid, thick, impenetrable. He sniffed for moisture, a clue to decay—none. No windows, grates, only the narrow air shaft, the doors, and the small openings overhead where the lights were located. Virgil climbed a wine rack, grabbing the mesh enclosure covering the light bulbs. Like the doors, the steel mesh was embedded in concrete.

He crawled the floor seeking a drain, although the dust was proof no water came down here. He found a sump pump, the electrical wiring denuded of insulation by time and wear. Back to the center of it all: the bed, clothes cabinet, toilet.

The lights blinked. Virgil followed the aisles between racks to the door. Aramenta stood halfway up the steps, waiting.

"You need anything?" she questioned.

"I want out."

A brief expression of irritation crossed her face. She turned to go, and Virgil shouted at her, his voice vibrant in his throat. She continued without glancing back. Virgil spun around, club in hand and bashed the walls between the security doors. He stood with legs spread, breathing hard, hands shaking. He examined the door, how it worked. Electric, the hinged area controlled by a long rod which went through the ceiling. He fingered the locking mechanism. It could be controlled two ways: with a key and by the electric device which closed the door and set the tumbler. He used a sliver of wood to jam the faceplate. There! When the door closed, it would not catch.

Filled with new hope, he waited. Time here was deceptive. He sat inside the passage between doors watching for Aramenta.

She came with food, set the trays at the top of the steps, and motioned for Virgil to get back inside the cellar. He did this, waiting for his opportunity. She threw the switch and the two doors moved in synchronized swings. Virgil crouched, watching her bring down the trays to place them in the lighted area. At that point she would be between doors, vulnerable. When she stooped to place the trays, he lunged at the door with all his strength.

Aramenta looked up, startled, and saw Virgil strike the door and fall back. He climbed to his feet, mouthing words, voice screeching, face flaming with anger. He held his shoulder where he'd struck the door and railed at Aramenta as she walked away with the stride of one unconcerned.

Virgil turned as two arms reached for a tray.

"Ayyyy!" Virgil raced at the figure and instantly the two arms disappeared. Standing over the trays, panting, Virgil massaged his bruised right shoulder. You ate my food last time, he thought; this belongs to me. He pulled both trays over to his things, using one box as a seat, another for a table. Warily watching the recesses of shadow, Virgil ate all he could hold. Only then did he place the trays with scant remnants, where the food could be reached.

No further attempt was made to get it.

Aramenta came again, glanced down at Virgil, checked the timer, and left him screaming at her. His throat was raw from yelling, every muscle in his body now ached from exertion.

When the lights in the cellar went out, Virgil sat propped against the door watching the dark. Exhaustion overtook him, he dozed fitfully only to awaken frightened, adrenaline flowing, prepared to defend himself against an unseen aggressor. The food trays were still there, exactly as he'd left them, scraps of food undisturbed. Again he nodded off and once more came awake tensed, fists knotted. A mouse was eating the balance of the food. Virgil kicked at the tray and the rodent scurried away.

At last the cellar lights came on again. Muscles cramped, bones throbbing, Virgil braced himself against the wall and got to his feet. He froze, hand against the wall—thump-thump-thump. Somebody upstairs? A visitor? Virgil ran into the cellar, club in hand, yelling as loud as he could, beating things with the board. Beams, racks, anything that would transmit his distress signal to the upper floors. He thrashed, banged, venting anger and frustration with every blow, praying that somebody up there would hear, question, demand to see what was happening! Spent, soaked with perspiration, now slightly chilled as he sagged to the floor gasping, he crawled back to the door. Aramenta was there, sitting on the steps beyond the outer door, a pot of coffee beside her. She lifted a cup, smiling, questioning.

Dully Virgil nodded. He threw the club aside and on hands and knees dragged himself to a box. He sat on it, leaning against a wall, head back, mouth open. When he turned to look at Aramenta, she was patiently waiting, coffee poured and ready. He reached out. She held back. *Damn you!* He stretched and she placed the cup at the tips of his fingers making him press hard against the bars to take it. Stupid woman!

"I have been thinking," Aramenta signed conversationally. "We must establish a plan. You may need books to study. Do you want books?"

He sipped coffee, the searing liquid burning his throat.

"First, it be smart to move from here to inside. Use bed. Hang up clothes. Baby then know you here to stay. Make home for you in there," Aramenta signed, her arthritic hands producing stiff motions. Old hands. Flesh like worn satin. Her hair was straggling, wisps of gray. It occurred to Virgil she was still wearing the same blouse and slacks she'd worn the day she tricked him.

"Baby think you not going to leave," Aramenta continued, "maybe come out, be friends. This must be first. You get him to come. He never comes to me."

She lifted her cup, staring into the liquid pensively. She put it down, face suddenly animated, "Maybe you sleep his bed, he come ask you to move! Use his things, he think this is not good, then he comes out to"—she searched for the sign and failing that, fingerspelled—"protest."

"This not work," Virgil signed with leaden hands. "I cannot catch him."

"He will come. Soon. You try again."

"No," Virgil reasoned, heavily. "He afraid. He hides."

"Talk to him."

"Talk?" Virgil glared at her. "How talk?"

"Hands," Aramenta indicated. "That why you here. Baby deaf. You talk with hands, he will see. Tell him you deaf too. Alike. Tell him. This will work."

Anger ebbed and flowed, Virgil's body racked with strain and lack of deep sleep. Vaguely, he was aware that she was still signing, motioning, gesturing. She looked at him as if he were not truly there, or as though seeing through and beyond him. She babbled with hands, sometimes lips alone, about money, much money. Rich, she told Virgil, he would be rich!

He studied her with detachment, accumulating cognition, slowly affirming his initial thought: Aramenta was crazy. She was beyond reason. There was no hope of penetrating the veil her madness had erected between reality and the fantasy of this plan!

"More coffee," Virgil signed, holding out his cup. He saw an expression of wariness cross her face. She motioned him to stretch and he did this. She poured the coffee.

He wasn't going to get out. As secure as any cell, the walls of this dungeon were built to withstand his efforts. He realized the timer, lights, exhaust fan, had been constructed with careful consideration to keeping somebody out—or in.

"Must know Baby's mind," Aramenta rambled. "Be smart, be dumb, be"—spelling now—"retarded?"

Virgil watched with unseeing eyes, examining her face for clues, her soiled clothing, the quivering fingers stumbling through signs, sometimes unintelligibly. Who might come looking for him? His parents? Surely not. If he were gone months, or a year even, they would not come. Not the attorney. He would think—besides, he wanted Virgil to go elsewhere. Of course, Miss Lee would tell everyone he'd quit, gone away. Everything he owned was here below. Who

244

would argue? Who would miss him? Marie, in a small Mississippi town and unlikely to ever leave, much less come looking for Virgil?

"What you think about plan?" Aramenta queried, eyes bright. Virgil was still staring at her.

Mad. Completely mad. She was old. She was oral. Somewhere in her mind this all made sense. She sat here evolving plots and contingencies, an insane keeper of an insane inmate. Was the other man insane? Baby? Thirty years old and she called him Baby? Virgil must be careful. He must be aware of what was happening to himself. He too could be warped by this.

"Why you not talk with me?" Aramenta's hands jerked angrily. "I try talk. Try tell you, help you! You not talk. Okay!"

She snatched up the coffeepot and supplies, storming up the steps. Virgil saw her pause briefly to shoot an angry glance down at him, then she stalked off.

The coffee going cold in the cup between his hands, Virgil stared at the wall of his enclosure. He wasn't going to get out of here. Not easily. Not quickly. His warden was too wary, the insanity too sure, the walls too thick, the doors too strong. If he was to escape he must outwit the woman, defeat her not with childish artifice—he would have to become a part of her madness. The key—Virgil looked toward the shadows of the cellar—the key was in there. The man. Baby.

When dinner came, Virgil waited inside the cellar as the door changed positions and Aramenta placed the trays. When he could reach the food, he confiscated it all.

You want food, he thought, come get it, Baby.

He ate only what Aramenta had placed on one tray,

watching, waiting, but Baby never came. Virgil completed his meal and began searching for him.

"Want food?" he signed to the shaded areas. "Come get!"

He did this with determination, his original fear of the man dissolving. He almost anticipated his adversary, meeting him face-to-face. "Come get," he commanded. When after thirty minutes or more, Baby had not appeared, Virgil began eating what was on the second tray. As he did this, he detected distant thumps, his only indication that Baby was there watching, hungry, and—angry.

"He not come to me," Virgil reasoned.

"He will."

"Three days I wait. I eat his food. He not come."

"He will," Aramenta repeated. She spooned sugar into Virgil's coffee. This morning—night—evening? Aramenta sat on a pillow she'd placed on the stairway. She gave Virgil his coffee.

"I cannot teach something I cannot see," Virgil argued.

"He sees you, he watches, he is hungry," Aramenta replied, pleasantly. "He will come soon."

Virgil observed Aramenta, her lips moving, both hands occupied with her cup of coffee. Talking to him? To herself?

Suppose she died? Went upstairs and had a heart attack? Would he remain here until someone came to see why she did not answer the telephone? Who would come? The attorney? Who? Or if the building caught fire? Virgil and this nameless other creature would be trapped like moles in their underground cavern as the flaming embers fell in on them, consuming their oxygen, turning toilet water to steam.

"I have decided," Virgil signed slowly, "I will do this thing. For money."

Aramenta's eyes narrowed suspiciously.

"How much money you pay for this?" Virgil asked.

"Much."

"How much?"

She looked away briefly. "This depends on you," she said. "How long this takes, how good you do this thing."

"How much?" Virgil persisted.

"I don't know."

"You cannot keep me here forever. You make deal now with me and I do this. No deal, I will not work."

Aramenta lifted her head, almost a toss, her eyes alight with a spark of success. "I pay you ten thousand dollars."

Ten thousand! Virgil disguised his disbelief. Who would allow a madwoman to give him anything? When he got out, told people, they would surely lock her away and there would be no money, he knew that.

"Not enough," Virgil bargained. Aramenta's eyes flickered irritation. "Twenty thousand," Virgil said.

Jaw set, lips thinned, Aramenta nodded. "I pay this. We have a deal." She gathered the things she'd brought down, cups, sugar.

Virgil stayed an overwhelming urge to yell. He tapped the bars with his cup. Aramenta turned, one foot a step higher than the other.

"I need poison for mice," Virgil signed. "I need clean things for bed. My clothes dirty. No toothpaste. I do not like this pillow. I want another. Do not serve beets again. Baby does not like. I do not like."

"Baby likes," Aramenta gestured, shortly.

"No," Virgil signed evenly, "Baby does not like."

"Who ate beets?"

"Mice."

Aramenta's back straightened slightly. She nodded. Virgil watched her disappear at the turn above the steps.

I get you, woman, I catch you. No money, you be sorry. Even if money, you be sorry you do this thing. I catch you. Hurt you.

He turned from the door, scanned his belongings. He had to begin. One thing he'd decided, he wasn't going to get out of here without the help of his fellow inmate. Virgil carried a box to the bed area. Filthy. He walked to a beam and tapped with rhythm, tap-taptap-tap.

When he returned to the door, Aramenta was there.

"Need soap, scour powder, broom, things which clean. New bed frame, mattress."

Aramenta nodded, departed. Virgil carried another box down the winding aisles. Wait, woman. I get. You see.

Chapter Twenty-one

In the total black of lights-out, Virgil knew the man was there, unseen, unheard, the odor of his body giving him away. Virgil worried at first that Baby might attack him as he slept. This never happened. Baby came not to fight, but to eat, driven by a primordial need which brought him forth. It was survival, not aggression, and had Virgil made the food available he was sure he could coexist with Baby and never see the man.

He had used food to tempt and, failing this, to torment. Virgil ate with animated, exaggerated mimes of pleasure. "You want," he gestured. "Come get. You don't come. I eat."

Like caged animals, food became the focal point of their existence. Virgil anticipated every meal, raged if Miss Lee was late even a few minutes. He complained bitterly when she forgot salt, or served portions too small, when it was cold or too spicy. He suffered a vague yearning which food alone did not satisfy. His only consolation was the realization that somewhere in the dark, Baby was suffering too.

Baby somehow skirted all Virgil's efforts to keep food away from him. As Virgil slept, or by frontal attack, Baby would secure some amount, eat like a ravaged animal, face-to-face with Virgil for a short time only to vanish again into the honeycombed passages he had developed over the years. Virgil had fits of weeping, rage and hatred of the elusive figure.

Depression became his most formidable opponent. His efforts to read culminated in a staring trance where he sat looking at a printed page seeing nothing, his loathing of Aramenta and pity for himself blocking out all else. He had begun to think of her as "Aramenta," dropping any title of respect. Despite his resolve to handle her more carefully, he often met Aramenta with screams of anger, moments when if he could have reached her, he would surely have killed her.

Virgil sat in the passageway waiting on Aramenta to come with coffee. He seethed with an emotion that simmered within him ready to erupt with any small inconvenience.

"Where my mail?" he demanded.

"No mail."

"Lie!" He made a vulgar sign. "Lie!"

"No lie." Aramenta calmly poured coffee.

"You lie," he fingerspelled slowly, "b-i-t-c-h."

She contemplated him a long moment, continued preparing their beverages.

"Marie write each week!"

"No mail," Aramenta insisted. Then with a gesture of sincerity, "I promise this. Mail come, I give to you. I promise."

He stretched for the coffee, took it. Sullen, glaring at the liquid, he sat on the floor, elbows on his knees, cup between his hands.

In the shadowed sanctum of his confinement, priorities began to alter, memories to waver. From his subconscious came instant and vivid replays of totally irrelevant events from his past. Doubts began to plague him. He would discover himself repeating things, a phrase, a lyric, in an endless, mindless chant.

He began praying, asking God to intervene in this madness. With renewed sincerity, bordering on slavering beggary, he appealed to God for understanding, forgiveness of past sins, assistance, anything! Where was God? Was he, too, deaf? From whispers to shouts, appeals to accusations, his pleas degenerated into a vicious assault on the heavens, damnation of the deities, contempt for "God's mysterious ways."

Virgil refused to go to the door. For several days he stayed back, seeing Aramenta waiting. She tapped the ceiling, bumped the floor, but would not enter. Baby repeatedly grabbed the food with Aramenta standing there. If Virgil was to do without, Baby would suffer. He blocked the food, not taking it himself, but refusing to allow Baby past to get it. It was futile. Sleep had to come, Baby always won. If Virgil had been sick, hurt, or dying, Aramenta would not have cared enough to come and see. Damn the woman. Damn them all!

He was being stupid, going as crazy as his captor. She was reducing him physically and mentally, and if he should die from it all, who would know? Or care?

Virgil reversed himself. He appeared at the door. Aramenta made no mention of the past days without seeing him. He had the infuriating sense that she'd known all along he was trying to trick her.

"I want hammer, crowbar."

"No."

"I need this!"

"No tools."

"I cannot catch this—*baby!*"

She offered coffee, cinnamon rolls. "No tools," she concluded.

With his bare hands, using dismembered racks as his only additional implements, Virgil began at the door and worked his way toward the sleeping area, destroying the racks, piling the debris in the passageway.

"What this?" Aramenta demanded angrily

"Take out."

"No!"

"Take out, damn you!"

She finally did, carrying the splintered wood up and stacking it in the basement. He drew satisfaction from her exertion.

"Why you do this?" Aramenta protested. Virgil refused to say, sitting in her presence without communication. Anything he could do to create mental anguish, this he would do.

"Why you tear up everything?" Aramenta questioned daily.

He sipped coffee, intentionally oblivious.

"Tell me this!" Aramenta ordered. "Or I turn out lights night and day!"

His heart leaped in momentary panic. Nevertheless, he did not reply, drinking coffee, letting her fret. He paid for it with interminable hours of darkness, not sure whether one day passed, or several. By feel alone, he groped from rack to rack breaking them down, tearing board from plank, prying hoops from casks and reducing them to curved staves. The pile of lumber filled the passage and still he continued.

The lights returned as he worked. Blinded, he paused. He saw overhead receptacles being withdrawn one at a time and realized Aramenta had been looking down through the openings all those days he'd attempted to hide. She could easily have seen him lying in bed, even bathing.

The cellar seemed larger as the racks and casks were destroyed. Vibrations came stronger through the floor. Movement overhead from the house seemed sharper. Virgil removed the final object between his bed and the exit, then started on the west wing. His hands blistered and raw, he reduced everything to nothing, carrying rubble to the doors, where Aramenta now labored to keep pace. She was no longer disturbed. She had deduced what he was doing.

The lights, now unfiltered, rebounded from floor to wall, making shadows recede. He found place after place where Baby had taken refuge. Inside casks, man-made hollows, the burrows of a creature determined to keep himself hidden.

When the lights went out, the bulb between the exit doors now cast a scant illumination in the cavernous cellar. Virgil slept so soundly, only the glare of light the next day awoke him. He smelled coffee.

"Smart," Aramenta signed cheerfully. "You smart. I knew you could do this. Very good thing you do now. Smart."

You bitch, you wait, you'll see how smart. Wait. Get you, break you, you pay for this. He smiled, nodded.

"I think," Virgil said, amiably, "this can work. We see. No place to hide, Baby must come to me. No hide; cannot get away."

"Very good. Very smart. Thank you. Thank you for this."

You wait, woman. Soon enough time for you to suffer for what you do. You be sorry.

*   *   *

253

"Mr. Beausarge?"

"Yes, Rosa." Randy held a finger on the list of assets he and Alec were checking.

"Mr. Bruce Matthew wishes to see you."

"Mr. Matthew is here?"

"Yessir."

Randy released the intercom key and looked at William and Alec. "He's here to cause trouble, you can bet on it."

"By what authority?" William questioned.

"He's scared Aramenta Lee is getting away from him," Randy said.

William pondered this a moment, then, "Ask him in, Randall."

The New York attorney came through the door smiling, his conservatively cut suit obviously expensive. He acknowledged introductions and his expression grew serious.

"Gentlemen, I am here on behalf of my client, Mrs. Aramenta Darcy, née Lee."

"All right, Mr. Matthew," William stated.

"I have had an extensive check run on her holdings and—"

"Aramenta asked for that?" Randy demanded.

"No. But that's neither here nor there, gentlemen. I've represented this lady for many years. I take it upon myself to protect her interests when her interests seem imperiled."

"Imperiled, Mr. Matthew? In what way?" William asked.

"Apparently, the estate has been greatly diminished in some way," Matthew said. "According to the will filed for probate, there are assets listed for audit which are not in fact the registered property of the decedent."

"We're going over that now, Mr. Matthew," Alec interjected. "You're right. But the matter will be corrected as soon as we have verified various holdings. The error was caused by an outdated list of assets. It was all we had with which to work."

Thank you, Randy thought gratefully.

"Gentlemen, let me be unequivocal," Bruce Matthew said. "I have waited quietly, asked for information which hasn't been forthcoming, and repeated efforts to reach my client have been frustrated. Now I learn her telephone is unlisted. I feel I must warn you, I am prepared to block probate of this will until I can arrange an independent audit."

"Who do you think you're fooling?" Randy snapped, standing. "You come down here trying to muck this up— don't give me that nonsense about your 'client.' It won't wash! You stick your fingers in this and Aramenta will send you packing so fast your head will swim, mister."

"I'm not sure the lady is competent to make that move," Bruce said.

"I beg your pardon?" William's eyebrows raised.

"Since her arrival here," Bruce noted, "she seems to have undergone a mental deterioration. Correct me if I'm amiss, but she is living in an empty mansion, is she not? Ordering food by phone, becoming reclusive and recalcitrant?"

William gazed at Randy.

"I don't think even a New York court of law will adjudge such behavior just cause for superimposing the attorney's will over that of the client," Randy fumed. "Now let me set you straight, Matthew. If you think this cumbersome ploy will weasel your way into the facts and figures, you can go to hell. Aramenta sent you home before, she'll do it again."

"You seem quite certain of that," Bruce said calmly.

"Quite certain."

"Okay." William shuffled together the papers in his lap. "I suggest we all drive out to see Miss Lee and get the matter settled once and for all."

Randy reached for the telephone and Bruce lifted a hand, smiling, "Don't call," he said. "Let's surprise her."

"I'll call," Randy retorted.

"Randall," William's tone dropped. "Let's go out there and take our chances. If she isn't in, we'll have lunch and forget it. If she is, we will—as Mr. Matthew says—surprise her."

They drove, William and Bruce chatting conversationally in the front seat, Randy seething in the rear. When they reached the Lee Mansion, William parked by the front walk.

"The place seems deserted," Bruce observed.

"We'll have to go around back," Randy said, leading the way.

They paused outside the kitchen and knocked. Aramenta opened the door, hands covered with flour. She glanced at the other two men, then looked long at Randy.

"This is my brother, William, Aramenta."

"A pleasure to meet you at last, Miss Lee."

"Ara-men-ta!" Bruce pushed past to hug her. She held her hands to the sides to keep from dusting him with flour.

"What is this, Randy?" Aramenta asked, coldly.

"There's some question concerning the estate, Aramenta," Bruce soothed. "We need a few minutes of your time."

"I'm busy, Bruce. What are you doing here, anyway?"

"Looking after my girl, Aramenta."

"I told you before, I am adequately represented, Bruce. I instructed you to go back to New York. What are you trying to do here?"

"Aramenta, there are some serious discrepancies in the valuation of the estate."

"I don't give a damn, Bruce."

"Of course you do! Let us sit down and I want to show you some grave questions which have come to my mind concerning—"

"Randy, what is this?" Aramenta's eyes flashed hotly.

"Bruce is of the opinion we're not protecting your affairs

adequately, Aramenta. In fact, he suggested you yourself may not be capable of looking after your own best interests."

"Well, of course, that isn't precisely the context in which I—"

"Bruce, you are dismissed as my attorney. That means totally, irrevocably, and henceforth. Is that clear enough? Any money you may have spent 'on my behalf,' as you put it, is your personal loss. If you try to meddle in my affairs again for any reason, at any time, I shall bring suit against you and your firm. This is unforgivable."

"Now, Aramenta, just a moment."

"No, Bruce. Not even a moment. Go back to New York, where you belong, and leave me alone. Randy, I expect you to see that he has absolutely nothing to do with my affairs hereafter."

"I shall indeed."

Bruce wheeled, face red, and for an instant Randy thought blows would pass. William took this opportunity to step between them.

"Miss Lee, Mr. Matthew is correct about one thing. There are some discrepancies we can't seem to resolve. Apparently, some of the assets listed in the estate are not valid. If we could get you to come down to the office—"

"Who are you?"

"William Beausarge, Miss Lee. I was just introduced to you by my brother, Randall."

"Who the hell am I paying here?" Aramenta questioned.

"Actually, the estate is handled by the firm of Beausarge, which includes my—"

"Gentlemen, since when does a law firm become a nonentity?" Aramenta glared at Randy. "I have been dealing with Randy and I shall continue to do so. I do not have anything to say to anyone else. Randy—Randy, if you cannot cope with my situation, I shall be forced to seek representation elsewhere."

"I think I can handle it, Aramenta." Randy was almost smiling.

"Good day, gentlemen."

They stood staring at the closed door. Bruce turned and left first, and William cocked his head, studying Randy.

"You've done a good job on her," William said. "She's sold. Let's go."

Heart ascending, Randy followed his brother back to the automobile, where Bruce Matthew sulked in the rear seat. Randy noted that William now sat opposite the steering wheel.

"I assume," Randy said with barely contained innuendo, "I'm in the driver's seat?"

He started the motor without comment from the other two men.

From a window, Aramenta watched them depart. She smiled for the first time in days. Randy had enjoyed that. Aramenta's obdurate attitude of loyalty would not soon be forgotten by that young man. If he had not been in complete control heretofore, he certainly was now.

She returned to the kitchen, the floor vibrant with rending wood down below. She checked her batter. Just right. She dusted her hands with flour once more, lifted a bit of dough, and proceeded to make Mother's rocks.

Her doubts about the wisdom of having Virgil locked up were resolved. For a while, she'd been worried. She had seen him cease shaving and bathing, becoming sullen and angry. He'd tried trickery and ruse, everything but what it would take to attain success—help Baby. Now he was rapidly clearing the cellar, showing initiative and wile.

Today, he'd actually been smiling and confident that he would make progress once Baby had no place to hide. Aramenta slipped the cookie sheet into the oven, washed her hands, and began a pot of coffee. Or would Virgil prefer iced tea? Despite the cool of the basement and cellar, all the physical exertion was taking a toll. He had appeared at the cellar door streaked with dust and rivulets of sweat.

She would make coffee and tea. He could have a choice.

That Bruce, really, what a terrible thing he was trying to do. All those years when so little had been involved he'd seemed such a nice man. Now the lure of riches, the stocks, and proxies—money twisted the best of men, evidently.

"The surest mark of a common man," Mother used to say.

If there'd been any doubt before, certainly there was none now—Bruce was acting very common.

Ah, well. She sniffed the aroma of baking pastry.

Ah, well. Blood tells.

She had to hurry! Virgil became impatient when the passageway clogged with timber. Aramenta had to haul it out as fast as it accumulated. She shifted restlessly from foot to foot, waiting for the cookies.

Mother wasn't always wrong. Goddamn Mother.

Chapter Twenty-two

From behind the final cask, Baby bolted into the open cellar. Crouched, crablike as he followed the wall, he ran seeking the farthest, darkest areas. The bones in Virgil's face pulsed with Baby's screams. He completed the demolition of the keg and carried the last of the staves to the passageway.

"What's wrong?" Aramenta was alarmed.

"Nothing."

"What's happening? Why is he screaming?"

"No place to hide," Virgil reported.

He returned for more debris. The mattress that had been on Baby's bed leaned against one wall. Baby scurried behind it. Virgil yanked the mattress and springs flat on the floor, and Baby cringed, his eyes filled with terror.

Yell! Yell and yell! I deaf, not hear. Stupid!

Virgil carried the remainder of the dismantled barrel to Aramenta. She stood at the outer door with an expression of horror that gave Virgil grim satisfaction.

"He hurt?"

"Not now," Virgil warned. "Will be, if he keeps doing this."

"No. Do not hurt him!"

"How will you stop me?" Virgil questioned.

"Do not hurt," Aramenta warned.

He made a vulgar gesture and walked away. The cellar reverberated with manic shrieks, the nude and bearded man now huddled in a far corner. Virgil walked toward Baby and the throb in his skull intensified. Dumb! Crazy! He walked faster, closing on the creature. Baby jumped and ran. He hugged the walls, past the exit, with Virgil following, back to the doorless bathroom. Virgil relentlessly pursued Baby who climbed into the tub, and then like a cornered animal attacked, teeth snapping.

"You bite me! Bite me and I knock out your teeth!"

Scratching, arms flailing, Baby knocked Virgil aside and slithered beneath the bed. Virgil began disassembling his bed, letting the spring and mattress deliberately fall on the screaming man below. He carried the slats, bedstead, and frame to Aramenta.

"What you do to him?" Aramenta accused.

"Nothing."

"Lie! You hurt him!"

"Not hurt, dumb bitch! Crazy! Crazy!" Virgil circled one ear with a forefinger. Again, "Crazy!"

Aramenta was at the bars now, closer than she'd ever been. Virgil could have darted at her, perhaps grabbing her. His head strummed with the echo of yelling. The sound must come to her ears as the ravings of a lunatic. Virgil saw her head shake, tears in her eyes, her knuckles bloodless from grasping the bars so tightly.

"Crazy," Virgil gestured again. "What I do with crazy man?"

"Not crazy. Afraid."

Disgusted, Virgil made a sign for coffee. Aramenta stared beyond him into the cellar.

"Make coffee," he commanded anew.

She turned and slowly mounted the steps. Good. Worry. Go more mad than you are already! Let Baby scream until his throat bleeds. Let him cry until Aramenta's ears rang with it. Punish her. Let them both suffer!

Virgil sipped the coffee, keeping a calm expression of total unconcern. He could only judge the intensity of Baby's affect on Aramenta by the varying degrees of alarm she reflected, sitting on the steps, hands trembling, eyes huge. In a while, go back there and beat the dumb smelly beast until he hushes. Virgil would never sleep when lights out if Baby continued!

But dark extinguished the cries. Virgil rolled over on his mattress and placed a palm to the concrete floor. He felt no vibration. When sleep came, it was deep and satisfying. He awoke when lights came on the next "morning." Immediately aware of Baby, he sat up. Baby was asleep, naked, on the other mattress.

Deaf, perhaps. But more was wrong with this man than deaf. He had a genuine fear of Virgil, cowering, clawing his way to the farthest retreat the open room would afford. Now the starkly white body was positioned, back to Virgil, on one side, almost fetally curled with Baby's arms around his head, knees drawn to his chest.

Virgil had a vivid recollection of himself before he learned signs, sleeping nude despite Mama's repeated demands that he wear pajamas. After the house was dark, Virgil would remove his bedclothing, burrow under the covers, and sleep with his own warm breath on chest and knees.

The lights blinked rhythmically. Aramenta was waiting with breakfast. Baby stirred, his almost hairless legs extending, muscles stretching as he turned on his back. One arm flopped to the side, Baby's mouth working. Virgil watched for word-shapes to the lips, then decided it was an unconscious move to displace stale saliva.

"Baby okay?" Aramenta asked.

"Okay."

"Not yelling."

"Yes, he is yelling," Virgil said, soberly. "You deaf, cannot hear him?"

Aramenta stared at Virgil a moment, then smiled.

"I want table for typewriter," Virgil requested. "Want lamp. Light not good for typing."

"Not much furniture upstairs now," Aramenta protested. "No lamp."

"You have much money," Virgil signed, sharply. "Go buy lamp. Buy table!"

She nodded.

"Need two chairs and table for eating," Virgil continued.

"No table."

"Buy table, damn you! Buy what needed. You want Baby always to eat from floor?"

Another short nod.

"More sheet and blanket for beds."

"All right."

"Candy."

"Candy?"

"Yes." Damn you. "Candy!"

Her eyes shifted, worried.

"Candy bars," Virgil amended. "Snickers, Mars, Hershey."

His demands would be met, he saw that. But Aramenta was upset, as though what Virgil asked was unfair, unreasonable. When she left him, he wondered why. Too expensive? That was not logical. Too heavy to easily carry? She could get a folding card table. What then? He sipped coffee, contemplative. Aramenta's body and dress suggested days of minimal care. He guessed that she was more and more reclusive, ordering what she wanted and seldom going out. This had continued so long now, she was afraid to venture out. Virgil hoped he was wrong. If Aramenta yielded her outside ties, he was in the hands of a steadily degenerating mentality. He sought to test her reason, asking advice about Baby.

"What would you do first?" he questioned.

"I don't know."

"Teach him to eat properly? Dress? What?"

"I don't know."

"He still doesn't come to me," Virgil complained.

"Go to him."

"I give him tray. I follow around."

"That is good."

"But does nothing!"

"He no longer screams."

"So?"

"He is getting better."

Angrily, "How long this to be? I do not wish to be here ten years! How soon out of this place? Tell me! How soon?"

As usual when there was an outburst, Aramenta's expresson inured. "When Baby like you. Then."

"Like me!" Virgil was twenty-six! He could be another twenty-six years making this animal into something human. Virgil fought for self-control.

"How I do this? How? You keep me here many years to do this? How do this quickly?"

"I don't know."

Tears sprang to Virgil's eyes. "If I fail, what then? I stay here forever?"

"You will not fail."

"I now pale like Baby, muscles weaker. I lose weight. You not see this is true?"

"You will not fail," she repeated, dumbly.

Before words, when there were only things with no names, he must have had thoughts. But Virgil could not remember them. When he tried to recall thinking during those first years of his life, he was engulfed with emotional images but no memory of thoughts.

Things were what they were: ball, milk, Mama.

Mama was *what* she was, not *who* she was. She was sustenance. She was anger, punishment.

He sat now watching Baby in a corner, squatting, eating from his tray with his fingers. What thoughts went through that strange mind? Baby's beard and matted hair made his head seem abnormally large atop the frail body.

Before Virgil learned signs, when he was under five, anger was his most vivid impression—it was the emotion most responsible for the formation of his personality. He'd spent years rationalizing, studying, evaluating, remaking those formative images of infancy. What images did Baby conjure, sitting there like a wild animal, eyes darting, wary, feeding himself?

Virgil tried to step back from himself, shed the sharply personal self-conceptual picture that came to his mind's eye when he thought of "Virgil." He knew now that the first five years of life were crucial for any human. For the deaf child, for Virgil, anger was the matrix. Often, as quickly as it erupted, anger subsided. From wrath to weeping. Mama would clutch him with breathtaking tightness, rocking to and fro, and she would kiss away his tears. It had left him frightened, confused. Avoiding anger became his prime consideration. Any change in environment was distressing. New situations, the introduction of strangers, toys out of place— all were indications of impending conflict.

He saw himself as though photographed unseen, a tousle-haired child, in short pants (which he detested) and smiling—always that simpering, idiotic smile designed to allay anger, set aside disfavor, alleviate confrontations he could not avoid. He remembered reacting with two basic defenses: adherence to a strict regimen which had been approval-proven, and the smile. If an activity had gone unpunished, or at least unnoticed, this he did without variance over and over again. When his infant actions displeased, often for no apparent reason, he ceased at once.

He blamed Mama for that. Shifts of adult temperament had fostered in Virgil a wariness and distrust he struggled to control even now. Because of Mama's handling of him in those first years, Virgil became acutely alert to the slightest modifications in his surroundings. A shadow, a modulation of rhythms underfoot, even a change in air current brought him to belly-knotting awareness. It was this awareness that fostered in Mama the fruitless hope that he was not truly deaf.

"He hears what he wants to hear," she once said.

At twenty-six, he understood what had made Mama the way she was. Maturity, books he had read, had given him comprehension. It was "natural," the psychologists reported, for many mothers to be alienated from their deaf children. She could not love what did not love her in return.

Had he not loved her? He couldn't remember.

Responding to a basic internal need, mothers drew maternal comfort and satisfaction from the development of the infant. He'd read that, too. Her need for the baby and her rewards for having the child were directly related to the mother's observance of structured responses—the smile, recognition of voice, and the baby's first words.

But after the smile, with a deaf baby, there was no response to voice, first words did not come for many years, if ever.

Virgil watched Baby carry his tray, circling Virgil as though beyond an invisible line, to the toilet. Baby rinsed the tray and took it to the passageway, where he left it. Following the man with his eyes, still sitting, eating, Virgil saw Baby walk along the wall, one hand against the perpendicular surface like a child drawing a stick along a picket fence. Now in a corner, Baby squatted, his body moving as if to an inner metronome, back and forth, back and forth.

Baby now examined his beard, to and fro, to and fro, the chin whiskers between both hands, separating each hair from the other as if searching for insects. Virgil had read of experiments with chimpanzees where the animals were caged without companionship. He remembered descriptions of rocking and a peculiar obsession with such things as the hair of the body, the chimps often pulling themselves bald. Virgil threw his fork on uneaten food, stomach churning.

He was getting nowhere with this! Flushed from his burrow, the animal was visible but no less feral. Virgil rinsed his tray and took it to the exit doors. He returned to the bathroom and ran a tub of water. Not too cold, not too warm. He put a bar of soap and washcloth on the tub. He removed his shirt. If he must live with this creature, the beast would be clean!

Baby saw him coming and tensed visibly.

"You bathe," Virgil signed. "Now. Smell bad! Stink!" He held his nose. Baby slowly came to his feet. "You put on clothes," Virgil continued, maneuvering Baby toward the bathroom. "Be human."

Baby moved sidewise, taking the line of least resistance, moving as Virgil's body dictated toward the toilet.

"Do this easy way," Virgil mouthed, "or hard way. You decide, stinky. One way or another, you are bathed."

Baby passed the bath area and Virgil cut him off, easing back toward the tub.

"Pig. Worse! Hog!" Virgil signed "big" and "pig." He held his nose again, face wrinkled. Baby's eyes flickered here, there, seeking escape?

Stunned, Virgil watched Baby step into the tub, slide down, chin whiskers afloat, grinning.

"Good," Virgil signed, stupefied. "Use soap."

Virgil sat on the commode watching as Baby took the washcloth, rubbed it full of suds, and bathed with care, oddly beginning with his feet and hands, then working himself over thoroughly. Only when Virgil advanced to hand him a towel did Baby react—withdrawing, tensed, eyes widening.

"Don't worry," Virgil mouthed. "I wouldn't interrupt you for anything. Keep going, stinky."

He'd done this before. Why should that surprise Virgil? Of course a man thirty years old must have bathed! What else had he done?

Baby began rubbing himself with soap again, starting his bath afresh.

Virgil stood less than four feet distant, and for the first time at this range, Baby was not trying to break and run. Savoring this, surprised at the elation he felt from the success of the bath, Virgil was grinning. Baby looked up now and then, eyes lingering, then continued his ablution.

In the first few days after the cellar was cleared of hiding places, Baby came to take a tray, then retreated. Virgil followed, eating from his own tray, moving as Baby moved, always as near as possible without throwing Baby into a panic. Gradually, Baby allowed him nearer. Virgil then began holding the tray on the table motioning at the chair while seating himself. Finally, Baby stood at the table eating and, at last, sat across from Virgil, dining as though he were alone.

Virgil kept meticulous notes of his progress. He made asterisks beside those foods which Baby most preferred, judging this by what Baby first ate. Bananas, apples, oranges. Fruits were highest on the list. But it was gelatin that Baby loved most, attacking the wiggly food with a gleam in his eye that transcended mere pleasure. These foods Virgil asked Aramenta to bring in greater quantity.

"Must eat balanced diet," Aramenta argued.

"Yes. Agreed. But for snacks."

Begrudgingly Aramenta complied. Virgil used the fruit to do what candy bars had failed to do—entice Baby.

"You want banana?" Virgil offered across the table when Baby finished his own. Baby looked first at the fruit, then Virgil, then the fruit again.

"Here. You have." Virgil placed the banana on Baby's tray. Baby hesitated, glanced at Virgil, then took it.

The next time Virgil offered a favored fruit, then placed it back on his own tray. When Baby did not reach for it, Virgil made a satisfied mental note—Baby knew the difference between mine and yours. Virgil lifted the fruit, an apple, offering it again, smiling. He held it in an open palm until Baby reached, paused, unsure. Virgil extended his hand an inch farther. Baby took the apple and stared at Virgil. Virgil nodded, smiling, making the sign for "apple" and "good."

At the next meal, Virgil pointed to his Jell-O. He could see the indecision in Baby, the almost imperceptible tremor of desire and the conflicting warning of "not mine." Virgil reached slowly across Baby's tray and took his spoon. He saw a temper tantrum about to erupt and put it back. He then used his own spoon, scooping it full of gelatin and extending it. He held it there until his arm ached. He put it back in his tray. After eating all except the Jell-O, he pushed the tray at Baby.

"If you want, take."

Baby wanted it all right, his spoon still in hand, watching Virgil.

"Take it," you yo-yo.

Baby reached out, pulled back as if anticipating punishment, then touched the gelatin with his spoon. Virgil nodded, smiled. He made the sign for "eat."

At Virgil's direction, Aramenta brought one tray heaped with food, the other empty. Virgil placed the empty container before Baby. From his tray he served equal portions. He extended Baby's spoon.

Following meals were served accordingly, but before dishing it out, Virgil would pause, eyebrows lifted, pointing at the food. "You want this? This? You want it?" He would serve everything but the Jell-O, which he kept on his own tray. Baby could barely eat for looking at the gelatin.

"You want this?" Virgil questioned, eating everything except the dessert.

Baby was shaking now, eyes flitting hither and yon, inner turmoil building, conflicts unresolved. Virgil ate with deliberate slowness, face pleasant, asking now and then, "You want some of this?"

Would he fight? Snatch? Run again? Attack? Virgil had brought him to this point over many meals, many days. He had carefully built toward this dinner and he waited now to see if it would succeed or fail. If Baby grabbed and ran, nothing had been accomplished. If Baby screamed, begged, it was at least a step forward from snatch-run.

"You may have this," Virgil said. "But you must ask for it, or reach and take it nicely. I will not give it to you. You want it?" He pointed at the Jell-O, eyebrows arched.

Come on, damn you! You know how to bathe! You know how to do some things! Try learning a bit of grace and charm, you animal! *Ask for it.* Cry and beg, at least. Any-thing!

Virgil ate the last of his food. Baby still sat, eyes glued to the untouched gelatin.

"You must tell me—you want this?" Virgil casually dropped his arm so his hand was next to the Jell-O.

Baby looked up, eyes brimming with tears.

"All you have to do is ask, dumb-dumb. You want the Jell-O, damn you? Ask for it!"

Baby shivered as though chilled, his clean spoon in hand, both fists clenched, eyes blinking. His lips pursed in a tragi-comic expression.

"Baby," Virgil pleaded, "ask. Ask, damn you. Ask for the Jell-O."

Baby reached for his bread, hand quaking, lifted it, put it down. He looked at his tray through tear-blurred eyes, lower lip now hanging loose. He picked up his banana, arms twitching as if suffering muscle spasms. He looked at Virgil, spoon in one hand, banana in the other, held as if both were weapons.

Hesitantly, Baby raised his banana, fingers uncurling, and held it out to Virgil.

Barely able to control himself, Virgil nodded. "Yes," he mouthed. "I don't mind if I do. It's a fair trade."

He put the banana on his tray. He pointed at the gelatin. "Would you like some Jell-O?"

Baby reached over and helped himself, eating from Vir-gil's tray. Numb, Virgil watched

Chapter Twenty-three

"I need scissors, comb," Virgil requested.

"You have comb."

"Yes. I have. Baby has none. I need another."

Aramenta nodded. Then, suspiciously, "Why scissors?"

"To cut hair," Virgil replied, irritably.

"Might hurt."

"Hurt what? Me? Baby? I need it! Get it!"

She studied his face, agreed.

"Basketball."

"What?"

He made a movement denoting the bouncing of a ball, then with both hands pretended to shoot a basket. He fingerspelled slowly, "Basketball."

"Why?"

"Why you argue? Debate everything? Why you do this?" Virgil raged. "I ask for things and you always argue!"

"I must go buy basketball!"

"Then *buy* it," he shouted. Goddamn her! "Buy what I need!"

Later, she delivered the comb and scissors. Neither were new. "I want these returned," she commanded.

"I need them."

"You ask and I give when needed. Return them."

"Give them to me," he said, extending his arm through the bars.

"Return this day," she warned, holding them beyond reach.

"All right!" Fool!

He pulled a chair into the best available light and put the scissors and comb on the table with his typewriter. He expected a physical fight, but he'd made up his mind to cut Baby's hair.

"Cut hair," Virgil said, using his fingers to make a snipping motion around his own head. He had been close to Baby, but had never touched him except in conflict.

Baby approached the chair, looked at the scissors, and sat down.

Done this before, Virgil thought. Like the bath.

Baby sat unmoving as his hair fell around his shoulders onto the floor. Virgil stepped back, winced at the effect, uneven, too close here and there, but at least cut. He circled Baby, clipping whiskers. The scissors pulled and Baby twitched, drew back. Virgil pushed away a lifted hand. "Sorry," he said.

The job done, Baby went into the bathroom and washed his face with hot water. Virgil watched him search the medicine cabinet, pawing through toilet articles. He found Virgil's razor. Then to Virgil's amazement, Baby shook the aerosol can of lather and squirted a handful. Baby smeared his face. Baby proceeded to shave with the expertise of any mature man.

Somebody had taught him these things. Had he forgotten? Or like an elderly man living alone, had Baby merely neglected such things letting them go by so often he seldom thought about it anymore?

The act of dressing came with equal ease. Virgil tossed Baby's underwear, trousers, socks, and shoes on the bed. Without protest, Baby donned the apparel.

Baby brushed his teeth without urging, using Virgil's brush, which thereafter belonged to Baby. Virgil demanded a new one from Aramenta.

"He is brushing teeth," Virgil announced. "He bathes, shaves, and dresses. Now open this door."

"Bring him out with you."

"Open door, he will come out."

"Let me see. Bring him to the door."

But Baby's eyes enlarged. He began to tremble, and when Virgil sought to bring him inside the security doors, Baby tore away, screaming, and ran to the rear of the east wing.

"Needs a mind doctor," Virgil angrily reported.

"No," Aramenta declined, "he is learning now very quickly. You are doing all that is right. Not long now. Keep teaching. You do good. Very good."

Goddamn you! Damn you, dumb— Virgil forced a smile. "I will keep trying." He left her to hide his wrath. Wait, crazy woman. Wait. You open that door someday and you die for this!

The basketball created a response that was fascinating, but perplexing. Virgil took the inflated orb inside and, without warning, tossed it at Baby.

Baby caught sight of the missile and dived clear, screeching. The ball struck the floor, bounced to a wall, and rebounded. Baby shrieked and ran.

"Ball," Virgil mouthed. "Won't hurt you. Ball! Here, see?

Bounces." He batted the ball toward Baby and Baby vaulted aside, terror shaping his face into a howling visage.

What was the cause of this? Virgil retrieved the ball and watched Baby cower as far away as possible. Virgil felt the cries pounding his temples. What image did the ball evoke? Some arcane memory? Something from the dim past?

He stooped, rolling the ball toward Baby, and watched the man high-step away, trying to crawl a wall to avoid contact. As if the ball might sear flesh or—

In that instant, Virgil realized what he faced.

He had read about this. In the months of his last two years of school, and after graduating, he had studied all he could find relating to deafness. To overcome his problems, to know the limits of his own ability, he had devoured every printed word he could uncover. He knew the causes, the psychological implications, the various physical ailments associated with his problem.

Now, watching Baby having a temper tantrum, a creature totally without control of himself, Virgil became aware of what Baby was.

It was something only recently understood, and still not completely so. When Baby was born, for whatever reason, he was deaf—or was he? He *seemed* deaf. Virgil was convinced Baby was, truly, without hearing. He had tried making loud noises when Baby was not looking. Baby was unresponsive unless reverberations clued him to the activity. Asleep, only light or touch awoke Baby. Yes, Baby was deaf. But more.

To test his theory, Virgil retrieved the ball and walked toward Baby. Baby cringed, drawing away, not from Virgil but from the basketball. Virgil put the ball behind himself, holding out a hand.

"Come. Come see. Come. It's all right. Come, Baby."

Baby allowed himself to be cornered and Virgil smiled, touching the man's shoulder, forearm, finally taking a hand.

He pulled gently and Baby jerked away. He began again. He coaxed Baby to the bed, where they both sat.

Gently, slowly, Virgil revealed the ball. Baby touched, snatched away, permitted himself to be forced to touch again, and again, until the fear dispelled. At this point, Virgil placed the ball between them. He pushed it on the bed and it nudged Baby's leg. Instantly, Baby knocked it back, sharply. Virgil repeated the action.

As suddenly as it had erupted, the terror was gone. By the end of the day, Baby was kicking, tossing, hugging the ball. Completely depressed, Virgil sat on the bed, anger and hatred for Aramenta bringing tears to his eyes.

Baby was afraid of new things. Experiences, objects, food, clothing, anything unfamiliar brought dread as a minimum, panic-stricken terror at the extreme. Whether this was a toy, or a strange face, or unknown surroundings, Baby would be subject to mindless screaming and unreasoning fear. It was an emotion born of a mental disorder. It was not harm Baby dreaded, nor was he apprehensive of danger necessarily. It was simply, irrevocably, a fear of the unknown.

"Autism," Virgil had read. With many of the outward symptoms of deafness or mental retardation, the victims until recent years were destined to lifelong confinement in an institution.

The autistic child exhibits screaming tantrums when his routine is altered, or when faced with any sudden change in environment, or if physically restrained. As with many such afflictions, today's child might be helped through an enlightened and intensive program of care and training. But not this poor beast. Baby was thirty years old! The pattern of fear, the childlike and psychotic responses could be beyond help.

Virgil watched Baby making laugh-face, bouncing the ball away, smiling, racing after the globe to kick it against a wall. The ball skittered toward Virgil, and with a fist he socked it back toward Baby.

Baby had not expected that. The ball going away was suddenly returning. It struck Baby on the forehead, snapping back his head. Baby stopped, stunned, and stared at Virgil. Virgil watched the expressionless face slowly return to a smile. Baby ran after the ball, came, and threw it at Virgil.

"All right, Baby," Virgil said. He tossed the ball away. Baby chased after it. "Now I know how to train you. Now I know what must be done."

He rebounded the ball off a fist and Baby shrieked, mouth wide, and turned to follow. A child. In a man's body, this was a child! Truly, this was a *baby*.

Virgil ladled food slowly to the impatient and hungry man. As he spooned, he made the sign for what he served. Apple, beans, potatoes, everything became a sign. When Baby ignored him, Virgil made the sign anyway.

Over several days, Virgil typed a list of every food he could remember. He triple-spaced these. He made a list of the five hundred basic signs needed for rudimentary communication. Henceforth, Baby must earn what he received. If he did not try, Virgil gave a clearly indicated choice: reward or punishment.

"Banana" Virgil signed, holding an imaginary fruit in one hand, making a peeling motion with the other. "Banana!"

Baby waited impatiently for the delicacy.

"Do as I do, damn you!" Virgil snatched Baby's chin around to face him.

"Do this, Virgil! Make sounds. Watch my lips. Put your hand on my throat. Feel that? Feel that move? Ahhhhhhhh. Like that. See my lips? Virgil!" A sudden snatch of his chin that hurt, because his eyes had wandered. "Watch my lips!

You must learn words. Say this, Virgil. Say, Ahhhhhhhhthor. Ahh-thor."

Virgil grabbed Baby's chin as the eyes drifted. "Do this! Like this. This is sign: banana!"

Baby's lower lip hung flaccid, uncomprehending.

"Baby, damn you! Banana! Make the sign. Banana!" He slapped Baby hard and the shock of the unexpected assault made Baby scamper backward, falling. His screams drummed Virgil's facial bones. "Banana! Make this sign: banana!"

Virgil seized Baby's hands, shaping one as if holding fruit, manipulating the other as if peeling it.

"Like that. Banana. Like that, you dumb—"

Whap! Baby recoiled, shrieking, neck muscles corded.

"Do what I do, damn you. Do it. Do it! Banana! Banana!"

At last Baby did.

"Do that again."

Baby repeated the sign.

"Banana," Virgil breathed. "When you want it—that is the sign, banana. Do it."

Baby made the sign, face ugly, discolored, screaming. Virgil handed over the banana. Reward. Punishment. Every little thing must evolve the same way. Years of reward and punishment. Success was hard won, failure lurked around every new corner of experience.

"Apple, Baby." Baby sulked, nose running. "Apple." Damn your sorry time. Do the sign. "Apple."

Virgil pressed the knuckle of an index finger into his own cheek and twisted. "Like that. Apple. Do it, Baby, damn you, do it! Apple. Do what I do."

Perspiration poured from their bodies. Each meal became a dreaded confrontation, Virgil teaching signs, Baby balking, finally learning, slowly doing, then receiving. More often than not, Virgil completed the chore and fell on the bed, staring up at the overhead light, panting, exhausted, too tense to eat.

The means for success came from examining himself as he had been during the first years of learning. Virgil tried to recapture the sensations, heartaches, and joys, the now vague images of what had once pleased and displeased him. He tried to imagine how Baby's mind constructed thoughts, reached decisions, and remembering how he himself had been before he learned words and signs, he eased the way for Baby and himself.

Touch was, as Virgil remembered, a treasured experience. Not always pleasurable, but always effective: fingers crawling under his palm in a dark theater, a touch of an elbow as he sat with Marie in a swing. His most pleasant childhood memories were built around bedtime—snuggling under fresh, sweetly clean sheets, the slowly accumulating warmth of his own body, his breath curling back into his face. Then Papa, or Mama, would come and tug the sheet and blanket slightly, reshaping it more nearly to the contours of Virgil's form, and once in a while, dearly, they would pause at bedside to pat his bottom, firm, loving touches that drove out demons and relaxed the mind.

Virgil crossed the room in the dark, feeling for Baby. When he touched flesh, Baby trembled, pulling away. Virgil rearranged the covers, smoothed them, tucked the sheet around Baby's shoulders. He put a hand on Baby's upper arm and with his other hand pat-pat-patted. He felt muscles giving, the tremor subsiding. Pat-pat-pat-pat— A long-drawn breath which flowed into a yawn escaped with a shudder that seemed to cast off the final knotted fibers of the body. Even breathing now, slowly inhaled, slowly exhaled. Pat-pat-pat— Baby squirmed into a more comfortable position. Pat-pat-pat-pat—

It was, thereafter, a part of going to sleep. Virgil tucked Baby in, caressed him, comforted, salving the hurts from the day of assaults and signs. He came to await that moment of complete relaxation when Baby's body throbbed with the rhythm of snoring, all anxieties gone, all cares aside, worries vanquished, sleeping like an infant.

"What is happening?" Aramenta questioned, serving cookies and orange juice along with coffee.

"Nothing."

She pushed the cookies near the bars. "You do not seem unhappy about this nothing."

He shrugged. "What can I do about it?"

"Stop lying for one thing."

"Lie?"

"Yes. Lie. I know you are both playing, I hear you. The ball bounces against the wall. I can hear this. I hear Baby laugh, too."

Mildly surprised, Virgil resisted the impulse to ask how the laughter sounded—odd, twisted, natural, pleasing or not?

"I play some."

"With Baby. Virgil, why are you lying about this? You are making great progress. I know this. I do not know why you would lie to me about it."

"More coffee?" Virgil extended his cup.

"I am proud of you," Aramenta's lips read. "What you are doing is a wonderful thing." He missed some of the next words as she turned to get sugar and cream.

"Since progress is so great," Virgil bargained, "let me out now."

"No. When you can bring Baby to the door without having to hold him, then I will open the door. We will take him to a doctor. They will continue what you began."

When those doors swung open and he saw Aramenta on

the steps, Baby would—what? There was no way to predict. Huddle next to Virgil, possibly, run back inside, probably, but the new experience, strange face—Baby could not be depended upon.

Virgil did not tell Aramenta his conclusions. Nor did he mention the signs. For what? If she asked to see, Baby might revert to insane screaming. Virgil masked his feelings, his seething thoughts. He had a plan now. One that would work. The doors would open, and when they did—

"Is there anything in particular you'd like for dinner?" Aramenta asked.

"Tacos."

"Tacos? Virgil, I don't know anything about tacos!"

He arose, stretching. "That is what I want." He turned his back, cutting off her communication. Ignoring her tapping for attention, he walked back into the cellar, where Baby was playing with the basketball.

Virgil wrote long letters to Marie. Endless pages describing his hatred and secret hope of killing Aramenta Lee. He told Marie about Baby, how he had learned, and now, after so many weeks, Baby had begun making a few hesitant signs voluntarily when he wanted something.

Aramenta asked to read what Virgil wrote and he refused. She offered to edit his work, and he shook his head. No, he would not fall for that again. Aramenta had used his writing as her excuse, her sly oral way to squeeze into his mind and life. She had set him up to hurt him, to use him for her own purpose.

She lied, saying she had not planned this. The cellar was too well constructed, too carefully designed—no, he knew better than that. She must have been thinking about it for weeks. He had no doubt, too, that she would keep him imprisoned for years if in her demented mind he did not meet her standards for Baby.

Each morning when Virgil awoke, his first thought was of killing Aramenta, each night it was his final conscious consideration before sleep. He dreamed of outwitting her, somehow tricking her into opening the doors and reversing their roles—she the prisoner and Virgil the jailer. He would cut off the lights and leave her to descend to the very pit of her madness. He would serve her salty food and cut off the water. He would drive the heat to unbearable limits by eliminating the exhaust fan and blocking the doors. Oh, yes, Aramenta would pay dearly. Her time was coming.

But then he thought about the money. The twenty thousand dollars. He knew it would never happen. A woman crazy enough to lock him away—she would be too crazy to deliver on her promise. But if she did, if it happened, if he truly *had* twenty thousand dollars—

Always his mind came back to the pain he would bring her, the punishment which would be hers. He began exercising, knee bends, touch floor, jumping jacks, keeping himself fit for that one instant when freedom beckoned and he could turn the tables on Aramenta.

If he could, he would lock her in here with this lunatic son of hers. Then she would see what it was like. She would know the loneliness, the fear, the depression that smothered the mind and sapped the body. She would scream as loud as Baby then—two of them shrieking, crying, begging. Aramenta, the madwoman, and Baby, the dumb lunatic.

Only he wasn't truly dumb. Virgil had come to realize this. Baby did things that surprised. Learning to dribble the basketball by watching Virgil. And the shaving. Virgil was sure that Baby had had a straight razor before. But observing Virgil, Baby had seen the how, not only of Virgil's safety razor, but the pressurized can of face lather as well.

Each day, Virgil went down his list of signs checking them off. Baby made many of these without the slightest comprehension of what the gesture meant. But it kept him sharp on "do as I do," which was the method Virgil employed.

"Love," Virgil motioned, hands cupped over the heart. Baby did this. "Like," Virgil mimed, bringing thumb and middle finger together and pulling away from the chest as though drawing out a string from a button. Baby made the sign, "like."

How many years would it take before meaningless signs were matched to significant emotions or thoughts? It was not like teaching the names of objects. Now Baby could sign any food, name a preference for water, milk, or juice. *Things,* Virgil recalled from childhood, came easy. Emotions and abstracts eluded the student. Baby signed "love" but had no idea why.

"Kill," Virgil signed, shoving a pointed finger under the palm of his other hand.

"Kill," Baby did by rote.

"Kill," Virgil repeated.

"Kill," Baby mimed.

"Kill the bitch."

Baby faltered, lost.

"Kill your mother."

Baby fumbled, fretting, fearing punishment for his failure. Seeing Virgil's expression, Baby shrank, one arm lifted to fend the anticipated blows.

Kill her. She pay for this. Money. Hurt. Baby's mother wish she never had such a baby. Baby's mother pay!

Chapter Twenty-four

Alec Smith sat with legs crossed, one foot jiggling nervously. His heavy framed glasses slipped to the tip of a large nose crisscrossed with broken blood vessels. He used an index finger to push up the spectacles as he continued:

"According to the IRS, Mrs. Arlington Edward Lee filed returns for the past seven years showing a net income of under fifteen thousand annually. The returns were processed by this firm, signed by your father, and the source was dividends from Marine Guaranty Bank stock, Axiom Insurance preferred stocks, and various smaller holdings."

"This doesn't make a bit of sense," William snapped.

Alec lifted a hand signaling for patience. "I traced the Marine Guaranty stock and the Axiom Insurance stock. According to the records, Mrs. Arlington Edward Lee owns 685 shares in Marine Guaranty, 6,000 shares in Axiom. Very meager, very modest."

"Where the hell did her other stocks go?"

Alec pushed up his eyeglasses, shrugging. "I don't know, but she doesn't own them now."

"That's impossible!" Randy stormed. "The list of assets in her file shows holdings of sixty thousand shares in Marine Guaranty, 180,000 shares of Axiom."

"That list is obviously out of date," Chad Mathis noted.

"Then what happened to them?" Randy demanded.

"She transferred them, apparently," Chad said. "Marine Guaranty's list of preferred stock holders shows the largest single shareholder to be one James Darcy."

"You mean, Mrs. Darcy."

"No, I mean *James* Darcy," Chad corrected.

"That's her deceased husband—Aramenta's husband. He was killed in 1945."

"That's what puzzles me," Chad grunted. "The stocks were transferred to James Darcy over ten years, beginning in 1958."

"What!" Randy circled the conference table to look at the list.

"Why the hell would she give stocks to a dead man?" William questioned. "If she did, were they properly recorded and taxed at the time?"

"I wouldn't know," Chad said. "I have no record of that."

"Jesus!" William threw up his hands. "Can you imagine trying to straighten this out? What does IRS say?"

"They don't say," Alec said. "They watch and wait."

"All right." William swiveled his chair. "Randall, this mess is yours. Obviously something is wrong. Now we can spend a bloody fortune running down assets, checking titles, and for what? For that idiot woman out there! I suggest you get in your little red wagon and scoot out to see this lady. Tell her what a screwball conglomeration this has become. If we have to do all the research involved, it is going to cost her an arm and a leg. If she wants to make it easy on you, us, and herself, she'd better get her ass down here and cooperate. Tell her, Randall, in no uncertain terms."

"I'll try."

"Randall," William's voice dropped, "I'm about ready to wash my hands of this nonsense. Are we all agreed?" He addressed Chad and Alec. The two attorneys nodded.

"I'll see what I can do."

Sure, they were ready to wash their hands. William had seen Aramenta was firmly in Randy's pocket and he knew his various connivances were doomed to failure. Why not wash their hands of it? Randy drove into the driveway of Aramenta's home, pulled around back, and parked. He was filled with an admixture of elation, for having won the war, and trepidation, because things weren't adding up. There had to be an explanation, but what?

"Aramenta!" He stood at the open back door, leaning in. "Yo, Aramenta!" Randy stepped inside.

Thump-thump-thump.

"Aramenta, are you home?"

Thump-thump-thump.

He walked through the kitchen, dining room, and into the hall. Thump-thump-thump—coming from the basement? For all the world it sounded like a kid bouncing a ball against a wall! Randy opened the basement door. The lights were burning.

"Aramenta, are you down here?"

"Who is it?" Distantly, alarmed.

"Randy, Aramenta! Where are you?"

She emerged from the wine cellar steps, almost running. "What do you want?" she yelled.

"I was looking for you—"

"Go back upstairs, please."

Randy laughed nervously. "Okay. What's going on?"

She was practically pushing, crowding behind, her hands on the railing. "Please go back upstairs. Randy, I don't appreciate you coming in without knocking."

"I knocked, Aramenta. I came to the rear door and called."

She was locking the basement door. *What the hell?* Thump-thump-thump-thump.

"What's that noise. Aramenta?"

"Let's go into the kitchen, please." Her expression suggested he had caught her in a den of iniquity.

"Aramenta, is somebody down there?"

She wheeled angrily. "Hereafter, if I do not respond to the door, whether I'm here or not, I would appreciate respect for my private property."

"That's clear enough," Randy said, face burning.

"I should hope so."

"I'm sorry, Aramenta. I didn't think. It was thoughtless. I guess, wandering in and out all these months, I momentarily forgot that this is, after all, your home."

She turned and walked into the kitchen. Thump-thump-thump.

"Aramenta, what makes that noise? I've heard it before."

"Plumbing."

"Plumbing? You once told me it was a dog. Don't I recall you telling me it was—"

"Randy, what do you want with me?" She was boiling.

He studied her anger, smiled to disarm her. "Don't I get an offer of coffee? Or am I that far out of favor?"

"I really don't have time today. What did you want, please?"

"I need to talk to you, Aramenta."

"Business?" she questioned, coldly.

"I'm afraid so."

"Go away, Randy. I am weary of telling you I do not wish to discuss the matter."

"Aramenta, I don't understand this."

"After telling you two dozen times, I don't understand either! You do wish to represent me, don't you?"

"I do. You know that."

"Then, damn it, how many times must I make my wishes known? I do not—repeat: do *not* want to worry with it."

Randy put down rising anger. "Aramenta, this estate is so tangled it may take years to sort it out. The IRS could freeze the assets, bank accounts, cash flow, everything, tomorrow! They could subpoena you into court to make you face your responsibility. Now frankly, I'm at my wit's end. My brother and my partners are equally as fed up. You want honesty? Here it is, Aramenta: either you give us assistance with this estate and the questions we have, or seek new representation. We cannot handle this without your cooperation."

He detected a momentary weakening. She stared past him a second, then stiffened. "Very well, Randy."

He waited for more. He said, "Very well, what, Aramenta?"

"I shall find a new attorney."

"You mean that?"

"Unfortunately. I'll call Bruce Matthew and have him meet with you. Perhaps he can manage without bothering me with minor details."

Breathless, Randy said, "Aramenta, he can't do it. Matthew will have to do what we are having to do—chase down every asset, verify it, evaluate it, a fortune being spent needlessly perhaps!"

"I shall conclude this discussion with a single question, Randy. Can you, or can you not, handle this estate?"

"As well as anybody anywhere, but—"

"Alone! Without my participation. Can you?"

"I can only make the effort, Aramenta. I can't assure you that you won't have spent the bulk of whatever your fortune may be, after taxes—"

"Good."

"Good? God! Aramenta, what the hell is happening to you?"

"I am busy!"

"Busy?"

"Yes. Have we concluded now?"

Randy ground his teeth together, muscles jutting at the jaws. He left without another word.

"She refuses?" William said.

"Adamantly and completely."

"Randall, what goes with this woman?"

"I don't know."

"You explained about the stocks?"

"I tried."

William gazed into space. "Is she legally competent?"

"I'm not a psychiatrist—"

"No, but are you a judge of human behavior? Is the woman imbalanced or not? Your estimation, Randall! Is she?"

Randy felt Alec and Chad watching him. He looked out William's office window, stalling, thinking. Was she?

"Well?" William thundered.

"I'm not sure."

"What did you say? Speak up, damn it!"

Randy turned to face them. "I said, I am not sure."

William threw his pencil on the desk and it bounced away. "Shit!" he whispered. "I don't have time for all this. I have other accounts—sane accounts!"

Alec rose, gathering his reports. "I'll leave these on your desk, Randall."

Chad walked out without comment. William stared at Randy, anger easing, flesh tone more normal. He broke into a smile as though they shared a private unspoken joke. Then he began laughing softly.

"What is it, William?" Randy asked, peevishly.

"I was thinking, little brother. How funny it would be, if after all this, you control naught. Zero!"

Randy walked to the door and turned. "About as funny as it would be—if I controlled thirty million dollars, I suppose."

He left William chuckling and closed the door harder than he intended.

Aramenta gave the envelope to Virgil. She saw his first burst of excitement sour. He looked up accusingly.

"You open my mail."

"Yes."

"Why?"

"To see what she said."

"Not right to do this!" Virgil signed, short, angry gestures. Then, face livid, Virgil questioned, "You mail my letter?"

"No." Calmly.

"Why? Damn you!"

"You are smart," Aramenta replied evenly, "you know why."

"Dirty damn woman!"

"I said I'd give you your mail," Aramenta said. "Now you have it."

"Open!"

"Yes, opened."

"You say you mail my letter and not do it!"

"Not until you write a letter that is sensible." She spoke this.

"What? Sign! I cannot read lips!"

Aramenta came down another step so he could better see her face. "Be smart. Write nice letter. This I mail. No other."

"Hate you!" Virgil seethed.

"That is too bad. Are you going to read the letter, or are we going to argue?" Aramenta asked. "If each letter makes us fight, you get no more mail. You want a letter mailed, write a letter I can mail—no talk about where you are!"

Virgil stomped out of the passageway screaming. Baby stood around the corner waiting. Virgil knocked him aside. The basketball Baby had held went bouncing away.

He threw himself on the bed, raging, venting his wrath with periodic shouts of vulgarities. He pulled the single, typed piece of paper from the envelope. So short! He read it once, quickly, again more slowly.

Dear Virgil:

Why not answers? Why do this me? You have girlfriend Mobile? Hurt think about. Cry sleep. Alonely self. Why? Love for you. Many time tell you. If you not love I wish ded. God hate deaf. Oral hate deaf. Ma Pa hate. Die from this. Be lone. Hurt me. Please say. Love. No love me. Please say. No talk boy here. Never! I never do wrong. Because love you. Please. Please love. Say this. Say come to you. Say. Please. Love,

Marie.

Virgil went to his typewriter, sat, shaking with hatred and anger. Many letters he had written. Many times Aramenta had not mailed them! "No talk of basement," she declared. He struck this. "No talk of 'wish you here' and 'come see me,' " she censored. He struck this. "Cannot write about Baby!" she said. Damn her! Cannot this, that—what then? Virgil put paper into the carriage, adjusted it.

He had tried tricking Aramenta, writing Marie that he met an old friend—naming someone Marie never knew. "Take this out," Aramenta demanded. In another effort, Virgil mentioned casually the time he and Marie went to Atlanta, where neither had ever been. Aramenta saw through that.

"You keep be foolish," she warned, "I stop trying to do this for you. No letters mailed no matter what letters say!"

His fingers trembled, poised over the keyboard. He had many long unsubmitted letters to Marie—diatribes releasing the pent emotions, letters he never gave to Aramenta, knowing she would only tear them into shreds. Besides, he did not want her to know his plan. Now Marie, suspecting he had met another girl, was waiting, anguished, afraid she was losing him.

Dear Marie:
Please do not think I have another girlfriend. I do not. I love you. I never go with another woman. I think about you every day. I know what a friend you are—more and more I know this. It is your love which keeps me strong. In my dreams at night we have a home, good jobs, and we are making a family. I want to hold you, kiss you. I am sorry you are so lonely. I too am lonely. But it won't be long, perhaps, before we can be together always. I pray to God for this. Give my love to your mother, Ilene, and your father, Ralph. Know that I love you. Do not worry! Soon I will see you.

He banged the wooden support summoning Aramenta, then waited at the passageway. When she appeared, he thrust the letter at her. "Okay?" he questioned. She studied it.

"No."

"What wrong with that?" Goddamn you! Crazy woman! Bitch!

She went upstairs and returned with certain lines deleted. Virgil snatched the letter from her hands and stifled a sob— she had caught every trap. He nodded, sobbing. "I do this, you mail? Promise?"

"Yes. Type it and give it back. Have you an envelope?"

"Yes." He walked back to the typewriter and composed anew:

Dear Marie:

I love you. I think about you every day. I know what a friend you are, more and more I know this. It is your love which keeps me strong. In my dreams at night we have a home, jobs, family. I want to hold you, kiss you. I am sorry you are so lonely. But it won't be long, perhaps, before we can be together always. I pray to God for this. Know that I love you. Do not worry! Love,

Virgil

He rapped the timber that would bring Aramenta, but she was already waiting for him when he reached the exit. He gave her the edited note. She read it several times, studying every word. Without smiling she nodded.

"You will mail?"

"Yes."

"Swear this to me."

"I said I would. I will."

"When?"

"Today."

"What is today?"

She smiled without reply, and left him clutching the bars of the door. November, December, January? Virgil stared through the bars choking back sobs.

The floor thumped steadily, Baby dribbling the ball like an automaton. Once learned, he seemed to dwell on a given activity with mindless repetition. Virgil watched, sullen, depressed, as Baby artfully bounced the ball hundreds of times without losing it once. Now and then the lingering smile on his face erupted into laughter for a reason Virgil could not fathom.

It had taken weeks to teach the five hundred basic signs, most repeated without recognition of meaning. From this to the alphabet, Virgil had slapped, demanded, slapped again, and finally rewarded Baby for forming the letters with one hand. Dumb! Stupid! Hands flickering rapidly, Baby could now race from A to Z in seconds. No comprehension, just rote. Then, surprising Virgil as Baby sometimes did, he switched from one hand to the other in midalphabet, completing the run of signs without hesitation. Ambidextrous. Like bouncing the ball—Baby had the ability once the wall of his disturbed mind allowed the information to enter and be assigned muscles needed to perform a task.

Virgil had seen men and women of low intelligence perform similar functions on assembly lines—monotonous, machinelike steps repeated thousands of times a day. Such people actually performed these dull jobs with greater efficiency than others with more intellectual ability.

When lessons were done, when dinner was over, after Virgil had released Baby from a chore, always it was back to the robot bouncing of the basketball. To alter the action, more for his own relief than Baby's, Virgil taught him how to bounce the ball from wall to floor and back to himself to be struck with an open palm. After only a few abortive efforts, Baby did this, supplanting the hand-to-floor routine Virgil nodded, satisfied. Against the wall, Aramenta could share Virgil's pleasure at the unceasing reverberations!

At dinner, Baby sat across the table, eyes on the food with only quick glances at Virgil for direction.

"Do this," Virgil said, "I love you."

"Iloveyou," fast signs, impatient, eyes on the food.

"You love me," Virgil prodded.

"Youloveme." Baby rocked to and fro.

"My mother loves me."

"Motherloves."

"No!" Virgil swatted a hand creeping toward the fruit. Baby's face twisted, lips pursed, chest indicating a whimpered protest. Virgil repeated, "My mother loves me."

Baby signed, "My mother loves me."

"Say something on your own, dumb-dumb."

"Say something your dumb."

Virgil sighed, dishing food onto Baby's tray.

"Keep your goddamned hands out of the food, Baby." Virgil tapped Baby's spoon. "Use! Spoon. Use!"

Baby picked up the spoon in one fist, eating off his tray with the other hand.

"Dumb animal!" Virgil slapped Baby off his chair. Baby came up, mouth wide, food on his tongue, screaming.

"Pig!" Virgil pointed at the chair. "Sit! You make me sick!"

Baby cringed, screaming, eyes blurred with tears as yet undislodged. Virgil stared at the unswallowed food and threw his napkin on his tray.

"Eat it! To hell with it!" He stood abruptly, his chair thrown backward. He went to the bed and lay down, staring at the wall.

Why lie to himself? He'd been here months. Not one person had come. Not Mama, Papa, the attorney Beausarge. Nobody! They didn't give him a thought. They didn't miss him when he was gone, nor did they want to think of when he returned. Except Marie. Dear, beautiful, poor Marie.

Waiting almost seven years for a groom who ran home to his parents and left her stranded with empty promises.

He had no friend. Except Marie. Deaf, plump, uneducated, couldn't-spell Marie. What kind of wife would she make a writer? She never read!

He remembered a time she came to him, a finger pinned to a line in a paperback novel. "What this?" she asked.

Virgil read the sentence: "She whispered sweet nothings in his ear."

He tried to explain, leaving Marie even more confused. "How do this?" she asked. "Whisper mean speak hush, soft. Sweet, good to taste. Nothing—is *nothing?* She does this in his ear?"

Marie distrusted words. Signs, in the simplicity of gestures, were fast, clear, sharp, unlittered with conflicting synonyms, except rarely.

"Orals be better to sign," she once said. "Say what mean. Orals never say what mean. Never! Mouth say one thing, hands say next thing, eyes say all lies!"

Marie had begged him to marry her the day before leaving school after graduation. "Must suffer," she had reasoned, crying, "do this together!"

Virgil had refused. He wanted to establish himself. He wanted to try writing. He wanted to make something of himself. He had no money, no job, could not afford a wife or family. All this he told Marie. All true, but also lies.

Truly, he deep down thought a secret thing. He thought about all the deafs he knew. Deaf—94 percent of them—marry deaf. Two deafs do not always make babies deaf. But always, their circle of acquaintances become concentric, shrinking until finally their world revolves around only signers, less and less orals, ultimately themselves alone. Virgil feared this. He had to try—had to make the effort—to be among orals, to be as they were. Writing would make this possible if he could succeed. If his printed words were pruned, trimmed, and polished, who could tell by reading that he was deaf and mute? One book—some made millions! He'd read that. If it took a lifetime, would it not be worth that day when his books went around the world and he was, to the readers, as oral and hearing as they themselves?

How could he tell this to Marie, who truly did not understand how a lover put sweet, hushed words, which were nothing, into a person's ear? It was like their effort at sex, the day after graduation. Marie had dressed, completely unashamed, face perplexed.

"Why people do this?" she had asked. "Not comfortable. Not feel good. Why then?"

Yes. Why indeed? Virgil had returned home, wasted himself for years, come to Mobile, and now—this dungeon. He rolled over, and slowly his thoughts were penetrated by what he saw. Baby sat at the table, a spoon in one hand, jaw slack, staring at him.

"Eat," Virgil gestured, impatiently.

The spoon hand fluttered, fell back to Baby's lap. They stared into each other's eyes. Baby's facial muscles sagged, body worn from ball bouncing all day. Virgil suffered a surge of remorse, shame for releasing his frustration on this demented animal. He sat up, sighed, looking at Baby. He forced a smile. He pushed a cupped hand to his mouth several times, signing, "Eat, eat!"

Baby turned to his tray. He dipped a spoon of Jell-O and held it out to Virgil, face blank.

A move to ease anger? Goodwill regained? Enticement to come back and eat too? Baby had never shared Jell-O for any reason! Not even to trade. Nothing was more favored than the gelatin.

Virgil went to the table. He allowed Baby to place the spoon into his open mouth. Virgil swallowed, smiled.

"Good," he signed. "Thank you." Baby spooned more. Confused, Virgil again let himself be fed. "Good. Thank you, Baby."

When the last of the gelatin was gone, Baby let his spoon hand fall to his lap again, mouth agape, staring at Virgil.

"You," Virgil pointed, "very good boy. Very good. This was good what you did. Good boy. I thank you for this."

Baby watched, face denoting nothing.

Chapter Twenty-five

Virgil clipped Baby's fingernails, toenails, and using a razor, trimmed the disastrous head of hair. When the time came, they would need to look presentable. Virgil stood back, examining the hair and nodded. "You beautiful," he signed. "Go see yourself in the mirror."

Baby arose and went into the bathroom. Virgil was sweeping up hair when it struck him—*Baby did it!* He had voluntarily done what he'd been told! Virgil stared at Baby, now standing before the medicine-cabinet mirror, looking at himself.

Trembling with excitement, Virgil patted his foot. Baby turned.

"Do you understand me?"

No response.

"You understand what I say now?"

Baby's mouth hung open, stupidly. Had it been a chance reaction? Like a dog which seems to follow a nonchalant human command?

"Come," Virgil signed. Baby came from the toilet, stopped before Virgil. "Like haircut?"

Nothing. Eyes without expression. Baby seemed to await further instruction. Virgil continued sweeping hair. He put this in a sack for delivery to the exit and removal.

Each time he thought he was making progress, something would happen to destroy Virgil's confidence. Baby would have a temper tantrum, rolling on the floor screaming, slapping himself. Or he would purse his lips, huffing, stomping his feet in an infantile expression of frustration. One moment Baby would perform an adult function such as shaving, the next instant he would squat in the center of the room, oblivious to Virgil, rocking from side to side.

Virgil completed sweeping and thrust the sack at Baby. "Put this at the door," he ordered. Baby took the sack, unmoving.

"Take it to the door," Virgil instructed. He busied himself, pretending to ignore the man. Baby held the sack, jaw dropping, seemingly incapable of translating the dictate. Or purposely ignoring it!

Virgil wheeled, abruptly, snatched away the sack, and with his other hand knocked Baby to the floor. "Dumb! You could do this if you would. You don't fool me! You can, but won't!"

Baby shrieked, sliding backward on his buttocks. Virgil kicked at him. "I tell you to do something, why don't you do it? I talk with you—why don't you answer me?"

Baby's mouth opened wider as Virgil advanced, following, kicking at the milk-white thin legs, the man's hips. "Damn you! Damn you!" Virgil screamed. Baby reached the wall, blocked, tears streaming, arms raised to ward off blows. Teeth bared, Virgil stood over the miserable, sniveling, screeching—

I'm sorry, Virgil! Forgive Mama, poor baby. I'm sorry!

Oh, God, what's wrong with me? Virgil, baby, don't cry, let Mama wipe your face. I'm so sorry. Mama is—what is happening to us! Oh, dear God, what am I doing to this child?

Virgil sank to his knees. He touched Baby's face with one hand. Baby's eyes, uncertain, frightened, confused—body shivering with dread, knees drawn up defensively. Virgil pushed a strand of cut hair from Baby's shoulder. "I'm sorry," Virgil mouthed. A knot was twisting Virgil's stomach. "I'm sorry, Baby," he said. He pulled the frail body nearer. "I'm sorry, Baby." He hugged the crying man so tightly that he felt Baby gasp for breath. "Forgive me, please, I'm sorry."

Virgil remembered reading, the autistic child was "psychologically unborn." The psychiatrists were not absolutely sure why, but they had learned that autism involved a mental barrier which somehow excluded everything and everybody around them. During the critical first year following birth, the parental reaction was "He doesn't like to be held, leave him alone. He's different! Let him be."

It was the totally wrong thing to do. Baby's mind, for some unknown reason, would not permit the accumulation of touch, love, and comforting motions which some doctors called "stroking." Without such strokes, the infant does not develop. He is, for all practical purposes, "psychologically unborn."

This cellar then was a womb. Virgil the instrument by which "birth" would occur; Baby was an unborn personality in an adult body. He *could not* develop, without the stroking. It was, Virgil became convinced, the crucial single ingredient missing when someone had first attempted to teach Baby how to shave, bathe, dress himself—learned responses only, which became those of a machine.

To penetrate the mysterious wall the mind of the autistic

child suffers, physical force, physical punishment was necessary. But equally as important, if not more so, the emerging psyche sought, craved, demanded *stroking!*

Virgil held the weeping man, Baby's tears falling on Virgil's shoulder. He made gentle swaying motions, patting, consoling, his chest vibrant with love sounds. He remembered his own preverbal days of confusion when Papa would take Virgil on his lap, Virgil's head on the man's chest. Papa talked, crooned, making sounds which Virgil's ears could not hear, but which he felt in the barrel of Papa's chest—the soothing, comforting hum-sounds which lulled Virgil, eased the pain of a scraped knee or a smashed finger. Love-hums, Virgil thought of them, even before he knew the words "love" or "hum."

Now, holding Baby, stroking away the tears, Virgil subdued the racking sobs of this lonely, muddled being. Virgil rocked him, crooning. He fought down his own bitter shame, his aching realization that he, Virgil, had just felt what Mama must have felt at such moments. Poor Mama—helpless, disappointed, hating herself as Virgil this instant hated himself. Frustration and disillusionment boiling over in misdirected anger and abuse—poor Mama.

Holding Baby, Virgil made love-hums. Rocking Baby, hugging him, Virgil too cried tears. For Baby. For Mama. For himself.

The temperature of the room seldom varied more than a few degrees. Physical activity brought perspiration, but when Virgil sat down to rest, the chill crept into his bones. Sleeping comfortably required blankets. Sometimes he went to bed only after making sure he and Baby wore socks to protect their extremities. Lately, moisture had accumulated in the cellar.

He tossed, restless, angry that he must endure this discomfort. He got up and in the dark made his way to Baby's bed, checking to be sure he had provided enough cover. Baby too was awake. Virgil massaged Baby's shoulders, urged him onto his stomach, and rubbed the man's back through the blankets. He ceased only when he was shivering, arms tired. Still Baby was awake. Virgil gave a final squeeze to Baby's shoulders and went back to his own bed. He was freezing! Damn Aramenta. Virgil curled, holding his feet with both hands to warm them. He considered a hot bath. Probably give him a cold, as cool as it was down here. He sighed heavily, resigned, resentful, and tried to put all thoughts from his mind so sleep would come.

Something touched the bed. He lay unmoving. Rats? There'd been no evidence of rodents since he put out poison long ago. Imagination? Something tugged the cover and Virgil turned quickly.

Baby was silhouetted against the distant faint illumination from the passageway doors. He was near enough that Virgil could reach him. He touched Baby's arm. Baby came closer. Taking Baby's hand, Virgil signed into it, "What?"

No response. Virgil touched Baby's face, shoulder. Again he signed into Baby's hand, "What?"

Baby pressed nearer, shivering. Damn that woman! They needed more blankets! Virgil lifted the covers, tugging Baby's arm. Immediately, Baby slipped into bed, huddling close, chilled hands and feet against Virgil's body. Virgil held him, gently massaging Baby's back.

Virgil awoke with the lights. He crawled over Baby and out of bed. Baby always slept later, but this morning he squinted at Virgil dressing, shivering. Virgil went into the bathroom and brushed his teeth, washed his face and hands, combed his hair. He walked toward the passageway as Baby snuggled back under the blankets, blocking light with covers over his head.

"Good morning!" Aramenta had coffee, grapefruit halves, toast, and marmalade. She served from a tray, pleasant.

"We cold last night. Need more blankets."

"All right. I'm sorry. I'll get them this morning."

"You mail my letter?"

"I did."

"No reply?"

"No."

Wrath against his captor was always scarcely beneath the surface. The sight of her made Virgil's belly knot, facial muscles tense, hatred boiling anew.

"How long since you mail the letter?" he demanded.

"I forget."

"One week? Two weeks?" He could not begin to guess himself. Time blended into an endless montage of seconds like minutes and hours like days. He held out his hands, palms down.

"I am becoming sick," he said. "See my hands? They shake like this all time."

Aramenta nodded, still pleasant.

"See bones?" Virgil pulled back his sleeve. "I am losing weight!"

"Then you must complete your work, get out of here," Aramenta suggested, mildly.

"I have done all I can with Baby. He needs doctor now. This is true. He cannot go longer without a doctor to help him."

"I think you are doing fine. But if you can get him here, show me he will walk out, I will open the door. Be happy to open door! Bring him. Do this now."

"He will not come," Virgil said, irately. "He has mind problem! He is afraid of all things new."

"When he will come to the door, I will open it."

"Open and go back from door," Virgil argued. "Then he will come out."

"I need him to walk out of there ready for more training. Don't you understand? He is doing fine, I know this. I watch from above sometimes. But he must come out and stay out. Do this. I open door then."

Virgil held the warm cup with both hands, absorbing heat from the beverage. "You love this baby?" he asked.

"I want to."

"Not truly. You love this baby, go call doctor. Bring help. Baby needs this now. Not dumb. Sick. Mind sick! Needs help."

"You are helping him," Aramenta noted, giving Virgil the grapefruit half. He had to turn it sideways to slip it between the bars. Juice dripped as he did it. Damn bitch!

Calmly Virgil said, "We not feel good last day."

"What's wrong?"

"Stomach pain. Both us. Baby, me."

"I'll get some medicine." She could not veil the concern in her eyes despite the vague smile of cheer. "Are you"—fingerspelling—"constipated?"

"No."

She chewed her lip a second. More spelling, "Diarrhea?"

"No."

"What then? What feels like?"

"Hurt," Virgil signed sharply, indicating the center of his stomach. "Vomit. Baby, me. Both vomit."

"Something you ate, maybe?"

"I don't know."

He could see her mentally listing the foods they had been served the past few days.

"Too much beans," she concluded. "I'll get some fresh fruits. Would Baby take aspirin?"

"Possibly will. Chew, like the vitamins."

Aramenta winced. "Chews the vitamins?"

"Does not seem to care. Taste bad. But he does."

Aramenta's eyebrows lifted and she nodded. "More coffee?"

Virgil had been plotting for weeks. His plan revolved around a ruse which, with a single sound, could be doomed to failure. He practiced with Baby, retreating into a certain corner of the east wing. Here in the shadows, Aramenta had no way of seeing them from above. It was the largest blind spot in the cellar.

For all of an entire day, Virgil would keep Baby there. Keenly alert to sound Baby might be making, Virgil had considered various alternatives—tying Baby so he could not move, even gagging him so he would not scream. But a whimper, a thud, how far did such sounds carry? Aramenta would know it was a trick if she heard a thump, a heavy sigh. Virgil had no way of knowing if these things were being produced by Baby. He could not know if other sounds existed in the room which might cover any noise of their making.

He had become convinced his only hope lay in tricking Aramenta so that she would come inside the cellar. If she came as far as the sleeping area, Virgil could run from the depths of the east wing, overtake her, and arrive first at the doors. There at last, he would escape. This, too, he practiced with Baby.

At a given moment, without notice, Virgil would leap up, race the length of the wing, turn, and dash for the locked doors. Throughout, he urged Baby to follow closely. After several faulty starts, many failures, Baby did this. If Virgil bolted for a far point, Baby jumped like a startled gazelle, close behind.

Impelled by this mindless reaction, Baby might conceivably follow Virgil to the exit, through the doors, up the steps, and out of the basement to freedom!

To the most minute detail, Virgil planned. He set aside clothing, a meager stock of food, invented ways to keep Baby quiet, occupied, and so contented that no sound would escape Baby's lips. It would become, ultimately, a test of Virgil's physical endurance. He must not only placate Baby through the hours of lights on, he must also stay awake nights with a hand on Baby's chest, alert to any sign of snoring.

How long would it take? A day surely, two probably, possibly three, four, even a week. Aramenta would be afraid. Justifiably so. They might be lurking around a corner, waiting. Possibly to attack her. To break for freedom, certainly. Virgil tried to think as Aramenta would. She would not be lured easily. She would have to be very sure something was truly wrong.

He must have something to precipitate action, to drive her mind frantic with worry. He had to provide her with evidence of danger, illness, and death. It must build slowly. Thus he had told her this morning that he and Baby were slightly ill.

He would damage the toilet so it would not flush. For several days they would use this, the stench would become horrible. He would make it worse by clogging the ventilator. He would put catsup in the tub, from above that would appear to be blood. He would remove the mattresses from the springs and put them in the corner where he and Baby must remain throughout. But over the springs, Baby's and Virgil's, he would form all their clothing bundled into a human shape, and cover this with a single blanket. From the light receptacles above, hopefully, to Aramenta it would seem two figures lay abed, unmoving—dead.

Virgil unraveled the strands of a large towel. He spent days stretching, shaping, soaking, and rolling the kinky material until he had a string which would go from the inner door, down the main room, around the corner all the way to the end of the east wing. He tested this. Tying the string to the door, the other end to his finger or toe. If Aramenta opened the door, he would feel it, dark or light, day or night.

Virgil deduced, there were two weak points in the plan. Food and sounds Virgil did not know existed. If Baby sighed, moaned, chanted, hummed, anything aloud not visible to Virgil's eyes—all would fail. If Baby could not be quietly restrained, convinced to forgo the trays delivered twice daily, all would be lost.

Food to Baby was more than sustenance for the body. Like a creature in a zoo, with the approach of feeding time, Baby began to pace nervously, anxious, anticipating. To ask Baby to leave food was to ask more than the slight discomfort of hunger pangs. To Baby, food transcended the needs of the belly alone. Food was a psychological requirement, a critical acquired symbol and easement.

Virgil hoarded as much fruit as he could, putting it in the clothing wardrobe, where Baby did not know it existed. Anything slow to perish, Virgil saved, hiding it for the moment when he could best begin. But even as he did this, he knew Baby would go for the trays, cry if restrained, whether hungry or not. Baby could not resist. He was a slave to what the food represented—a momentary relief and satisfaction. Like a fat man feeding his soul, not his belly, Baby would defy all commands, risk any punishment for food.

Virgil had considered this, evaluating his alternatives ranging from murder to—what?

When Baby came to get in bed with Virgil, he signaled hope for both of them. At some point in all of this, Baby had gone from the completely selfish creature Virgil had first encountered to caring about someone other than himself. Baby came to Virgil's bed because he was cold. But more, he came to touch another human, seeking warmth deeper than that which would dispel the chill of the room.

For only one thing will a starving man yield his last morsel. In all the animal kingdom, only one thing could overcome the basic biological fight for food and survival. Virgil must conquer Baby's physical and pyschotic need for food with the only weapon at Virgil's disposal: love. For love and love alone, man could be induced to bear anything! Including, if need be, starvation.

And if he failed—

Virgil must consider this. Somehow, for some reason, Baby might move at a critical moment. Aramenta might hear them *breathing!* Failure was a probability, not a possibility. And if they failed—

Aramenta would become aware of all Virgil's elaborate preparations to fool her. She would think of the catsup-blood in the tub, the stink of urine and feces. She would be angry, raging, more insane than ever. If they failed, Virgil could expect nothing less than a skeptical, demented, for-ever-wary jailer. Nothing short of true death would get her to open the doors.

If they failed—Virgil was sure—he would be here for years.

Before going to bed, Virgil rubbed soap under both arms and left it unwashed. He had already fouled the commode. Catsup had been accumulated in the shaving-soap mug in the medicine cabinet. It was time to commence. When lights came on the next day, Virgil was perspiring, feverish, the soap having caused this—a trick he had learned in school to avoid class.

"How do you feel this morning?" Aramenta questioned. He saw by her expression she was more worried than she would like him to know. Virgil sat, perspiring, pale, accepting the coffee with exaggerated trembling of his hands.

"Not good." He smiled. "Baby sick again today. Up all night. Vomit."

"The flu, perhaps," Aramenta suggested. But if she did not have it, how had these isolated men caught a virus?

Virgil nodded, shivering, drinking the coffee. The hot liquid combined with the soap in his armpits brought sweat pouring from his face. As he sat before her his clothing became drenched.

"I'll make soup, bring it down later," Aramenta said.

"Good. Baby may like that. Never have soup."

As Virgil ate breakfast he was keenly aware of Aramenta's eyes, darting, concerned, alert for any clue which would indicate this was only another trick.

It was the same at supper. Virgil served Baby all he would eat, then returned both trays with uneaten food he'd saved. The soup had come and been rejected as though neither could eat it, when, in fact, Baby never saw it.

At lights-on the following day, Baby relieved himself in the filthy commode, expression sour, nose wrinkled. Virgil did the same. This was the last "morning" of normalcy, if his plan worked. Aramenta was waiting with coffee, milk, cereal.

"What is that odor?" she asked.

"Sick. Baby, me. Both sick. All night."

"Your stomachs, still?"

"Yes. Baby still in bed. Need clean sheets. These all wet."

"Wet?" Behind her calm expression, in the depths of her eyes, Virgil saw alarm rising on wooden wings.

"Sweating," Virgil said. He trembled his hands so violently he spilled coffee, came up apologizing profusely.

"It's all right, Virgil. All right! Here, use this napkin. I'll pour more."

Head hung, shaking, face wan and unshaven, Virgil

slumped, sipping the fresh cup, holding it with both hands. Suffer, woman. Worry. Make your heart hurt. Worry until you are sick to your stomach!

The plan had begun.

Chapter Twenty-six

Randy walked the graveled drive, circling the house. Aramenta's rented automobile was in the back, windshield littered with leaves from a huge pecan tree, the tires showing spatters of dust where rain had fallen and the blotches dried. He climbed steps to the rear porch and stopped at the kitchen door.

"Aramenta?"

She sat at the bay window. Randy stepped inside. She gazed at him with eyes which gave no indication of recognition. Randy sat across the table from her. He studied her face, alarmed. She looked ill.

"Aramenta, are you feeling well?"

"Yes," a throaty reply.

"Aramenta, we're running into things on the estate which you need to know about. It's confusing us all."

"Us all, who?"

"Members of the firm. Alec Smith is handling taxes. He thinks we may have filed incomplete returns. There's also some question on the stocks and bonds listed as part of the estate. We believe your mother deeded them away before her death."

"To whom?"

"To James Darcy."

"He's dead."

"I know. But the strange thing is, the transactions appear to have taken place in the late fifties and early sixties."

"I don't know anything about that."

"Aramenta, would you consider coming downtown, spending a day or two with me at the office, going over these things?"

"No."

"The will is up for probate, but it's stalled on these things, Aramenta."

"I don't want to go downtown, I don't want to talk on the telephone with a bunch of idiots. I don't want to go to dinner or the theater. I want to be left alone. Why is everybody bothering me?"

"Who is bothering you?"

"People. Your brother. People who have found my unlisted number somehow. They come to the house trying to sell things. I don't want that."

"Aramenta, bear with me a little longer. The whole mess will smooth out and be over and done with. But this problem with the taxes and the stocks—"

"Can you handle it, goddamn it, can you handle it?"

"I'm doing what I can, Aramenta. But I need your help. Some of these questions may never be resolved, but others you might know. Why would your mother bequeath holdings to your husband? To a man dead fifteen years when she did it?"

"I don't know."

"It is very complicated, don't you see?"

"I don't care." Aramenta stood, face sallow, holding the table for support. "I don't want to hear about all this, Randy. How many times do I have to tell you that?"

Randy heard again William's question, "Is the woman legally competent?" Standing here now, wearing soiled clothing, shaking, fatigued, close to a breakdown, she was not exactly the Rock of Gibraltar.

"Aramenta," Randy held his tone low, soothing, "I'm worried about you."

"Don't worry about me," she countered hoarsely, "worry about the estate! Please—please leave me out of it."

"I don't think we can leave you out of it," Randy counseled. "I'm probating the will, fighting IRS, wrestling with innumerable details, but things aren't stacking up."

"Give it away!" Aramenta shouted. "Donate it all to charity!"

"For what purpose, Aramenta? To regain your anonymity? So you won't have to be involved? You don't know what you're asking. Such a move would turn idle curiosity into instant notoriety. The newspapers would hound you forever! You'd become the freak who gave away a fortune. There are some things you can't run away from in life—money, inherited power and influence, the right of succession. You were born to it, Aramenta. You can do what the Duke of Windsor did, abdicate, but did he ever truly escape?"

"Born to it," she whispered. "Blood tells—"

"As a matter of fact, it does," Randy said, too sharply.

"Damn her."

"Damn who?"

"Goddamn her."

"Your mother?"

"Yes."

"Aramenta, I don't profess to know what made your

mother tick. I told you, I'd never been able to see her. But lady, look at yourself. You are standing here in an empty forty-one-room house. The damned place is cold! You have allowed yourself to withdraw, sucked in your being, holed up here like a hermit. What's wrong here? Are you ill?"

"I don't know. Maybe. Maybe I'm crazy."

"Aramenta." Randy closed his fingers over her hand. Cold, clammy flesh, bony. "Aramenta, sit down and listen to me."

Slowly she sat. He still held her hand.

"Aramenta, this house has had an adverse effect on you. I see you deteriorating everytime I come out here. You are shaking, icy cold, nervous, and hypertense. If you will allow it, I'll put you on a plane to Paris this day."

"No. I can't."

"Why can't you?"

Her lips quivering, tears rose in her eyes.

"Aramenta," he said, tenderly, "let me help you."

"There's nothing you can do."

"Not true. If you allow it, I can help you. Is there some problem I don't know about?"

A tear fell, spattered on the table; with one thin finger, Aramenta smeared it.

"I want you to sit there without blowing your stack, Aramenta. I want you to know what is happening in my head."

She gave no hint of comprehending. As though his hand on hers allowed her to draw strength, she sat, head down, tears hitting the table only to be swept away by one finger.

"My brothers, the senior partners, are delving into the estate. I made some mistakes. I tried, foolishly, to handle the entire matter alone. Alec Smith is one of the best tax men in the legal profession, here or anywhere else. He thinks the estate is much smaller than I assumed. He says most of the stocks have been signed over to James Darcy, your late husband. This makes no sense whatsoever, Aramenta.

"Due to this and other puzzling factors, the estate is in danger of being splintered. By IRS, by my own firm, by stockholders who may demand that you liquidate rather than come in and alter their corporate situations abruptly.

"I know this is a lot of mumble-jumble legal crap. I know you don't want to worry about it. But someday you may hate me for not pursuing the matter. It could cost you millions of dollars. I can't do this alone. To pull it all together, it's going to take your intervention.

"However, I want you to know I probably won't be managing the estate, or the financing and investments, or the voting of stocks by proxy. I'm losing all that, Aramenta. Better, more experienced men will handle it. So I have no further motive than your personal well-being. It is you, the woman, not the heiress, that concerns me at this moment."

She sobbed quietly.

"I'd like to take you out of this house, Aramenta."

"I can't."

"Why can't you?"

"Too much. To do."

"Forget it, for Christ's sake," Randy urged gently. "Come with me this minute! Leave your clothes, leave everything. We'll go out and buy a whole new wardrobe, everything! Go home to Paris, Aramenta."

She shook her head. Tentatively, she tugged her hand. He let it go and she pulled it like a limp rag to fall in her lap.

"I don't know what else to say," Randy confessed. "I am completely stymied. William has virtually taken over—"

"I won't allow that!"

Randy tried to smile. "You may not have any more to say about it than I do. This is going to sound ludicrous in light of everything, but you may not be rich at all, Aramenta.

You may be limited to whatever you receive on the annuity and your trust fund, plus what you get for this house and the furniture."

"All right." She almost sounded relieved.

"No, it isn't really," Randy said, rising. "I would have liked to see you take a stand, Aramenta. I had visions of you—and me, truthfully—marching into corporate meetings wielding your votes like a banner. I've been sitting up nights redesigning the Marine Guaranty Bank motto, logo, and investment procedures."

He laughed shortly, a sound without mirth. "I've been a kid dreaming about playing attorney."

Aramenta took his hand and pulled him back to his chair.

"All my life I've lived for the present," she said. "Dominated by the past, obsessed by it, and living every moment solely for the present instant only. I never thought about the future, did you know that? Never did I think of what a great day tomorrow might be, or how much better-off I'd be next year, or the next. I somehow got through each day, hardly ever without thinking about the past, however. Like a woman riding backward in a caboose, seeing where the train has been, knowing where she was in relation to it, but never considering where the tracks led."

Randy waited for the point to this. When she said nothing else, he patted her hand, stood, and left.

Randy drove to the hospital too depressed to go back to the office. He couldn't abide William. Nor the constant resentment and anger of Alec or Chad over Randy's mishandling of the Lee estate. He'd made a hundred costly blunders. He'd filed holdings in Aramenta's name that she did not own, snarled the probate of the will with self-created complications—and now this curve-ball legal snafu which nobody understood.

He pulled into the parking lot of Providence Hospital and went inside. He walked up to the third floor, down the hall to Dad's room, and entered without knocking.

It was one of those cool, pale-aqua cubicles so popular with such institutions. The sickly aroma of antiseptics and the pervasion of illness and death never seemed to ebb.

"How is he?" Randy whispered. The nurse smiled, put down a magazine, and rose. A noncommittal response, professional cheer, the woman guarding herself from truly caring about the patient when death was so probable. Her starched skirt whisking, she left Randy sitting, looking at Dad.

"Thought I'd stop by and see you," Randy said, voice low. He spoke expecting no reaction. Dad's eyes peered without vision at the acoustical-tile ceiling. What did you say to ears which don't hear? Or did they? Dad's eyelids fluttered, closed, slowly opened.

"Wish I could talk to you," Randy said softly. "I have a problem."

Flutter, close, open, blue eyes that once were quick to smile, always saw the better side of things. Kind, gentle, loving eyes.

"You remember the Lee estate? You gave it to me to manage about ten years ago. Pay the household bills, that sort of thing. Mrs. Arlington Lee died, Dad. Soon after your first stroke. I had to probate the will."

Why was he saying this? Because, like confession, he needed to purge his mind and seek assurances even if only from his own voice? Randy told Dad about Aramenta, the house, the peculiarities of the woman. His voice grew bitter when William entered the case, and then subdued when he admitted his failure to execute the will properly.

Flutter, close, flutter, open. A slight twitching of the pupils horizontally.

"I know William has always been your favorite, Dad. I don't blame you for that. William was so much older, more like a friend than a son, I know. After Mom died, you must've looked down and seen a second boy and realized it was me. I'm not bitter about it. I'm not, really. But I was always the kid, don't you know? William and you—like two fathers. I waited all these years to be given cases and nothing came. I did all the legwork, the research, hoping and waiting.

"I really thought I had something with this Lee estate. I have to tell you, I had delusions of grandeur. I saw myself sitting on the board at Marine Guaranty—becoming somebody, something. You can understand that, can't you, Dad?"

He had the feeling Dad was looking at him. It only lasted a moment. Then the eyes fluttered, closed, slowly, ever so slowly, opened.

"I lost out, Dad. William took it away from me. Alec jumped on the taxes, Chad assumed the stocks, and William is already talking about mergers. Not smart mergers, just power plays. But he can make them look smart. Anyway, the result is, I'll be back to law."

The nurse leaned through the door. "Time's about up, Mr. Beausarge."

"Okay. Thanks."

He took one of Dad's hands, cold like Aramenta's were. He stroked the back of the hand, and the blue and purple veins collapsed and slowly pumped up again.

Randy stared at the hand. Two fingers, tap—tap— He looked at Dad's face and an electric sensation shot through his body. Dad was looking at him, pupils wavering, but definitely looking at him!

"Hey!" Randy whispered, grinning. "Hey, Dad!"

322

The lips tried to move, barely parted, a tube up Dad's left nostril restricting mobility.

"Doing all right, are you?" Randy asked.

A hissing sound from Dad's throat, a long exhalation. Trying to say something? Randy leaned over looking into Dad's eyes. He could almost feel a superhuman effort taking place in this broken body.

Slowly, the hand came up, reaching—for Randy's pocket. The pen? The ball-point pen? He took it out, exposed the writing nib, and put a tablet he carried beneath the pen.

The quivering hand grasped the pen like the hilt of a knife, more as though to stab than to write.

"I'm afraid we may be tiring him, Mr. Beausarge, if you would like to come—" The nurse halted, watching.

With great effort, eyes again on the ceiling, Dad moved the pen and it slid off the pad. Randy placed the hand again. Marks. Meaning nothing. Scribbled. No, wait! "I" or "L" or a numeral "one" possibly.

"The number one?" Randy asked. The hand lifted, fell, lifted, fell—two taps.

"All right, Dad, number one."

He tried to anticipate what the hand was attempting. "Is that a B, Dad?" Two labored taps.

Carefully, pen clutched, a mark down, a mark across.

"Tee?" Randy said. Tap. Tap.

"Mr. Beausarge, I think we should let him rest now."

"Yes, I will, nurse. One moment." Randy leaned over his father. "Anything else, Dad?"

The pen fell away. Randy pocketed it, stood there a moment, then nodded curtly to the nurse and departed.

Ranting of a clogged mind? A moment of lucid recognition that soon passed? He pondered the pad, the uncertain scrawl. One-Bee-Tee. If the taps meant "yes," but each move might have been an effort to correct the misunderstanding caused by the first mark.

He pulled into his driveway, waved at the kids, who came for a hug and kiss before scampering back to their friends.

"Bobbie?" he called inside the front door.

"In the kitchen!"

He walked in, sat at the breakfast bar, and told her what had happened.

"One-bee-tee," Randy said. "I think."

"I dunno, darling. Would you hand me the potato peeler out of that drawer?"

He poked around, looking; she reached past his hand and got it, going to the sink to peel carrots.

"One-bee-tee," he repeated. "I think."

"No telling," Bobbie said. "How soon before you'll be ready to eat?"

"Not soon."

"I'll force-feed the kids then, and we'll have a private dinner alone later, how about?"

"Okay," he agreed. He went upstairs to take a shower, decided to call the office, and went to the telephone. He could never remember that number. Taking a directory from the bedside table, he looked up the number and dialed. As he waited, he realized the office was probably closed. He fingered the cover of the directory idly. It was one of those plastic things where a series of sponsors buy ads, and housewives dutifully rush home to cover their telephone directories.

He stared at the cover. "One-bee-tee!" He hung up the phone. How stupid of him! For weeks he'd been working with the Marine Guaranty logo—"First Banker's Trust!" It was the parent company that ultimately became Marine Guaranty Marine Guaranty still carried the 1BT symbol on their stationery.

Then it came to him. Like a sun reaching the apex of a mountain crest to throw light into a darkened valley. He ran downstairs, told Bobbie he was going to the office, and despite her shrieks of protest, drove away.

Randy entered Dad's office, which was the largest of any in the firm. Against a wall in color-coordinated file cabinets was all the data on Dad's accounts spanning fifty years. Randy scanned the alphabetical directory and stopped at "F," where he opened the drawer. A complete series of files on First Banker's Trust. These he examined perfunctorily. He closed the drawer after withdrawing a single folder marked TRUSTS, and he sat at Dad's desk.

DARCY, JAMES LEE.

Randy returned to the files and found the listing. There was an entire drawer set aside for DARCY, JAMES LEE. He located the particular file he wanted which listed holdings, properties, etc. He paused, dialed Bobbie to tell her he wouldn't be home until very late.

He began at the beginning. The date the trust was established, 1950. There were four trustees: Mrs. Arlington Edward Lee III; her daughter, Aramenta Lee Darcy; Randy's father; and—sweet Jesus—Randall Beausarge!

His outburst of enthusiasm mellowed as he read, slowly covering the history of the trust from its inception. He found a birth certificate and the name—James Lee Darcy, son of James and Aramenta Darcy.

He discovered a thick sheaf of correspondence from doctors, between doctors, Dad and the deceased Mrs. Lee. Physicians' reports, psychiatric evaluations, a chronology of heartache and a fortune spent trying to help a child who confounded the medical science of his time.

Why hadn't Dad told Randy he was an executor? The answer was in the files—Dad was respecting Mrs. Lee's wish for secrecy. Letters and notes of conversations between Dad and Mrs. Lee, the woman's anguished confessions of failure, of a unique and terrible problem to which she was devoting her life. Then Dad had a stroke and Mrs. Lee died.

Randy skipped nothing. He completed the files at five A.M. Taking the key folders, he drove to an all-night restaurant, where he sat thinking it through, drinking endless cups of coffee and eating doughnuts.

He had won. But he had none of the exhilaration victory would be expected to bring. He was numb, stupefied, considering the information he now possessed.

Why should Dad have revealed any of this to Randy? What had his youngest son done to encourage the elder Beausarge? Had he shown initiative, drive, ambition? No, he'd sat around without complaint, waiting, as though pennies would someday rain from heaven. When his big chance came, Randy was not prepared or capable of handling it.

He was victor. He could snatch William around by the nape of his thick neck! He wouldn't. In fact, it was imperative that he somehow stabilize the firm, draw them closer together, use the others as his allies, and mend his fences with William.

Randy paid his tab. The sun was rising. He'd need no sleep this day! He felt great. He must see William, let the others know he was executor of the trust fund that controlled it all. He would have to meet with William, get them on the right track for settling the estate and probating the will.

Dad was out of it now. Mrs. Lee deceased, Aramenta could exercise equal power but no greater than Randy's where the estate was concerned. And until she signed, he was the sole administrator. If she never signed it did not matter.

Aramenta—yes, Aramenta. All her problems were solved. She could go home now.

He would have to locate James Lee Darcy. The files gave no clue as to the whereabouts of that unfortunate soul.

Aramenta would know. After all, he was her son.

Chapter Twenty-seven

Aramenta crawled along the concrete slab which served a a roof for the wine cellar. She pulled a light fixture out and avoided looking at the blinding bulb. One eye to the place where it fit and she had a view of the cellar, a circle of floor, part of a wall, now shadowed for lack of the light she'd withdrawn.

Hands shaking, she replaced the fixture, crawling to the next and the next. Over the toilet she had bent low, peering, a putrid odor assailing her as fetid air rose from below. Horrible! In the bathtub, smeared dark stains; the commode had not been flushed in days.

Dear God. Oh, God—she clawed at another fixture, frantic now, yanking it free and putting her eye to the hole. Nothing. Once more, as though not believing what her senses had told her for the past two days, she went back to the lights over the sleeping area. Virgil's bed, rumpled, a still form unmoved. Baby's bed, the mattress lying flat on the floor, the body under covers, a shoe visible at the far end of the blanket—no movement.

She sank against a post, face streaked with tears, arms and legs perspiring, dirt intermingling with body fluids. The sound of her own sobs came back dully to Aramenta's ears, her chest a fiery pain from tension.

She had thought at first it was another of Virgil's tricks. When neither tray was taken, she had subdued the instant acceleration of concern—he was attempting yet another foolish ploy! The trays remained in the passageway all of that day, and when the lights went out, still they were ntouched. She had sat on the steps, watching, waiting.

She had gone to the timer, extended the hours of light, began the systematic process of checking through the over-head portals, withdrawing the fixtures, leaning down to see what she knew would be there—the men futilely trying to hide.

Virgil could forgo food, she knew that from the time he'd tried before. But Baby, never. She had put an ear to the holes, listening. There! A movement? A scrape of shoe on concrete? The drumming in her own ears drowned it. Aramenta had waited—waited—waited two hours! Nothing. Not a whisper, not a sigh, absolute silence.

For a day they might somehow do this. Virgil might gag Baby when Aramenta walked overhead, or stood at the doors. For a day, yes. But two days—Baby would not be kept away from food, could not be restrained into total silence, not for two days! She had studied the beds, looking down, watching for a movement, a clue to trickery. Again she examined the bathroom, every object, every minute detail with careful scrutiny. A dirty washcloth lay crumpled in a corner, thrown there wet. It was now hard. The bottle of Kaopectate lay empty in the lavatory, the top beside an unused soap dish. Not one thing had been moved in forty-eight hours.

To flush them out, to force movement, she cut the lights and pressed an ear to the hole, alert, waiting for hours. She crept back as though they might hear her footsteps, feeling her way through the dark, listening. She sat upstairs soaked with the cold sweat of ascending fear, visions of her crime becoming images of tragedy.

There was no faking Virgil's sickly pallor, the shaking, the outpouring of perspiration the last time she'd seen him, two days ago at breakfast. She had lured him into stretching for his coffee and felt his hand as she gave it to him—the flesh was searing hot! All right. He had a slight fever. She'd given them aspirin. The half-used bottle was spilled beside the bed in which Virgil slept.

What demonic god would allow this to happen? With success only days, weeks away? Illness which struck them down so fast—what could do this? They were weakened, yes, certainly, a lack of sunlight for months in Virgil's case, but what of Baby, who survived all these years?

Food poisoning? Something she fed them? She could not deny this might be. What she fed them she did not always eat herself. Their trays were prepared with careful consideration of balanced diet, sufficient roughage, adequate fruits and vegetables with good rich red meat! Neither too bland nor overly spicy, she had taken great care to see that their bodies received proper nourishment. And the vitamins. The best she could buy, sold to her with assurances that these were not harsh, but more than adequate. Sunshine was essential, Aramenta knew that. But she also knew that diet and vitamins counteracted this loss. Men who served as laborers in mines, far from sunlight, worked away the day and came out at night to return to their homes—healthy. Pale, but healthy!

It was the food trays which most convinced her that Virgil was not tricking her, that a tragedy had transpired and it was of her making. The food ignored. If Virgil could train Baby to do this, surely he could have gained his freedom by simply bringing Baby to the door and proving his control. God, please! God, don't let them be sick. Gone—yes, perhaps a tunnel Virgil had been burrowing, digging for freedom all this time. But she knew better. After two days somebody would have appeared by now, the police, somebody with questions and Virgil standing angrily at their sides.

They weren't gone. They were there. Sick, dead, hiding— they were there.

If it was a trick? Aramenta had not missed the loathing in Virgil's eyes, the seething hatred that had accumulated and deepened all this time. She had never worried about that. When he was free, when he had his money, he would forget, if not forgive. In the passion of his imprisonment, the petty irritations piling atop other grievances, yes, he hated her. She would have hated him in reversed roles. But as she knew he would, he had finally and resolutely set to the task at hand.

Had he not taught Baby signs? Had Aramenta not secretly and excitedly sat here atop the room below watching the enactment of a miracle? Baby had been mastered with a brilliant blend of force and gentleness. Virgil had lived up to every expectation. A few more weeks and he would have been free! She had already made that decision. She had dwelled on Virgil's claim that "now it takes a doctor to go further." She was not a fool—she would have let him go very soon. Very soon.

Oh, God! Weeping, pained with the sustained pull of abdomen and pectoral muscles from sobbing, *oh, God!* What had happened here? How had she allowed this to happen?

Like Mother—no different—Mother began and Aramenta concluded this terrible thing. Worse, she had used Virgil, done to him what Mother always did to others—what Mother wanted, others did. Force, by physical or mental methods, welded others to Mother's goddamned will!

Please God—please—don't let them be dead.

The trick. Yes, she must consider—hope—it was a trick. Then? In that cellar, what then? If she opened the doors and they lurked there, what would they do. Attack? Run? Tear her flesh and hair, shred her clothing, pummel her body with fists and feet? Could she expect any better?

Call somebody. Yes, do that. Randy, the police, a team of doctors—call and let them open the doors.

She could not do it. Admit them to see a sight even worse than the one she'd attempted to hide all this while? No, she could not do that. The Lee name. Grandfather, Father, all those honorable Lees disgraced doubly—by Mother and now Aramenta.

Better that she be attacked. Better that they kill her in a savage burst of wrath and frenzy, than to bring the world in to see what Aramenta had wrought. If—dear God please no—*if* they were lying there, bodies cold and unyielding, the victims of her horror, Aramenta would set the house afire. From top floor to lower she would build the fires to ensure the ultimate and complete destruction of this house of madness. She would retreat before the flames, to the basement, where she would kindle more fire. To the wine cellar—with Brother's pistol to escape the inferno and open the gates of hell.

She dragged herself to her feet. Tears no longer came, but her body continued the dry racking sobs. She moved as though every muscle threatened to fail her, as if she might any moment fall dead from fatigue and anguish, and would that God should be so kind. She climbed the basement stairs, one at a time, each step accomplished with both feet side by side before attempting yet another.

"Why?" She heard the voice; it was her own. "Why, Mother?" What miscreation of genetic factors had produced this tortured and evil house? Would it not have been better that they died, all of them, in their cribs?

Aramenta reached her bedroom—Mother's bedroom. She labored, every fiber of her being resisting, fear like crystals of sand in the texture of her muscles. Movement a direct result of will and effort, producing physical pain.

Oh, yes, Mother. You win. I am an extension of you. I should have fought, like Annette, died like Arlington. I should have resisted and struggled and been strong enough to defeat you! Yes, goddamn you, soon enough I will find your miserable soul, and if you exist out there and death can be compounded with yet another death, I will kill you, Mother. I am coming! I will kill you if the soul can die beyond mortal death alone.

Her hands moved as though disembodied from her arm, opening the commode next to the ornate bed. She fingered Brother's pistol, cold steel. She saw her own hand take it up, oddly steady and as though beyond the control of her will.

If they were there, let them go free. It was done. For good or ill, it was over. If they were determined to hurt her, let it be so. If it was murder, she would absolve them by committing this with her own hands so they would be guiltless. But if they were dead, Aramenta would this day die and this edifice of her Mother's life would descend into the cellar with a shower of cleansing flames, this Aramenta swore.

Spasms had replaced the sobs. She stood stupidly staring at her reflection in the smoked-glass mirror. Yes. That was Mother. Mother as Aramenta remembered her. She raised the pistol, pointing at that domineering, tyrannical woman. She knew that expression well, the thin lips curled at some imagined misdeed. Mother's eyes afire with some inner fanatic reasoning.

"Blood tells, Aramenta." She heard Mother's voice, saw the lips move. "Blood tells! Born to it. Flowing through the veins and as inescapable as the fates of man."

The pistol was aimed now at Mother's smoked-glass image, rising to a point midway between the uplifted eyebrows and the bared teeth. Aramenta's fingers tightened. Mother did not seem afraid. The trigger pulled back slowly, savoring the final instant of Mother's awareness before a bullet shattered her face forever! The hammer drew back with a slight click, Aramenta's arm as steady as steel. Kill her. Kill the goddamned mother. Kill her!

The gun recoiled, Mother's icon splintered, shards of mirror splitting Mother into a thousand splinters which hung in place a fraction of a second before cascading to the floor.

There. Dead.

Aramenta smelled the acrid fumes of spent powder, an aroma not altogether unpleasant. She walked to the broken glass and looked down. A hundred assorted pictures of herself returned her gaze. She looked miles away, like the effect of peeking through binoculars from the wrong end. The flickers and pieces of Aramenta were almost smiling.

She went down the basement steps, drawing huge drafts of air, swallowing against dry flesh, preparing for what must ensue. She stopped at the head of the cellar stairs.

God, please. Let them not be dead. God, please, let them not—

The outer door opened, the inner door closed. Aramenta took the heavy key from her pocket, pistol in hand, squinting toward the bars. Hoping, praying, mumbling like a condemned being going to execution. Please God—please God—please God—

The odor gagged her, even as she stepped over the untouched food trays. Nobody could stand that! Acrid, penetrating fumes akin to ammonia which burned the eyes and seized the lungs in half-breath. Aramenta inserted the key and turned it, the shaking now returning to her hands, shock and horror making further progress a supreme effort of will, mind over body.

Please no, God—please—let them be—

She pulled the door open, groaning with dread, every breath a moan which reverberated through the empty cellar. Holding the gun as far forward as her arm allowed, she walked slowly toward the toilet, the stench mounting, eyes blurred with tears, her voice a dirge, echoes making a chorus of whispers: Dear God, please, God, let them be—don't hurt me, listen to me, please God, let them be—

The gun was a jittery, shivering, wobbling object outstretched. She seized it with both hands. The stink! The horrid, unbearable—

Aramenta stood over the bed so violently spastic now that she could not force her hand to the blanket over an inert form. Her mouth wide, sheer terror now so uncontrollable, dread becoming so powerful—they must be dead! Must be! She turned, seeking a more acceptable alternative than lifting the cover to see Virgil lying there. Baby! My Baby! My poor Baby! She was screaming, the piercing rebounding shrieks returning to multiply and divide, screaming, screaming!

From the shadow came an object. Aramenta wheeled, panic grabbing her muscles, tightening. Coming at her! Two! Oh, God! Oh, God!

Her hands gripped the gun, all reason gone, the roar of an exploding shell thundering in her ears, the flash of muzzle fire blinding. No. No, she did not do that. The gun was for her, the bullet for her brain. No, a calm voice within a shattered body now, no, no, no—she had not pulled the trigger.

Randy parked in the rear. He gathered the files, psychiatric studies, history of the Darcy trust, and walked onto the back porch. He rapped the kitchen door and waited. Another knock. He turned the knob and pushed it open.

"Aramenta?"

He hesitated. The last reprimand for his intrusion was still vivid in his mind. "Aramenta, you here?"

Nothing but the hum of the refrigerator. Randy stepped inside. She could be ill. At her age— He walked through the kitchen, put the files on a table, on through the dining room and into the hall.

"Aramenta? Hello!"

He jumped; the sharp, distant, but distinct sound of a gunshot! Randy's heart seemed to have paused, his first thought that of suicide. Aramenta had been so depressed, so erratic lately and— Randy ran toward the bedroom. Empty.

From the cellar came screams, bedlam. Randy returned to the hall—only hurt herself? He ran to the rear, to the basement door, and as he reached for the knob, it flew open and struck him in the face, chest and one leg, knocking him against a wall and to the floor.

"Virgil!" The deaf man hesitated only an instant, then with a second man behind him raced for the front door.

"Stop! Stop! Virgil! Stop!" Aramenta screaming hysterically. She reached the top of the steps as Randy stood again. She pointed a pistol, her face dirty, contorted, crying, babbling.

"Aramenta," Randy said it very calmly, "what's going on here?"

"I didn't mean it—to shoot—it went—I didn't mean!"

Virgil was snatching at the front door handle. It was locked, he fumbled with the key, the other man a picture of fear.

"Let me take that, Aramenta." Randy seized the pistol, hand encompassing the cylinder so that it could not turn if the trigger were pulled. "Let me have the gun."

The front door opened. Virgil knocked open the screen door and was onto the porch now.

"Virgil! No! Stop! Don't take Baby! Don't take my baby! Virgil! Leave my baby!"

Randy saw the pale, unshaven—Baby? Virgil was on the front porch, gesturing, "Come! Come! Come!"

"No, Virgil!" Aramenta was shrieking like a wild woman. "Leave my baby! Don't take my baby, Virgil!"

Virgil ran back to the door, seized Baby's arm, and pulled. Baby resisted, staring at the sunlight and trees, an automobile passing in the distance.

"Come!" Virgil was yelling. Randy saw Virgil snatch the man's arm and stumble outside. The man pulled back, his arm coming up, elbow next to his body, hand limp and posed, staring, eyes wide.

"Not Baby," Aramenta was still crying. "Leave Baby, Virgil. Please don't take my baby."

Aramenta suddenly ran from the hall toward the kitchen. Randy advanced, seeking to intervene. Virgil was on the front steps now, frantically making signs, one hand gesturing as though speaking, the other constantly urging, "Come, come, come."

Aramenta returned to the hall. She pushed Randy aside, now walking slowly, half-steps toward the man standing uncertainly in the doorway. She held a banana, peeling it with a motion which suggested she did it as though to make it appealing.

"Banana, Baby? Want a banana?" She curled back another section of peel, holding it out. Baby's eyes darted from Virgil, to the outdoors, to Aramenta, to the banana.

"Come to Mama, darling. Come to Mama. Mama loves you. I love you, Baby. I'll look after you. Come back. Come get the banana."

Randy saw Virgil's hands flutter to motionless poses as Baby moved toward Aramenta, cautiously, eyes going from the fruit to her face.

"I love you," Aramenta was signing, speaking, the banana proffered, luring. "My Baby. My sweet, poor baby. Come to Mama, darling. Come along. Come on."

Like a master encouraging a cowardly dog which fears punishment, Aramenta cried, banana out, one hand making the signs as her lips formed words of comfort.

Baby reached for the fruit and Aramenta held out her other hand, touching his hand for a moment before he gained the will to take the fruit greedily. Aramenta inched closer. She touched his chest and shoulder, her fingers trembling, voice choking, sobbing, touching him as though until this instant she was not sure he existed in truth.

"My baby. My baby. He did it. My baby. My darling baby. Come with Mama now. Are you hungry? Hungry?" She made a gesture toward her mouth. Baby nodded and Randy saw Virgil's jaw drop.

"Want something to eat now?"

Baby nodded. Aramenta's fingers touching his face, stroking his hair, weeping, consoling, assuring him, luring Baby toward the kitchen, past Randy. Slowly, daring not to grab yet, not to clutch and hug, but Randy saw this was only by will—she wanted to.

"Mama will make some breakfast. Cereal, with strawberries. Would you like some cereal? I know you're hungry, aren't you, my darling? I know—" she sobbed. "I know you are hungry. Mama will feed you. I'll look after you, yes, I will. I'll—"

Randy turned to stare at Virgil. Virgil's face was a stark, pale mask. Anger? Confusion? Hatred? Randy couldn't be sure. He saw Virgil's eyes go to the rear of the hall, the basement. Randy looked back at the open door.

"Need a ride, Virgil?"

Virgil was shivering, barefoot.

"I said, how about a ride?" Randy stated.

Virgil shook his head.

"You have no shoes, Virgil. Your shirt is torn. We can go to my house, let you wash up. You can borrow some of my clothes until we can get to a store."

Virgil made a vulgar sign.

"You know, Virgil," Randy said, taking Virgil's arm and gently guiding him toward the car, "you are quite a fellow."

Randy had fleeting thoughts of the irreplaceable file folders he'd left on Aramenta's kitchen table. But he dared not leave this man. He eased Virgil into the front seat, keeping a smile on his face to subdue Virgil's glowering intensity.

Forget the files. Aramenta would want to read them anyway. It told of the case history, the shift of wealth, the status of—Baby.

"Hungry, Virgil?"

Virgil glared at Randy, eyes wild. Randy put a cupped hand to his lips as he'd seen Aramenta do a moment ago. He repeated, "Hungry?"

"No."

"You'd like coffee, though. Right?"

"No."

Randy drove toward home. Hope to God the kids were gone! That Bobbie was there to help with this.

"Okay, Virgil, we're going to my house."

"Police," Virgil's lips formed.

"No. Not yet," Randy said, firmly. "First you eat, bathe, dress. We'll go buy some new clothes. When you've shaved and eaten, we will talk. I think we have something to say to each other."

"Go to police!" Virgil mouthed, a sound emerging from his throat.

"I think we'd better discuss it, Virgil. It may mean a difference in the rest of your life. I'm not sure, but I think—I think—you are a very wealthy young man, Virgil."

Chapter Twenty-eight

"You could go to the police, of course," Randy said, putting his elbows on his desk, fingers laced. "You have a case, Virgil. They'd go out and arrest Miss Lee, put her in prison. What she did was wrong in the eyes of the law and she'd be convicted."

He watched the sullen, unyielding eyes for a glimmer of mercy, a hint of forgiveness. Anything to denote a change in determination.

"If you did that," Randy reasoned, "Miss Lee would be in prison. The boy—Baby—would be in an institution. I don't believe you really want that, Virgil. You'd have your vengeance and little else."

"What?" Virgil missed the meaning.

"You would have revenge. No money. Understand?"

Virgil nodded.

"What you've done is nothing short of a miracle, Virgil. A wonderful thing. You brought that poor twisted young man out of the cellar, out of the dungeon of his own mind." How much did Virgil understand? Randy watched, waiting for his words to strike a responsive chord.

"When he was born—Baby. When Baby was born, the doctors could not handle such things. They said he was xenophobic. Do you know that word?" Randy wrote a block-letter note, spelling, "XENOPHOBIA."

He questioned again, "You know this word? It means a fear of strangers, an unreasoning fear of strange things. This is what the doctors thought was wrong with Baby twenty-five years ago."

Virgil wrote, "Autistic."

Randy saw the word and nodded. "Amazing. That is exactly what it is, Virgil. You knew that from studying the deaf?"

"Yes."

"Aramenta told me you knew the problem. She said you worked miracles—that's what it was, a miracle, Virgil. It would be a shame to destroy that miracle. Putting Baby away in an institution would make him revert to what he was, don't you agree?"

Virgil glared at the attorney. Begrudgingly, a short nod.

"What you've done here," Randy said, "is give new life to Baby. He was born in the cellar. You know that. Born. Right there in the cellar."

Short, quick nod.

"Now he has a chance, with professional therapy, to go on, learn more—who knows what may come of him someday?"

Virgil's gaze dropped to his lap, lips twisting. Randy waited for visual contact again.

"You saved his life, Virgil. You gave him life. I don't think you want to take it away again, not truly."

Virgil swallowed hard, looked away. Randy waited, hopes rising. When he caught Virgil's eye once more, he continued, "It goes further than Baby, you know. Aramenta Lee was a desperate woman, frantic, afraid, lonely. She never felt loved, she never felt like her life had a purpose. She once told me she existed only for the present, never the future. Now with her son she has something to live for, Virgil. She will spend the balance of her life devoted to her child, just as Baby's grandmother spent thirty years of her life trying to help him."

A crystal gleam of reflected light in a shimmer of tears and Virgil looked away again. Dare Randy make his offer? He decided to try.

"Aramenta Lee says she owes you money, Virgil. For services rendered. I think she mentioned a figure of twenty thousand dollars."

"No!" The croak from Virgil's throat was pitched high, came sharp, loud.

"What is the amount then?"

"Want fifty thousand!"

"Fifty thousand? That's a great deal of money, Virgil. That's more than you'd make in ten years with your earning capacity." Randy saw anger rising. "Frankly," Randy said, "I think it is not enough."

Virgil faltered.

"I was thinking in terms of a hundred thousand, Virgil."

Disbelieving, Virgil jabbed a finger at paper and Randy wrote, "$100,000.00 (one hundred thousand dollars.)"

The enormity of the sum sank in. Randy said, "Of course, if you elected to sue her, a civil suit, you'd probably get more, you know. Money, and make her go to jail, possibly."

"More?"

"Yes. But we're back to Baby again, aren't we? Do you want to do that to Baby? Let me tell you how I've been thinking."

Virgil was staring at the figure again.

"I've been thinking," Randy said, "if you took a hundred thousand dollars, not all at once because the taxes would take too much—but we would open a savings and trust account for you. I can take care of that. We'll build it to the total of a hundred thousand, after taxes so that you have the entire amount of one hundred thousand dollars. At current interest rates, you'd get close to seventy-five hundred a year from that. The rest of your life, for as long as you live you could exist on the interest so long as you don't touch the principal. You understand what I'm saying?"

"Yes."

"I think Aramenta would be happy to give you a small cash sum until this is arranged, and—do you drive, Virgil?"

"Yes."

"You have a driver's license?"

"Yes."

"I think we can buy you a new car, too."

Skeptically, "When?"

"Tomorrow. Today. Right this minute."

Randy saw the light of assurance flitting, disappearing from Virgil's face, the muscles tensing again.

"Listen to me, Virgil. You may go to your grave and never again do something as fine as what you have done with Baby. You may live to be a hundred and never again affect any two people as you have affected Miss Lee and her son. In time, you will become extremely proud of this. You will look back, remember, and feel a great warmth for the man you helped. Someday, who knows, that man may walk up to you and personally thank you for what you have done. Now, you deserve this money. A hundred thousand can make you independent for the balance of your life. You can get married, raise a family, write—anything within the limits of the interest power."

Virgil was looking at the numerals, $100,000.00.

"There is one thing, Virgil."

Distrust again in the deaf man's eyes.

"I need you to sign a release. It says you consider the money payment for a service rendered. It says you will never press charges against Miss Lee and/or James Lee Darcy."

"Who?" Virgil's lips pursed.

"Baby. His name is James Lee Darcy."

Virgil took a deep breath, gazing into space. His eyebrows raised, lowered, lifted again, and he looked to Randy once more and nodded.

Randy pushed the intercom key. "Rosa, bring your notary stamp and ask another secretary to step in here as a witness."

The task done, the case won, the day saved, Randy relaxed, smiling. He'd sent Rosa to the bank for Virgil's cash money, which he'd demanded—a thousand dollars. Plus a cashier's check for five thousand more to buy the automobile. Cheap at the price and Aramenta better damn well know it.

When Rosa returned, giving the crisp new bills to Virgil, and the check, the deaf man arose, shook Randy's hand quickly, firmly, and went to the door. Randy caught up and touched Virgil's shoulder.

"What do you plan to do, Virgil?"

"Go home."

"Home?"

"See Mama. See Papa. Then—"

Randy saw another swallow, an effort to control his emotions, then Virgil said, "Go see only friend."

"Only friend?" Randy laughed. "You have made a few friends here, Virgil!"

"No," Virgil said. "Only friend. This one I marry."

"Oh, ho! Well, congratulations!"

He watched Virgil walk the hall and stand before the

elevators examining his check. Randy turned to a row of men awaiting him and smiled.

"The board of Marine Guaranty, I presume," Randy said, lightly.

"Yes, Mr. Beausarge," Rosa replied.

"Come in, gentlemen," Randy invited. Then to Rosa, "Ask Chad, Alec, and William to come down now, Rosa."

"Yes, Mr. Beausarge."

As the men passed, shaking his hand, Randy saw Virgil step into the elevator, where, for an instant before the doors closed, their eyes met.

Virgil did not smile.